I0747046

EBOLA

Also by Millicent Eidson

MayaVerse Series Titles

Anthracis: A Microbial Mystery (Book 1)
Borrelia: A Microbial Mystery (Book 2)
Corona: A Microbial Mystery (Book 3)
Dengue: A Microbial Mystery (Book 4)

Book or Story Collections

Microbial Mysteries: A Story Collection (Book 0)
MayaVerse A - D Book Collection:
Anthracis, *Borrelia*, Corona, Dengue Microbial Mysteries

Short Works

Monuments: A Ten-Minute Play
Red Thread
Pariah

EBOLA

A MICROBIAL MYSTERY

Millicent Eidson

Maya Maguire Media - Vermont

Dedication

To public health and healthcare workers who have suffered infections, injuries, and death from Ebola or violent attacks while doing their duty.

Praise for Millicent Eidson

"Millicent Eidson's unparalleled talent shines through in this remarkable work, ensuring a thrilling reading experience. I confidently predict that this offering will be warmly embraced by the literary world, solidifying Millicent Eidson's place among the most esteemed authors of our time."—**Midwest Book Review**, *Anthracis:* **A Microbial Mystery**

"Dr. Eidson's medical thriller serves up unique and carefully drawn characters, fascinating and chillingly realistic threats, and enough Happily For Now resolutions to satisfy any women's fiction or romantic suspense fan. You won't want to miss this new entrant into the genre."—**Amazon Reviewer**, *Anthracis:* **A Microbial Mystery**

"This 2nd book in the Maya Maguire series follows the intrepid CDC veterinary detective as she tries to track down the mysterious tick microbes causing *Borrelia* infections. Her travels lead her from her home in New Mexico to the European sites of other outbreaks. Meanwhile, Maya is dealing with her own professional and romantic issues. This is a fascinating insider's look at the increasingly menacing diseases arising from animal microbes worldwide."—**Amazon Reviewer**, *Borrelia:* **A Microbial Mystery**

"The author's background as a scientist working for the CDC gives you an insider's view of this public-health agency at a time of crisis. I recommend Corona to all fans of medical mysteries."—**Amazon Reviewer, Corona: A Microbial Mystery**

"The mystery, the characters, the setting, and the uncanny timing of this book make it a compelling read. I would recommend it to anyone who loves medical thrillers, mysteries set in Hawaii, mysteries with diverse characters, books with a strong female protagonist, and fictional tales related to climate change."—**A.M. Reade, USA Today Bestselling Author, Dengue: A Microbial Mystery**

PROLOGUE

"We are called to assist the Earth to heal her wounds and in the process heal our own—indeed, to embrace the whole creation in all its diversity, beauty and wonder." *Wangari Maathai Nobel Lecture, 2004*

Afi Mountain Wildlife Sanctuary, Nigeria, West Africa—May, 2022
The 420-pound silverback pokes at the stiffened body of his twelve-year-old son on the forested hillside near the Cross River. The stench of diarrhea and vomit permeates the ground nest of sticks and clumps of grass. The patriarch can't linger. It's time for him, as the dominant male, to lead his small troop in a search for fruits and herbs.

Blood dripping from his nostrils and staining his reddish fur, a a three-month-old gorilla lies inert in his mother's arms. The young mother opens her mouth for a high-pitched scream, and another female gorilla joins in.

The silverback twitches his ears and stretches up to his five-foot height, glancing into the canopy as the deluge begins. They must rebuild their nests in the treetops for the rainy season.

The torrent cascades off the leaves and triggers a swarm of flies, already invading the dead gorilla for their own nourishment. The silverback roars and pounds his chest, startling a greater long-fingered bat, roosting upside down from a branch of the bloodwood tree. The nocturnal carnivore shakes its wings and defecates more guano shiny with fish scales, and Ebola virus, to the nest below.

Emitting a low-pitched growl like a deep rumble, the silverback heads off into the forest to find their next meal. Reluctant to leave, the others glance back to the dead body. The mother cradles her infant, the baby already in transition to the spirit world.

ONE

Dr. Stefan Duda pushed through the mesh of vines and sponged his face with his handkerchief. Born in Poland and living the good life in Norway, he wasn't adapted to the intolerable hothouse of a Nigerian wildlife sanctuary.

He'd hoped for more moderate temperatures during a spring health planning meeting in Guinea organized by the World Health Organization. But Guinea and Nigeria weren't far from the equator. Temperate breezes were too much to expect this deep in the jungle, two hundred kilometers from the Atlantic.

Dr. Jan Kreischer was ahead, out of sight. Stefan's colleague, who recently completed his internal medicine specialty at Universität Hamburg, was five years younger and pumped for this special trek. Jan had disregarded their guide, Dr. Biko Okeke, and grabbed the lead up the steep trail of Afi Mountain.

Stefan tugged out a water bottle from his pack. "Just a quick break." He spoke English as the only language in common with Biko, a newly minted Nigerian physician and Igbo tribesman, who'd arranged the weekend excursion for them.

Biko was conflicted about whether to hurry after Dr. Kreischer or stay behind with Dr. Duda. Only fifty lions survived in Nigeria so he wasn't concerned about a major predator threatening Jan's life. But illegal hunting with wire snares across the trails was widespread in the sanctuary and he feared the man getting injured.

Biko noticed drops of sweat on Dr. Duda's pale face. He must have shaved his beard recently, as evidenced by the lighter skin. Wise choice, along with the cargo shorts, loose dashiki shirt, and safari hat Biko had recommended.

"Keep walking?" Biko asked. The forest was too silent. He climbed over the thick root of a locust-bean tree and picked up the pace.

Stefan had been a champion swimmer in an earlier life and maintained his level of fitness. Once hydrated, he had no trouble keeping close to Biko. After about ten minutes, he spotted Jan Kreischer kneeling at trailside, poking a rotting gorilla body with a stick. Stefan's fingers instinctively went for the mask in his pocket.

"Get back here," he ordered, and Jan complied after a few more minutes examining the animal. Biko handed each of them N95 respirators to prevent the transfer of zoonotic diseases, those capable of jumping across species.

Since the COVID pandemic, all trips to see the critically endangered gorillas required masking. Gorillas shared ninety-eight percent of human DNA and the Cross River species had fewer than three hundred individuals in the wild.

Stefan's mask helped counteract the overwhelming odor of rotting flesh from the decaying carcass, swarmed by ants and carrion flies. He noticed Biko eyeing a second dead gorilla, this one a baby nestled on a leafy bed.

Biko regretted leading a gorilla trek with the COVID public health emergency still in place. An earlier tour group might have introduced the disease to the jungle animals. Many of his fellow countrymen believed that Nigerians were naturally protected from the Chinese virus, and some of the four million people in Cross River State relied on bush meat from wild mammals for their diets.

But Biko prided himself on being a sanctuary ally. Along with his younger sister Nneka, who worked as a guide, he had assisted in the distribution of posters warning villagers against eating gorilla carcasses. Their meat was viewed as a gift of free food from the local deities.

Stefan snapped into epidemiologist mode. All dead animals and people were data points, not formerly living beings for mourning. "We should take samples." But they didn't have protective clothing, scalpels, or test tubes, let alone a way to refrigerate their specimens.

"These bodies will be gone once we return." Biko waved his arm toward the top of an African corkwood tree and its fan-like leaves. "Do you see the Egyptian vulture? It is a young one."

Through thick mist beginning its descent down the forested hillside, Stefan made out beady eyes and a sharp black beak. The bushy head of reddish-brown feathers crowning a white face didn't generate revulsion like other vultures with faces of naked red flesh. Two larger ones with whiter plumage and yellow heads screeched as they swooped for a landing on the same tree. The younger bird emitted an arresting growl that Stefan had never heard from an avian species.

Something brushed his bare legs, then painful pinches as ants swarmed and began to bite.

"You're right, Biko, there's nothing we can do. Jan, let's get out of here." Despite his experience in pathology labs, Stefan gagged with the stench, enhanced by the cloying fog. *Let nature take its course.*

TWO

A plastic water bottle, tossed by a Paris street protestor with the force of youthful rage, smacked Maya Maguire on her nose the minute she stepped out of the limo. Mark Zielinski, her vacation host, tugged her back down to the leather seat.

"Are you okay? Let me look at it." His voice was tender, more aligned with his closet poet than his high-powered legal career that paid for the Paris trip.

Mark fingered aside the thick swoops of Maya's shoulder-length black hair. Her nose was already turning red, in contrast to the hue of her youthful skin made more golden by strolls in the Jardin des Tuileries on the other side of the Seine. No fresh abrasions joined her forehead scars from the fallout of several public health investigations. He kissed the small flat mole near her left eye.

"It only hurts a bit," Maya said. Through the tinted window, she eyed a huge sign carried by two husky women. They looked older than most of the college-aged marchers, perhaps pushing thirty like her. **MARCHE CONTRE L'INACTION CLIMATIQUE.**

"Pleading a handicap so we could drive through a climate protest wasn't a good idea." She eyed a raging bonfire of scrap wood on the sidewalk in front of the Musée d'Orsay. "Makes us look like part of the hated elites."

She should have lobbied harder for them to park on a street farther way from the demonstration. Fully recovered from her lengthy COVID recuperation at Mark's New Mexico ranch, she could have pushed his wheelchair.

Or their chauffeur would have done that for them. The Frenchman forced his door open into the surging crowd, then formed a fist with his left hand. He arched his arm up toward the overcast sky, and slapped his left bicep.

"Bras d'honneur," Mark whispered. "French version of fuck you."

The chauffeur opened Maya's door and helped her to the sidewalk, then Mark slid over on the seat and stepped out.

"Monsieur Zielinski," the driver said, "would you prefer your cane or the wheelchair?"

People shouting in French surged. Their yellow fluorescent vests made the driver jumpy, reminding him of earlier anti-government protests that had turned violent. A waving mass of colorful flags obscured the view across the river, but the noisy tumult seemed confined to the Left Bank.

"Maybe we should have gone to the Louvre again," Maya said.

They'd braved a mass of other tourists to see the *Mona Lisa* yesterday, and Mark had no desire for a second visit. "Let's try the cane. If I get tired, they'll have a wheelchair for me to borrow."

As boys in soccer jerseys surrounded them and began to rock the vehicle, the driver retrieved the cane and waved it, shouting, "Merde!"

"Bonne chance," he said while handing the cane to Mark. Then he jumped in the front seat and sped away. Maya looped her hand around Mark's left elbow and guided him through the crowded crosswalk.

On the fifth floor, they paused to admire Monet's *Mount Kolsaas in Norway.* "I've never seen a winter scene by Monet before," Maya said. "While I was working toward my master's in public health degree, I frequented all the New York museums."

"You've been to Norway, right?"

"Three years ago, but just to Oslo. I helped my colleague Stefan Duda with a *Borrelia* investigation."

Mark frowned. "*Borrelia*? What's that?"

Maya laughed and gently tapped her fist on his large head topped with dark brown hair, now grown out into a short ponytail at his neck. "You can't have Alzheimer's when you're barely past fifty. Remember my tickborne disease investigation when you got my car accident charges dropped? That was *Borrelia*."

Mark took her left hand, missing its baby finger. "Yes, I do, and the subsequent stun grenade at the Lyme disease demonstration. I thought you might quit such a hazardous profession."

Maya had been through too many years of grief and therapy to allow any setbacks. "After Manolo's death and my China incarceration, nothing can knock me off track."

She smiled at Mark's rugged countenance, more aligned with his role as a New Mexico rancher than his position as a powerful attorney and philanthropist. Other than his dark features, he had little in common with her deceased husband, who had been younger than Mark by almost two decades. Both were raging extroverts—a counterbalance to her innate tendency to be in her head, trying to make everything into numbers she could analyze.

Maya refocused on Monet's next painting, the *Poppies at Argenteuil*. Its vivid field of red flowers beneath a cloud-flecked blue sky made Maya yearn for an escape from the fervor of a big city.

Last fall, she'd investigated a dengue fever outbreak in Hawai'i. She always felt grounded when connected with nature, even in the face of deadly mosquitoes. And that's what motivated the protestors, too. Protect the planet's environment and creatures before the tipping point of runaway droughts, fires, sea level rise, and pandemics.

A young woman shoved them aside and slapped a poster onto the painting's surface. She yelled in French too quickly for Maya to understand, but her white tee-shirt said **+4° L'ENFER**.

"That means hell, right?" Maya struggled to remember her Duolingo lessons during the months of trip planning.

Mark nodded. "She may be referring to what Paris will be like with increased temperatures. But gluing something to a famous painting—that's taking it too far."

Three guards brushed past them to hustle the vandal away and museum staff guided everyone else out of the gallery. Maya remembered the barriers and safety glass over the Mona Lisa. Would museums have to do that with all their artwork?

She grabbed a table in the art nouveau Café Campana near the massive translucent clock built into the museum's north face. Golden lamps floated down from the high ceiling and panels on one of the coppered walls glowed with the vibrant blue of an imagined fish tank.

A bustling waiter stopped by their table. Maya ordered the quiche saumon épinards and Mark the salade César. Within minutes, the waiter opened a 2021 pinot noir, the most expensive on their list other than champagne.

After approving the choice, Mark lifted his glass in a toast. "Here's to a magical week with you in the City of Light. It sure was worth extending my trip beyond the legal conference."

Maya returned his toast with a grin, then handed him her phone. "Take a picture—I want to send it to my parents."

She posed in front of the massive clock, a remnant of the museum's initial incarnation as a nineteenth century railway station. At five foot six inches, her head blocked only the bottom of the Roman numeral VI. Mark smiled, remembering the significance of her red sundress. In Chinese culture, the color symbolized good fortune and happiness.

No question, Dr. Maya Maguire was an intriguing mix of the exotic as a Chinese orphan, combined with the earthiness of someone raised in Arizona, and the challenging brilliance of a veterinarian working in public health. An expert in all species and the spillover of their dangerous diseases.

The waiter dropped Maya's side salad to their table and she twisted with impatience in her model pose, all the protest turmoil suddenly making her hungry. "Mark, dépêche-toi, s'il te plait."

"I am trying to hurry," he said. "It's hard to see your face with the glare coming through the clock." He snapped the picture.

Only two days left on their joint vacation, Mark reflected as he waited for their main course. They'd broken past any awkwardness because of their initial attorney/client relationship and their age difference. They'd bonded during months of physical therapy for his spinal injury from a spooked horse and her long COVID infection.

But despite his best intentions, their physical relationship had not moved beyond first base. He'd hoped that Paris would drive disease data and statistical analyses out of her head, plus dreams or nightmares of a dead spouse.

Still, the trip had been a success. After a week in Paris, all work set aside, she seemed reborn as a confident, sexy woman at a major transition point in her life. In June, her Centers for Disease Control and Prevention training program would be done, and she'd made no decision about next steps. She was fond of both New Mexico and Arizona where Mark maintained offices, and her parents still lived in Flagstaff. Odds were she'd remain in the Southwest.

Maya's phone rang as the waiter delivered the main courses. She picked it up and held it close to her ear. "Stefan, this is a surprise. Where are you off to these days?"

His voice was so weak, she barely recognized it. "Conakry, Guinea. I've got Ebola. Unlucky Friday the 13th."

THREE

Stefan shifted his phone away from his face, overcome by a spasm of hiccups. Biko, geared up with personal protective equipment required by the Conakry hospital, handed him a cup of water.

Stefan was grateful that the fog in his brain had mostly dissipated. "Thanks, Dr. Okeke, you're the best." Covered head to toe in PPE, his Nigerian friend was recognizable only by his black-framed glasses and goatee.

Stefan glanced around the isolation ward of the international hospital, crowded with other conference attendees infected with Ebola virus. The stench of diarrhea was overwhelming. Over loud cries for help, he could barely hear Biko's voice. He couldn't imagine the conditions in one of the public hospitals.

"I appreciate your care," Stefan said, "risking your own health."

Biko shook his head. "I am immune from my infection in 2016."

Stefan took a quick sip from the cup, the cool liquid soothing his throat. "We don't know how long acquired immunity lasts."

With a start, he remembered Maya and brought the mobile to his ear. "Sorry, brain's been fuzzy. Didn't mean to leave you hanging. I hope we're okay after what happened in China."

"It's been a whole year, don't worry about that." Her timbre had started low but became more strident. "What the hell is going on?"

Biko placed a damp cloth on his forehead and Stefan relaxed into the pillow. "A dumb-shit internist poked at a dead gorilla and got infected with Ebola. He spread it to the rest of us."

"Have you talked to Kondrat?"

Just like Maya to be worried about his family. "He hung up on me."

"I don't believe it."

Stefan couldn't accept it, either. But they'd had a fight before the trip about all his travel. Kondrat had threatened a 'divorce' if he didn't slow down, not that they'd ever legally married.

He heard Maya's muffled voice. "Mark, can I use your international dialing plan for Oslo?" Then she came back on the line. "I'll call Kondrat, maybe I can provide some reassurance. How are you doing?"

Stefan breathed a sigh of relief. The offer meant she forgave him for arranging the dangerous China bat expedition. And she'd seen in person how prickly Kondrat could be about their frequent separations due to work. She knew how to handle him.

He mustered his strength to answer her question, if he could remember all his signs and symptoms. "Fever, headache, sore throat, and joint pain. Really weak. Not nearly as bad as some others, like my colleague Jan Kreischer."

Biko stirred at his bedside. "Don't forget the seizure."

Stefan ignored the prompt. "Thanks, Maya, let me know what Kondrat says." He ended the call and dropped the mobile to his bed. Hopefully, she hadn't heard what Biko added. There was a limit to how much he wanted to freak out his family.

FOUR

In the critical care unit, the nurse almost wasn't quick enough to offer the stainless-steel bowl as the patient vomited over the side of the hospital bed.

"Add an antiemetic to the treatment regimen for Dr. Kreischer," Biko said to the nurse. "If we don't get this vomiting under control, he may go into shock."

Jan appeared semi-conscious as his body continued to heave. When he shifted to lean back against the metal headboard, blood began to leak around his IV line. Biko moved quickly to apply a gauze sponge and the nurse bandaged Jan's arm.

Biko checked the chart. "His platelets are too low and he's anemic. I'm concerned about a coagulation problem. I'll prepare orders for a transfusion of platelets, plasma, cryoprecipitate, and red cells."

Biko leaned across the bed in Jan's line of vision. "Dr. Kreischer, do you recognize me? I was your host for the gorilla trip."

Jan's gaze remained vacant and he didn't answer. As the initial case, it appeared he was the source of infection for the others. Jan was also the most advanced in his clinical course, on the road to organ failure if they couldn't turn things around.

Biko put a hand on the plastic chair to steady himself, weak with guilt over leading the excursion. He'd been excited to attend a big conference in Guinea only months after completing his community health and primary care residency. His training at the Lagos University Teaching Hospital was a respected pipeline for those interested in public health.

Several weeks before the meeting when the registration list was shared among attendees, Stefan contacted him about the Nigerian gorilla sanctuary. He and Jan offered a generous donation for gorilla protection and Biko's education program if he'd lead a quick trip before the meeting started.

Biko had protested. The drive from his apartment in Lagos to the sanctuary could take eight hours one-way, and when their gorilla tour was completed, the flight to Conakry for the meeting would require another day. He finally acquiesced, proud to demonstrate his home country's progress in conservation.

On Monday morning when the meeting kicked off, Jan's generic 'dry' symptoms began, which were similar to Stefan's current condition. Jan tested negative for COVID and felt confident he wouldn't spread his mild viral infection to other attendees who all wore masks throughout the proceedings. Unfortunately, there were numerous social events with meals and drinking.

Late Thursday afternoon as the conference ended, other attendees began to fall ill, and Jan crashed. Real-time rapid laboratory tests confirmed Ebola virus species *orthoebolavirus zairense*.

Biko updated Jan's treatment regimen and reviewed the status of other patients. On duty at the hospital for almost 24 hours straight, he headed to the anteroom and removed his PPE.

Outside the hospital, Biko could see the narrow blue-topped spires of the Grand Mosque, the largest in West Africa. Its loudspeakers broadcast the Azaan, Muslim call to prayer. Although he himself was Christian, many meeting attendees were Muslim. He hoped there would be additional prayers for them today.

Like Stefan, Biko was a World Health Organization employee. He'd been ordered to check in at twelve o'clock with Dr. Vazir Shah, the Regional Director for Africa. The man valued punctuality, so a bit longer to wait.

He stood beneath the shade of a palm tree, trying to relax. Guinea was so close to the equator, the temperature didn't vary much year-round. But the weather this week had been unusually warm, approaching 40° Celsius.

Struggling to catch his breath, he stared out into Sangareya

Bay. A fellow med student had taken him sailing once in the Lagos Lagoon. How he'd love to escape onto another boat right now.

His mobile buzzed with the alarm and he placed the call. Dr. Shah was a rare Sunni Muslim from South Africa, speaking only English and Afrikaans, so Biko spoke in English.

"Good afternoon, sir," he said after the secretary patched him through.

Dr. Shah avoided the usual niceties. "What's the count at your hospital now?"

"Nine hospitalized, two in critical condition. No deaths, but with a fatality rate of fifty percent, that may change soon."

"And you believe the index case was Jan Kreischer, exposed a week ago on your gorilla tour."

"Yes, sir. We did not send anyone to test the gorillas, so we are not sure." He regretted allowing Jan to surge ahead on the trail.

As a new physician, Biko had been uncomfortable giving orders to his white colleagues. He appreciated their attendance at a meeting about the health care economics of West Africa, but also felt a twinge of resentment that his continent required so much outside help.

"Tell me again why you weren't wearing masks." The tone lowered, becoming ominous.

Was he about to be fired? "I feared heat exhaustion as we climbed the trail, sir. Neither of them were adapted to a rainforest environment. We had our masks ready to put on, once we spotted the gorillas."

"You could be wrong about the exposure for Dr. Kreischer," Dr. Shah said. "The average incubation period is a week so the timing of your outbreak is on the shorter side if related to the animals. Perhaps there's Ebola brewing in Conakry from another source. Guinea had an outbreak with sixteen cases and twelve deaths just a year ago. Where was Dr. Kreischer before the meeting?"

"I picked them up last Thursday night at the airport in Lagos. They flew in from the Democratic Republic of the Congo where they were working on dengue fever."

"The DRC had Ebola cases last year as well. I'll advise their hospitals to be on increased alert."

Dr. Shah cleared his throat, then continued. "I'm most concerned about the Conakry attendees returning home using many different modes of transportation. It may be up to three weeks before they start to show symptoms."

"And the precise ways in which Ebola virus can spread has some uncertainties," Biko said.

"Yes, but close contact is a risk factor. It's a logistical nightmare, with over a hundred conference participants, plus employees of the hotel and local venues for dining and drinking. At each destination, health staff need to triage those getting off planes and trains. We have an emergency situation report ready to issue this afternoon."

"Should we consider vaccine for our hospital staff?"

"Your outbreak is still small. I will discuss it with Guinea's health minister, who must make the request to the International Coordinating Group in Geneva."

Presumably WHO would have someone else manage the vaccine campaign—Biko was already overwhelmed at the Conakry hospital. Because of his previous infection, he was unlikely to be at personal risk. However last fall, a nurse relapsed from her 2016 infection and died. Four others who attended her funeral became infected and died too.

He needed to pace himself and stay healthy to combat the outbreak. A huge international disease threat required multiple countries to marshal their resources, and he might have set it in motion.

FIVE

Maya hung a damp washcloth on the towel rack, refreshed from the cool water on her face. She had first met Stefan's partner when she and Stefan studied public health together at Columbia University.

Their friendship was enhanced during her *Borrelia* investigation in Oslo where the couple lived. But she was still unsure exactly how to handle Stefan's request that she talk to Kondrat. She knocked on the door connecting her Paris hotel suite with Mark's.

"Come in," he shouted.

He stood at his balcony railing in front of the Eiffel Tower, sliding glass door open and white curtains billowing in the breeze. She tugged him a step back from the edge and slipped an arm around his waist.

"Sorry I made you cut our Musée d'Orsay visit short, but Stefan sounded bad. I needed to get my thoughts together in a quieter place, before trying to call Kondrat."

"Not a problem, we can go back tomorrow."

She leaned her head against his shoulder. "I'd love that. It's been a great trip, although the view from the top of the Eiffel Tower was a bit overwhelming."

His fingers caressed her ear. "So that's why you appeared nervous in those selfies we took looking down to the Seine."

A fear of heights was relatively new. But last fall she had a nightmare, imagining her husband tumbling from a sandstone arch they'd visited in Arizona to celebrate their engagement. His crushed, bloody body seemed too real. The dream had been rich with the memories of pungent pines, carried by a light breeze that felt fresh on her skin.

She shivered. She'd been proud to conquer panic attacks after Manolo's COVID death and the dengue outbreak in Hawai'i. After all, she was now twenty-nine. It was time to develop some self-confidence. And Manolo no longer haunted her dreams every night. A little vertigo while on the Eiffel Tower or a hotel balcony—no big deal.

"I need to make my call to Norway now."

Using his cane, Mark took slow steps into the suite's living room, then handed her the phone. "Take your time. I'm turning on the TV news to find out if the demonstrations will muck up traffic again tomorrow."

She frowned at his aggrieved tone. "You don't think they have a point? They're worried about climate change threatening the planet and the need to support low-wage workers."

He opened his mouth to respond but she waved her hand and headed for her suite. Touching base with Kondrat was more urgent.

She'd texted him through WeChat when they first got back to the hotel so he'd accept a FaceTime call from a strange number, and he answered immediately.

Almost three years since she'd last seen Kondrat in person, but he hadn't changed a lot. Still thin, but muscular and tanned. His close-cropped copper hair gleamed in the sunlight of his back patio. He had served fantastic meals there when she worked with Stefan in Oslo.

"Hei min venn," she said, remembering a Norwegian greeting. She hoped Kondrat still considered her a friend. Stefan was unrelenting when focused on a public health goal, whereas Kondrat was driven by his emotions and the protection of their family.

"Are you still working with Young Friends of the Earth Norway?" she asked.

He nodded. "Good to see you, Maya. Yes, Natu rog Ungdom, we call it. But only part-time, arranged around Paula's schedule."

"What's she up to these days?" She remembered their daughter fondly, who was eight on Maya's Oslo trip. The couple had adopted her from a Moldovan institution for kids with learning disabilities.

She had thrived in Norway and Kondrat deserved more of the credit than Stefan.

"Ballet lessons year-round, skiing in the winter. Right now, she loves to garden with me." Kondrat looked strained, as if he were pretending everything was fine. "And you, Maya, what are you doing in Paris?"

"Playing tourist." Their brief delay in discussing Stefan might be deliberate for both of them, but it was too important to postpone.

"I talked to Stefan this afternoon," she said. "He sounded weak, but hanging in."

"He paints everything with a rosy tint, even when it's not justified." Kondrat's exasperated expression vied with his loving inflection. "Did he tell you how he caught Ebola?"

"Yes." But Guinea experienced periodic Ebola outbreaks from exposures in-country, so she wasn't sure they could rely on the gorilla story.

"He was gone for two outbreaks, meningitis in Niger and dengue in the Congo." Kondrat took a long drink of his red wine. "He finally had a few days before that meeting in Guinea. Instead of coming home, he flew to Lagos for the gorilla trip."

Maya understood the logistics. Those countries were in the same region, and with the conference only lasting four days, Stefan would have been home in Oslo soon. Now, his hospital release date was uncertain. She assumed he'd recover, but with Ebola, there were no guarantees.

Her role wasn't to speculate but to reassure. "The hospitals in Conakry have lots of experience in caring for Ebola patients, and I believe he's in one of the best."

She decided not to provide any odds of bad outcomes like death. Published studies indicated the case fatality rate was over sixty percent. Zaire virus, the type they had in Nigeria and Guinea, was the most lethal.

"Do you think I need to fly down there?" Kondrat asked. "The school year hasn't ended for Paula, so I can't bring her to either set of grandparents in Poland."

That was a subject she could be firm on. "You'd never be allowed to see him—the isolation is strict with Ebola. And there's nothing you could do to help him."

Tears streamed down Kondrat's cheeks. "I feel so helpless. All his trips around the world for terrible infectious diseases, and he's never been sick before."

Like Maya, Stefan was an epidemiologist, not a front-line human health care provider. That provided considerable protection from infection. But they still needed to take precautions when interviewing ill people or investigating the source of their diseases.

Maya ignored Kondrat's complaint about Stefan's work/life choices. She had a difficult time balancing those herself. Until the trip to Paris with Mark, she couldn't remember when she'd taken a week-long trip just for fun.

But she understood Kondrat's vexation. "Talk to him and his caregivers. His morale while he recovers will be important."

"You're right, thanks Maya." Kondrat carried his wine glass into the kitchen. "I need to pick up Paula from her dance lesson. Why do you think Stefan called you, by the way?"

Maya smiled. "After the China trip, I think he's looking for any excuse to re-establish our friendship."

"I'm glad he did, so we can reconnect, too."

As the call ended, Maya set Mark's phone on her bed and got up to stretch. If she helped to heal the rift in Kondrat's and Stefan's relationship, that would be a major accomplishment for the day. She recognized a strong bond at its core, so her intervention might have been unnecessary.

She opened her laptop for a quick review of her emails. Mark didn't like her doing that, insisting that she put work behind her. But leaving emails unchecked would make her more nervous than facing hundreds when back home.

One had been sent from Faye Simpson, the retired New York City Public Health Veterinarian. **<Maya, do you know about the WHO alert on Ebola? NYC is gearing up for plane flights.>**

Stefan's little excursion was spreading its tentacles.

SIX

Mark, yearning for progress in his relationship with Maya, ordered the chauffeur to stop the car under the tree canopy. "Let us out here, we'll walk."

Crêperies lined Rue du Montparnasse on both sides. Strolling families filled the narrow street, absent most cars. Lesson learned from the Musée d'Orsay—don't force your way through a crowd of Parisians, inviting them to take out their anger on his expensive vehicle. The rental company charged an exorbitant fee to remove paint thrown at the limo on their museum trip.

Mark maneuvered the brick pathway with his cane. As Maya laced her fingers through his, each of her touches shot lightning from his head to his toes.

An advantage of delayed gratification—her slightest breath in his ear practically made him orgasmic. He hoped the whiff of the forbidden didn't play a role—she was young enough to be his daughter, if he'd ever had kids. And too many wealthy men fetishized Asian women, thinking they were submissive. Clearly they hadn't met Maya.

At the corner, she paused beneath the green trellis dripping pink flowers, almost too vibrant to be real. "How about this café?"

"I don't like the traffic noise," he answered. "I'm up for walking further."

She almost tripped as she focused on the old six-story buildings fronting the street. "Trees growing on those wrought-iron balconies, so beautiful."

He never tired of trips to Paris, an exciting combination of big city energy with old world charm and pockets of nature. Seeing it again through virgin eyes was wonderful. Not that Maya really was a virgin, but her experiences couldn't compare to his own.

"Is this okay?" Maya paused at a small table in the street, protected from traffic by a line of low wooden fencing.

Mark spotted the waiter, a guy closer to Maya's age and enviably fit. "Bonjour, monsieur," Mark said. "Pouvons-nous nous asseoir à cette table?"

The young man nodded. "Bien sûr, you may sit at this one. Here is the menu."

Mark plopped into the wicker chair in frustration. Parisians switched to English too quickly when they recognized an American accent. Quite a change from three decades earlier when he studied abroad and they ignored anyone with imperfect French pronunciation.

Maya's French proficiency remained limited despite daily practice. Her eyes had glazed over when Mark asked the chauffeur in French which parts of Montparnasse Ernest Hemingway and Pablo Picasso favored. It devolved into a lengthy history discussion that Maya didn't follow.

She pointed her finger at the menu. "I'll have la gallette aux épinards."

Mark smiled. "A tasty combination of strong flavors, the buckwheat and the spinach. Will you share a bottle of Chenin Blanc? I wish we had time to visit Touraine, a glorious wine region."

Maya swirled her hair between her fingers, inadvertently revealing the small scars on her forehead. He didn't know the details for all of them.

"I can't be hung over for my flight to New York tomorrow. This week has been awesome, but work awaits." She grinned. "You haven't been a fan of me checking emails."

"I hoped the vacation would provide a well-earned break. Let's see, I'll pretend it's still breakfast and have jambon et oeufs."

On her phone, Maya studied the restaurant's reviews. "Look at the egg in this photo. It's soft, not fully cooked. That's dangerous for bacterial infections like *Salmonella*."

Mark grimaced. Most of the time, he enjoyed this new assertive Maya, more self-confident than the timid stats nerd who first came to his attention four years earlier in the Arizona anthrax attack. Her mother hired him after the FBI detained Maya, accusing her of being the firefighter who starts fires to become a hero putting them out.

Their in-person interactions increased the following year when her car hit the already-dead body of a Jicarilla elder on a remote New Mexican highway. After Mark got the charges dropped, their sole remaining legal contact was an informal consult about sexual harassment from Dr. Russo, that entitled prick she worked with. Mark still burned with anger at the guy, and the fact that he got away with it.

To her later regret, she disregarded his advice to bring in the police and file an official workplace report. She had an exasperating tendency to obsess over a decision before taking action. But the death of her husband and unborn baby from COVID brought her closer to Mark in shared disability and redemption.

"Seeing germs everywhere can be a bit much," he complained, then brushed her palm in apology.

She ducked her eyes. "You're right, my parents say the same thing. I'm sorry."

They placed their orders, agreeing on cider instead of wine. Exuberance replenished the vacation atmosphere when a band strolled by. Four young men in dark pants, light blue shirts, and brown berets led the crowd in lively folk music, played with an accordion, saxophone, drum, and flute. Scruffy backpackers and families with kids danced in the street.

"What's going on with your friend and Ebola?" Mark asked as the food arrived. "I remember that huge scare a decade ago."

"You're probably thinking of the 2013-2016 outbreak in Guinea, Liberia, and Sierra Leone. An estimated thirty thousand cases with over ten thousand deaths. Infections spilled over to other African nations plus the US, UK, and Italy. Other outbreaks followed, but nothing to that scale."

How did she possibly have those details at her fingertips? She must have been researching late at night. "I hope Stefan is recovering."

He knew Maya became heavily invested in her friendships, especially when someone's health was in jeopardy, their own relationship an example.

"Communication is challenging but I think so."

"Glad to hear it. Have you talked to Dr. Grinwold about staying in New Mexico when your training is up in June?"

Maya traced her fingers over the sweet crepe listings on the dessert menu. "Yeah, he offered me the permanent position of State Public Health Veterinarian."

"That's fantastic! You'll accept it, right?" Mark was cautioned by the stillness in her expression.

"Those jobs don't open up very often, and New Mexico has been without one for a while. CDC funded my three training years, so it made sense for him to avoid spending state money before it was needed."

Maya coughed as a smoker at the next table lit up. Mark knew she hated it. Her secretary's husband died of lung cancer and they bonded over losing spouses at a relatively young age. But Europe was more laissez-faire about smoking outside, a common feature of the cafés.

Putting on her N95 mask, always at the ready, Maya set the dessert menu on the table. "If you don't mind, I'd like to call it an evening."

Irritated at their romantic dinner cut short by the smoker, and her avoiding a question about the New Mexico position, Mark called the chauffeur. Despite his momentary displeasure, he adored Maya's intelligence, drive, and emotional depth. She wasn't hard to look at, either.

With his money and influence, other women were available. But Maya's unattainability enhanced her appeal. He always loved a challenge.

On the other hand, her work obsession was excessive, and spilled over to their relationship. She was polite and never nagged him, but he refused to feel guilty about choices that posed any health risks, like a bad diet or horseback riding.

Public health people shouldn't be in charge of public health decisions, the most important lesson he learned from COVID. Only elected officials should decide on school closures and mask requirements. Lives saved wasn't the only goal—the health of businesses was equally vital.

Issues to keep to oneself, if one hoped to score with a particularly sexy public health vet.

SEVEN

Maya kept one hand on Mark's elbow as they pushed through boisterous Sunday night crowds and waited on the sidewalk for their ride. Hopefully at some point, she could come back and wander around as an ordinary tourist to experience the city without Mark's limo, fancy restaurants, and high-class hotel.

She regretted that their route wouldn't cross the Seine, magical at night with sparkling reflections from the lights of nonstop tour boats. But as the chauffeur dropped them at the hotel, nothing compared to the glimpse of the Eiffel Tower, a glowing golden beacon. She could stare at it for hours, but hurried to help Mark to his room.

As he relaxed on his sofa, she opened his drapes wide so they could relish the view, unobstructed by trees. "Can I get you anything to drink before I head to bed?" she asked.

"You know me, I can't fall asleep without my favorite Scotch."

She grabbed his bottle from the bar and poured him a couple of ounces. He liked it neat, only rarely on the rocks. After she handed it to him, he tugged her down, then held the glass close to her lips. "Don't make me drink alone," he said, expression plaintive.

"No thank you. Alcohol gives me rebound insomnia when it wears off. I told you, I need to be rested for my early flight."

She pulled out her phone to check the time and the screen displayed a WhatsApp message from Kondrat. **<Please call immediately.>**

Tilting it toward Mark, she asked, "Can I use yours again?"

Too busy getting ahead on her work so she could have the week off, she never figured out an international calling plan. Before the trip, she agreed with Mark to minimize her time on the phone, so she hadn't anticipate the need.

He handed his over, and she closed the door between their rooms for privacy during an anticipated emotional discussion with Kondrat. On FaceTime, his brow scrunched and moisture flooded his eyes.

"The call cut off while I talked to Stefan's doctor in Conakry, who told me he's broken out with a rash and his skin is peeling away. He's so vain, can you imagine how he'll react to any facial damage?"

"Why didn't you talk to Stefan directly?"

"They wouldn't put me through. Stefan has severe headaches and is kind of out of it."

"I'll text what I find out." But after hanging up with Kondrat, her call to the hospital failed to connect.

Her immediate instinct was to change her schedule—Guinea was closer to Paris than the States. But her wiser angels weighed in. How could she help in Conakry? Surely the phone connection problem was a short-term issue and they'd get through in the morning. Some countries had evening blackouts, perhaps affecting landlines or cell service there.

She texted Kondrat the situation and suggested they touch base tomorrow. Then she rejoined Mark in his half of the suite. He'd changed into a white silk robe painted with dramatic black whoosh-es of Chinese symbols.

"Here's your phone, thank you. No luck getting through to the hospital, but I'll contact them when I'm in New York." Always attracted to silk, she fingered his sleeve. "I haven't seen this before."

Unwilling to send him the wrong message, she pulled her hand away. "Listen, the call with Kondrat freaked me out and I really need to turn in."

He recaptured her wrist and drew her closer. "I saved this for our last night. By now, I hoped we'd be more relaxed around each other." He leaned in for a kiss and she turned her head to accept it on her cheek.

Overwhelmed with intense sexual tension, she couldn't deny a strong urge to melt into his arms. It would only be natural after spending so much time together during her COVID recovery. He was a good guy, she was sure of it, and wouldn't take advantage of her like Enzo Russo.

One finger on her chin, he swiveled her face in alignment with his, then lowered his lips to her own. Commanding but gentle, and a wave of electricity flashed throughout her whole body, concentrated in her groin. *Please, please, take me.* Despite the powerful thought, she remained silent. What was holding her back?

When he drew her closer, she froze just before full-frontal contact. She shifted her hands to his chest. "I…I can't, it's not the right time." Maybe it was her mind stuffed with worry about Stefan.

He didn't look happy but stopped immediately, unlike Enzo who'd used his larger size to pin her down.

"You know I'd hoped for more on this trip," Mark said, his voice pleading.

That's why she'd paid for her own plane ticket. He'd already booked the hotel suite and insisted on handling the meals and museum visits. They'd argued about it, but he refused when she tried to offer him euros.

"Mark, I'm not saying never, just not now. I don't want to lead you on or promise something for the future. You're special to me but it doesn't feel right at this moment. I can't explain it. I'm sorry."

He flashed his most brilliant smile, a winner with juries. "You're calling the shots, I'm in no rush. Some things are worth waiting for."

She turned for the door. "See you bright and early. Seven still okay?"

He nodded and tightened the belt on his robe. She guessed that he was naked beneath it. Oh, what she wouldn't do to give into the impulse.

"Fais de beaux rêves, ma chère," Mark said.

"I hope so." If Ebola didn't haunt her dreams. "Merci, Mark, bonne nuit."

EIGHT

All weekend in the Conakry hospital, fuzzy memories of his eleven-year-old daughter flitted through Stefan's mind. Because of her learning disability, whenever Paula became frustrated while reading, she'd pound the couch with a toy plastic bat.

In his fevered state, his head morphed into that cushion and he raised his hands to block the imagined blows.

Then his surroundings became visible again—beds in the isolation ward were full of patients, some crying out in pain and others too quiet. A young man in a nearby bed haunted him with tear-filled, blood-red eyes.

Pale light filtered in through clerestory windows and cheered him up. Like others who lived in northern climes, his moods were tied to sunshine. Scandinavian design emphasized lots of windows and connections with nature. Reaching his family—his top priority.

He called out to a PPE-clad hospital worker rushing by. "Can you help me?" When the man turned, he recognized Biko.

"Dr. Okeke, where's my phone?"

Irritated by the interruption, Biko was relieved to see that it was Stefan, looking much healthier.

He smothered his guilt that he played any role in Stefan's and Jan's Ebola infections by guiding the gorilla trip. The WHO leaders had concluded that these new illnesses were likely related to the outbreak last year. Cases could go undetected for months in a city like Conakry with 2.5 million people.

"How are you doing, Dr. Duda?"

Biko checked Stefan's chart. "Your altered mental status was caused by hypoglycaemia which we controlled with a continuous infusion of dextrose. Your blood glucose level an hour ago was in normal range."

Stefan propped himself higher on his pillow, relieved that his foggy brain wasn't related to something more serious. He tried to remember Ebola virus disease treatment options. "EVD monoclonal antibodies—are they available here?"

Biko nodded. "Yesterday we gave you an infusion of INMAZEB, a combination of three human monoclonal antibodies."

"Would have been nice if you'd requested my approval first," Stefan snapped.

Never having treated a fellow WHO staffer before, Biko was shocked by Stefan's lack of gratitude. The treatment was only recently stockpiled at the hospital and still unavailable to many Africans. Stefan's recovery likely benefited from the antibodies in addition to stabilization of his blood sugar.

Disinclined to back down after lengthy shifts with little sleep, Biko answered in a similar tone. "I would never allow a patient to dictate their treatment, and neither would you."

Biko's displeasure was clear by his wrinkled forehead, visible under his face shield. Stefan admitted that fighting with his health care provider wasn't a prudent choice. Involving the patient in medical choices was more common in westernized countries, and he'd prefer to be alive than stand on the principle of informed consent.

"Don't get me wrong," Stefan said in an attempted apology. "I certainly don't disagree with your decision. Thank you for your care."

Biko made a slight bow. "You are most welcome, but what is that American expression? Do not count your chickens. In the efficacy study, mortality a month later was reduced to 34% compared to 51% of those who didn't receive INMAZEB. Beneficial, but not a guarantee."

Stefan smiled. "I promise to be a model patient. How is Dr. Kreischer doing?"

"We are struggling to maintain sufficient fluid and electrolyte support to replace what he lost through severe vomiting and diarrhea. His body-wide pain is extreme. We had to increase his daily morphine dose."

A deep, violent moan ricocheted through the small room. Biko pivoted to greet a nurse running toward him at full-speed.

"Dr. Okeke, that's Dr. Kreischer. We need you now."

Biko followed her to the last treatment bay. His mask didn't protect him from the gagging fecal odor as fresh blood pooled on the floor under the white curtain.

NINE

The limo idled in bumper-to-bumper traffic on the autoroute to Charles de Gaulle airport. Maya crossed and uncrossed her legs in concern over the chance of missing her flight. If only the airport was closer than 35 miles. Public transportation workers had called a day-long strike for better wages, so Parisians who lived in the suburbs all took to their cars.

Maya's phone showed a temperature of 81°, unusual for an early hour in the month of May. Limo windows rolled up and blasting air conditioning didn't prevent exhaust fumes from filtering in. Maya adjusted her mask, seating it tightly around her nose and chin. N95s protected wearers from more than COVID.

Neither Mark nor the chauffeur wore masks. She hoped that fuel emissions from the mass of crawling vehicles wouldn't irritate her throat, requiring her to remove the mask for a drink from her water bottle. A catch-22, increasing her exposure.

At the airport, Mark ordered the driver to park nearby. He wanted to ensure that everything went well at the ticket counter and baggage check.

Mark kept her calm in the long line. Airport workers joined the strike, so the single desk clerk refused to understand anyone speaking a language other than French. She sympathized with his plight—few Americans were multilingual like many citizens of the European Union. The sole burden of communication was on him.

The employee let slip the hint of a smile when Mark intervened in French about Maya's tickets. She'd flown from Albuquerque to Paris via Atlanta, but the return trip included a layover in New York. Mark verified all her flights and her luggage retrieval at JFK.

Ashamed about the level of her self-taught French, Maya was grateful for his help with the harried ticket clerk.

"Merci, monsieur. Vous êtes merveilleux," Mark said before they headed for the security check. As Maya eyed the even lengthier line there, Mark was sensitive to her edgy angst and didn't prolong the farewell.

"Keep me posted on what you decide about your job with Dr. Grinwold." He squeezed her hand.

"You'll be the first to know. Well, after my parents, of course."

His laugh transformed his face into that of a schoolboy. "I never want to get in the way of your mère formidable."

Maya knew that her mother respected him too. "Thanks again for an incredible week. I can't imagine a better guide to this captivating city."

"I'm happy to be whatever you need me to be." His statement was generous but his expression sad. Perhaps if they didn't consummate their relationship in Paris, it wouldn't happen anywhere.

"We apologize for the delay due to computer issues." At the flight attendant's broadcast over the plane speakers, Maya anxiously peered out the nearest window to spot the gangway being reconnected.

Careful not to poke the passengers on either side, she arched her arm around to rub the small of her back. Eight hours trapped in a flying sardine can would not be her favorite part of the vacation. Even worse, a delay before they got into the air.

She hadn't intended to be a tease, and fretted over Mark's demeanor in the terminal. No one else had attracted her physically, mentally, and emotionally after Manolo's death. At fifty-two, he was old enough to be her father, but she never thought of him that way. He was two decades younger than her parents who'd adopted Maya as an infant later in life.

Ultimately, her relationship with Mark shouldn't be rushed. If she decided to leave New Mexico in July when her training finished, it would be better if they weren't deeply involved. As a scrupulous planner, her indecision about her next job confounded her.

Too many conflicting feelings. Santa Fe offered a moderate four-season climate with a magical multicultural history and ambiance. She'd never tire of hikes and cross-country skiing, the Indian Market in August, and farolitos in December.

Dr. Grinwold wasn't the warmest of bosses, but other health department staff were special friends. However, the New Mexico plans she'd made with Manolo were difficult to put behind her. Easier since the mind-bending dengue investigation and thrilling landmarks in Hawai'i, but still....

Advice from Faye, her oldest veterinary public health advisor, would be helpful. She looked forward to her NYC layover, plus she could see the Miranda family if they were open to it. They'd grown close during her brief courtship and marriage—she missed them with an ache as big as the Grand Canyon.

Her father-in-law had joined her for Manolo's memorial service on the first anniversary of his death, but the frost hadn't thawed on her relationship with Ramona. His sister still blamed Maya for reckless work travel, exposure to COVID, and infecting Manolo.

All of that was enough to lock in a knot between her shoulder blades as she awaited takeoff. Stefan's illness had escalated and she couldn't reach his doctors to learn his treatment plan until the plane landed in New York. Although antibiotics were useless against a virus, the Food and Drug Administration had approved two monoclonal antibody treatments about a year earlier. They prevented the virus from entering human cells, leading to reduced mortality.

Despite Mark's admonition to take a break in Paris, she'd snuck in some late-night Ebola research since the call from Stefan. But she still didn't know how soon the monoclonals should be given, their availability in Guinea, or their success rate.

Clueless on how to access Wi-Fi on her phone when in the air, she'd have to postpone further research until they landed.

The captain finally announced their approval for takeoff, flooding Maya with relief. Once the plane achieved altitude, she got out to stretch near the restrooms. The pin in her right thigh from a childhood accident was painful when she was seated for too long.

Her muscles relaxed as she dropped back into her seat, determined to snooze. But the conversation behind her was alarming.

The male voice inquired, "Do you want a lozenge for your sore throat?"

The female replied, "Yes, please. And give me a drink from your water bottle."

"Fingers crossed we didn't get exposed to any of those meeting attendees who came down with Ebola," the man said.

"This is only a cold and we were masked," she answered.

What were the odds that Maya would be on the same flight as someone returning from the conference where Stefan got infected? But Paris might be a logical connection. Apologizing to her seatmate again, she climbed over him to the aisle.

Dawdling as she retied her tennis shoes, she snuck quick glimpses at the couple. They both wore masks, until the woman removed hers to take a long swig from a plastic bottle and wiped her forehead with a tissue before bringing her mask back up.

Maya continued down the aisle, stretched a few moments more, then strolled back to her row. From behind them, she could see their laptops open to medical articles. More evidence that they were health professionals returning from the meeting where Stefan became ill.

Tempted to engage them in conversation, she realized that others wouldn't appreciate hearing passengers discuss Ebola exposure. Should she tell a flight attendant? Her public health brain said yes.

Passengers had been forced into unwelcome quarantines in the earlier big outbreak. Best option—text Faye the minute the plane landed and ask for her advice. Faye no longer worked for the city health department but likely knew the regulations and policies.

Meanwhile, with a full plane, there was no chance of changing to a safer seat.

TEN

Faye clicked the TV remote and lifted her swollen feet to the otto-man as Bosco, her tortie polydactyl kitty, jumped into her lap. She stroked her nails against the couch fabric and Bosco grabbed at Faye's fingers with her catcher's mitt front paw of six toes. The familiar music and character headshots from *General Hospital* attracted both cat and human attention.

Faye identified with Willow's identity crisis on the show. Imagine, discovering as an adult that your mom wasn't really your mother. Faye had felt so alienated from her family, she sometimes imagined she'd been switched at birth. Growing up in a Colorado Pentecostal ranching family where sexual difference was deviant, she didn't realize until vet school that she was bisexual. More recently, she fell in love with a trans female. Dr. Taylor Lewis—Black, brilliant, and beautiful.

Her phone pinged with a text from Maya. **<Just landed at JFK, flight DL989. Passenger with sore throat was at Guinea meeting with Ebola. What should I do?>**

Faye turned off the TV and brushed aside her geriatric pet, adopted when a neighbor passed away. Heart racing, she texted back. **<Health department is already screening international passengers. Force your way to front of line and tell them. I'll contact Dr. Moskowitz.>**

Since Faye quit her job as the city's Public Health Veterinarian in July, she hadn't spoken to the Health Commissioner. Thirty-seven years of service tanked over a dengue virus dispute. Faye clicked on Moshe's name, then FaceTime. Pretending that she liked him, she pasted on a smile, teeth closed to hide a lack of childhood dental work and way too much coffee as an adult. At sixty-seven, it made no sense to spend the money on improved dentition now.

Moshe's face was pallid, anchored by watery blue eyes. With COVID cases way down from their peak around the New Year, he must feel more in control. At least until she told him that Ebola might threaten the Big Apple.

"Moshe, it's good to see you," Faye gushed. "You remember Maya Maguire from her internship several years ago? Her plane just landed at JFK, flight DL 989. There's a symptomatic passenger from the Conakry meeting where they had Ebola transmission."

His grim expression so familiar from COVID days reappeared. "No one's reported compatible symptoms since we started screening yesterday." Both hands combed through his dark curls. "I don't have enough staff to manage this. Would you consider an open-ended contract to help out?"

Faye's mouth dropped open, then she snapped it shut. Perhaps their fight over dengue surveillance was behind them. Or he was desperate.

"I…ah…sure, why not? I assume you need me at JFK right now."

She'd enjoyed the time off for frequent excursions with Taylor, her committed partner even though they didn't live together. But Taylor was seventeen years younger and still worked full-time as Chief of Staff at the Staten Island hospital. During endless daytime hours, Faye felt guilty for sitting out public health crises when agencies were short-staffed. She still had epidemiologic skills despite occasional problems with high blood pressure and swollen feet.

"Why would I ask for your help if not necessary?" Moshe said. "Get your butt in gear."

No longer his employee, she should be offended. She always joked that his imperial manner was compensation for his stature. But her adrenaline ramped up at the idea of being needed.

"Email your Ebola protocols—I'll join your staff within the hour." She cut off the call without saying goodbye.

ELEVEN

The second the plane landed, Maya climbed over the aisle passenger and ran to the forward galley.

"Keep your seatbelts on until the plane has reached a full stop and the captain has turned off the seatbelt sign," came the stern loudspeaker announcement. A flight attendant, eyes bulging, faced Maya. "Ma'am, you must return to your seat."

Maya showed the man her CDC ID and the text chain with Faye.

"Only a sore throat?" The attendant's expression was skeptical. "That could be any of us."

Keeping her voice low to avoid freaking out others, Maya continued. "Early Ebola virus infections can have nonspecific symptoms. These two must disembark first for separate screening by the health department."

The attendant agreed. "Stay here and I'll get them for you." He spoke into the intercom. "Please remain in your seats momentarily for some passengers to exit."

Maya provided her seat number and the description of the couple behind her. Then they appeared with their carryon luggage, concern reflected in their postures and arched eyebrows above their masks.

Ready with her ID, Maya said, "Follow me for an interview about your recent travels."

At the other end of the airbridge, a young man met them carrying a laptop. "Dr. Maguire?"

Maya nodded and the masked staffer led them to the side. A second one coordinated the deplaning crowd.

"I don't understand what's going on," the female passenger complained.

The staffer opened his computer. "Our Commissioner asked me to review your travels. We're doing this with all international passengers. What are your names?"

"Todd and Virginia Mason. Why were we singled out?" The husband held his wife's arm protectively, then glared at Maya.

Did he recognize her as sitting in front of him? She didn't know the protocol and was unsure whether to reveal what she'd overheard. The staffer immediately took the temperatures of all three of them with a forehead thermometer—only the woman's was elevated at 102.5.

The staffer invited them to sit down for the interview. The Masons were married PhD economists employed by Columbia University and had attended only the Conakry meeting. No side trips. The wife started with her scratchy throat on the last day of the meeting, then a headache and sore back during the long flight. She vomited once in the airplane bathroom.

"More than nine hours—a long time for someone who's pregnant," the husband said.

Maya's heart softened with sympathy. They had the Columbia connection and the wife was traveling in early pregnancy. She'd been hyperaware of the couple's movements and conversations but somehow missed the escalating symptoms. Must have dozed off.

"Your clinical status is compatible with many infections," the staffer said, "but given your exposure to Ebola at the meeting, you need to be hospitalized for lab testing and isolation until we get the results. Do you have a preference for a hospital?"

They appeared about to protest, then the wife shivered and the husband pulled a jacket out of his bag. "Staten Island," he said.

Dr. Lewis, Faye's partner, was the Chief of Staff. When Faye arrived, she could give the hospital a heads up. The health department staffer called for emergency medical services.

Shouts about missed connections escalated from the long line snaking the wall with a single screener.

"Perhaps I can do something?" Maya waved in that direction.

The staffer handed her the laptop. "Sure, you've heard the routine. I'll stay here until EMS arrives."

Maya joined the second staffer who, clearly stressed, wiped sweat from her face and grimaced.

"Thank God, I could use the help. I've screened eleven people so far. They cleared fever checks and report no symptoms. None were in Guinea." She gestured to the group behind her, still not allowed to move toward the customs area.

"Will you require self-monitoring?" Maya asked.

"Yes. Tell each one that they must take their temperature twice daily and report symptoms to the health department."

"For how long?" Maya asked.

"Not sure yet. Dr. Moskowitz is consulting with the onsite CDC Port Health Station for those details. It's been a while since we worried about Ebola exposures on a plane."

The staffer showed Maya a seating chart provided by the airline. "Those I've already cleared sat more than two rows in front of or behind the couple you reported. We have different requirements for those sitting closer."

The fist of pain between Maya's shoulders intensified, but she stretched and took some deep breaths to ease it. "Unfortunately, that includes me."

She hadn't been sure what standard they'd use for Ebola. The two-row protocol applied to measles, rubella, and tuberculosis with proven aerosol transmission. Ebola infection usually required contact with blood or body fluids from an infected person or animal, or contaminated objects. Scientists still argued over the role of respiratory transmission through larger-sized droplets or smaller-particle aerosols from an infected person with coughing, vomiting, or diarrhea.

Someone behind Maya yelled, "You can't keep these older folks standing." She texted Faye. **<Where are you? The passengers are ready to revolt and I need your advice.>**

Faye called back. "What's up?"

"Symptomatic passenger and spouse are headed to Taylor's hospital."

"That's good—they have a special unit and procedures."

"For the passengers we already interviewed," Maya said, "we have their contact information, they didn't sit nearby, and they're asymptomatic. Have you heard any guidance for them?"

"They can proceed through customs and head home. Someone from the health department will follow up next week to see how they're doing."

"I wish CDC and the city had more staff," Maya said, "but I guess they're meeting other flights."

"I'm sorry, sir." The staffer sitting next to Maya raised a hand and spoke in a commanding voice. "You were in an area of the plane with heightened concern."

Maya glanced over to take in a family of three including a teenager with a partially shaved head and a nose ring. The girl jerked her hand to her face, then vomited on Maya's tennis shoes.

"Uh, Faye, I've got to go, we sure need you," Maya said.

Faye faded in and out. "Yeah, I'm the reinforcements. I can see you all on the other side of the customs booths. Be there soon."

TWELVE

Stefan shifted on his hospital bed, frustrated with his inability to do anything. Additional staff rushed by. Finally, Jan's awful moaning stopped. They probably increased his morphine dose.

Before their joint dengue investigation in the Democratic Republic of the Congo, Stefan had never met Jan, who reminded him of a puppy dog in training. Stefan enjoyed Jan's enthusiasm for work and play, but his tendency to act without thinking was a concern.

Only a couple weeks earlier, they'd shared an afternoon at the Lola ya Bonobo sanctuary near Kinshasa. The chimp-like animals, closest relatives to humans, entertained them by slamming tree branches against the wire fence. Jan danced in a wild circle outside the enclosure, encouraging a male bonobo to copy him.

Stefan's daughter Paula would have loved seeing the mom bonobos show off infants on their backs. Kondrat constantly lobbied for their family to come along on work trips. The sanctuary guide explained that the youngest orphan bonobos were cared for by staff members acting as surrogate mothers.

Because of COVID, the facility had canceled a much-advertised revenue generator allowing visitors to hold the babies. Jan was particularly disappointed at the policy change but Stefan understood their decision.

The evening after the bonobo exhibit, they had grazed at a Congolese buffet. They first sampled fufu, a sticky paste of boiled cassava, yams, and plantains. Then liboke, fish boiled in banana leaves and chile before grilling. A Soukous band in the back corner played local music loud enough to attract dancers and Jan struggled to make his voice heard.

"Bonobos, check. Gorillas are next on my list. A Nigerian physician is one of the attendees at our Conakry meeting, and they have a sanctuary. We should ask him to take us there."

Stefan wondered about hiding bonobo and gorilla sightings from Kondrat, who'd kill him for going on the adventures without his family. But the largest apes were on his bucket list, too. So he'd acquiesced to Jan's proposal, regrettably at this point as he sank lower on the hospital bed. He clutched at his abdomen, a ball of pain, rivaled only by the sledgehammer in his head.

Eyes closed, trying to reconstruct the bonobo memories, Stefan lost track of time. He didn't rouse until Biko's gloved hand touched his arm.

"Dr. Duda, I have bad news. With Dr. Kreischer's coagulation disorder and fluid loss, we couldn't save him."

Stefan shoved himself into a sitting position, unable to accept Jan's loss. "But surely you gave him the monoclonal antibodies."

Biko's entire body yearned to rip off the PPE and hurl it at Stefan. The last thing he needed was someone doubting his therapeutic acumen. He took a deep breath. "Bloody feces is a strong predictor of a fatal outcome. Despite INMAZEB and supportive care, we could not save him."

Stefan slid back down. Only a week and a half since Cross River, and they never even saw live gorillas. He should have listened to Kondrat and flown home to Oslo for a couple of days before the Conakry meeting. But Jan was passionate about photographing great apes and he might have arranged the trip with Biko anyways.

Losing a young person with such a vibrant life force seemed unreal. Perhaps if Stefan closed his eyes, he'd be back engaging with the bonobos, this time with one arm around Kondrat and the other hugging Paula.

THIRTEEN

She'd never jogged in her life, but Faye broke into a run and tightened her N95 mask when she spotted the teenager vomiting. No need to scare people with full PPE before Ebola confirmation. She commandeered an airport worker mopping the floors, then handed him her extra mask and gloves.

"Clean that up, please, but make sure it's in a separate sealed bag."

The guy frowned but complied with her authoritative voice and posture. If Maya was alarmed by her contaminated shoes, she didn't show it, typical of a young woman who seethed internally but remained buttoned up to the outside world.

"Hi, I'm Dr. Simpson," Faye said to the man holding the teenager's shoulders. "What have we got here?"

He turned his attention from Maya to Faye. "Supposedly we sat near another passenger who might have been exposed to that Ebola virus. Our daughter is exhausted and upset."

"I ate too much bagged popcorn on the plane." The girl brushed at her mouth with the back of her hand.

Faye handed her a sanitary wipe from her daypack. "You're not being singled out. It's standard procedure to monitor those at risk of certain diseases."

The woman slipped her arm around the girl's waist. "We need to get home. Tell us what to do."

"Where did you go on your trip overseas, and what's your next stop?" Faye asked.

"Paris, all the tourist spots," the father said. "We live in Brooklyn—that's where we're headed now."

"Give me a second to get oriented," Faye said to the family.

With a minimum incubation period of two days, it was impossible for the girl to have clinical signs so soon, even after nine hours on the plane. Faye was tempted to require laboratory testing, but they hadn't been in Conakry. The chance of confirming infection at this point was zero. However, any of the passengers could be infected from their flight exposure, even if it was too early for symptoms and a confirmatory test.

"Did you advise passengers seated farther away to do self-monitoring?" Faye asked Maya.

"Yes, and we told them someone will follow up near the end of the incubation period."

"These folks waiting behind you—they're the ones you're done with?"

Maya nodded and Faye joined the airport worker who controlled the cleared group. "Let these folks proceed through customs, get their luggage, and continue their journeys."

"About time." A male voice emitted from the pack. "I missed my connection—who's going to pay for that?"

Faye turned back to Maya, the health department screener, and the family. "For those in the five rows of concern, we'll do active monitoring. Require the same conditions as the self-monitoring group but flag their names for health department daily contact."

Refocused on the family, Faye added, "I agree that your daughter's vomiting is unlikely to be related to potential Ebola exposure on the plane, so I'm allowing you to go home. Lab testing isn't justified at this point but we will establish a direct active monitoring program. Please take the next 24 hours to recover at home. Someone from the health department will stop by tomorrow to confirm your status and discuss any plans for travel, work, or use of public spaces."

The man reached into his wallet for a business card. "I'm an assistant district attorney for the City and I have a court case in the morning."

Faye wrote Moshe's name and phone number on the card and

handed it back. "I advise taking the day off work so the department can make a more definitive decision. If you want to appeal my decision, contact the Commissioner."

She shouldn't sic an aggressive ADA on her old boss but he always wanted to be in control, so let him. That's why they paid him the big bucks.

As soon as the family left to join the other passengers headed for the customs counters, Maya muttered, "He should be grateful you didn't slap them into quarantine."

Maya usually was less harsh, surprising Faye. A long flight and anxiety over Ebola potentially invading the homeland had everyone on edge.

"Yeah, but you're in the same boat," Faye said. "You sat close to the Conakry couple."

"I'm not ill," Maya answered, her voice tense. "I'm glad no one requires quarantine. What a nightmare with the legal and logistical issues."

Faye glanced at the crowd still in front of them, more than a hundred passengers. "While you two continue interviews, I'll sort them into separate groups so we can handle them more efficiently." She texted Taylor about the couple on their way to the Staten Island hospital, then announced the rows of concern and moved those passengers to a line along the wall.

Maya handled those at lower risk. For the five closer rows with eight passengers each, Faye counted 34—no one missing other than the Conakry couple, the family of three, and Maya. In small clusters, she informed them about Ebola signs and symptoms and the need for temperature monitoring plus health department follow-up. Then directed them one-by-one to the other staffer.

She went back to Maya's line with those seated farther away and screened them for symptoms and travel histories, taking handwritten notes. When one masked woman moaned and sank to her roller bag, holding her head, Faye quickly shifted.

"Ma'am, are you okay?" Faye asked. "Do you have anyone traveling with you to help?"

The woman raised her head, eyes bloodshot, voice raspy. "No, I'm alone."

"Let me move you to the front." She helped the woman to her feet, held her arm, and pulled her luggage. As they walked, she continued her questions. "When did you become ill?"

"A few minutes ago."

Good, she hadn't been symptomatic on the plane. Ebola was one of those diseases that were more contagious as the signs and symptoms worsened.

Faye stopped by Maya, who'd finished with another passenger. "This lady just began to feel sick," Faye said, "which isn't surprising considering the time everyone's been standing. Can you interview her now?"

"Of course." Maya adjusted her mask and turned to the woman. "What was your overseas itinerary?"

The woman lowered to her bag again and held her hand to her forehead. "Sorry, this headache is intense. I'm a People, Culture, and Inclusion officer for Doctors Without Borders and I was at a health planning meeting in Guinea." She showed a text message on her phone about the WHO alert. "I hope I wasn't exposed to Ebola."

Faye's knees weakened as she reviewed the plane's seating chart. This new suspect case had been seated sixteen rows ahead of the possible Ebola case and her husband they'd sent to the hospital. Their whole game plan with only five rows of concern was now a cluster-fuck.

FOURTEEN

At the news of Jan's death, Stefan's eyelids fluttered and his breathing paused. Biko feared he'd lapsed into unconsciousness again. Then to his relief, Stefan trembled and reconnected his gaze.

"Jan's family in Germany," Stefan said in a weak voice. "Will you notify them?"

"Of course," Biko said. "Do you know how to reach them?"

"Lilly is his younger sister living with their parents in Hamburg."

"I will contact the conference organizers." Biko's exasperation heated his skin inside the protective suit. Stefan had worked together with Jan for weeks in the Congo but was offering few details to help Biko and the hospital locate Jan's family. As if there wasn't enough work caring for critically ill patients.

"Dr. Okeke, Biko—can you give me any kind of estimate when I can head home to Oslo? My family is quite anxious about it all."

The hospital could use the bed but Biko had to be honest. "It depends on your clinical course. The virus can persist in immunologically privileged sites, where immune cells are less likely to attack it."

"For Ebola, what are you talking about?"

"The interior of your eyes, central nervous system, and testicles. Even when you're feeling healthy, you can transmit the virus."

Stefan searched his memory for training lectures and journal articles. "I've never tackled Ebola so I don't recall the details."

"Viral RNA has been detected in seminal fluid more than three years after illness. Some cases, including yours, may be related to undetected virus in the semen of men who survived the 2014 outbreak in Guinea."

All of Stefan's muscles weakened at the news, but he had no sexual contact with anyone while in Africa. His health had never been in jeopardy from his job and now he posed a risk to Kondrat. What Jan had done in his private moments, Stefan didn't know.

"Ah, that's a shock. How long do I have to worry?"

"You must avoid unprotected sexual intercourse for at least six months," Biko said.

Manageable, Stefan thought. He'd been Kondrat's partner for more than a decade and had limited sexual contacts before that. Using a condom again—it was possible.

"Anything else I should know?"

"In addition to sexual dysfunction, there are many other complications such as loss of hair, vision, hearing, and memory. Also depression and anxiety."

Stefan rarely experienced a down day, but the possibility loomed like a fog around his hospital bed. "Besides sex, are there other ways I could spread it to my family?"

"All bodily secretions for several weeks—sweat, tears, saliva, vomit, feces, and nasal blood."

The news overwhelmed Stefan—he couldn't threaten Paula.

"Back to my original question. When can I get out of here?"

"When you're clinically improved and viral RNA is no longer detected in your blood. We will re-evaluate at the end of the week."

Despite his stress, or perhaps because of it, Stefan napped until jerked awake by another patient's screams. Faint light, tinged the color of blood, seeped through the high windows. With Oslo two hours ahead of Guinea, Paula was probably sleeping while Kondrat consumed his latest Nordic crime thriller.

This time when Stefan reached for his phone, he found it on the hospital tray. Biko must have remembered his request. Thank God he was cared for by someone he knew, making the trauma of hospitalization more tolerable.

"Hallo." Kondrat's speech was flat, as if answering a call from a telemarketer.

"Kondrat, are you in bed?" Stefan ignored his partner's frosty greeting and turned on the charm. "I miss you so much, kochanie."

"Don't 'sweetheart' me," Kondrat answered.

"All right, I promise not to flirt. What's your current novel?"

"*Everything is Mine* by Ruth Lillegraven. The protagonist has a less-than-ideal marriage, imagine that."

Perhaps an Ebola update should wait for Kondrat's mood to improve, but Stefan knew little of patience. "You'll be happy to hear I'm feeling better. My physician will do another lab test in a few days, then decide when I can fly to Oslo."

"That's wonderful news." Kondrat's intonation softened. "Paula's asking about you."

Stefan decided to avoid any delay in presenting the semen issue. They'd always been honest with each other, no matter how uncomfortable the topic. "There's a slight complication. To avoid risk of Ebola transmission, I have to wear a condom for six months."

Kondrat's usually higher-pitched voice dropped into a growl. "Who were you fucking over there? Don't worry, a condom's unnecessary. You're not coming home." Then he hung up.

FIFTEEN

Taylor Lewis headed to the isolation suite after receiving Faye's text about the Masons' Ebola exposure in Guinea. Sometimes when greeting new patients, Taylor donned a black wig in alignment with their trans female status.

The Cher imitation was Faye's preference but Taylor often chose dreads at work. With a favorite mauve for lipstick and fingernails, Taylor usually passed for female despite XY chromosomes and intact male genitalia. Their height and husky voice might confuse others, but decades of estrogen had softened facial lines and provided small breasts.

When wearing personal protective equipment, Taylor went with a bald, shaved head. No need to add unneeded fake hair to make the suit more claustrophobic. The EMT radioed that the patient vomited enroute, and Taylor verified that all of the response team had completed the required training. For their first possible Ebola case, there would be no breaks in protocol.

Under the supervision of a trained observer, each team member donned their PPE, including a single-use impermeable coverall, double gloves with extended cuffs, and disposable boot covers extending to mid-calf. The powered air-purifying respirator, or PAPR, included a full-face covering and head-shroud. With the news about vomiting, disposable aprons were added to reduce contamination of the coverall by bodily fluids.

As they awaited the ambulance near a special unloading area, Taylor projected on a wall screen the Occupational Safety and Health Administration's Bloodborne Pathogens standards for viral hemorrhagic fever exposures.

Upon arrival, the ambulance staff kept the woman on the gurney despite her insistence that she could walk. In an exam room with negative air pressure to avoid virus escape to the building, Taylor administered the initial screening questions about the Conakry meeting, then noted the couple's temperatures.

"You're fine," Taylor told the husband. "At this point, you need to be in a separate area."

"That's not happening." He clutched his wife's hand.

Taylor's decades of experience with upset patients kicked in. "I'm sorry, sir, but you won't be far away and I'll update you."

A nurse led the husband down the hall and Taylor checked Dr. Mason's chart. As a health care economist, she should be familiar with the medical world, but tears streamed down her face. Compared to studying it, everything upended when ensnared in the system due to illness.

"I understand this is frightening, but you're in good hands here," Taylor said. "You made it home and will be offered the best possible care. First we need to confirm what we're dealing with. We'll take a couple tubes of blood and get them to our health department for rapid testing."

Dontrell, the young lab tech, asked Dr. Mason to make a fist, cleaned the inside of her elbow with antiseptic, and applied a tourniquet to her bicep.

"Can you make it a little looser?" Dr. Mason poked at her upper arm.

Dontrell's dark eyebrows scrunched, a level of concern apparent to Taylor through the face mask.

"It has to be tight to block blood flow so I can see your vein," Dontrell explained, then inserted a needle. Unable to bring blood into the hub, he adjusted the angle several times without success.

"Ow, that hurts," Dr. Mason complained. "And my fingers are tingling."

The tourniquet might be too tight with potential damage to nerves and blood vessels. Taylor debated whether to take over the venipuncture, but that would demoralize Dontrell, and Taylor's skills were unlikely to be fresh compared to a tech who did the procedure daily.

With a new needle and a second vein, Dontrell drew two tubes of blood. He released the tourniquet and removed the needle. At that moment, Dr. Mason muttered, "Thank God you're done," and vomited all over Dontrell's arm and hand.

Startled, Dontrell palmed the needle in his contaminated hand and snagged a cotton ball with the other one as blood pooled inside Dr. Mason's elbow. Blood still oozed and Taylor handed over more cotton balls, then applied a strip of adhesive tape.

Grabbing a towel, Dontrell cleaned up yellow fluid tinged with blood from Dr. Mason's pants leg. Taylor called for a nurse from the hall. "Please escort Dr. Mason to the next room. I'll be there in a moment."

"It's just stress, I'm sorry, I'd be more comfortable at home." Dr. Mason grabbed the towel from Dontrell and patted her mouth with a clean end.

"You need a complete clinical evaluation and the lab results." Taylor assumed a conciliatory but authoritative tone.

Once Dr. Mason had left, Taylor surveyed the area contaminated with blood and vomitus. "Get those specimens to the city lab asap. I'll find someone to take care of this mess."

Before marking the tubes, Dontrell headed to the sink to wash the blood and vomitus from his PPE. Then he froze like a marble statue as he opened his hand clenching the needle. "Uh, Dr. Lewis, I've got a tear in my gloves."

Taylor took Dontrell's hand. The hole went through both gloves and blood glistened from the base of his thumb. An Ebola needle-stick—Taylor forgot how to breathe.

SIXTEEN

The lab worker trembled, eyes glued to the penetration of his protective bubble, hand injected with the blood of a possible Ebola patient.

"Dr. Mason might not have Ebola virus disease, and this blood could be your own, not hers." Taylor squeezed Dontrell's shoulder. "Let's head to the changing area and get you out of this gear, then clean your hand."

A nurse supervised Dontrell doffing the PPE, then wound management. Taylor labeled the blood tubes and ordered an environmental services staff member to clean the exam room. Next, Taylor removed their own coverings and delivered the specimens to the hospital lab. Finally, they checked in on Dontrell, playing a video game on his phone.

"You should stay in our isolation suite," Taylor said.

Dontrell rotated his hand. "Aw, doc, everything's fine. It was a stupid mistake."

"I agree, you probably have nothing to worry about. But let's play it safe."

The nurse poked her head back into Dontrell's room. "Dr. Lewis, we have another patient who took those same flights from Conakry and then Paris."

When it rains, it pours. "All right, let me gear up again." Taylor gathered the hospital team and repeated all the procedures with the newly admitted Doctors Without Borders staffer. The older woman was travel-stressed, sweating, and weak. Taylor kept her overnight for observation and fluids, along with a blood test. Fortunately, no more mistakes with PPE protocols occurred.

At eleven PM, shift changes and new workers in place, Taylor took a break in the hospital cafeteria. A cup of black coffee was calling but at the late hour, herbal tea won out.

"Are you dumping all your Ebola patients on me?" Taylor asked when connecting to Faye on FaceTime.

With the airport in her background, Faye frowned, her round freckled face more deeply wrinkled than ever. "I don't know what you're talking about."

"Two of your ill Conakry passengers ended up here," Taylor said.

"The health economist couple said they were headed to Staten Island. Is the husband showing symptoms, too?"

Taylor always enjoyed teasing Faye, who gave as good as she got. Some other doctors wondered why Taylor partnered with a portly white senior citizen. But then, they didn't know how lively Faye could be, in everything she did.

"No, although we kept Dr. Mason's husband just in case. I'm talking about the woman working for Médecins Sans Frontières."

"Oh yeah, Doctors Without Borders. We had to expand our targeted plane rows when we found out about her. Didn't realize she's at your hospital—guess everyone wants the best."

"Shh, keep it down." Taylor relaxed with the potent herbs in the tea. "Those snooty Manhattan docs will get jealous."

Faye rubbed her droopy eyes. "On the second flight from Paris, we identified five more passengers who originated in Conakry—I'm not sure which hospital took them in."

"Seven total—that's a lot of Ebola suspects. But our system is better prepared than the last time health care workers brought the virus here from Africa. Hopefully we'll head off the hospital transmission they had in Texas a few years back."

Taylor didn't bring up the potential exposure of the lab tech with a needlestick. Until their recent long-term commitment, Faye wasn't the type to unduly worry. But now she was cautious about either of them taking risks. After all, they weren't getting any younger.

Faye's camera shifted to include Maya in an airport café.

"Hi, Dr. Lewis." Maya's chin rested on both hands.

She looked more fried than Faye. When they were all together in Hawai'i last September, Maya had confessed her discomfort with long flights and difficulty sleeping on them. Taylor guessed that Maya had been awake for more than 24 hours.

"Good to see you again, Maya. When will Moshe allow you two to go home?" Taylor couldn't avoid coloring their tone with disrespect. Faye's rantings likely influenced Taylor's opinion, but some pedantic Zoom meetings during COVID played a role. Dr. Moskowitz was full of himself, giving orders to hospitals instead of pursuing partnerships.

"I just checked in with him. A new shift is greeting the flights, and I'm taking a taxi with Maya back to my apartment."

"He should count his blessings you volunteered to help him out." But Taylor respected Faye enough to let her make her own decisions about this temporary contract.

According to Dr. Mason, attendees at the Conakry meeting started their travels on Friday, so the arrivals of concern should taper off. Of course, some may have stayed extra days in West Africa for multiple reasons, and passengers at risk could still trickle in.

"Moshe will notify other states through a CDC Epi-X report," Faye said. "Then we'll hear if patients show up in any other countries or US cities."

"I'll keep you posted on those in my hospital. Is Maya still planning to spend some time in the Big Apple?"

A worried frown flashed across Maya's face. "I sat right in front of Dr. Mason on the plane. I'm not sure it's safe for me to stay with Faye if I'm incubating Ebola virus."

But in that case, she shouldn't fly home until Taylor sorted out what was making Dr. Mason sick. Taylor swallowed a twinge of resentment that anyone might jeopardize Faye's health, after the fear of almost losing her to dengue fever last fall.

"My fingers are crossed," Faye said with a smile. "There's still no consensus that Ebola is spread through the air, and we'll mask around each other as much as possible. I'm hoping that at some point, the three of us can paint the town before Maya has to head home."

"Me, too," Taylor said. New York, with all its travails, would be much safer if it didn't have Ebola.

SEVENTEEN

Stefan's muscles cramped from lack of movement and worry about Kondrat prohibiting his return home. Kondrat often reacted from immediate emotion and calmed down later—Stefan chose to remain optimistic. Using condoms for several months was no big deal, but he should have found a way to broach the issue more gently.

Careful not to dislodge his IV line, he swung his legs to the side of the bed and stood up. He stretched his long arms up along the wall behind the bed, then squatted with his back against the wall. Nothing better than moving again. The man nearby with the reddened eyes sobbed about the pain in his knees, and the nurse adjusted his morphine dose. With a sudden bout of dizziness, Stefan sank back into his bed.

Biko was nowhere in sight. Other staff might have answers but Stefan trusted his WHO colleague, even if he was occasionally prickly. Biko clearly felt guilty about the gorilla expedition, but Stefan and Jan were the ones who pushed for it. Although WHO downplayed the animals as the source, Stefan would place money on the gorillas. Next time he talked to Maya, he'd ask her to research Ebola in nonhuman primates.

Whether the outbreak flared up from simmering disease in Guinea over the past year wasn't Stefan's primary concern. Question number one: How could he convince Kondrat he hadn't slept around, so he'd be allowed home?

Using PubMed on his phone, Stefan found a study in Sierra Leone from 2016 in which Ebola survivors were discharged on average 20 days after symptom onset, when symptoms abated and they tested negative. Only hospitalized four days so far, he had a long way to go. Staying bedridden in this hell-hole for another two weeks with nothing to do except listen to dying patients would drive him insane.

Stefan glanced to his side, afraid the nearby patient could hear his unsympathetic thoughts. He honed in on the study's details. Minimum hospitalization time was 12 days—could he hang on for another week? The maximum of 45 days would never apply if he didn't have another seizure.

Question number two: What was the level of evidence for semen being a threat? There must be a way to alleviate Kondrat's freak-out. But another Sierra Leone study published last year provided no consolation. Maximum duration of viral RNA in the semen—696 days. That didn't necessarily mean the guy was contagious—perhaps the detected particles were dead viral fragments.

So why did Biko recommend condoms for only six months? Three-quarters of the Sierra Leone patients still had indications of virus in their semen at that point. Men over 35 years of age, which included Stefan at 37, stayed positive for a lengthier period.

But viral persistence wasn't the only problem. More than half the male survivors experienced longer-term symptoms of sexual fatigue. Stefan couldn't fathom not wanting sex with Kondrat, but if he continued to feel like crap, that might be understandable.

Nothing in his research was reassuring. Sometimes it was worse for doctors to be patients. They knew too much.

EIGHTEEN

A furry paw poked at Maya's nose with the desired effect—she opened her eyes. "Bosco, you cutie pie."

Pale yellow light from the spring morning filtered through Faye's lace curtains, along with the brake squeal and clanging crunch from a garbage truck compacting the city's waste. Maya got up from the couch and looked out the window. Brilliant red tulips and golden double-frilled daffodils greeted the dawn from a curbside flower box.

The tortie cat brushed Maya's bare calves beneath her short gown. Bosco's food bowl was empty, and Faye had shown Maya where the food was stored. She gingerly opened the kitchen cabinet to avoid waking up Faye. Then she dropped a handful of the dry food into the dish and rubbed her hand over the length of the cat's body.

"You're so soft, gatita bonita," she told the cat, then settled back on the couch with a cup of water. Her brain felt pillow soft from insufficient sleep, but her adrenaline was on a New York level of intensity.

Before they turned in around midnight, Faye mentioned that the doorman delivered the New York Times early. Maya undid three locks, then opened the door to find the paper on the floor mat.

Multiple public health issues filled the front page, including an accelerating wildfire risk and a warning that the evolving coronavirus could lead to repeat infections. But the primary headline focused on Saturday's massacre of ten people at a Buffalo grocery store. CDC was forbidden from studying gun violence for almost 25 years, but finally funding was restored.

Maya released a deep sigh and took another drink of water. Only four years into her epidemiology career, she wasn't capable of evaluating the overall public health infrastructure. But her work load had been affected by lack of money and personnel, especially during the pandemic when so many staff burned out or quit in frustration over opposition and threats.

Those factors could determine her own decisions after her CDC training concluded next month. Staying in New Mexico had its advantages. Dr. Grinwold valued her statistical skills and she owed him a lot. The learning curve to become the official State Public Health Veterinarian wouldn't be steep. In fact, life would be simpler because she'd lose the second boss at CDC headquarters in Atlanta.

Just last week when she checked in with Dr. Grinwold from Paris, he'd complained that program funding was down despite the pandemic. CDC resources directly impacted a state's preparedness level. He expected to have a sufficient budget to keep her on board, but couldn't finalize the position until he knew her salary expectation.

If she didn't accept Dr. Grinwold's offer, other options might be limited at this late date. In a prolonged 'go with the flow' frame of mind, she'd made no effort to job-search. Physicians were preferred for public health leadership and a MPH degree was the entry card for worker bees. Sometimes agencies didn't recognize the value of a veterinary epidemiologist.

She got up and rinsed her cup, then studied Faye's diplomas on the living room wall. University of Northern Colorado for her undergrad and master's degrees, followed by the University of Colorado for her DVM degree, 32 years before Maya.

Just then, Faye strolled into the living room in her cheetah-patterned pj's and fluffy slippers.

"Does it ever bother you that we needed a master's on top of our vet degrees to get accepted into EIS?" Maya asked. Unlike the vets, physicians who dominated CDC's Epidemic Intelligence Service program didn't require any advanced public health or research training before they started.

Faye shrugged. "So we're more valuable from the get go—I have no problem with that. Our additional degrees make it easier for health commissioners to justify a vet for a public health position, especially in leadership."

Maya nodded. At the moment, she wasn't really focused on a new job anyways. Did New York, other states, and CDC have sufficient resources to fight an Ebola outbreak on home soil?

"I assume you have coffee going," Faye said with a wink.

Maya flushed. "I, ah, I didn't know you had a coffee maker." As a tea drinker, she hadn't checked.

Faye laughed. "Just pulling your leg. For years, I picked up a cup on my way to work. Never had the motivation to grind my own beans."

"Now that you're mostly retired, what do you do?" Maya asked.

"Go for a walk at my favorite time of day. Care to join me?"

"Sure. I never hung out in this end of Manhattan during grad school. Does Dr. Moskowitz need your help with Ebola follow-up today?"

Faye shook her head no. "If we get confirmations, he might need me, but for the moment, it's under control."

Maya grabbed a change of clothes from her suitcase and was ready in fifteen minutes. Neither of them fussed with makeup or hair.

A couple blocks away, they found a place to buy a cup of green tea for Maya and black coffee for Faye. Faye pointed out the entrance to MOCA, the Museum of Chinese in America, among the myriad shops in Chinatown. "We should make a point to visit while you're here," she said.

"I'd like that," Maya said. "I heard about that fire two years ago which threatened the museum's collections."

"One more blow during COVID." Faye led them to a covered structure with benches in the street outside a restaurant, now empty in the early hours. "The pandemic hit New York harder than any other city in the world, and Chinatown was targeted by so many people as the source."

Maya recalled the guy in Santa Fe who threw a beer can in her face while blaming her for the pandemic. "In Arizona, my dark hair and skin didn't make me self-conscious even without many Asians. My parents took me to Chinese cultural activities and we hung out with other adoptive families."

Faye leaned back and rested her feet on the opposite bench. Her typical office position, feet up on a chair or the desk. Maya had heard its informality drove Dr. Moskowitz crazy.

"Would you be more comfortable in someplace like New York where you'd be less conspicuous?" Faye asked.

Maya loved living close to her parents, happily retired in Flagstaff. But cutting the cord could be beneficial. Working in New York would enhance her renewed bond with Manolo's dad.

"I should call Sebastian," Maya said. "I didn't give him a heads up about my visit because I wanted to check our schedule first." But with Ebola, she should stay away until the incubation period for her possible exposure had passed. Manolo's sister still blamed her for the COVID infection that killed him. She couldn't risk that again with another disease and another member of his family.

"Let's find out if there was transmission on your flight before you spend extended time in closer contact with others." Faye's words confirmed Maya's own conclusion.

Increasing traffic drowned the sweet songs of birds greeting the morning. A Tesla driver stuck behind a delivery truck leaned hard on his horn, reminding Maya that magical moments in New York could vanish in a heartbeat.

"When do you think the Ebola results will be available?" Maya asked.

"I'm not sure if the specimens were set up last night. Moshe said a handful of passengers from other flights were hospitalized. The lab has a lot on its plate."

"So it's unlikely we'll know anything today. Maybe I should avoid prolonged time indoors with you too."

Faye slapped her hand on the table. "Don't be ridiculous. You're not experiencing symptoms, are you?"

Maya did a quick self-screen. Still a bit fuzzy-brained from insufficient sleep, but otherwise fine. "It's too soon because my exposure to ill passengers was only yesterday."

"We've been masked, except when you ate and drank, and Ebola is unlikely to be transmitted without symptoms. It's not the same as COVID, which you can spread for a couple of days before you feel sick."

No risk to Faye or the Mirandas, Maya thought. At least, not now.

But Manolo's sister wouldn't appreciate that. The tiniest chance of spreading an exotic disease to her son, almost seven years old, wouldn't be tolerated.

NINETEEN

Within one day, WHO had provided contact information for Jan's family. Biko located a crab apple tree outside the hospital walls for some shade to place the call. Stepping away from dying patients made the outbreak slightly less real, and more tolerable. Until a young woman answered the phone with "Lilly Kreischer, Guten Tag" at the Gustave Mahler Museum after he struck out at the family residence.

Biko knew little German but recognized the greeting. He hoped that Jan's sister spoke English.

"Fräulein Kreischer, this is Dr. Biko Okeke from the World Health Organization. I'm a colleague of your brother, Dr. Jan Kreischer." He hesitated, trying to form the words. He had some practice during his medical residency in informing family members of the deceased, but not enough to feel comfortable.

"I'm calling from Conakry, Guinea, where Dr. Kreischer attended a medical conference with me."

"Ja, ja." Her voice became strained and nervous. "We expected he might be home on the weekend, but then when we could not reach him, we assumed he was kept longer for his job. Working for WHO, his plans change frequently."

"Yes, our duties provide unexpected challenges, including health risks. Unfortunately your brother was confirmed with Ebola infection. I hoped the hospital or WHO had contacted you sooner, but things have been chaotic over the past few days."

In his pause to pronounce the final, damning words, Lilly jumped back in. "Thank you for calling now. Can we fly down to Guinea to see him? How is he doing?"

"I am so sorry—I cannot give you good news. He passed away yesterday. We are still waiting for a pathologist to perform an autopsy."

A passing breeze, or perhaps her scream, was loud enough to loosen crab apple blossoms to sprinkle his shoulders. The color was bright pink, normally cheerful, but today the darker red of closed blossoms reminded him too much of blood. He should have verified Lilly was in a quiet place before revealing the awful news. But if she wasn't alone, perhaps that was better.

An older woman came on the line. "This is Lilly's supervisor. What are you calling about?"

She'd overhead enough of the call to speak in English, and Biko rapidly provided information about the WHO office which would assist in returning Jan's body.

Unsure how else to help Jan's family, Biko said goodbye. Stefan was on the road to recovery—hopefully Biko wouldn't need to go through this terrible ritual a second time.

That evening in the upscale Conakry restaurant, Biko's forehead beaded with perspiration. Suddenly dizzy, he propped up his head with one hand. Then he asked his dining companion, a minister with Guinea's Ministère de la Santé et de l'Hygiène Publique, to repeat her question.

His fluency in French, the official language of Guinea's educated citizenry, was only to the level of university classes, and opportunities to practice had been few. He instinctively knew to avoid looking into the eyes of a Muslim woman or someone of higher social status, so he focused his gaze on the linen-covered table.

"For the moment, we have sufficient resources," Biko answered. "It is only five days since Dr. Kreischer's greatest period for transmission, when he was showing symptoms before hospitalization."

His stomach twisted into a knot. His tongue enjoyed the rich flavors of the konkoé, the smoked catfish and vegetable stew. But he should not have ordered the Sauce d'arrachide ou Kansiyé. Too spicy with its mix of peanut butter, garlic, and hot chili peppers.

"Over the next two weeks," he continued, "I expect a surge of cases due to direct exposures from Dr. Kreischer. Those people may then expose others. To use an English expression, I fear we are only seeing the tip of the iceberg."

"Inshallah, we will not have thousands of deaths like the Titanic which inspired your expression." The Minister's white teeth flashed in a grim smile, as bright as the gold glimmering from her ears, neck, and wrist. She tapped her fingers in time with the chant of an older griot in the corner. The storyteller plucked the large 21-string kora, made from a calabash gourd that rested between his knees.

This time, Biko dared to look more directly at the Minister. Few other women dined at the upscale restaurant. She wore an elegant black turban adorned with intricate embroidery. Her niqab veil sat on a plush, gold cushion, no longer covering her mouth and nose.

"I share your hope." He took another sip of his bissap. The mint in the purple-colored hibiscus drink would settle his stomach. "I discussed the vaccine on Friday with my supervisor, Dr. Shah. Has he spoken with you about the process?"

She nodded. "I will start the request tomorrow. WHO recommends submitting it within seven days after confirmation of the outbreak, so we are ahead of the game."

"What is the caseload in other hospitals?" Biko asked.

"Constantly shifting, and the counts are unreliable. Everyone has a different case definition—some waiting for laboratory confirmation and others relying just on clinical signs."

When Dr. Duda felt better, Biko planned to request his epidemiologic skills to document and control the outbreak, especially if the dead gorilla was the cause of this mess. As the senior physician in age and experience, Stefan shouldn't have lobbied for the trip.

"Female patients prefer female physicians," the minister said, "but we have a shortage. Would you mind assisting with supervision of patients in the women's section of your hospital?"

In Nigeria, Biko had cared for equal proportions of Muslims and Christians, but in Guinea, most of the population was Muslim, with greater preferences for gender segregation.

"I assume you will have a female nurse to assist me."

The minister nodded.

Biko shivered. Restaurants like this one that catered to western visitors or the elite class tended to overdo it with their air conditioning. When he reached for his credit card, the Minister waved her finger.

"Assalamu alaikum. This is the least we can offer in thanks for a visiting physician who puts his life on the line for our patients."

Biko arrived at the women's isolation ward close to midnight and found no female nurses on duty. Weary and impatient, he regretted not checking in on those patients sooner. An emaciated young woman, perhaps no older than a teenager, grabbed for his hand as he passed by her bed. She spoke to him in Fula, a dialect used by millions of people in Guinea, Nigeria, and other African countries.

"I am pregnant—I have pain."

If at home in his Lagos hospital, and not faced with Ebola isolation, Biko would find the girl's husband or female relative close at hand. As he determined next steps, blood in her pelvic region spread out on the covering sheet from the size of an ink spot to the dimensions of a rare steak.

He yanked the sheet back while calling out at the top of his voice, "Nurse, I need help! Infirmière, aidez-moi!"

Her total absence of a clitoris and vulvar labia shocked him. He remembered that more than ninety percent of women in Guinea underwent female genital mutilation, starting at age four. Fortunately, rates were much lower in Nigeria except for certain regions. Her scar tissue could lead to prolonged and obstructed labor, resulting in the loss of a child.

Given the size and low position of the infant, she appeared ready to deliver. Before he could ask her any questions or stop the bleeding, her eyes closed and she stopped breathing.

TWENTY

A skateboarder nearly knocked Faye over as he raced through the crowds on the Brooklyn Bridge pedestrian promenade. He vanished before Taylor could yell a reminder that he belonged in the special bicycle lane.

Taylor instinctively looped an arm around Faye, then the second one around Maya, as they approached a boisterous group of teenage boys. The narrow walkway was jammed by vendors selling ballcaps, t-shirts, keychains, and other New York souvenirs.

"I appreciate your sharing an iconic experience." Maya adjusted her surgical mask. "But maybe this wasn't a good idea." Unmasked pedestrians invaded her personal space and ramped up her anxiety. Screeching brakes from the vehicle traffic under the platform triggered flashbacks of a pickup truck colliding with her bicycle when she was a child.

"You're not in any official quarantine," Faye said, "and you're following the City's advice to monitor your symptoms including temperature checks. We need this break to clear our heads."

Taylor understood Maya's concern. They'd worked almost non-stop since Maya's plane arrived yesterday afternoon with the two ill women from the Conakry meeting. Maya's body likely thought it was four AM, way past time to be sleeping. As much as Taylor wanted to support Faye's attempt to entertain Maya, calling it quits on the evening would be a welcome choice.

"You both pulled another eight-hour shift at JFK, and I'm fading too," Taylor said. "Let's take in the view from the base of the tower, then head on home for some rest."

As Maya's phone buzzed with a new text from Mark, she

thanked Taylor for wrapping up their jaunt. Mark had called midday to verify that Maya was comfortably ensconced with Faye in New York. She'd shared the news about Ebola, swearing him to silence until the City or CDC issued a press release. Now he wouldn't leave her alone, urging her to take it easy and get tested.

Maya typed a quick **<Don't worry, playing tourist now>**, then Faye led the way along the path over the traffic lanes which offered an unobstructed view north along the East River. Faye pointed to the left. "Can you see the Empire State Building?"

Maya nodded, remembering her overnight near there last August when she flew out for Manolo's funeral service. Her stomach tightened at the possible pushback if she tried to visit his family again.

She crossed to the southern viewing platform and spotted the thin spire of Freedom Tower, One World Trade Center. A tiny greenish figure floated above the dark water in the distance. "Is that the Statue of Liberty?"

"You got it," Faye answered. "Did you ever go to the crown? It's closed since COVID. Such a shame people can't do it anymore."

Maya sucked in a calming breath. "Yeah, one of those classic experiences for which photos are no substitute." The number of green copper pieces and rivets had been impressive, but she didn't plan to repeat the claustrophobic climb, even if it reopened.

Taylor pried a ringing phone out of tight jeans. "It's your boss, I mean your ex-boss."

Why is he calling Taylor and not me? Faye wondered. But Taylor had a more central role with patient care.

"Good evening, Moshe." Taylor decided against using the speaker in the busy area. Better be careful with the words on the call, as well.

Moshe rushed ahead with the news. "The two women you have there in Staten Island—our lab reports them as Ebola. At the moment, your lab worker with the needlestick is negative, but I recommend retesting again in a couple of days to be sure. We have four more confirmed cases in other Ebola treatment centers."

"I'll ask our staff to reassess biosafety. Do you have additional results for our hospitalized husband?" Taylor assumed the man was in the clear or Moshe would have mentioned him.

"Negative. He's still healthy?"

"Asymptomatic when I checked on him. As a precaution, we've got him in isolation."

"What's the clinical status of your patients?"

"Stable, for the moment."

"All right. I'll convene a discussion early tomorrow with the state and CDC about next steps. We will likely update our monitoring plan for plane passengers."

Taylor glanced over at Maya. Those decisions would impact her, too. In the haunting light of the bridge LEDs, her eyes had rounded and her skin took on a sallow shade.

Maya guessed the bad news—first American Ebola cases in eight years. And twisted viral filaments might be replicating in her blood.

TWENTY-ONE

Biko spent the morning finalizing the release of Jan Kreischer's body to his parents, who'd flown down to accompany it home. A long way to go for a ritual, but they seemed to take comfort in placing their hands on the sealed casket. They were wide-eyed at the tented triage area in the parking lot and the moonsuit-clad staff hurrying to and from the hospital entrance. Maybe it was good that they saw firsthand the dedication of those trying to save lives from Ebola.

At noon, he sank to a chair next to the bed where Stefan dozed. Biko's limbs felt tethered to the earth by steel struts. He'd arranged for his own rule-out Ebola test, but the results weren't back yet. His headache intensified, but it might be stress from managing both the men's and women's Ebola isolation units. With the pregnant woman's death, the Minister had come through with more female nurses to assist on the women's side.

Stefan's eyes fluttered open. "Biko, it's good to see you." He looked at his phone. "Thursday—I've been here a week."

"How are you doing today?" Biko asked.

Stefan propped himself higher on the bed, adjusting the pillow to cushion the thick metal railing that substituted for a headboard. He pulled his arms out from under the sheet and studied them. "No rash." He assessed his gastrointestinal system. "No nausea, vomiting, or diarrhea."

Biko handed Stefan a clinical glass thermometer. "You know the routine, in your armpit."

"I thought this was one of the better hospitals," Stefan groused. "Where's the digital infrared scanner?"

"You should be grateful for my expertise instead of complaining about our resources," Biko snapped back. The hospital's air conditioning had been out for several hours due to one of Conakry's intermittent power outages, and Biko's forehead dripped sweat into his eyes under his face shield.

He held out his hand for the thermometer and Stefan gave it back. "37 degrees Celsius—normal," Biko said. "We need the bed, so I'm kicking you out. I'd like your help."

Failing to allay Kondrat's anger and fear on daily phone calls, Stefan had nothing better to do until Kondrat allowed him to come home. Besides, his insatiable curiosity was piqued by the chance to work on his first Ebola outbreak. "I didn't intend to sound like an asshole. What can I do?"

"More than 300 suspect cases in isolation throughout Conakry require follow-up. Our case definitions are too broad, so we classify as suspect cases a lot of other diseases with similar symptoms. Those include malaria, typhoid fever, influenza, meningococcal disease, and other bacterial infections."

On his phone, Biko pulled up the materials developed by the World Health Organization for case and contact definitions during the 2014 outbreak. "WHO has a committee evaluating these, but they are not prepared to release updates until the fall."

Stefan rubbed his own perspiring face with his upper arm, covered by the short-sleeved gown. "Won't the Regional Director make the ultimate decision?"

"Of course, but I respect your opinion." A decade older than Biko, Stefan had battled disease outbreaks all over the world from multiple viruses, bacteria, and parasites.

"Less than half of the suspect cases are getting laboratory-confirmed," Biko continued, "resulting in a lot of noise in our data. With too much misclassification of other diseases as Ebola, our healthcare system is overwhelmed."

A familiar issue for Stefan during the height of the pandemic. "So your isolation beds are filled by non-Ebola patients who don't need that level of protection from person-to-person spread."

Biko nodded. "Once you are out of the hospital, we can plan your work."

Despite his eagerness to make a contribution after everything Biko and the hospital had done for him, Stefan was worried. "Do you think I pose a risk to anyone when doing case investigations?"

Biko wished he had a clear-cut answer. "Recovered patients are the best investigators and caregivers. You're unlikely to be reinfected, but some people may fear being close to you."

"How about virus isolation? If it's positive, we know I can transmit."

"I will draw a blood specimen but it will take several days for the result. I was serious about needing the bed for other patients, so I will discharge you to your hotel. You must remain there until I clear you. At that point, you will use PPE and should pose no threat to others when you start work again."

"I plan to sleep alone," Stefan joked. If he needed to kill time before safely returning home, at least it would be for a good purpose.

Biko compared his own symptoms of headache, loss of appetite, lethargy, and aching muscles to the case definition on his phone. Only three of them, plus high fever, were required to qualify as a suspect case. At 38 degrees Celsius when he checked last hour, he definitely had a fever, but not high enough by some standards.

He chose to be optimistic. Probably nothing more than heat exhaustion from the workload. Guinea's infrastructure including the hospital's climate control was overwhelmed by the warming planet. Or maybe just corruption and incompetence.

TWENTY-TWO

Maya exited the subway at 72nd Street and walked one block north along Broadway. On a Friday night, the Upper West Side sidewalk was jammed with people enjoying the remaining hour before sunset. Several days into her New York stopover, she'd recovered from her trip, and her pulse buzzed with the city's energy.

She dodged a few puddles from the light rain that had just lifted. Then she paused to admire the ornate balconies and rounded towers of the Beaux-Arts condo building, now illuminated by golden rays of the setting sun as damp fog wafted toward Central Park.

A famous actor's wife had been confirmed with Ebola infection, and Moshe had tasked Maya to verify that the husband remained asymptomatic and quarantined at home. On her second visit, the doorman waved her through to the elevator. Renowned for their charitable work in Africa, the couple had attended the meeting in Conakry to announce a sizable donation for regional hospitals. Fortunately, the wife remained stable during her hospitalization with high fever, difficulty swallowing and breathing, and hiccups.

Until her flight home to Santa Fe on Sunday, Maya represented CDC on Ebola control. In the hallway of the 7th floor, she pulled her PPE out of her pack and donned it, hoping to avoid contact with other residents who would likely freak out.

She rang the doorbell. No answer. Double-gloved, she tried to rap on the wooden door loud enough for Mr. Lund to hear. At the dinner hour, it was unlikely he'd be napping. Maybe he was on the phone or watching TV, oblivious to the knocking. She removed her headgear and put her ear to the door, but heard nothing. Then she used her phone, only to receive a recorded message.

The next call went to Faye. "I can't meet you and Taylor for dinner. My last contact isn't answering his door."

"Someone new?" Faye stood on the deck of the Staten Island Ferry with her arm around Taylor, both headed back to Manhattan after meeting up at Taylor's hospital.

"It's that actor, Todd Lund. He was here in his apartment this morning. He's not allowed to leave his residence because of his wife's infection. Their sleeping together meets the definition of a contact requiring quarantine."

"Did he object when you told him that?"

"No. I verified a normal temperature and he agreed to keep a symptom diary. He knew I would be checking back again tonight."

Faye pulled her raincoat tighter against the cool breezes of New York Harbor and glanced at her companion. Taylor wasn't in a position to help them with this one. "Moshe was adamant about our requiring quarantine enforcement for definite contacts of confirmed cases."

"Not that easy when we're allowing them to stay at home." Maya leaned on the floral-papered wall of the building's corridor. She squashed a moment of guilt that she remained free and unrestricted. After all, she sat on a plane in front of a confirmed case and interviewed others.

But that only required self-monitoring, according to the NYC policies updated this week. The vomit on Maya's shoes from the teenager returning from Paris could have been defined as contact, if the vomit touched her bare skin and the girl tested positive for Ebola. Which she hadn't, at least not yet.

For the public panicked by Ebola on the home front, those distinctions were splitting hairs. On last night's newscast, a medical doctor from a local teaching hospital advocated locking down anyone on a plane from Conakry.

"When we met with Moshe Wednesday," Maya said, "he didn't say what to do with someone who broke quarantine."

That omission had surprised Faye, knowing that Moshe could be a martinet. Perhaps the lower COVID case counts had him in a better mood, and he assumed that everyone would take the threat of Ebola seriously.

"Don't hang around the building in your moonsuit," Faye advised. "No need to cause undue alarm. Can you wait near there until I find out Moshe's instructions?"

"Yeah, I'm feeling a bit famished. I'll stop at the corner hot dog stand, then come back to try one more time." Maya's heart rate stabilized as she removed her PPE and headed out to the refreshing evening.

Ten minutes later, cooler and calmer with some food and a Coke, she said hello to the doorman and asked him if Mr. Lund was in.

"I don't think so," he answered, "but you're welcome to check."

This time, she knocked at the door without donning her PPE. If Todd answered it, she'd step away and ask him to wait while she geared up. Her loud hammering on the door drew a startled peek by an elderly man next door. Maya tried to call Todd one more time, but it appeared he'd pulled a disappearing act.

Her imagination leapt between his gallivanting around town, impatient with any restrictions on his life, and his dying body on the floor, bleeding out from Ebola.

TWENTY-THREE

After exiting the ferry, Faye led Taylor to a bench at the Battery Playscape. On a chilly evening with the sun slanting low through the fresh spring leaves of the trees, few children took advantage of the granite slides. Faye appreciated the peace and privacy of the perennial gardens.

"Moshe, we have a problem," she said when her call connected.

"I should have stuck with city staff rather than rely on you." His voice harkened back to its old irritated tone.

Faye's gaze drifted up to catch Taylor's. She hadn't told Moshe that she had him on speaker. She covered the phone with her other hand and whispered to Taylor, "Remind me again of your advice to enjoy my retirement."

Taylor smirked and whispered back. "You can still change your mind about the contract."

Faye concentrated on maintaining a professional demeanor. "Todd Lund, that actor from the bank heist movies—we've got him under quarantine uptown."

"He's funny as hell," Moshe answered, "and my wife likes the way he looks."

"Maya's assigned to his in-person checks, and he's not answering his door."

Moshe's sigh was loud. "I guess it was too much to hope we'd pull off all these quarantines without a hitch."

Faye sympathized. "Remember when that nurse was detained at Newark after returning from treating Ebola patients in Africa? She won her legal case against Governor Christie for a violation of her constitutional rights."

Moshe's sigh became a grunt. "Public health's always the bad guy from our 'overreach' on COVID."

Remembering that Moshe had tricked her into quitting after decades working for the City, Faye found it odd to be on his side. Over half a billion confirmed COVID cases worldwide, including six million deaths. Almost a two-year drop in life expectancy. How much worse would that be if they hadn't established vaccine, mask, and distancing requirements?

"What should I advise Maya?" Faye asked.

"Verify with the hospital that he hasn't shown up to see his wife, then get the police to meet Maya at his residence."

"All right, she will meet them there."

Maya and the doorman waited for the police to help in tracking down Mr. Lund. They cooled their heels making small talk. Not Maya's strongest skill, but any opportunity for public health education shouldn't be passed up.

She understood the doorman's skepticism of government. Without her adoption, she might have had a life of poverty and oppression under China's onerous restrictions. Limited crime there came at a tremendous cost to personal freedom.

A beefy middle-aged patrolman pushed in through the main door. With his fiery, thinning hair and ruddy complexion, he could pass for a close relative of her Irish mom. "When's the last time anyone saw Mr. Lund?" he asked.

"This morning. He mentioned ordering food delivery." Maya turned to the doorman. "Did anyone drop off groceries or restaurant takeout meals for him?"

The man shook his head no.

Perhaps he was ill and unable to place a phone call for help. Maya's breathing rate increased with every minute Mr. Lund's status remained uncertain.

"We don't require a 24-hour wait to file a missing person report," the policeman said. "But I'm not breaking down a door just because you want to lock people in their homes against their will."

The doorman reached into his desk. "No need, I have a master key, if I'm authorized to use it."

The policeman led their procession into the apartment. Maya looked away from the underwear and pajamas tossed on the bedroom floor. She hung back as the policeman inspected the bathroom.

"Unless he's become invisible, he's not here." The policeman smiled at his own joke, then looked pointedly at the doorman. "I'm not spotting a cellphone or a wallet. I'm guessing Mr. Lund snuck out."

"Don't expect me to be his babysitter." The doorman straightened his spine and spread his legs in a wide stance, attempting to match the cop's height and bulk.

Finding no dead body, Maya had already calmed down. She tried to reduce the level of testosterone threatening to spill. "Could you show me the other building exits?"

The doorman nodded.

She pulled out two of her CDC business cards and handed them over. "Thanks for your help. I'll report this to the health department. If you see or hear anything, please let me know."

Faye and Taylor relaxed on her couch at eleven PM with Maya in the side chair. Faye punched the button on the remote and turned on her TV. The missing actor was headline news after the press release.

"Todd Lund of the international crime caper films is nowhere to be found," the male anchor said. "He and his wife, Madison, recently returned from a philanthropic trip to Guinea, West Africa. His wife is hospitalized at New York-Presbyterian with an Ebola infection, and Todd was at home in the Upper West Side under quarantine."

The picture on the screen showed the two of them, impossibly handsome and well-dressed, handing out aid packages in an impoverished community. The goats were as pushy as the humans in grabbing foodstuffs.

Faye wasn't sure she agreed with Moshe's decision to go public, causing greater scrutiny of their quarantine policy. If he wanted to keep his job, she hoped he cleared it with the mayor.

The female anchor's lips turned up in a barely perceptible smile, probably intended to reassure. "But no one's authorized to use force in bringing Mr. Lund in. The health department wants to verify that he's—"

"Hold on a second." The male anchor's hand went to his earpiece. "Let me patch this in."

On a split screen, Todd's grinning face came into view as he held his phone, speech slightly slurred. "Someone told me I've done a Jason Bourne. Look guys, I'm up here at the Harlem Night Market for a lively evening of food and music. Didn't mean to freak anybody out."

"Thanks, Todd," the male anchor said with an ingratiating voice. "We assume the health department can find you at home tomorrow?"

That wouldn't satisfy Moshe, but short of transporting through the airwaves to Harlem, Faye was out of options.

"You bet." Todd threw his arms around two other men, all three dancing in the street with wide eyes and gaping grins. Then he leaned forward and vomited blood on his phone, filling the screen with a vibrant, gory red.

TWENTY-FOUR

Stefan, released from the Conakry hospital and on his way to meet an Ebola response team, slowed his scooter to dodge a car-sized pothole after a moment of dizziness. He parked it, removed his helmet, and wiped his brow.

Thank goodness he'd cut his thick brown hair before the trip to Africa. A week of hospitalization hadn't prepared him for Guinea's intense heat and humidity.

He'd chosen the lightweight machine because it was easier to maneuver than a motorbike. And renting the scooter allowed him to avoid a sedan crammed with other staffers investigating cases of Ebola virus disease. Although he was probably not at risk of reinfection, he relished the fresh air and the privacy.

In the football field edging the ocean, a ragtag group of boys kicked up red dirt as they maneuvered the black-and-white ball. Like other Guineans, their passion for the game showed in their vigorous play. No adults hovered nearby, and this didn't appear to be a school function. The kids should have been dressed in uniforms rather than t-shirts and shorts. Then he remembered it was Saturday.

Shouts of "passe le ballon" and "à moi" settled down to shoulder slaps and "bien joué" when they took a break. None of the boys wore masks. They teased one child who scraped his knee and used a handkerchief to stop the blood. All acted oblivious to any risk of Ebola or COVID.

Stefan took a step toward the bleeding boy, then hesitated with his lack of supplies. Ebola-contaminated blood leaking from Jan and other patients replaced the oceanfront scene in his vision.

Appearing healthy and energetic, the kid booted the ball. As others chased it, the boy paused to wipe his brow with the bloody cloth. Just catching his breath—unlikely to be infected.

Last year, Stefan's daughter put her fleet feet to good use playing on a school team. Fortunately, her coach restricted the eleven-year-olds from heading the ball. Sports provided pleasure and risk, plus challenging decisions for parents. Hopefully, Stefan's work in Conakry would finish soon so he could see one of Paula's games before her school year ended in June.

He pulled Monday's edition of *Le Lynx* from his bag. The satirical newspaper featured a sketch of Ebola looking like a multi-headed snake, similar to its appearance under the microscope. The virus wielded a sword, threatening to decapitate Guinea's president. Mamady Doumbouya, a military officer, led a coup in the fall to seize the presidency from Alpha Condé, Guinea's first freely elected president who had served for eleven years.

"La Guinée déclare une nouvelle l'épidémie d'Ebola," read the headline. The cartoon surprised Stefan, who knew about increasing threats of censorship for journalists. Former President Condé was released from house arrest last month, so perhaps the new president wasn't as ominous as he appeared with his height, red beret, and dark sunglasses.

Stefan had a few minutes before his meeting about Ebola contacts. When his virus isolation test came back negative and he moved to a hotel, he was determined to keep his promise to help Biko and WHO with the outbreak. But first, a personal priority. Kondrat hadn't answered the phone when Stefan tried to reach him at breakfast. This time, as Stefan relaxed watching the soccer game, his partner picked up.

"Elsklingen min, it's wonderful to hear you," Stefan said, the rush of excitement making him woozy.

"I already told you to avoid terms of affection." Then Kondrat's tone softened. "Who are those kids in the background? Are you out of the hospital?"

"Yes, my blood is clear." Stefan decided not to repeat the caution about virus hiding in the semen.

"We can't wait for you to be home."

Kondrat's kinder attitude startled Stefan. Kondrat may have assumed the negative test meant Stefan posed no risk at all. Perhaps a partial truth was his best response.

"Medical and public health personnel are overwhelmed here. I volunteered to help as repayment for my excellent care and rapid recovery."

Biko's warning for Stefan to take it easy flitted through his mind. The single seizure early in his hospitalization was a bad omen, but one that hadn't been repeated. And Biko didn't prescribe complete bed rest, since he expected Stefan to pull his weight.

Kondrat's deep sigh came through the phone. "Your news comes at just the right time—Paula pesters me every night for updates. I'm so sorry for freezing you out. It's not fair you should have to put yourself at risk again."

"Nei, nei, there's no chance. Ebola immunity is wonderful—I'm the ideal person to give Guinea a hand now."

"Okay, możesz zostać."

Stefan smiled at Kondrat giving him permission to stay, but wondered about his switch from Norwegian to Polish, the native language for both of them. Kondrat sometimes did that when deeply affected—he sounded resigned, no longer wanting to fight.

"Tatuś, my science fair is next week!" Paula's voice blasted the phone call.

"Of course I will try to get home for it, but I'm a doctor helping sick people. Listen to Pappa—he has enough love and hugs for both of us. Can you put him back on?"

"I'm here," Kondrat said.

Stefan checked the time again. "I really have to go now. Muszę iść. Kocham cię." He paused for Kondrat to say 'I love you' also. When it didn't happen, Stefan added "Ser deg senere" in Norwegian, promising to catch up with Kondrat later. His phone beeped an alarm for the meeting and he disconnected.

In ten minutes, dodging vendors scurrying down the road with trays of plastic water bags, Stefan approached the popular farmers market. A vehicle ran the traffic light and almost collided with three children crossing the street. He took deep breaths to settle his shock over the deluge of sensations, then parked near a massive billboard.

It advertised the national lottery with an attractive woman dressed in a shimmering white shirt and jeans. "La fortune aux Parieurs, les Bénéfices à la nation" was the enticement. Fortune for gamblers, profits for the nation. With half of Guinea's population living in poverty, Stefan pondered who was getting the benefits.

Avoiding judgment of what gave people joy, he focused on finding the public health team. The cacophony of Guineans hawking their wares almost drowned out autos and motorbikes. Trash littered the sidewalk and multiple cars honked at a man with only one leg who ventured into traffic on his crutches. Jamming the roadway edge, women in bright print dresses balanced baskets of fruit on their heads.

Stepping deeper into the market, Stefan wandered amid huge bowls overflowing with nuts and roots, next to bags of flour and shelves crowded with bottles. He didn't spot anyone official amongst the array of umbrellas sheltering purveyors of colorful clothing and jewelry.

He rounded a display of smoked fish to find a young woman writhing on the dirt floor, dust coating the red beads and gold thread woven into her thick braids. Blood trickled from her mouth and nose. A man in a moonsuit crouched over her, then spotted Stefan and yelled "Stay back!" Stefan struggled to don the PPE from his pack as the man slipped a phone under his own face shield. "Je dois appeler une ambulance!"

"Non, trouvez ma mère," the woman whispered weakly. "J'ai peur."

After the screams, bloody deaths, and limited help that Stefan encountered in the hospital, reputed to be one of the better ones, he understood her terror.

TWENTY-FIVE

Faye moved closer to the TV screen. The network had cut away from the shocking live video of Todd Lund vomiting blood on a Harlem street.

"Uh, I hope someone will take care of that," the female anchor joked with a rueful expression. Just then, Faye's phone rang, and she answered a call from Moshe.

"I won't stand for it," he shouted.

Faye clicked off the TV and put Moshe on speaker without informing him. "Are you talking about Mr. Lund?" The actor was Maya's responsibility, not Faye's, but she wouldn't remind Moshe of that.

"Of course I am." His audible anger vibrated all the way to Maya in the chair, who trembled in response. She bottled up resentment that he implied she goofed up. CDC participated in the Ebola team as a guest of the City, and she feared straining agency relations.

"Dr. Moskowitz, I'm sorry." Maya stepped closer to Faye's phone, nerve endings on fire. "When I saw Mr. Lund this morning, he seemed so cooperative with your orders." In her four years with CDC, she'd never been responsible for enforcing a home quarantine.

Taylor's mouth opened as if they were about to jump in, and Faye raised a hand to stop them. Although Taylor garnered respect as a hospital Chief of Staff, Faye fought her own battles.

"A team's on the way to collect Mr. Lund," Moshe said. "At least he was out on the street—maybe he hasn't exposed many others."

"No harm, no foul," Faye replied with a hint of sarcasm, bristling like a porcupine at Moshe's imperious tone.

"That's not for you to judge," Moshe shot back. "You need to visit all the contact homes tomorrow. When you locate each person, call the FDNY EMS to transport them to the nearest Ebola isolation unit, even if they currently appear to be healthy."

Faye had never given orders to the Fire Department. She'd have to check with the other contact team to determine the total number of people Moshe expected them to detain. Could the two teams really get it done? Especially in the face of potential backlash against such a strict public health order.

On Saturday, the lighter traffic might make it easier to get around to all five boroughs. But Faye was dead tired. She'd decompressed for only a few hours off duty since she met Maya's plane on Monday.

"I'll notify the Chief tonight," Moshe said, "about my approval of the transfers."

Faye decided she'd had enough. "You're forgetting I'm retired, Moshe. Use your own paid slaves."

"And you've forgotten we have a contract," he snapped. "Maya's with CDC—she doesn't get time off."

Taylor knew that CDC Commissioned Corps officers were on duty 24/7, but Maya was a civilian CDC employee. She couldn't be compelled to work overtime. Knowing Maya, she'd likely volunteer to do so, from what Taylor had seen of her work ethic in Hawaii.

In addition to the two women ill on Maya's flight from Paris, Taylor now managed two additional patients. Dr. Mason's husband, quarantined in a separate room from his wife, finally tested positive, along with Taylor's lab tech from the needlestick.

Whether Taylor's hospital could also assist in hospital quarantines of currently-healthy people depended on Moshe's definition of exposure. The number would be huge if Moshe extended it to airline passengers like Maya who sat close to anyone infected.

"Dr. Moskowitz, this is Dr. Lewis." Taylor despised how the Health Commissioner spoke to the two women in Faye's living room, but didn't let it show. "My unit is equipped for ten patients, so if someone else from Staten Island needs quarantine, I can take six more."

The hospital had set aside isolation units in 2014 when Dr. Craig Spencer returned to New York from Guinea with Ebola, and added additional ones for COVID.

Maya jumped into the call. "Are we expanding the definition of exposure? Will I be included?"

"You never had direct physical contact with a patient, correct?" Moshe asked.

Maya tried to remember the moments when Dr. Mason and her husband joined her at the front of the plane. In the crowded situation as they preceded other shoving passengers, did she bump into them at all? If it happened, it likely wasn't skin-to-skin, so low risk. She preferred to be out tackling Ebola than confined to a hospital room, so she chose to be optimistic.

"No touching that I recall," she answered. "If we're sticking to the CDC definitions, I should be okay." Even without full PPE, she took comfort in being masked around the Masons most of the time on the plane and during the interview at JFK.

"One step at a time." Then Moshe's volume diminished from a full carillon to a single bell. "Other than Todd Lund who's a likely case, we have no proof of continuing transmission here. Let's get those with the highest risk exposures off the streets, then take it from there depending on disease spread."

Maya accepted his directive. Most scientists agreed that Ebola virus infected people through direct contact, not through the air, food, or water. Having been raised Catholic, she believed in her soul that she wouldn't become a Typhoid Mary, spreading the virus to others. After COVID, God wouldn't curse her with that role a second time.

TWENTY-SIX

The young woman lying on the packed clay of the Conakry farmer's market tried to stand but failed. Stefan, as directed by his team member, stayed back until he was geared up with PPE.

"I'm Stefan Duda. Are you Mohamed? My clinical skills are rusty but tell me what I can do."

"Keep them all away," came Mohamed's order in French-accented English.

Stefan stood and waved his arms to shoo the crowd back. "Ebola, reculez!" Magic words—everyone scattered. He was reluctant to cause panic, but couldn't quickly think of another way to move a large group of people all by himself. Where was Alphonse, the second team member he'd been scheduled to meet?

Grabbing a towel from his bag, Stefan slipped it under the woman's head as Mohamed spoke in an urgent tone into his phone.

"Merde!" Mohamed swore. "I can't get an ambulance, and Alphonse insists on continuing interviews with healthy contacts. He's only a data collector like you," he added in disgust.

Stefan didn't argue the point. Fear sometimes overcame duty, and patient transport was a major problem in previous Ebola outbreaks. "How about your vehicle? You and I have protection—we can take her to the hospital."

"Alphonse has the keys. I will not let him get away with this insubordination." Mohamed opened his phone again as a middle-aged woman rushed in and threw herself across the younger woman's body, their clothing a riot of color. "Qu'est que c'est passé?" Her voice faded as if swallowed by the wind.

"Maman, je meurs," came the weak answer.

Stefan hoped her daughter wasn't dying, but couldn't be falsely reassuring. "We'll get assistance now."

The older woman nodded, tears streaming. As she kissed her daughter's face, Stefan tried to pull her away, but failed. A week's worth of bedrest from his Ebola infection left him no match for a mother's determination.

A second man in a moonsuit stopped about twenty meters away.

"Alphonse, get over here to help," Mohamed ordered.

Instead, Alphonse tossed a set of keys into the air before vanishing among the stalls. Stefan caught them.

"Everyone is afraid," Mohamed said. "Before she collapsed, she told me that she and her family cleansed the body of sa grand-mère last week."

Liberia required cremation of Ebola-infected bodies—perhaps not Nigeria. Stefan asked, "No cremation orders to prevent spread?"

Mohamed shook his head. "I can do nothing. We should take them both to the hospital."

Stefan lifted the young woman by her shoulders, the mother cradling her head. That left the heavier end for Mohamed, but he looked stronger than Stefan felt.

They maneuvered the women into the backseat of a rusting Chrysler, the daughter moaning as the mother sobbed. When the vehicle without seatbelts nudged into the crowded street, Stefan let fly a silent prayer to Saint Faustina, a Polish woman canonized for medical miracles.

TWENTY-SEVEN

Biko met the car with Stefan and the two women at the emergency entrance. He hoped he wouldn't get into trouble for admitting them. This hospital was reserved for foreigners, wealthy locals, and government officials. He wanted to maintain good will with his more senior WHO colleague, who promised to take responsibility for the decision.

For the next half-hour, he stabilized his patient while Stefan located a cot for the mother in the parking area's tent city, divided into sections for those with mild, unconfirmed symptoms or exposed but not yet ill. A sign in large black letters warned **DO NOT ENTER! HIGH RISK AREA.**

"How is she doing?" Stefan rejoined Biko at the daughter's bedside.

"Like Dr. Kreischer, she has a coagulation disorder which we are managing with vitamin K and a blood transfusion." Biko hoped that their team would achieve a better outcome for this patient. Losing a WHO physician like Dr. Kreischer was a stain on Biko's record.

Stefan noted the fluid lines and thanked Saint Faustina that the woman no longer faced a risk of dehydration and metabolic disturbances. Her beribboned braids against the white sheets provided the only hint of brightness and life in the sterile environment.

He was not optimistic about the mother housed in the parking lot's oppressive heat, made worse by the tight walls of the canvas tent to avoid public terror over the virus wafting through the city.

"How did your contact tracing go today?" Biko asked.

"I never started," Stefan said, embarrassed by their lack of progress. "This is what greeted me when I arrived at the farmer's market."

"You should get back to it."

Biko was right. Stefan's own skills were better suited to epidemiology than critical care. "The man who brought us here didn't wait," Stefan said. "My scooter is still at the market."

"I will call a taxi, but put away your PPE or he will refuse to drive you."

Stefan acquiesced. Ebola fear was out of proportion to its risk of spread, but justly deserved for its horrific outcome. "Biko, can we review these case definitions before I head back out to the field?"

Biko agreed. "Let us step outside. I need a breath of fresh air."

Free of their claustrophobic PPE, they sought a spot in the shade. A new makeshift poster attached to the outer wall of the hospital showed photos of patients and staff who had died there, along with hand-scrawled descriptions. Jan Kreischer was listed, without a picture. The impromptu memorialization tugged at Stefan's heart, reminding him of their mission.

He angled his phone to Biko. "This is the WHO decision tree I'm using with our surveillance team. We need to isolate anyone potentially exposed if they develop a sudden onset of high fever. As a clinician, how do you define high fever?"

Stefan favored a higher number to cut back on misclassification from other diseases, but they might miss some real Ebola cases whose fevers weren't elevated yet. He wanted to reduce the pressure on hospital staff with their limited isolation beds. "Unless you disagree, I will use 39.4 degrees Celsius, or 103 degrees Fahrenheit."

Biko shrugged his shoulders. Too tired to quibble, he was distracted by a series of aerial yelps. A bird flew by with a heavy yellow beak and a long tail. Its feathers were brown streaked with silver, except for a whitish underbelly. He recognized it as a Western Plantain-eater, one familiar to him during his nature walks in Nigeria's Cross River valley.

If only he could escape his medical duty and get back there.

Perhaps rewind recent history, the gorilla trip, and all these Ebola deaths.

Biko shifted the glasses on his nose, attempting to see more clearly the WHO information on Stefan's phone. "How is exposure defined?"

Stefan glanced at his screen. "Contact with a suspected, probable, or confirmed case less than 21 days ago. That includes sleeping in the same household, direct physical contact, and touching blood, body fluids, clothes, or linens during the illness. Also, breastfeeding."

Given Stefan's concerns about reunion with his partner, Biko was surprised he didn't mention sex, but WHO probably included it under direct physical contact.

Stefan added, "We're also checking on those with exposures at laboratories and hospitals."

Biko was glad his responsibilities did not extend to larger policy and disease control implications, but he needed to understand the next steps. "Will you include someone based on symptoms alone, who did not have known exposure?"

"They are about half of the suspect cases so far. High fever with at least three of the following: headache, loss of appetite, stomach pain, vomiting, diarrhea, lethargy, aching muscles or joints, difficulty swallowing or breathing, hiccups."

"Those certainly fit me," Biko said in a wry but exhausted tone. "I have headache, loss of appetite, and lethargy, but my temperature is only 37.8 degrees."

Stefan wanted to reassure Biko. With the lower temperature, his clinical signs could be due to his workload. "Mon ami, you should take a break. Maybe your problems will correct themselves. Based on your experience this week in the hospital, can you think of anything else to consider in our definitions?"

"Include anyone with unexpected bleeding like our new patient, or someone who dies suddenly with no obvious reason."

Stefan could see why the system was overwhelmed. People without Ebola infection might meet one of those suspect case definitions.

"Our hospital is full," Biko said. "How will you triage these suspect cases?" That was the surveillance team's problem, unless all of them were dumped into Biko's lap.

"The interviewer files a report," Stefan said. "Then the surveillance team collects a sample for lab testing, fills out a case notification form, draws up a list of contacts, arranges for hospital care if needed, and finds transport."

Biko's lips felt chapped and his mouth dry. His throat yearned for Bouye, a creamy drink made from baobab fruit. It was sold at the local market, but he could not take time away from patient care. He had no option but to head back into a hospital awash with diarrhea, vomitus, blood, and tears.

He answered a call, listened for a moment, then handed his phone to Stefan. "It is the health minister. The confirmed case count now exceeds 250, with more than twice that many under investigation. It has been three days since she requested vaccines, and you must find out why WHO is failing us."

TWENTY-EIGHT

STREET VOMIT = JAIL! blared Saturday's New York Post headline. Taylor bought a copy at a corner newsstand while jogging to work via Battery Park and the Staten Island Ferry.

The **Health Commissioner off the rails on Ebola** subheading loomed over an unflattering picture of Moshe —washed-out skin color, hand waving with a pointed finger, and teeth bared in a snarl. Taylor smiled at the slam and wondered where the rag got the photo.

Slipping the newspaper into their daypack, Taylor paused to answer a call from Faye.

"Hello darling, you and Maya off to play health cops?" Taylor joked.

"That's on hold," Faye said. "We have a Zoom meeting in half an hour with the mayor's office, state health, and CDC. No one's happy with Moshe's decision."

Taylor's phone rang with the screen indicating New York-Presbyterian. "I'll get back to you after this call from another hospital," Taylor told Faye, then quickly answered the incoming line. "What's up?"

"Taylor," came the raspy voice of a woman who, like Faye, didn't know when to retire. "We have Mr. and Mrs. Lund. Our workload is manageable, but under these new rules from Dr. Moskowitz, the contacts might overload us."

"I share your concern." Taylor was headed to Staten Island to check on their Ebola patients. The isolation unit's healthcare personnel were also monitored for fever and other symptoms twice a day. Maintaining surveillance for the next three weeks would be a challenge if some developed symptoms from other illnesses but they met the Ebola definitions. Isolating at home would be easier for minor illnesses, at least until Ebola was ruled in or out. But that would violate Moshe's new edict.

"Aren't you dating a health department ex-employee?" the other chief of staff asked. "Perhaps you can use your connection to weigh in on their public health order."

Taylor never discussed Faye with coworkers but they'd attended a number of events together so their relationship wasn't a secret. Still, it was startling to hear a request to take advantage of it. Besides, Faye had been forced to retire by Moshe, so she wasn't in the best position to lobby, even if Moshe did put her on contract for the Ebola emergency.

Then Taylor remembered Faye's imminent Zoom meeting. Perhaps Taylor could advocate on behalf of the hospitals, if Faye shared the link.

"Let me see what I can do." Taylor hung up and tapped on Faye's number using FaceTime.

She came into view and Taylor recognized her midcentury kitchen. Taylor loved every wrinkle in Faye's round, freckled face and her vanishing eyebrows. Fierce passion and intelligence radiated from her pale blue eyes. Taylor hadn't dated much and didn't favor a 'type,' but the 'opposites attract' paradigm appeared to work for them.

"I need to join your Zoom call," Taylor said. "The impact of Moshe's decision on the hospitals must be considered."

"I can find out if that's okay," Faye said.

"Seeking forgiveness is a better strategy than asking for permission," Taylor answered.

Faye stroked her fingers through the curls on her forehead. "Winner, winner, chicken dinner. I'll forward you the email with login info."

Taylor pivoted and raced back home.

For the Zoom meeting, Faye used her laptop in her bedroom with the door closed to avoid audio feedback from Maya on her own laptop in the living room. Both also wore headphones.

In the brief silence as everyone logged in, Faye reviewed the thumbnail images with the names and titles under each. Moshe Moskowitz, the NYC Health Commissioner, was all too familiar with his pale face and glowering expression, contrasted by the smiling and wide-eyed countenance of Antonio Romero, the mayor's young assistant.

Sally Haefner with her 70s-era Afro was the recently-appointed New York State Epidemiologist, someone Faye had never met. Besides Maya, CDC was represented by Kenzo Ito, Viral Special Pathogens chief. His white-streaked hair and unlined face was stern like a Samurai warrior, experienced with battles, not diplomacy.

Faye wasn't prone to anxiety, but her muscles tightened as Taylor popped onto the screen. Moshe would guess Taylor learned of the meeting from Faye, so she hastened with her introduction.

"I hope you don't mind my inviting Taylor Lewis, Chief of Staff for our Staten Island hospital. Dr. Lewis took in some patients I triaged at the airport. I thought Dr. Lewis' hospital management perspective might be helpful."

Moshe's thick eyebrows drew together. "I am consulting with government agencies, Dr. Lewis. I'll get back to you when we have a decision."

Antonio jumped in. "Speaking on behalf of the mayor, I don't mind Dr. Lewis joining us. After all, the healthcare facilities are impacted by this revised policy."

"I'll allow Dr. Lewis on the call," Dr. Ito said. "But your health department can't unilaterally make such a huge change by enforcing hospital quarantine for all Ebola contacts. Especially based on one scary newscast."

Faye recognized the importance of being in the room where it happens. She sighed, relieved that the focus had shifted away from Taylor's presence, but concerned about the fight over agency prerogatives.

Moshe's face matched the newspaper photo. "New York City

makes its own decisions. You forget that CDC is here on my invitation."

Maya was CDC's field rep for the team. Was Moshe threatening to throw her out? Faye tried to ease the tension with gratitude and compliments. "I, for one, am delighted that Dr. Ito authorized Maya to help us. Every extra expert is a tremendous benefit when Moshe and his team are working themselves to the bone."

Dr. Ito didn't temper his fury. "Moshe, you poured on jet fuel by referring to Mr. Lund as a 'person under investigation' or PUI in your news release. It's stigmatizing and implies he's guilty of something. I told you CDC is transitioning to the term 'suspect case.'"

"Calling him 'suspect' won't reduce his complaint that he feels like a criminal," Moshe snapped back. "Until you get around to updating the national case definition, we're not changing."

Antonio spread his hands wide and like Faye, adopted a conciliatory tone. "Let's not debate semantics. Bottom line, Mr. Lund violated Moshe's public health order to stay home. The mayor wants to nip this Ebola outbreak in the bud. Dr. Lewis, does our hospital system have room for contacts and suspect cases along with the confirmed ones?"

Taylor squirmed, balancing pros and cons, including uncertainties on how to pay for the quarantines and whether the hospitals would eat the cost. "I think we can manage it, depending on the number you send us. I'll give you a final answer after checking with the other facilities."

Fingers crossed, they'd all agree. But if not, the load would fall heavier on a few.

"The team's monitoring 54 people at their homes," Maya said. "Most appear to be following our isolation requirements, which should reduce any problems. However, in their second or third week of isolation, that cooperation might break down."

Faye nodded. She remembered all the trouble they had getting people to stay home for ten days with COVID, before CDC finally changed it to five days in January. "Twenty-one days is a heavy lift."

"If we look at recent history with a different virus," Maya said,

"COVID isolation only applied to symptomatic cases, not their contacts."

"A ridiculous comparison," Moshe shouted. "Ebola has a case fatality rate of 80 to 90 percent! And it's a foreign disease. I won't allow it to be established here in New York."

Antonio asked, "Dr. Lewis, can our hospitals support Moshe's public health order?"

Taylor reluctantly agreed. "Isolating exposed people in a hospital so they can't spread Ebola to others should reduce the overall number of infections, a huge benefit to our medical teams. Based on Maya's data, I believe our hospitals can pull this off."

Dr. Ito shook his head. "Regardless of hospital capacity, public health agencies in the past faced public outrage and lawsuits when imposing Ebola quarantines for potential exposure rather than symptoms. We have to consider the nationwide consequences of such an extreme decision."

Dr. Haefner, who had remained silent during the initial arguments, weighed in. "I agree with Dr. Ito to continue with isolation of exposed contacts at home. My 57 counties outside of the City need a consistent policy, and many won't have sufficient healthcare beds to isolate Ebola contacts before they develop clinical signs."

Taylor opened an incoming text and read it aloud to the others. **<Todd Lund at New York-Presbyterian confirmed with Ebola, vomited ten liters already.>**

Moshe slammed his fist on his desk, explosive like a gunshot. "Never again. All those exposed will be isolated in a hospital. No more vomiting on TV to make us look inept."

"The mayor supports Moshe's decision," Antonio said. "Sorry we won't be in lockstep with the state and CDC."

Taylor studied Faye and Maya's expressions. Faye had long practice in rolling with the public health punches, but Maya's face displayed shock. She likely never had been embroiled in such a consequential battle between agencies.

Dr. Ito's shoulders went back as he sat up straighter and enunciated. "You'll hear from the CDC Director and our attorneys next."

TWENTY-NINE

After a reaming over the phone from Guinea's health minister about the missing Ebola vaccine, Stefan used his handkerchief to wipe sweat from his face. The sweltering temperatures outside the hospital made him feel fragile.

He hoped that the manufacturer wasn't withholding the vaccine to demand more money. Trying to recoup their research costs, companies often charged more initially, especially for a vaccine with lower worldwide need. But it might just be bureaucratic hoops delaying delivery to Conakry. His apologies to the minister didn't calm her outrage.

Putting his phone in his pocket, Stefan told Biko, "I need to find out what's happening from Dr. Shah. Once we get the doses, we should prioritize healthcare employees like you so we can maintain clinical staffing."

Stefan studied Biko for his reaction. Accustomed to being in the lead for decision-making about the use of WHO resources, Stefan nevertheless had honed his ability to compromise after more than a decade in government positions. At least in his work life—he flinched with guilt about his lack of ability to accommodate his family.

Biko shuffled his feet and hugged his arms. "I worry about my colleagues. They're already exhausted with overwork."

Stefan nodded, although he was cautious about the vaccine's effectiveness for healthcare workers if already infected. Biko looked worn out—could he be one of them? Stefan called Dr. Shah and put him on speaker.

"She shouldn't be so impatient," Dr. Shah said. "WHO received her request on Wednesday and it was circulated to the review group on Thursday. I expect the decision by Monday. Then UNICEF will organize delivery within a week, so you should have it by the end of the month. However, it often takes countries an additional week or so to implement the vaccinations."

Would that be too late? Stefan resolved to help Guinea get ready to start vaccination sooner than that timetable.

"I assume we should prioritize Conakry," Biko said.

"Yes. The comités de veille surveillance teams have not identified a large problem outside of Conakry."

"Is there any new information about undesirable side effects from the vaccine?" Stefan asked.

"Nothing to dissuade a decision." Dr. Shah audibly harumphed in exasperation at the question. "Severe joint inflammation and pain are the primary issues, as well as swelling and redness at the injection site, headache, fever, and fatigue." He added, "Send me details of your proposed plans," and hung up.

Encouraged that the wheels were turning, Biko nevertheless was cautious. "It will require considerable lab testing to distinguish those with vaccine reactions from those with Ebola virus disease."

Biko had doubts about Guinea's capacity to keep up with the lab work, but he wouldn't show weakness to Stefan or their boss on the phone. Besides, as the epidemiologist on the WHO team, Stefan would have more responsibility for successful implementation and evaluation. Biko had enough to do managing ill and dying patients, especially when he felt so poorly.

"If we use the vaccine for pre-exposure prophylaxis," Stefan asked, "will your hospital staff cooperate?"

Biko mentally reviewed the hospital staff he knew. They should be eager for vaccination, but he was uncomfortable speaking for all of them. The vaccine had been created by taking a gene from the Ebola virus and adding it to the vesicular stomatitis virus, which caused cattle infections.

Many Africans feared being experimental subjects for drugs developed by the White man. Some Ebola cases had popped up in other countries related to travel from Conakry—was the vaccine under consideration there?

"I assume there are informed consent forms," Biko said. "I cannot assure you of complete cooperation, especially because vaccination does not eliminate the need for personal protective equipment."

He himself was unsure about the need to get vaccinated, given his previous infection. He could not afford any downtime from patient care due to an adverse reaction, and his PPE might be sufficiently protective. "Besides our hospital staff, who else?"

"Laboratory workers, and those like me on case investigation teams."

All groups protected with PPE. Biko wondered if they should extend vaccinations to the families and neighbors of infected cases. He remembered a concept from one of his public health classes. "Ring vaccination strategy creates a ring of immunity around the outbreak. That includes post-exposure treatment of contacts, as long as they are not ill already."

Stefan nodded. However, until they received the first vaccine shipment, he had no idea if they'd get sufficient doses. "That's a possibility. But you're right, if given after exposure, it may be too late."

Biko led the way back into the hospital, barely cooler with its whirring ceiling fans. If he refused to take the vaccination because of possible side effects on top of already feeling lousy, it might imply a lack of faith in WHO and jeopardize his employment. He regretted his reluctance, molded by an aching body, spongy mind, and too many mournful laments.

As Biko sagged against a wall, Stefan reached out to support him. "Are you all right?" he asked, voice both sympathetic and stern. "You won't be eligible for vaccination if you're sick."

THIRTY

With her plane from New York arriving late to Atlanta, Maya hurried off the flight into the busy Hartsfield-Jackson airport. She headed immediately for the Plane Train and the next terminal. If there were no more delays, she'd make her connection to Albuquerque.

Despite the rushing crowds of Memorial Day travelers, she finally felt truly alone with her thoughts, not answerable to anyone. No wannabe boyfriend in the adjoining room of a Paris hotel suite, no senior mentor and purring cat to interrupt her sleep on the Manhattan couch. Most important, after intense collaborative work, the NYC Ebola outbreak appeared under control.

The last passenger at the gate, she grabbed her seat just before the flight attendants closed the doors. Then she expelled her deepest breath since leaving New Mexico.

Not a single new case had been diagnosed after she and Faye got all the contacts into hospital quarantine. With an incubation period of 2 - 21 days, someone might not show symptoms yet even though most infections revealed themselves within a week or so after exposure. Maya was tired but had no other signs she was carrying Ebola virus home.

The political wranglings had been draining. The CDC Director and the State Health Commissioner huffed and puffed at NYC's radical move. The tabloids splashed daily headlines about city government overreach. But the Mayor continued to back Moshe's decision, and the citizenry's relief about avoiding Ebola exposures on bus and subway lines provided popular support.

Her phone pinged with a text from Manolo's father. **<Sorry we couldn't connect during your visit.>** A couple of days ago, when she called Sebastian to say hello, he agreed that seeing each other in person was a bridge too far. She needed to keep his relatives safe, particularly Johnny, the only grandchild after Maya's pregnancy loss.

Just as the flight attendant announced the plane pushing back from the gate, she texted Sebastian, **<I miss you all so much, but I'll be back>**.With no work commitments when her CDC Preventive Medicine Residency ended in a month, she would have plenty of time for visiting friends and family. She swallowed hard with that thought. Did it mean she'd reached a decision to delay taking a new job right away?

Arriving close to midnight at Albuquerque's Sunport, she was heartened by the laconic cowboy lounging on the seat in the baggage area. A young woman strolled by him and said, "Howdy."

Maya giggled. Dave Schwartz, despite the wedding ring on his finger, was ruggedly attractive at thirty-five. He politely nodded, tipping his hat back to reveal brown hair and piercing hazel eyes. Then he spotted Maya and hurried to her.

"Gal, it's been too long." He embraced her in a teddy-bear hug.

"We've got to stop meeting like this." She placed a kiss on his unshaven cheek. "I'm always hitting you up for a place to stay after these late arrivals."

He grinned. "You have enough on your plate without arranging for transportation to Santa Fe. Besides, Bo misses your cuddles."

Half an hour later when Dave pulled his truck into the gravel parking area at his Bernalillo ranch, his Black Lab raced out, almost knocking Maya off her feet. She dropped to her knees for an energetic roughhouse. Once inside, Dave offered her Braxton's bedroom with its teenage sports hero posters.

"He won't mind," Dave said.

"I'm sorry that I won't see your family." Maya unzipped her suitcase on the floor.

"Yeah, Emilia and the kids send their regards."

"Why didn't you join them for their holiday weekend at White Sands?"

"I'm working on an *E. coli* outbreak related to a petting zoo."

"You and Dr. Grinwold getting along?"

"He's anxious we stay on the same page because one kid died from HUS and others may need kidney dialysis if they survive."

Good thing she'd be back at work tomorrow. HUS, hemolytic uremic syndrome with kidney failure, could be a major complication of infections with *Escherichia coli* 0157:H7 bacteria. Her boss, the State Epidemiologist, was crusty under normal circumstances. When children were in jeopardy, he was much worse.

Tensions between health and ag, represented by Dave Schwartz as the regional USDA veterinarian, sometimes simmered below the surface. Different constituencies, and Maya had been in the front row seat of interagency battles recently.

Travel weariness kicking in, she sank to the bedspread. "That's terrible news. What animals?"

"Lambs at the petting zoo last month had matching bacteria to the human cases. We also found it in soil from the school playground a couple hundred yards away. The only human cases are in school kids, and none of them had been inside the petting zoo."

Maya knew that the bacteria could survive several months in water or soil downstream from infected animals. Challenging to control that risk.

"I've written up a proposal for an experimental treatment of the sheep herd that supplies the petting zoo." Dave stepped away for a moment and returned with towels which he dropped on the bed.

"Daily feedings of probiotics to beef cattle can reduce their fecal shedding of *E. coli*. I'm proposing to try it for sheep. Also, the heat from composting can eliminate the bacteria from manure. I recommended the petting zoo adopt that practice."

"You're always on the cutting edge. I'd love to work with you on that."

Dave brushed hair from his eyes. He looked unkempt and shaggy—probably had little time for grooming during an important outbreak. She wasn't the only one allowing her job to take over her life.

"Have you reached a job decision?" He spoke casually, as if he didn't want to influence her choice.

She stood and gave him another hug. "Just rolling the options around like a bag of marbles in my brain."

He winked. "Between the two of us, someday we might make a big scientific breakthrough. Possibly a Nobel Prize."

His remark reminded her that neither of them did the work for recognition. Awards went to those working in laboratories, not epidemiologists or animal health specialists. "Will you have time to drop me by the Rail Runner terminal tomorrow? Whatever time works for you."

"No problem." He headed for Braxton's bedroom door.

Her skin prickled with goose bumps. A year ago, Mu Jian joked they'd win a Nobel Prize if they confirmed bats as the origin of COVID in China. That sleuthing led to imprisonment in a COVID hotel by the Chinese government, before Mark paid her ransom.

With Ebola demands in NYC, she hadn't spoken much to Mark since he flew home to New Mexico ahead of her. She'd still be locked up in China without his intervention, and she vowed to see him again as soon as possible. After Stefan's phone call from Guinea about his Ebola infection, her vacation with Mark in Paris hadn't turned out exactly like either of them expected.

THIRTY-ONE

Protected from the sweltering sun by a shade tree in the moldy brick courtyard walls of the Musée National Conakry, Stefan relished a few minutes off his feet while relaxing in the café. Next to an artisan selling wooden masks, he ladled Ghanbouda sauce over the small white mounds of Tô cassava flour.

Biko remained silent, not eating, head in his hands. With assistance from a larger team, they'd administered Ebola vaccinations to at least 200 healthcare workers using several of the museum's rooms, mostly empty because of an Islamic purge of its art work.

The museum's location, adjacent to one of Conakry's hospitals, didn't expose those getting vaccinated to Ebola or any other diseases circulating in healthcare facilities. Museum staff were accustomed to hosting meetings and cultural events in its rooms and outdoor area, alongside its remaining collection, including statues surrounded by a railing of colonial helmets.

"Who's that one?" Stefan waved his arm toward a bronze monument on a high pedestal, depicting a grandly dressed man cuddling a naked African boy.

Biko looked up. "Noël Ballay, a doctor and first Governor of French Guinea. Recognition of his colonial beneficence." He sounded strained, with just a hint of sarcasm.

Stefan assumed its location within the courtyard allowed it to escape the fate of other statues worldwide that were no longer deemed culturally sensitive.

He eyed the huge billboard that had just been erected outside the museum gates. **BEWARE, EBOLA IS REAL** in red letters, above the statement 'We share the grief of the bereaved families and friends of EBOLA victims and we remain firm in our support for the speedy eradication of this virus.' Photos of national heroes killed by Ebola were followed by **The A B C of Ebola: AVOID personal contact, BEWARE of Ebola symptoms, and CON-TACT the appropriate health facility for any EBOLA case**.

Stefan was surprised by its placement. The museum risked stigmatization by allowing both the vaccination clinics and the billboard. Attempting to energize Biko with conversation, he said, "I'm thrilled we got the vaccine shipment so quickly. Perhaps WHO is making up for inefficiencies and infighting during the previous Ebola outbreak here."

Biko had received his dose that morning. He was grateful for the bureaucratic improvements, but he pushed away the food that Stefan nudged his way. Between his sore throat and difficulty swallowing, eating held no appeal. He covered his mouth with his sleeve as he belched, then blanched at the spots of blood on his white shirt.

Stefan leaned forward, hands on Biko's cheeks. "Open up—I need to look." He snapped on a pair of gloves and eased back Biko's gums. His own health wasn't at risk, he reminded himself. You almost never caught Ebola twice—the general scientific consensus. So Biko shouldn't be infected either.

"Your gums are bleeding," Stefan said in a low voice to avoid alarming the nearby vendors.

Biko shrugged and his expression remained stoic. "A vaccine reaction?"

"Not on the list I've seen." Stefan reconstructed the timeline. May 6—gorilla contact. Today, May 31, was outside the recognized incubation period if the animal was a source of infection. But they had unprotected exposure to Jan Kreischer at the health meeting during Jan's nonspecific early symptoms, plus contact with other patients, usually when wearing PPE. Biko had been dragging for days, so an exact estimate of time between any Ebola exposure and symptom onset was impossible.

"I'm taking you to your hospital," Stefan said.

It made no sense to Biko that he'd break with Ebola so long after Stefan did. The range of incubation periods was broad but he'd been careful during patient care.

"They need us here as vaccinators," he said.

Stefan adopted the harsh cadence of his Polish grandfather. "Not if you have Ebola. Other staff can take over—we're leaving now."

THIRTY-TWO

Taylor settled long, denim-clad limbs on the bench seat in Washington Park, then took a bite of a lemon poppyseed muffin. Faye adjusted her Mets cap to block the sun as she devoured her raspberry spandauer, tossing errant almonds to the hovering pigeons.

"We did it." Taylor raised a chai latte in salute. "More than a week with no new Ebola cases."

Faye bumped her cappuccino against Taylor's cup. "I'm happy to end the month with success. Moshe didn't extend my contract, so I have a life of leisure again."

She leaned over to stroke Taylor's cheek, cherishing shared moments in the world's most wonderful city. "Maybe we can spend more time together."

Taylor frowned, then swallowed as if hesitant to answer. "I'd love to, but something's come up. I might be heading to Ghana."

Faye swiveled her head, distracted by a truck engine on 5th Avenue. She must not have heard Taylor right.

"Why?" Then she remembered that Taylor's parents had emigrated from Ghana before their deaths in the Lockerbie crash. Perhaps Taylor had extended family there.

Taylor sloshed the liquid in the cup. "Last night, the US Agency for International Development asked me to coordinate an Ebola vaccination campaign there."

USAID had tracked Taylor down on the request of Taylor's Uncle Kumi Kyeremateng, a chief in the outskirts of Accra, Ghana's capital. WHO staff had started a vaccine campaign in Guinea, and with new cases popping up in Uncle Kumi's area, USAID wanted to use it there as well.

No one knew how Ebola had jumped from Guinea across three other countries to Ghana. Maybe through infected long-distance truckers—they were suspected as one source of HIV spread. Taylor wasn't an epidemiologist and the number of mostly travel-related NYC cases hadn't warranted a vaccine campaign. But USAID wasn't asking for help in outbreak investigation, just outbreak control.

Taylor took another sip and continued. "Ghana pilot-tested Ebola vaccine during the 2014-15 outbreak, and it was a major failure. Ghanaians felt like they were guinea pigs. If the vaccine was so safe, why wasn't the president distributing it in his home region? Monetary rewards to receive vaccine made them more suspicious."

"Okay, but what does that have to do with you?" Faye uncrossed her legs and tossed the remains of her pastry to the birds.

Sometimes Faye's impatience irritated Taylor, who brushed errant crumbs from the bench. But Taylor loved her and wanted to get her on board for an upcoming separation.

"Ghana has new cases and they will try the vaccine again. One of my relatives is a local chief and coffee producer. He thought I could provide a respected source of information."

"You're an American, so why would you be trusted? Especially as a trans female."

"You have a point, which is why I haven't given USAID an answer. I'll probably need to travel as cis male."

Oburonis was the name Ghanaians gave to people who looked different, particularly for those from overseas, with lighter skin color or LGBTQ+.

After the USAID call, Taylor had reached out directly to Uncle Kumi, who felt that Taylor's Ghanaian heritage and personal relationship to him would be helpful, even if Taylor was viewed as a foreigner. Uncle Kumi valued Taylor's experience implementing dengue vaccinations in the Philippines, but didn't know about their gender orientation.

Taylor was tempted to honor the request although the trip would be challenging. Except for a grandfather's funeral, Taylor hadn't visited Ghanaian relatives in years. Not having been born there, Taylor didn't speak any of the local dialects, but English was the official language as a legacy of UK colonization.

Faye squirmed in her seat. She wasn't normally superstitious. However, since she and Taylor reconnected after the pandemic, they'd only been apart once when she went to New Mexico and Hawaii for the dengue outbreak. She had caught a life-threatening infection and Taylor supervised her care in Kona. They'd pledged to stay enmeshed in each other's lives, even while maintaining their different apartments.

She hadn't been out of the US except for the investigation of Middle East Respiratory Syndrome in the UK and Saudi Arabia almost 10 years ago. But she had experience in providing human vaccines, and a second set of hands couldn't hurt. Would Taylor want her to come along to Ghana?

THIRTY-THREE

Stefan stepped out of the Conakry hospital into a stifling, late May afternoon. He cradled Biko's phone, thumb poised over **Nneka Okeke.** Before Biko lost consciousness on the hospital bed, he'd handed over his phone and password, begging Stefan to reach his sister. Inexperienced in ICU care, Stefan was forced to stand aside as hospital staff stabilized Biko and drew blood for an Ebola test.

What would he say on the call? Until he saw the lab results, he could only report Biko's condition, not the cause of it.

He hated to burden the girl, only nineteen years old, when things were still uncertain. While they were hiking three weeks ago to visit the gorillas, Biko had mentioned his sister was a forest guide, taking a break from her studies at the Federal College of Forestry Mechanisation. Last spring, she'd been one of 39 students abducted from the school by bandits.

Held in the forest for two months, the students were beaten with sticks and guns. A pregnant classmate miscarried. Nneka was so weak that she'd been hospitalized. She was one of the lucky ones. Of more than a thousand Nigerian students kidnapped in the last decade, many had been raped and some murdered.

Nneka was Biko's only remaining close relative and Stefan needed to comply with Biko's request. Stefan's thumb touched the phone screen.

"Nwa m," came the clear tone. She followed with a question that Stefan couldn't follow. He guessed it was in Igbo, Biko's native language.

"Uh, this is Stefan Duda, your brother's WHO colleague. We've been working together here in Conakry on an Ebola outbreak."

"Yes, of course, Dr. Duda. My brother respects you tremendously and has learned a lot from you. Why are you calling me on his phone?" Before Stefan could respond, her voice raised an octave. "Is something wrong?"

Stefan swallowed, trying to break the news with compassion. "Biko has been quite courageous in caring for Ebola patients, and unfortunately collapsed about an hour ago. He was vaccinated this morning, and perhaps it's only a strong vaccine reaction. But I suspect he's ill with Ebola, despite his infection a few years ago. We should have confirmation by tomorrow."

"My God, how is he doing?"

"Unconscious, but stable." Stefan rushed to reassure her. "He's in the top hospital and receiving the best care Guinea has to offer. I became infected early and was released in eight days."

"I should come there. Let me check the flights."

Stefan was uncomfortable advising on such an important decision, but he knew the hospital wouldn't allow her to see Biko. "No visitors are permitted, and I promise to keep you informed."

As Stefan awaited her answer, he studied her photo on Biko's contact list. Luminescent dark skin, large bright eyes, and multiple Bantu knots of hair encircled by strands of small colorful coral shells.

"I understand. Besides, I must meet my work commitments. Nigeria raises money for forest conservation with park tours, which I lead." Her tone was quiet and strained. "I insist that you call me every night with updates."

"Of course, and the minute he wakes up, I'll get him on the line for you."

Deadly microbes continued to take their toll as medical and public health experts like Stefan fought them off. Far-away loved ones were helpless to comfort relatives at death's door. The world experienced that too often at the height of the COVID pandemic. Reminded of Kondrat's conflicted feelings when Stefan was hospitalized, he broke at the pain in Nneka's voice.

THIRTY-FOUR

Mark shared a lane with Maya at the Santa Fe city pool during its Saturday morning lap swim. Three weeks since Paris, she was healthy and strong in her red Speedo. He'd lost sleep over her interviewing people exposed to the Ebola virus. Now she was working on an *E. coli* outbreak. But she assured him she wasn't at risk—the bacterium was less likely to be transmitted directly between people except in a family or a daycare setting.

He paused at the shallow end to catch his breath. Slamming out a brisk crawl stroke, she completed two lengths of the pool in the same time he finished one doing the backstroke. His heart raced with the exertion, and sharing a fun activity with Maya.

By July 1st, she'd have to accept a new job because her CDC-funded preventive medicine residency had a time limit of one year. Only three weeks to go and as far as he could tell, she had no plans to move away from Santa Fe. But she also hadn't mentioned accepting Dr. Grinwold's offer of the State Public Health Veterinarian position.

Doing so was the only option that made sense. She was bonded to her New Mexico health department coworkers and lived within a day's drive from her parents in Flagstaff. If she stayed, he'd have time to continue his courtship. With any luck, they could plan a wedding for Christmas, one of the most romantic times of the year in Santa Fe with the farolito lanterns sparkling from adobe walls and warm luminaria fires brightening strolls through snowy streets packed with carolers.

"Taking a break?" Maya's smile dazzled after she touched the wall.

"I think I'll call it a day. But don't cut your workout short—I'll wait for you." His arms had been strengthened by months of weightlifting and maneuvering his wheelchair, but he still hadn't lost his pandemic paunch. He wasn't confident of boosting his bulk out of the pool, so he headed up the steps in the shallowest corner and pulled his towel from a hook before settling down to the bench.

As he tilted his head and tapped lightly to dislodge water in his ear, he chastised himself for contemplating marriage to someone he hadn't bedded. He couldn't be sure, but he guessed she'd only been with one man, her deceased husband.

She was inexperienced, naively liberal, and work-obsessed. But she sparkled like an exotic jewel in appearance and personality. Her being a hair on the shy side, and prone to bouts of anxiety, made him want to protect her. She'd never be a trophy wife, nor did he want one.

He draped his towel over his shoulders, trying to warm up. Before all this speculation about long-term plans, he'd have to get to first base.

Maya inhaled deep breaths as she hopped out. One mile, 70.4 laps in the 25-yard pool, 32 minutes. Not bad given the interruption of Paris and NYC. Mark looked lost in thought. He was appealing despite being in a different generation. She liked it when he appeared pensive and vulnerable. It reminded her of their quiet times reading and writing poetry at his ranch during her COVID recovery.

They'd held hands and shared affectionate caresses, as well as friendly kisses on the cheeks or forehead. She respected that he allowed her to set the timing on their physical and emotional relationship, although she doubted he often let anyone take the lead on anything.

Mark's dark hair, eyes, and complexion were similar to Manolo's, as well as his optimism. The age and weight differences with her husband were no big deal, and she couldn't help imagining what it would be like to make love with him.

Mark's ruthless side was valuable to her when she had legal

troubles, and it aided his business success and financial stability. He applied that relentless drive to good use with his clients and philanthropic organizations. But Maya at twenty-nine, now widowed for almost two years, wasn't ready to be part of his world full-time, or to make commitments of any kind.

Mark looked up, beaming his confident, compelling grin. He rung out the water from his short pony tail tied at the neck with a length of leather. "How about lunch at the ranch? Carmen's been asking after you."

Maya always enjoyed the ranch manager's motherly chatter and unassuming support. Before getting involved with Mark, she'd nail down whether he and Carmen had ever been lovers. It would be impossibly awkward if they had.

"I'll have to pass. I'm meeting Dave Schwartz to help him take poop samples from some sheep."

She smiled at her choice of words. If they made Mark uncomfortable, he wasn't the right guy for her.

THIRTY-FIVE

Wearing a navy skirt, Faye shuffled her sandaled feet in time with the music. She didn't care if her toes turned rusty in color as she swayed in the cattle corral just outside Accra, Ghana's capital. More accustomed to doing field work in pants, she'd changed her clothes in the airport restroom to dress like other women in respect of Ghana's traditions.

The animals, now confined to a shed, mooed along with the pounding of a drum decorated in red and black. Some men played smaller drums and one banged on a small metal pipe while the women danced.

The only white person in the area, and the only one not dressed in colorful native robes, Faye tried not to feel self-conscious. The multi-hued women's dresses, matching their turbans, wrapped their bodies leaving shoulders bare. Similar material in deep blue draped over Taylor's left shoulder like the other men. Taylor had worn kente cloth once before to a West-African inspired musical in Central Park.

"His outfit is called a ntama." Taylor gestured to his Uncle Kumi, a balding elder of redwood stature draped by a robe with a complex black-and-white pattern. "It indicates high status."

"They treat you like a king," she whispered back.

"The Akan are the largest ethnic group in West Africa, and there's a lot of pride associated with returning relatives."

"What language are they singing in?"

"Twi. My parents spoke it to each other when I was a child but didn't expect me to learn it. I was born in New York, and they were into adapting."

One barefoot woman danced nearby with bands around her ankles and upper arms in the same patterned orange, blue, and green material as her dress. While hopping, she undulated her hands like ocean waves.

Uncle Kumi raised his left hand to pause the celebration and stepped forward to shake Taylor's right hand. "Akwaaba, wofase. Thank you for coming. Two of your cousins died this week from Ebola, and the US Agency for International Development said you will help us get it under control."

Faye finally understood the expressions of people gathered to welcome them. Excited, but somber.

Taylor bowed. "I'm sorry for your loss, and honored you asked for me. Can we start by interviewing the immediate families of the deceased? Dr. Simpson is a veterinarian with experience in human disease investigations and has come to help."

Uncle Kumi cocked his head and answered in a graveled voice. "A female veterinarian, who does not look very strong. How unusual." He didn't extend his hand.

His tone didn't surprise Faye. She'd faced a similar attitude in Saudi Arabia when working with men to investigate camels infected by coronavirus.

"You cannot talk to anyone until after our funeral service," Uncle Kumi said. "The government cancelled this evening's wake, after the families spent long hours creating caskets to represent their professions. A book for the teacher and a man's dress shoe for the cobbler. Can you plead with the health ministry to allow us to gather tomorrow?"

"I will check," Taylor answered. "Are the family members here today?"

"No, they are extremely distressed. If you recall, the higher gods called abosom punish descendants if the rituals to honor their relatives are not strictly observed."

When Faye and Taylor boarded the plane last night in New York, they knew about Ebola cases in Ghana but not about any in Taylor's extended family. Since the decision for Faye to join Taylor on the trip, she'd been reading about Ghana and the challenges with previous Ebola outbreaks. Several Zoom briefings with USAID staff updated them about the local situation and culture.

The traditional practice of family members bathing and caring for the corpse was a major risk. Those activities might have occurred before the family got any Ebola confirmation. But that was the kind of question they must pose to the immediate family members, not Uncle Kumi in a public setting.

"Uh, given the calls and arrangements we need to make," Taylor said, "we should probably head to our lodging now."

"I am sorry you cannot stay longer for our celebration of your arrival, but of course I understand that you require rest from your travel." Uncle Kumi waved over the uniformed chauffeur who had met them at the airport in a Mercedes-Benz. Within thirty minutes, they pulled up to the front of the luxurious Tang Palace Hotel in the prestigious South Airport residential area.

Taylor and Faye checked in beneath monstrous chandeliers reflected in the golden floor tiles of the lobby. The bellboy accompanied them to an executive suite with curtains pinned back, offering views of Accra from a large balcony. In addition to the king-sized bed, the room featured a sofa and two guest chairs upholstered with rich leather.

"I can't believe USAID would spring for such an expensive hotel room like this one," Faye said. She and Taylor were unmarried partners of dissimilar age—sharing a bed might be forbidden. Even worse with Taylor being trans.

"Uncle Kumi insisted that I'm his guest," Taylor said.

"Perhaps we should book a separate room for me," Faye answered. "You know, just for appearances." She also wondered whether accepting the offer might compromise any public health recommendations that conflicted with Uncle Kumi's preferences. But she was in the uncomfortable position of playing second fiddle to Taylor on this investigation. She hoped that Uncle Kumi's refusal to shake her hand wasn't influencing her perception of him.

Taylor tugged her close with a hug and a kiss. "Don't worry

about it. The work itself will be stressful—I want you by my side at all times, especially at night."

"What if Uncle Kumi asks for extra doses of the vaccine?" She attempted to sound calm but cautious. "Or wants to hide cases and exposures?"

"I will do the right thing, no matter how my uncle leans on me." Taylor's voice turned tense and lecturing, a tone unfamiliar to Faye.

Unwilling to prolong the argument, she sat down on the bed and kicked off her shoes, tempted to lean back against the thick pillows for a short nap. Neither one of them would be in top form without some kind of rest after the overnight flight. But all she could think about was Uncle Kumi's personal and political clout inadvertently exploding Ebola virus into an epidemic.

THIRTY-SIX

Consciousness budding, Biko twisted on the Conakry hospital bed. An old man with a white beard and carrying a staff hovered in his visual field. His long-deceased great-grandfather—had he joined his ancestor in the afterlife? Too young, he told himself in alarm, much left to do. His heart raced as if he were running.

Although comforted by a blurry image of the goat farm near the Niger River delta, he pivoted from his elder and dashed into the mud-walled home. Carvings of Igbo deities on either side of the portal mocked his panic.

In a corner of the main room, he paused at the altar to his Chi spiritual guardian, decorated with offerings of china, glass, and food. He prayed for a different fate, and a soothing warmth spread through him. A hand grasped his forearm and he saw the old man clearly. Agwu, the god of medicine and healing.

Biko concentrated on forming speech. "Can you cure me of Ebola? Or are you here to show me my destiny—am I already dead?"

"Nwa m, how can you talk to me if you have passed on?" The voice was female, lilting, and humorous.

Liquid pitter-pattered his arm like a spring rain shower. He wiggled his fingers, intending to pry open his eyelids. A cool washcloth wiped his eyes, then the sterile, bleach-drenched hospital cubicle came into view, blocked by the petite form of his sister. Tears streaked her cheeks and dropped to his body. She handed him his glasses.

"Nneka, what are you doing here?" His hollow tone emanated from the tunnel of barely-regained consciousness. He raised his arms to embrace her, but they refused to obey his command. A wave of pain swept his muscles and his stomach turned over, threatening to erupt even though he was certain he had not eaten.

"After ten days in this bed, you are finally getting better since I arrived yesterday." Her round face took on the serene expression of Mami Wata, the water spirit of good fortune. "Once I get you home to Nigeria, you can finish recuperating."

Biko laughed that his sister, younger by seven years, had adopted a tone of authority. "And who gave you the expertise," he asked with a tender inflection, "to decide when I am to be released?"

"I am an optimist. The doctor will stop by soon. Everyone was excited when you started to move in your sleep this morning."

Biko adjusted his head on the pillow, hoping to reduce his dizziness. "I regret distracting you from your studies. Is it June already? You must prepare for end-of-year exams."

"Yes, it is June 10, but I am not in school." She frowned. "I am taking time off to be a forest guide. Do you forget?"

The awful month a year earlier when she was held hostage flooded back. He had been unable to focus on completing his medical residency, knowing that many kidnapped girls were forced to marry their captors. Fortunately, the families as a group scraped together sufficient funds for a ransom when the government refused to help. The University of Lagos allowed him to repeat his missed rotations before he started his job with the World Health Organization.

He turned his head side-to-side, another attempt to clear his mind. The fuzzy hair on his head and ungroomed goatee distracted him—never before had he failed to keep up with grooming. "Nneka, I hope you do not guide gorilla treks. Someone on our trip may have been the index case for this Ebola outbreak."

"Not yet. International tourism is below pre-pandemic levels, but it is increasing. We have many requests for tours of the Wildlife Sanctuary this summer."

"Please keep visitors away from the animals. Do you know if Nigeria has investigated Ebola in them?"

Nneka mopped his brow, beaded with sweat. "You worry too

much. We have no cases in Nigeria, although I heard about some in Ghana."

"Ghana? How did it get there without showing up first in Sierra Leone, Liberia, or Côte d'Ivoire?" Outbreak control wasn't his responsibility, but it felt like Ebola danger had exploded as he convalesced.

She laughed. "Ask your friend Stefan Duda. The staff say he stopped by every day to check on you."

Biko remembered none of those visits, and his colleague should have been deployed to Ghana. Had Stefan refused a new WHO assignment just to stay nearby in Conakry? Biko appreciated the gesture but Stefan could have made a cataclysmic workplace mistake if refusing any direct orders, just to keep an eye on him.

THIRTY-SEVEN

"About time you showed up." Dr. Grinwold dismissed his staff from the late Friday review of New Mexico disease cases and pulled out a chair for Maya.

She ducked her head and blushed, ashamed to let him down again. "I apologize for being late. I drove up from Albuquerque as fast as possible but got pulled over by a state trooper for speeding." She immediately regretted the explanation—telling your boss you broke the law wasn't in the 'good employee' manual.

His bald head gleamed under the office fluorescents, and he rubbed it with a meaty hand. "Well, that's your first ticket, other than the time you were charged with the Apache elder's death."

He must be really pissed if he brought that up. He knew full well that the elder was already dead from alcohol and cold weather exposure before her car hit him, and Mark had made the charges go away.

That was three years ago when she was still a newbie Epidemic Intelligence Service officer. Unfortunately, the incident's impact had carried forward in time, weakening her influence with Sandia Pueblo on the dengue investigation last summer.

"Again, I'm sorry. Did Stephanie give you my message? I lost track of time while the state lab demonstrated how they test the soil and sheep fecal samples for *E. coli*."

Dr. Grinwold grunted. "I didn't realize you had that much interest in laboratory science."

Maya attempted to get them back on a scientific footing. "I prefer being out in the field tracking down disease but looking at mosquito larvae under the microscope in Hawai'i—that was fun."

"How's the petting zoo investigation going?" Dr. Grinwold appeared genuinely interested despite his impatience at her late arrival.

"The scraped downslope soil tested negative. Dave's experimental diet change and treatment of the sheep seem to be working—no shedding of *E. coli* in new stool samples. They're unsure if they can afford to implement those changes longer-term or on a wider scale."

"One more time that you've achieved excellent cooperation with the USDA and state ag." Dr. Grinwold's smile exposed his teeth, canines eerily long like a puma's. "One of the best outcomes of your four years here."

Then his tone turned forceful. "Your CDC assignment runs out in three weeks and you need to make a decision about my State Public Health Veterinarian position."

Bolts of anxiety flashed through her limbs and chest as the room began a slow spin. Why did the opportunity trigger a panic attack? She replied in a timid voice, "You're really kind to hold the job open for me. I know you need someone for that function."

"You've provided that expertise even though paid by CDC. However, if you don't stay in New Mexico, I want to get a new veterinary epidemiologist hired as soon as possible. Is there another vet you can recommend?" He grinned—his attempt to ratchet up the pressure was transparent.

"I hate to put off your kind offer, but I'm still thinking about it."

He tapped his finger on a file folder. "If it motivates a decision, New Mexico can be as interesting as New York. We might have Ebola."

Maya took several deep breaths to counter a brief spasm of fear. "Not another traveler from the meeting in Guinea? It wound up more than a month ago." Relabeling the feeling as excitement, she had to admit some jealousy that Faye's Ebola work extended beyond NYC to Africa.

"No. A primate facility in Alamogordo has a dozen dead crab-eating macaques. Tests are underway."

Maya scrolled through her mental notes about nonhuman primate diseases before responding. Macaques rarely died from cold sore lesions caused by Cercopithecine herpesvirus type 1, but it killed exposed human handlers. Other potential monkey viruses included simian immunodeficiency virus, similar to HIV in humans, and the virus that caused simian hemorrhagic fever.

Could the monkey deaths be from tuberculosis? Mexico had higher TB rates. Human cases in the border states occasionally showed up due to unpasteurized, contaminated milk or cheese.

"I can think of several possible viruses plus TB," she said. "Why is Ebola on the differential list?"

The crepitus skin around his bulging brown eyes crinkled. "Back in the dark ages before you were born, this monkey colony had asymptomatic Ebola infections during that famous outbreak of *Orthoebolavirus restonense*."

She recalled it from vet school. In 1989, imported macaques from the Philippines died with bleeding and organ failure from infection with a newly-discovered Ebola strain. The virus was named after Reston, Virginia, its first US location.

To avoid transmission to humans for the first time on American soil, Army scientists pinned the animals with mop handles for sedative injections. After euthanasia, they disinfected the air by cooking formaldehyde on electric frying pans.

As described in the media, the fear had been intense. Subsequent studies indicated Ebola virus, even Reston, wasn't easily transmitted through the air, although its potential was still evaluated like on the plane flights Maya investigated. And the Reston virus, unlike other Ebola strains, infected only a small number of humans as evidenced by antibody titers, but they didn't become ill.

"I heard about the macaque deaths in Reston," she said, "but New Mexico had cases, too?"

"A few facilities like ours found monkey and human infections, mostly asymptomatic, traced to Sumatra. Then in 2008, an alarming expansion of intermediate hosts occurred when pigs from the Philippines tested positive along with hog farm workers."

Dr. Grinwold opened the folder and shoved it toward her, indicating his notes. The thrill of a new challenge sharpened Maya's focus but she sighed as she traced her fingers over his sloppy scrawl.

His neck and face turned red. "I didn't have time for Stephanie to type them up."

She laughed. "If I have any trouble, I'll ask for her help. Would you like me on scene tomorrow, or should I wait until Monday for the lab results?"

He twisted in his swivel rocker, then checked the continuous glucose monitor on the back of his left upper arm. Maya was impressed that he had admitted his diabetes problem publicly.

She remembered when he wore the monitor on his abdomen so no one would know about his health issues. The change was probably due to Nancy Bingham finally retiring as Arizona's State Epidemiologist to move into Dr. Grinwold's adobe ranch on the Santa Fe outskirts. His life partner had him on a healthier diet and daily walks.

In response to what he saw on the monitor, he pulled a bottle of apple juice from his desk drawer. "A bit hypoglycemic."

He paused for a couple of awkward minutes until Maya said, "I can come back later."

"No," he answered with a decisive tone. "I'd like you in Alamogordo tonight. Some backyard farmers near the primate facility claim their piglets are dying."

THIRTY-EIGHT

At four o'clock, Stefan provided his last Ebola vaccine in the museum courtyard. After eleven days of effort without a break, his brown hair tickled his ears and shaded his eyes—no time for personal grooming. He had hoped to gain a sense of satisfaction for the thousands of potential lives saved, but his emotional victory lap was interrupted. Three young unvaccinated health workers remained, begging him for more doses.

"Don't worry, the Minister of Health assures me she'll get a new shipment within a week." The heat, long hours, and frustration left him sweaty and eager to escape.

He wanted to take a photo of the women with their tearful eyes and wringing hands, but it wasn't appropriate to ask them. He'd post their passion for vaccination on social media to chastise all those promoting vaccine falsehoods, leaving everyone vulnerable to deadly microbes decimating their communities like a tsunami.

He said goodbye to the other vaccination staff members and hopped on his motorbike. One of them had recommended Tayaki Beach for an evening at the shore. First, he was delayed by a massive street protest against Guinea's military government, black smoke filling his lungs from a burning vehicle. Then he got lost on remote dirt tracks.

In about an hour, tired and hungry, he spotted the shore beyond a network of rice fields. He paid a toll to enter and park, then tied his tennis shoes together and draped them over his shoulder. Dodging plastic bottles and other rubbish carried in by the tide, he relished the sand massaging his aching feet.

With deep breaths, he inhaled the salt air. Shouting "C'est à moi," children competed to catch male fiddler crabs, each one brandishing a purple claw bigger than its body. Finding a thatched-roof bar, he settled on a bench with a glass of palm wine.

There was nothing more relaxing than the sound of youthful laughter—he ached to be reunited with his daughter. He hadn't seen Paula since early March—would she and Kondrat forgive a three-month absence?

Not for the first time, he regretted the hike to see gorillas in Nigeria. If only he'd flown home to Oslo for the weekend before the Conakry meeting, Jan Kreischer might be alive and the Ebola outbreak eliminated, including his own infection and now Biko's.

It was still hard to accept that hundreds of dead people were all his fault. Would they ever have an answer to the regrets that roiled his stomach?

They included a whole series of 'if onlys,' like an elaborate chain reaction of dominoes. If Jan hadn't been so adamant about the side excursion, if Biko hadn't agreed to guide them, if Stefan hadn't approved the hare-brained plan. And they still had nothing but circumstantial evidence that Jan was infected by the gorilla or that he was the index case.

Low clouds purpled, a breeze rustled the palm fronds, and the lights of Conakry in the distance began to sparkle. His phone rang and he tugged it out of his Bermuda shorts' pocket.

"My brother is fully alert now," came Nneka's voice. Stefan needed special dispensation to allow her in the hospital wards, geared up with PPE. But after he procured thousands of vaccine doses from WHO, he had clout to spare.

"That's wonderful news. I'll be right over." He glanced at the sand between his toes and sniffed the sweat under his arm. "Give me an hour to clean up."

Stefan's stomach grumbled as he maneuvered his bike around locals and tourists bar-hopping on a busy Friday night. He'd taken the time for a shower and change of clothes, but no dinner yet. In the hospital's changing room, he quickly donned full PPE, so familiar a uniform that he couldn't complain about it being uncomfortable even with the inadequate ceiling fans.

A miracle—Biko sat upright sipping a pinkish drink from a cup held by his sister.

"Mon ami, tu es magnifique!" Stefan bumped his fist against Biko's and nodded to Nneka.

Biko smiled broadly. "I cannot believe you are still here in Guinea. Did you hang around just for me?"

"Someone had to take up the slack on our vaccination campaign while you napped."

Biko knew Stefan was kidding, but felt beholden after Nneka informed him that Stefan purchased her plane ticket from Lagos. He tried to move his legs, but they shifted only slightly. Still too weak to assume doctor duties.

"Perhaps next week, I will recover enough to assist you with vaccinations, if the clinical caseload doesn't require me here at the hospital."

Nneka exploded. "I did not come all this way to return home alone. Surely WHO will allow you sick leave or vacation time after all you have been through on their behalf."

Stefan gestured to the other cubicles, most of them empty with drapes pulled back. "As you see, the Ebola case count has dropped, and I used up all the vaccine this afternoon. Unfortunately, we're not 42 days beyond the last case, so the outbreak isn't officially over. But I will call Dr. Shah tonight and insist that we both head home."

Biko scrubbed at the worry lines on his forehead. "Are you certain? With my limited WHO experience, I cannot be perceived as a slacker at this point in my career."

"Local authorities and the Ministry of Health can mop up the outbreak. That always increases community buy-in for our burial, quarantine, and vaccination recommendations. And there are still the Africa CDC, UNICEF, and the Red Cross staff to help. You and Nneka should fly back to Lagos as soon as the clinicians clear you."

Biko remembered Stefan's partner giving him grief about the

trip. "Thank you for facilitating the reunion with Nneka. I hope your own family reconnection goes well."

Stefan pulled out his cell to check the time. First, Dr. Shah. Then, Kondrat. Two important phone calls—what could go wrong?"

THIRTY-NINE

Taylor awoke at dawn, red light dappling the white duvet through the window. Grabbing a cashmere hotel robe, Taylor headed for the view framed by drapes they'd never closed.

A scarlet cloud cradled the sun's golden orb. Perched in the branches of a baobab tree, a fluorescent-blue Abyssinian Roller screeched "Arrg." Then it plunged in a spiral toward the street below, spreading its two long tail feathers.

The bird dive-bombed a businessman's head and flitted into the bushes, probably in pursuit of a rodent or snake for breakfast. Red sky at morning, sailor's warning—Taylor shuddered at the ominous portents.

Dropping the robe to an armchair, Taylor crawled back under the covers, enveloping Faye's small body. Go for a run or pleasure a partner? Easy choice. Beginning with the back of her knees, kisses rained upward to her nipples, when Faye arched her neck and lazily opened her piercing blue eyes.

"Dr. Lewis," she said with a Colorado drawl. "Interested in a trail ride? This filly is raring to go."

After years of taking female hormones, erections were hit-or-miss. Or maybe it was the normal declines of aging with an upcoming fiftieth birthday. "Let's use that giant soaking tub," Taylor suggested, imagining other ways to make Faye happy.

Faye checked the time on her phone, then leapt out of bed and grabbed Taylor's hand to lead them to the bathroom. "No rest for the wicked," she said. "We have one hour."

Later, bodies pleasantly thrumming, both donned work clothes and boots for their first day in the field.

"I miss your Cher wig." Faye winked to show she was teasing. She adored Taylor's body no matter how it was decorated. "Are you worried whether your family would accept you as a trans woman?"

"Not just my family. Traditional gender roles are well defined among the Akan people. Uncle Kumi already asked why I never married. He has two wives and wonders why I haven't done the same."

Faye's skin prickled and she pulled down the sleeves of her chambray shirt. "Did he say anything about your relationship with me?"

"No, perhaps he was being diplomatic. But while I'm here in Ghana, I must behave in accordance with my sex assigned at birth."

Asshole. Faye immediately regretted her characterization of Taylor's closest relative. "Is there a chance Uncle Kumi knows you're trans and he's trying to protect you from discrimination?"

Taylor answered the ringing phone and confirmed that Uncle Kumi's chauffeur was waiting for them in the lobby.

"I don't know how much he understands, but I think he's looking out for me." Taylor pocketed the room key. "Ghana's working on a bill imposing a prison sentence for someone convicted of being Queer. They're also considering a requirement for conversion therapy."

Faye resented Taylor feeling forced to pass as a cis male in 2022, but then remembered Taylor did the same at the funeral of the Catholic child who died of dengue last year. As a hospital chief of staff, Taylor was a diplomat, juggling multiple expectations of patients and employees.

"I guess you're right to be careful." She suddenly recalled an airport sign warning that Ghana didn't welcome paedophiles and sexual deviants. Sleep-deprived from the long flight, she had focused on the new continent and its Ebola outbreak, not her own and Taylor's safety related to gender or sexual orientation.

Out the hotel window, the sky had turned the color of slate. Taylor opened the door to the hallway as Faye grabbed her PPE bag. She cautioned with a grimace, "I think we're about to get slammed."

FORTY

Slipping her tennis shoes and socks into her daypack, Maya swirled her bare feet in the white gypsum grains of the Dune Life Nature Trail. With the sun just peeking over the eastern horizon, the sand was soothing, cool on her skin like the mid-seventies air temperature.

It was worth leaving her Alamogordo motel room at 6:30 to relish a few moments alone in White Sands National Park. She'd never managed a visit to the park with Manolo before he died. Lying in the dunes as her dad covered her body with sand—that was her last memory of the area.

Pausing at the trail's crest between two head-high sand pedestals formed by the roots of skunkbush sumac, she inhaled the crisp, fresh air.

Back home from NYC for a week-and-a-half, her bone marrow had generated new red blood cells to carry additional oxygen at the higher elevations. Besides, the park was only at about 4000 feet compared to Santa Fe's 7000. No reason to be out of breath, other than not having a clue about her future. The thought of 104° forecasted for early afternoon increased her sense of weakness.

Nothing pierced the brilliant-blue sky other than a cluster of white buds topping the fifteen-foot stalk of a soaptree yucca. Catching a rare flash of bright color, she bent to study a small green-leafed plant bursting with pink flowers. Desert sand verbena, according to the park guide on her cell, used for medicinal purposes by Native Americans. Would it heal a widow's lingering grief? Dropping to her knees, she sniffed the plant's vanilla scent.

Toddler giggles interrupted Maya's meditations. Turning back, she spotted a child struggling to keep her footing while guided by a boy who appeared to be about eight.

Behind them, a shorter woman in jeans exclaimed to another larger one in khakis, "This is the largest gypsum dunefield in the world! Now do you think it was worth the flight from Maine with the kids to see this?"

Maya glanced at her phone to check the time. At 8:30, she was due to meet up with Dr. Ben Smith, the new State Veterinarian. If she took the job as the state health vet, he would be her ag counterpart. Their work together on anthrax in Arizona had been collegial.

Forty-five minutes would allow her plenty of time to reach the hog farm north of town. Reluctant to leave her nature walk, especially if her life path took her out of the state, she nevertheless rotated to a seated position, dripped water from her bottle over her toes, and slipped back on her socks and shoes.

Closer to Tularosa, the life-affirming green of irrigated fields on the left side contrasted with pale dirt and sagebrush on the right bounded by barbed wire and a FOR SALE sign. Better to invest in the farmland, she thought. Parking her Prius in the hog farm's driveway, she spotted the linebacker bulk of the middle-aged African-American vet, his bare arms resting on the metal pig corral. He turned to smile, then swung open the gate, allowing her to drive in.

"Maya, it's great to work with you again." After she closed her car door, he pushed back his tan cowboy hat and leaned down to envelop her in a massive hug.

"Dave told me you shifted positions from Arizona to New Mexico," she said. "He's thrilled to have a partner like you in Albuquerque."

Ben laughed. "I think he's buttering me up to head off any turf battles. But our state and USDA goals mostly were aligned in Arizona, and I assume that won't change now that we're in the same neighborhood."

Maya had only seen her veterinary colleagues fight once, over the migrants coming across the Arizona border with Mexico. Ben's faith led him to humane outreach, whereas Dave's more conservative rancher background dwelled on the negative impacts from crime and school overcrowding.

"Why did you jump states?" she asked.

"Kids are grown, I'd invested enough years in the Arizona system to qualify for a pension, and my wife wanted a cooler climate. Plus New Mexico politics are slightly saner than Arizona's."

"You followed Nancy Bingham's reasoning when she retired to Santa Fe."

"Yes, we had fantastic health-ag coordination when she was Arizona's State Epidemiologist." Then he frowned. "With her partner, Fred Grinwold, I'm not so sure."

Maya resented having to defend Dr. Grinwold's taciturn nature, bordering on belligerence if he thought someone was jeopardizing public health. But underneath the bluster, he was principled and kind. "If Dave can achieve a détente with him, I have complete faith in you."

She grabbed her gear and followed Ben to his truck, where both pulled on coveralls, rubber boots, masks, and gloves.

"What breed of pigs do they have?" She followed Ben toward a metal-roofed building.

"Tamworth. They can withstand temperature extremes and their meat is less fatty, so it's popular in modern diets. But they're slow growers and prefer grazing to confinement, so not good for commercial production. Perfect for a hobby farm like this one catering to high-end restaurants."

Passing outdoor pens with long-legged adult hogs appearing to weigh at least five hundred pounds, Maya commented on their color. "Red—pretty unusual."

Ben nodded. "The breed's color origin is unknown, perhaps from matings with wild pigs overseas."

Once inside the shelter, Maya enjoyed the prancing piglets with their curly tails.

"This farm has rarely experienced piglet mortality," Ben said, "so ten yesterday raised an alarm."

"Did you take samples already?"

"Yes, I drove down last night and processed those." They rounded a pen with two piglets, one twitching and the second appearing deceased. "Damn, these weren't housed close to the others."

Maya wondered if Ben and Dr. Grinwold were jumping the gun on suspecting Ebola in the pigs. Even though the farm was a half-mile downwind of the primate facility where Dave had confirmed multiple Ebola Reston cases in the monkeys last night, a mechanism of transmission would be required. Some laboratory studies had indicated pigs could be infected by introduction of the virus into the nose or throat.

Ben left his equipment outside the pen and entered, closing the gate behind him. The piglet appearing dead with a blue snout abruptly jerked one leg. The one leaning against the wall had clear nasal discharge and an intermittent cough. Then she spotted a third in the corner partially hidden by straw. Its body was hunched with the hair standing erect.

"There's nothing I can do to save these," Ben said after his exam. "Fill up three syringes with sodium pentobarbital, then come hold the animals."

The first two piglets hardly squirmed in Maya's gloved hands as she knelt in the straw and Ben put an end to their suffering through an ear vein. The third recumbent pig required a heart stick. Then they both went to work drawing blood samples to submit for antibody testing.

"Are you going to perform a field necropsy?" she asked.

"I'd feel safer doing that at the lab." They placed each pig in a black bag, then he led her to the back of his truck where he loaded them in coolers along with the others he'd collected yesterday. "It's more likely this farm has an outbreak of porcine reproductive and respiratory syndrome virus."

"The China outbreak found the pigs were coinfected with PRRSV and RESTV."

Ben smiled. "You did your homework."

"The pig die-offs in the Philippines and China didn't confirm an inciting exposure," she said, "although multiple species of fruit and insectivorous bats tested positive for Reston virus."

Once again, she reflected on the role of bats asymptomatically harboring so many of the world's most deadly viruses. "What else do we need to do here?"

"I instructed the owner about disinfection, and biosecurity would be improved by keeping the hogs indoors even though this breed doesn't like it."

Maya considered collecting serum samples from the people working the farm. "It's probably premature because we don't know what's killing the piglets, but I'll ask Dr. Grinwold about human testing. Let me know ASAP what you find. In the meantime, I'll join Dave this afternoon at the primate facility."

They helped each other remove their PPE and bag it up. Ben offered her a drink from his water cooler and shook her hand goodbye. "I'm praying that this is nothing unusual. I really don't want to muck about in bat caves."

Maya laughed. "Not to worry. Believe it or not, I'm an expert." Her bat sampling skills for COVID were hard-won in Thailand and China, but at least this time there would be no government agency locking her up for it.

FORTY-ONE

Blue strobes flashed off the casino's purple walls as Stefan celebrated Biko's return to consciousness and the successful vaccine campaign. He concluded his karaoke song by shouting every note through his surgical mask. Reddened face dripping sweat, he bowed with a flourish as if concluding a performance at the Old Globe Theatre. When the deejay stopped playing "As It Was" by Harry Styles, the next inebriated expat tossed her long blonde hair, shoved Stefan aside, and grabbed the microphone.

His chair now occupied by a drunken patron, Stefan took the new singer's seat amongst a cluster of Afrikaners, bellowing for their companion like elephant seals in heat. She swung her wide hips in time with the pounding drum beat and belted "Rumors" by Lizzo and Cardi B.

Imbued with regret from the Styles lyrics, he mourned his trusting relationship with Kondrat, clearly damaged based on Kondrat's frosty tone on each call. Temporarily lowering his mask, he tossed back a shot of Sodabi from the bottle on the table, its 50% alcohol searing his throat and bringing stars to his eyes.

His vaccinations and masking had worked until now, so a little COVID risk was worth taking, two years into the pandemic. COVID worries weighed like a pea compared to the elephant of Kondrat's wrath.

"I can see why this palm wine was banned during colonial times," he muttered to the man next to him.

"Nee, nee. This is healthy—it treats my arthritis and will improve your digestion." His companion, built like a water buffalo, shoved closer the platter of grilled pineapple splashed with cinnamon.

Stefan agreed that the drink was powerful enough to vanquish joint pain, but the tropical fruit's acidity burned a hole under his sternum and irritated his throat. He pulled out a wad of 20,000 Francs Guinéens from his wallet, admiring the turbaned woman and doves on the front of the note. Each one was worth only a couple of euros, so he peeled off a dozen and threw them on the table.

"Sien jou later, vriend," the portly South African shouted as Stefan exited and the singer took a bow to thunderous applause and catcalls.

Stefan ignored the electronic beeps, clatter of chips, and cheers escaping the casino. He continued out to the facility's verdant grounds and settled into a lounge chair beneath a palm tree, kicking off his sandals to dangle his toes in the grass. At nine PM, Stefan savored the light breeze on his face and arms—the temperature might have dipped below ninety.

An hour earlier on the phone, Dr. Shah had complimented Stefan's efforts and approved his going home. "You tracked almost three hundred cases and supervised administration of a thousand vaccine doses. Infections are dropping and we can turn disease control over to the locals."

Stefan's conscience refused to be consoled. "But 214 people died—we didn't do enough."

"We're not God. There are limits on what we can achieve once an outbreak is surging. You'll contribute again in the future, if you maintain your own health and sanity."

Stefan had deferred to the wisdom of his superior and booked a flight to Oslo for the next day, then fortified his courage in the club. At this point, he could no longer postpone calling Kondrat to beg for forgiveness and approval to move home. In Norway, Kondrat likely had Paula asleep in her bed while he devoured one of his Harry Hole detective novels by Jo Nesbø.

A multimammate rat scurried across his left foot on its way to the safety of a bush. The prospect of catching Lassa fever flashed through his brain. The small cut on his big toe from the beach excursion could be a source of exposure if the rat's feet were contaminated by virus from its droppings. Returning with a second deadly infection from West Africa would be fatal to his relationship. A third of Lassa patients became deaf—he'd avoid hearing Kondrat's rants but not the vision of his partner's distress.

Despite a flash of dizziness, Stefan leapt up from the chair and ran into the sprinklers on the other end of the lawn to wash away any virus. He brushed aside the thought that Ebola still hid out in his semen.

Collapsing to the wet grass, woozy and out of breath, he felt like Executive Officer Kane in *Alien* when the screeching, sharp-toothed Xenomorph burst from his chest.

FORTY-TWO

Maya squirmed under the baking sun at the entrance gate of the Tularosa, New Mexico primate facility. A stern female guard scrutinized Maya's credentials. When the examination lasted more than a minute, Maya wise-cracked, "Do I look like an eco-terrorist?"

Big mistake. The woman flashed an evil eye, then picked up the phone for a lengthy, hostile discussion. "You didn't tell me she was coming," was the gist of it.

Whether the heat had encouraged her loose lips, Maya wasn't sure, but she regretted the quip. Perhaps it was just her good mood prompted by rewarding disease detective work with her favorite veterinary colleagues.

Finally, Dave appeared on the inside of the metal fence topped with rolls of barbed wire. He doffed his dusty brown cowboy hat and apologized to Maya and the guard for the oversight. He winced with apparent pain when he shook the guard's hand.

Maya noticed the bandage on his middle finger as she strolled with him to the adobe-colored building. "What happened to you?"

"The scalpel slipped when I necropsied a macaque."

"That's not the news I want to hear." Maya's tone matched the guard's. "I'm not leaving here without your serum specimen."

Dave responded in kind. "Even if I was really exposed to Ebola Reston, it's too soon for my immune system to generate detectable antibodies."

"It will provide a background level for comparison. Workplace safety, particularly with RESTV killing the monkeys, requires it."

"Is Fred Grinwold requiring you to be a vampire today?" Dave's lips curled up in a slight smile.

"Yes. He called and requested human specimens when I finished up at the pig farm with Ben."

Dave held open the door to the anteroom and they both donned full PPE including face shields.

"Ben sends his regards." Maya pulled on her latex gloves, realizing they were protective but not impermeable to puncture. "Unlike your monkeys, he still doesn't have any lab confirmation of Ebola infection."

"All right. Let me show you around the facility. Then I'll ask the staff to stop by their break room for you to take their blood samples."

As they entered the first area, the animals housed singly in cages began to scream. "They're sensitive to the deaths of other monkeys and human strangers in their midst," Dave said.

"I sure wish this type of biomedical research wasn't necessary," Maya said quietly.

"Animal welfare organizations have lobbied the FDA to lift its requirement for testing new drugs on animals," Dave answered. "Here, they're studying Alzheimer's, Parkinson's disease, and autism. No other animal model comes close to the human brain, and the newly-developed organ chip technology using human cells isn't a good replacement when studying the neurologic system."

Maya surveyed the burgeoning chaos of rattling cages and leaping monkeys. Their fur ranged from gray to brown except for the white belly, thick eyebrows, and tufts on either side of the upper lip. Facial skin was brown to pink around the eyes and on the nose. Some of the monkeys appeared beagle-sized and their tails were at least as long as their bodies.

"This species is *Macaca fascicularis*," Dave said, "known as the long-tailed macaque or cynomolgus macaque. These are the same ones implicated in the 1989 Reston virus discovery in Virginia."

A monkey reached out to stroke the hand of the animal in the next cage, then resumed tearing out its own hair from its torso. Another spun in rapid circles and a third sat listlessly, thumb in its eye.

The one behind Maya tugged off her hairnet. Dave laughed. "Stand farther away from their agile hands. These are the only Old World monkeys using stone tools to crack open oysters, crabs, and palm nuts."

They turned back to the anteroom for a clean hairnet, then proceeded along another walkway. "Where do they come from?" Maya asked.

"Paperwork indicates a breeding facility in Arizona, but RESTV got in somehow. A few Cambodian officials are under investigation for trafficking wild monkeys. Each one has a value up to $40,000."

The characteristic smell of animal feed and waste penetrated Maya's mask. At least this time she wasn't pregnant like at the mink farm in Denmark when she almost passed out. These cages and floors were gleaming—the employees worked hard to maintain a healthy environment. But it hadn't translated to the animals' mental health.

A staff member opened a cage and used a long pole with a rubberized band to hook a monkey around its neck and drop it to the floor, where the animal half-walked and was dragged to a short metal chair bolted to the cement. Tossed a snack, the monkey climbed into the chair and inserted its head in a restraint as the staffer slipped off the pole.

Looks barbaric—Maya's immediate reaction. "It's more cooperative than I might have guessed," she said.

The staffer nodded. "They're trained and rewarded for this, so it's familiar."

Maya noted the small white plastic cube attached to the animal's shaved head. "What's that for?"

"It's a cranial implant which helps stabilize the head for procedures and allows us access to the brain. This animal had it implanted into the skull yesterday, so I'm checking for wound healing and no infection. Next week, we'll insert a probe for the study of brain neurons."

Maya had limited experience with lab animal research and once again was glad she'd chosen to specialize in epidemiology. She understood the benefits of such work and had met several USDA vets in addition to Dave who monitored animal welfare. But she'd prefer to avoid a repeat experience of looking into the face of a creature that shared 93% of her DNA yet had no free choice of where it lived or how it spent its life.

"Do you ever get used to this?" She blushed, not intending to say it out loud.

The staffer, taking notes on the monkey's health, apparently didn't hear her. Dave answered, "My dad's mom died of Alzheimer's when I was five. I barely knew her, and she never knew me. Each time we visited the nursing home, she repeated the same questions about where I came from, at least until she couldn't talk at all."

Then he headed for a supply cabinet. "Let me show you how I collect the macaque serum specimens." He cornered another staffer who reinforced a monkey with treats to stick its right rear leg through the cage. Dave drew blood from the femoral vein. "You can help me sample this room."

If Maya could draw blood from humans, monkeys trained for the procedure shouldn't be too challenging. After all, they weren't likely to faint at the sight of a needle. She was a bit slower than Dave, only completing two rows of cages to his three, but they had their serum samples for Ebola testing within an hour.

She labeled her final tube to match the monkey's tattoo and cage numbers, then heard an alarming growl. As she looked up, the animal reached back for a handful of its feces and flung it through the bars at her face. Startled, she reared back and raised her head too high—some of the stinky warmth splattered her neck.

"Shit," she exclaimed, not intending the humor. At least the clear plastic face mask had protected her eyes, nose, and mouth. The staffer led her to the sink in the anteroom where Dave, alerted by her shout, joined them. He helped her change all her gear and insisted she wash her neck with soap for twenty minutes.

"Looks like we need a blood sample from you too," he joked, before his face turned more solemn. "But perhaps we should worry more about herpesvirus simiae."

"The monkey cold sore virus?" The class lecture about herpes B flooded her mind. Mild lesions in monkeys could kill infected monkey handlers within a month of exposure. Flu-like symptoms would be followed by blistering on her neck and swollen lymph nodes. Without treatment, she'd develop confusion, respiratory distress, and death.

"We can submit your serum sample for B virus testing along with Ebola," Dave said, "then test you again three weeks from now. You already drew blood from this animal, and I'll make sure its saliva is collected as well."

"I remember something about antivirals."

Dave nodded. "There are two which can be used prophylactically before you develop symptoms, and a third after symptom development."

"Any side effects or risks?"

Dave's face wrinkled in a grimace. "When do we ever get the benefit of drugs without risk? Both can affect the kidney and liver, plus mental health. Anxiety, depression, trouble concentrating and sleeping."

"Yikes. Maybe I'll wait for the monkey's test result because it might be negative. My skin is intact, so it's not like a puncture wound." She grabbed his arm. "You're more at risk. We should check for herpes and Ebola on the monkey you dissected."

"Georgia State University has the herpes testing facility, but I'm not sure how long it will take."

Maya took a drink from a water bottle to calm her nerves before they began the serological sampling of staff ordered by Dr. Grinwold. If she accepted his offer of the State Public Health Veterinarian position, her work would be confined to New Mexico. Even without the challenges of a CDC employee's occasional international travel, she'd need to weigh the rewards of solving outbreaks against personal health threats.

FORTY-THREE

The limo screeched to a stop, narrowly missing the truck in front. "I am so sorry," the driver apologized. "This traffic is not unusual, but I know you Americans aren't used to it."

"You ain't kidding." Taylor hugged Faye's shoulders as they quavered in the back.

Faye gulped, her fingernails digging into the leather seat. She hadn't imagined more congestion and bad driving than New York's, but every drive in Accra left her anxious. Not a useful mood when trying to ingratiate herself with the local populace.

Once the highway cleared, their journey continued, interrupted one more time on a rural road when a masked man waved them over. The chauffeur forked over a wad of Ghanaian cedis, then pulled up within twenty minutes to the central meeting grounds of an Akan village outside Accra.

"Medaase, wofase," Uncle Kumi said as he reached up to hug his nephew. Then he bowed to Faye. "Thank you, Dr. Simpson, as well. You both have been so helpful this week."

Faye smiled, happy she'd made progress in persuading Uncle Kumi of her value. "I'm glad to be of assistance. Do you want me to meet with the women in their huts, as usual?"

He waved over a teenager to guide her. Translation from the Twi dialect wasn't often needed because of English dominance during the colonial period, but the girl would be helpful with introductions.

Faye left Taylor with Uncle Kumi and the men to discuss Ebola risk and possible vaccination. Wearing a surgical mask, she accompanied her guide to the first of four single-room houses built of clay bricks, each home positioned at a corner of the courtyard.

This fihankra compound was slightly wealthier than others she had visited, with its corrugated iron roofs rather than thatch.

Greeting three young women, one with a child at her breast and the others with toddlers, Faye handed them a laminated card she'd developed with Taylor and their local health department on Monday. In black and white, it depicted an Akan girl standing in front of a map of Ghana colored red. The text said **End EBOLA Now**, with the large letters in black except for the word Ebola also in red. At the bottom were symbols of partner organizations like WHO, UNICEF, and CDC.

"I heard your Papa died last week from Ebola," she told the sisters, referring to their grandfather. "I am so sorry." She knew the women had performed a ritual cleansing of the body, washing it three times, drying it, and dressing it in clothing appropriate to his profession. Then the bedding and clothes had also been washed, potentially exposing them to Ebola.

Uncle Kumi had reported no additional illnesses in the village, so to avoid alarm, she and Taylor decided against full PPE. She'd seen a negative correlation earlier in the week between the amount of protection they wore and their success at convincing residents to accept vaccination. One curious toddler in his mother's arms tugged at Faye's mask, and she hoped her choice of no moonsuit was a safe compromise.

When the women consented to vaccination, Faye checked her thermal lunch box to verify that the ice had melted and the vaccine vials were now thawed. She donned latex gloves, cleaned each arm with alcohol, and injected 1 mL into each woman's deltoid.

Protocol required fifteen minutes of monitoring for adverse reactions. If needed, Taylor had additional drugs to help someone who developed breathing difficulties from anaphylaxis.

As they waited, Faye reapplied her mosquito repellent to discourage the swarming horde. Then her teenage guide demonstrated the ritual of Ghanaian tea preparation. In an earthenware pot resting on three large stones circling a wood fire, the young woman brought water to a boil. She added cinnamon sticks, cloves, and grated ginger, followed by black tea leaves, and brewed it for several minutes. After she removed it from the heat and let it steep a litle longer, she strained the tea into cups using a piece of fine mesh.

Faye politely declined the offer of sugar and milk. She sipped the tea to avoid burning her lips. The caffeine provided a pleasant jolt to counteract the warm fogginess of the hut as condensed water escaped through a narrow roof vent.

When the rituals of hospitality were complete, the guide signaled they needed to move on to the next hut. The eldest of the three sisters handed Faye a bottle of Asaana, the African non-alcoholic cola. "This is to cool your throat on your walk," she said.

The second sister slipped on Faye's wrist a bracelet of hand-painted glass beads. Solid blue beads alternated with forest green ones stroked with white lines like the crest of ocean waves. Her favorite nature colors.

When Faye completed additional interviews and vaccinations in the remaining huts, she rejoined Taylor and Uncle Kumi. The bottle of Asaana now empty, she reluctantly accepted Uncle Kumi's offer of brukina, a fermented mixture of cow milk and millet. On a scorching summer day, she didn't welcome an alcoholic high, but preferred not to offend him.

"Only two men admitted sufficient contact with the corpse to motivate vaccination," Taylor said. "The deceased had been a fisherman. For the funeral service in honor of tradition, they posed his body next to a stream with a net in his hand."

"I was more successful," Faye teased her partner. "I vaccinated seven women." All week, they'd kept a running scorecard in their hotel, with Faye the clear winner. A little game they played to distract during the occasional blackouts that drove their bodies apart in a bedroom without air conditioning.

FORTY-FOUR

"I'm glad you made this your first stop." Oslo's leading cardiologist addressed Stefan as she bustled into her office and booted up her computer. "Let me show you your ECG. Just like the one you had in Conakry, it's looking normal."

Stefan relaxed into the guest chair and twirled the silver troll cross that circled his wrist on a band of leather. He'd been wearing it that night when he collapsed on the casino lawn, and figured it brought him good luck. Mild stable angina brought on by stress, alcohol, and exertion, the doctor at the Conakry hospital had told him, before Stefan said goodbye to Biko and Nneka.

The cardiologist pulled up cardiac magnetic resonance images. "We'll take more time to study this MRI in detail, but I'm not spotting any evidence of myocarditis. That can be linked to severe Ebola infections like yours. Unless something changes, I see no need for an endomyocardial biopsy."

"Tusen takk, doktor." Stefan also breathed a prayer of thanks to Thor, god of strength, for his hardy constitution.

"If this gets worse, see me. We'll do another ECG at your annual checkup. And I advise some vacation time. I understand you've been working almost nonstop for several months."

"Kjæreste, I'm back." Stefan called Kondrat from his hotel room after the medical checkup. He wanted to share the good news, but then he'd have to admit the angina attack. Would it soften Kondrat's heart or only freak him out more?

"Good," Kondrat answered. "Paula is at school, but you can see her on Sunday."

"Baby, are you sure I can't move back home? I promise to be careful—I will pose no Ebola threat."

"If you had come back after the Congo instead of your gorilla jaunt, we'd have no issues."

Clearly they had bigger problems than Ebola. Stefan's lengthy times away from Oslo, prioritizing public health over his family, gradually wore down Kondrat's commitment. This detour had been worse—not for his job but instead a stroll in the jungle to see a great ape.

But the door had opened a crack. Surely once they saw each other in person and Stefan enveloped his partner in a hug, Kondrat would change his mind.

On Thursday, Stefan unpacked his suitcase in the furnished two-bedroom rental, only five blocks from the Bygdøy Peninsula home he owned with Kondrat. Convenient for short walks to reconnect with Paula.

A horseshoe above the red-painted front door was intended to scare away evil spirits. He'd been lucky to find the apartment so quickly, much nicer accommodations than the city center hotel he'd used initially. Given Kondrat's refusal to allow him home, he needed all the good luck he could muster. A bit unnerved by the bout of angina, he was superstitious about living alone.

He still hadn't told Kondrat about his collapse in Africa. He would not use fear to bribe his way back home.

With New Mexico seven hours earlier, Maya was likely at work. He dialed her cell. "My venninne, I got your text. So happy to hear that your Ebola and herpesvirus threats are behind you."

"Yeah, but the lab just reported my colleague Dave Schwartz has a positive titer to RESTV, probably from a slip of the knife during a macaque necropsy."

Stefan sighed and sat down on the dining room chair. Too many personal impacts from Ebola. First his own hospitalization, then Biko, and now one of Maya's best friends. None of the infections were fatal, takk for alt.

Perhaps Kondrat was wise to ban Stefan from his bed. Even with condoms, why take a chance on spreading Ebola? Certainly this apartment was more comfortable than the lumpy couch at home. But he ached for the warmth of Kondrat's body nestled next to his. If sleeping in adjacent rooms, one or both of them might be tempted to initiate sex.

Stefan refocused on his phone call. "Will Dr. Schwartz get any treatment?"

"He's feeling fine. Just like the other Ebola strains, there aren't any antivirals for Reston. Because that type has never made a human sick, there's little need to worry."

Stefan took a deep swig of his coffee and turned on his charm. Living away from his family through the summer and fall would be more bearable with a buddy.

"I just moved into a fabulous two-bedroom until I'm non-contagious to Kondrat. I remember how much you loved it out here on the Peninsula, with the Norsk Folkemuseum and all the neighborhood flower gardens."

He hesitated, uncertain how to balance an enticing offer of relaxation and friendship with a recognition of Maya's upcoming second wedding anniversary. But they'd been friends since grad school. Tackling *Borrelia* and COVID outbreaks together cemented the connection, even if she held her imprisonment by the Chinese authorities against him for a few months.

Nothing to lose by making the offer. "If you get time off at the end of your CDC training, you'd be welcome to spend it here."

Maya's voice developed a girlish lilt. "You're kidding! Getting a chance to come back to Norway—that's incredible. I'd been leaning toward moving on, trying something new. You're like my genie with a magic lamp—will you think I'm crazy if I say yes on the spot?"

FORTY-FIVE

Next morning's headline in the Daily Graphic took up a quarter of the newspaper's front page. **BUSHMEAT SELLERS HURT BY EBOLA HOAX.** As she nursed her cup of oolong tea, Faye read about street market vendors who feared a ban on the sale of bat meat in Ghana, similar to the one imposed last month in Guinea.

"I wish we had a larger impact before heading home," she said while pouring Taylor a cup. Taylor's dark skin above the waist-high towel still beaded moisture from the shower after an early morning jog through Accra.

"I disagree." Taylor's expression was relaxed, satisfied. "We talked Uncle Kumi out of the large funeral he had planned with the bodies on display. I can't imagine the number of infections that might have caused in his village. And we administered more than a hundred doses of vaccine in just a week's time."

Faye was less of an optimist than Taylor. In her career, she'd faced too many bureaucratic nightmares and failures in scientific communication to fully relax in the face of public health challenges. "According to a survey released yesterday, a third of Ghanaians will never consider vaccines of any kind. There's a total reliance on traditional medicine."

"Uncle Kumi arranged for press coverage of my vaccinating the President last night. That's a major accomplishment."

Faye flipped through the newspaper. "So why isn't that photo on the front page?"

"Anything related to foreign medicine is distrusted by many who remember colonial authority, even after sixty years. There's only so much we can do to counteract it. We were successful at training community health workers who are going door-to-door on vaccine and Ebola education."

A hotel pamphlet for Osu Castle, also known as Fort Christiansborg, sat on the hotel room table. Uncle Kumi had insisted they visit a culturally important site before the farewell feast scheduled for their last night in Ghana. Neither she nor Taylor were in favor of a final big gathering with lots of people, but no new Ebola cases had been reported from Taylor's extended family or the area Uncle Kumi managed as chief. And Uncle Kumi agreed to host an outdoor celebration in a local park with no bushmeat.

"Did the lab work from CDC come back confirming species *Orthoebolavirus zairense* for this outbreak?" Taylor asked.

Faye nodded, then dipped a piece of koose, a deep-fried bean cake, into her hausa koko, a spicy millet porridge. She'd ordered the traditional Ghanaian breakfast from room service while Taylor took a run. Might as well take advantage of the amenities paid for by Uncle Kumi.

"CDC reports no current outbreaks with the other Ebola viruses—Sudan, Taï Forest, or Bundibugyo," she said. "And the Reston virus is only in New Mexico."

She'd spoken last night to Maya, who dodged a bullet when the monkey that pelted her with feces came back negative for Ebola and herpes B. Maya had experienced a sleepless week wondering whether to start an antiviral treatment.

"Did Maya investigate a pig die-off there?" Taylor mixed sugar in their bowl of porridge to sweeten it, a rare treat for someone fixated on a healthy diet and exercise.

"She says those have another virus."

Taylor toasted Faye with the teacup, then picked up the pamphlet. "Good news all around. Let's dismiss Uncle Kumi's chauffeur and travel on our own to tour this relic of the slave trade."

Finally free of Uncle Kumi's long leash, Taylor kicked back on the top level of the double decker bus, still outfitted as a bald man in a blue-striped white tunic and pants. Passing as a cis male was a necessity at times in the US and particularly important when in Ghana. But after decades of hormone therapy and fun evenings in the gay dance clubs, Taylor's feminine style was hard to suppress.

Just before they had flown from NYC to Ghana, Taylor and Faye celebrated her dodging Ebola infection from her patient interviews. They'd belted show tunes and boogied among the mixed-gender crowd at The Manhattan Monster dance party.

Lost in the memory of that lively evening and unaware of other bus passengers, Taylor slipped out a stanza of "Cold Heart" by Elton John and Dua Lipa.

In the steamy reality of the Accra tour bus, Faye's hand restrained Taylor's gyrating shoulders. "I hope that cold heart you're singing about isn't mine," she whispered.

But Faye wasn't the only one paying attention. A punk-looking teenage boy in a black tee-shirt and short, spiky dreads leaned across the aisle. "Hey man, you a guy or a girl?"

Chilled, Taylor refused to answer. A scowling middle-aged man pulled the kid back into the seat next to him. "Leave him alone," he ordered. His son continued to complain about missing his skateboard at home in Atlanta, but everyone soon refocused on Jamestown with its landmark lighthouse and Independence Square with its monuments and sports stadium.

Along with the pair from Atlanta and a crowd of other visitors, Faye and Taylor hopped off in Osu to tour the sprawling castle. Under the scorching sun, its white walls were so bright that they shaded their eyes despite wearing sunglasses.

The area had alternated between Portuguese and Scandinavian control starting in the sixteenth century. The castle was first used for trade of gold and ivory, then Danes and Norwegians profited from selling slaves.

Up close, some of the buildings were streaked by black stains and peeling whitewash. The mood became ominous when a guide led them to a dungeon below ground level with walls three-meters thick, dirt floors, and a barred window.

Until 1850 when the British slave trade was abolished, the room imprisoned fifty African slaves regardless of age and gender for up to six months. They had no sanitation, pending their shipment overseas.

Back in the flagstone, palm-treed courtyard, the guide pointed out locked towers for retention of rain water, not for the slaves but for others living in the castle.

Additional dungeons had ceilings so low, they had to duck to enter. A large one housed 350 men in total darkness. The dank stone walls gave off a musky odor of fear, triggering in Taylor a bout of nausea. With no windows, the guide's flashlight illuminated their way.

"Can you turn off your torch for a moment?" Taylor asked. "I want to imagine what it was like for those imprisoned here."

Taylor began to wonder about the wisdom of the visit. In the dark, all of the good mood from a successful Ebola control week vanished when bathed in the thick air, moist like tears from the terrorized.

"Turn it back on," Taylor ordered suddenly, wondering whether any family members were descended from slaves or slave masters in the US or West Africa. Akan ancestors had purchased other Africans to clear the dense forests, and also sold them to the Portuguese in exchange for guns. But an estimated ten percent of slave ships from West Africa bore Akan slaves.

As they left the dungeons behind, Taylor ran fingers along the rusted iron gates, trying to imagine the hopelessness of those confined below. The upper floors of the castle with its chapel, bedrooms, and staterooms depicted the living standards of British rulers in the 1800s and the residence of Ghana's first president, Biko Nkrumah, starting in 1960. Because of its association with slavery, it was abandoned as a presidential palace in 2005. The guide pulled out a 50 Ghanaian cedi note stamped with the image of the castle and its red staircase.

From the highest level of the building, the gentle breaking surf was visible below. "I need an injection of nature right now," Taylor said. They were guided down a steep winding staircase to a final dungeon so short, no one could stand, where the bodies of dead slaves remained buried in the dungeon floor. The guide indicated the heavy Gate of No Return where the slaves were dragged to boats on the beach, no chance of ever returning to West Africa.

The tour ended in a beautiful, tree-lined park with flowers and peacocks. Relaxed and freed from imagined scenes of slave torture, Taylor slipped an arm around Faye's shoulders and fingered her dangle earrings purchased yesterday in a gift shop.

Faye stepped away, adopting the accent of a hectoring old lady. "Taylor Lewis, cut that out. You know that public displays of affection are frowned upon." She dropped her voice to a whisper. "Once we're in the hotel, I'm willing to share my souvenir. Jewelry looks good on you."

Taylor glanced around and nodded. After following others in the group down a path in the cliff, they reached the water and dipped their toes. "I'd love to strip off all my clothes to wash away the castle's sadness," Taylor said.

Surrounded by other beachgoers covered up with sarongs and kaftans, Faye said, "I can't imagine how they'd respond to nudity."

The week of playing a male role was more than enough. They were flying to the US tomorrow morning. As the sunset cast a golden path to New York along the dappled surface of the water, Taylor yearned to celebrate their freedom from enslavement to societal norms, and spun Faye in an exuberant circle.

A horse's snort and hot breath interrupted their embrace. A Ghanaian man in a blue-black uniform, POLICE emblazoned above his left pocket, leapt down from the saddle and pinioned Taylor's arms. Faye fell to the sand and cried out. A second policeman on foot pushed her aside.

"There are complaints," the first policeman said ominously. His dark beret reminded Faye that they faced an unfamiliar legal system.

As Taylor was handcuffed and led to the street, Faye grabbed their shoes and attempted to follow, dialing the number for Uncle Kumi.

How could Taylor be arrested just for the brief contact? Maybe someone on the bus heard the kid's remark and alerted a guard once the tour was over.

With someone spying on them, thank goodness she hadn't handed Taylor her earrings, a historic symbol of slavery, and more evidence that Taylor was trans. Their occasional touches, when Taylor's gender was unclear by Ghanaian standards, could have been the trigger.

She shuddered, feeling the weight of her parents' wrathful God who condemned anyone to hell for the slightest deviation. Whether it was the Pentecostal deity or the Ghanaian narrow-mindedness, Taylor had done something out of line and was about to be jailed.

FORTY-SIX

Manolo tugged Maya in for a passionate kiss, stirring her to shift closer and wrap her arms around his body. Then he shoved her away and she fell out of their bed onto the tile floor. The alarm clock said 5:15. Rubbing a painful elbow, she flipped on the light. No one else there, just a mess of covers.

The dream was disturbing in its hostility, although not the first time he'd generated fear rather than longing. She picked up her dream diary from the bedside table and jotted down notes to share with Dr. Kim. Was Manolo's violence due to her guilty conscience about possibly moving on with Mark?

She usually went into work by seven, so decided against trying for more sleep. The restless night cemented her decision about accepting Stefan's offer. Manolo's memories always crowded in more when she was sleeping in their shared bed. A longer break overseas, not just a quick week in Paris, might clarify her future options.

She sympathized with Stefan's frustration at not being allowed to move home, but also understood Kondrat's unreasonable fear about Ebola. If Kondrat caught it from Stefan, he could spread it to Paula. Nothing was worse than the parental terror of harming one's child. Stefan knew that too. He'd stayed on in Conakry for the vaccine campaign to extend his time for clearing the virus.

At eight o'clock, she slipped into the State Epidemiologist's office, eyes downcast, shoulders slumped. "I'm sorry, Dr. Grinwold, I can't accept your new job. I need a break."

His dour yet resigned expression indicated he'd been expecting the news. "The ag staff were grateful for your help with their Ebola investigations of the primate facility and piggery. I don't have anyone else who can juggle both the animal and human aspects. Sure you won't change your mind?"

She shook her head. "Since my time off for recovery from COVID and Manolo's death, I've been totally focused on work. Not that I'm complaining. But if I stay here, I don't think I can let go of the memories that haunt me."

"Find a different apartment," he ordered in a gruff tone, then softened. "No, no, I understand. Nancy's been warning me this might happen."

Maya's lips crept up in a slight smile. Dr. Grinwold's partner always had a motherly connection with her. Nancy was her biggest champion in the face of accusations that Maya spread anthrax in Arizona.

Before leaving Santa Fe, she'd have to thank Nancy for Dr. Grinwold's attitude adjustment. Besides, he was just looking out for her. Her savings wouldn't last too long past the end of the year if she wasn't bringing in any income.

Back in her office, she called her parents in Flagstaff. They were disappointed she'd turned down the New Mexico position but relieved that she planned to put her furniture in a Santa Fe storage locker. That could mean she might not be gone for good.

"When your lease expires," her dad said, "we can drive over to help with the move."

"Stay with us while you figure out next steps." Her mother's demand was typical of the brusque former astronomy assistant.

"Actually, a colleague in Norway asked me to visit. Oslo is one of my favorite places, so I told him yes. It's a low-cost trip—he's offered to share his apartment at no rent, and he's nervous about being alone while recovering from Ebola."

Neither of her parents had ever traveled overseas, so when she reassured them Stefan posed no risk to her, they decided to support her decision. One potentially stressful confrontation under her belt.

During her lunchtime swim at the pool across from the health department, she let her choice settle as she slammed out the laps to accomplish a mile. Halfway to her goal, Mark ducked under the lane rope to join her. He grabbed both of her shoulders and planted a kiss on her cheek. "I hoped to run into you here."

Maya had missed him, and she wanted to complete what they'd started in Paris before Stefan's call about Ebola derailed the vacation mood. But after hearing about Norway, Mark might not be interested any longer. "Can we talk tonight?" She tried to inject a cheery tone but failed to pull it off.

Mark's fleshy face drooped—he likely guessed that she was leaving. He'd made no secret that he wanted to take their relationship to a more intimate level, and had encouraged her to take Dr. Grinwold's job offer.

His face brightened with an idea. "Santa Fe restaurants are lovely, but it's been months since you've been out to the ranch. Carmen can whip something up, then leave us alone to talk."

Maya smiled. "It's a date. Now I've got to finish these laps and get back to the office. See you at seven."

The golden sun slanted its evening rays through Maya's lace curtains as she packed an overnight bag. One of her favorite times of day in the Southwest. The quick decision to leave New Mexico felt rash, exciting, totally unlike her. But right in line with what she was planning for her visit to Mark's Pecos ranch.

They'd danced around the nature of their relationship long enough—all her fault. Fortunately he was a gentleman and hadn't forced the issue. Sometimes overbearing on behalf of his law clients, but kind and patient with her.

She ached for the touch of another man. Manolo had been her first. The second anniversary of their wedding day, which was followed within a few months by his death, loomed ahead. And then next February, her thirtieth birthday. Why shouldn't she indulge in a night of passion, even if her future path with Mark was uncertain? She tossed her bag in the backseat of her Prius and headed for the highway, windows rolled down and foot on the gas.

At the ranch, she shared a delicious dinner of elk steaks and garden vegetables with Mark. Carmen had conveniently disappeared, after Maya cornered her to make sure she wouldn't be stepping into a relationship between the attorney and his house manager. Then she stopped by the main floor bathroom to brush her teeth and check her appearance in a cowhide-framed mirror crowned with an eight-foot length of cattle longhorns.

She brushed light makeup over several forehead scars from various misadventures. The missing baby finger was startling but didn't compare to the ugly keloid scars from her leg injuries. None were a surprise to Mark, who'd seen her in a swimsuit.

That was an advantage of waiting years to consummate their relationship. Both of them were curious and eager. Until Manolo died, she'd only viewed Mark as the older, attractive attorney who kept saving her bacon from legal troubles. Her passion for her husband had never wavered.

But she'd bonded with Mark last year during her COVID recovery at the ranch, and he had many of Manolo's best qualities. Dark hair, eyes, and skin had always been her type. The two men shared a dedication to helping others through their work, yet leavened with a sense of humor. Unlike her, neither man dwelled too much on everything that could go wrong. Differences in age and weight, plus Mark's ruthless streak, were not something she needed to ponder. Tonight, she only intended to see if they were sexually compatible—no commitments for the future.

The kiss on the lips Mark had given her when she arrived at the ranch lit a fire in her groin that spread throughout her body. Promising start to the evening. She fingered the sky-blue silk negligee in her bag before heading out to the front portal and Mark.

The setting sun bathed the Pecos hills with a soft, ruby light. Doves cooed from the nearby barn and horses gently neighed. A glorious, peaceful moment, uninterrupted by mysterious microbes. But public health wasn't totally out of mind. She'd brought condoms.

Mark unwound himself from Maya's arms as she moaned and shifted positions in the bed without awakening. He hoped she was recalling their multiple orgasms. At the bar in the living room, he poured a double shot of Scotch, savoring the silence. Just after midnight, the waning gibbous moon peeked out above the southeast hills.

Maya had been worth the wait. She'd been upfront about wanting to make new sexual memories to override the upcoming Manolo anniversaries. Mark had no problem being a substitute, as long as this wasn't a one and done.

Maya turning down the state job was a major disappointment, but public health veterinarians with her epidemiologic and statistical training weren't falling from the trees. Dr. Grinwold would likely hire her when she returned from Oslo. After all, her things would be in Santa Fe storage and her parents lived next door in Arizona.

His only competition—her job and her dead husband. Plenty of time to lure her back to the Land of Enchantment.

FORTY-SEVEN

Uncle Kumi's chauffeur pulled over to park along the street lined with rundown, metal-roofed homes and small businesses opposite the police station. Behind a fence, its one-story sea-blue buildings were clearly visible.

When Faye stepped out of the limo, few trees cut the heat as she dodged a man on an overloaded bicycle. With a spritely step she didn't feel, she lifted her feet to avoid kicking red dirt from her dark tennis shoes onto her black pantsuit. Ahead, Uncle Kumi led the way in an elaborate chief's robe, bright orange quilted with turquoise squares. A coral-colored beaded necklace reached to his waist, and he adjusted his black cap embedded with large gold stars.

After their identifications were reviewed by an armed guard, they entered a reception area. "I want to talk with my nephew, Dr. Taylor Lewis," Uncle Kumi insisted in his most stentorian tone. "He was kept here overnight, and I have waited long enough."

Uncle Kumi should have been allowed to direct the conversation, but Faye was too impatient. "Dr. Lewis is my American colleague. We're both here for the Ebola outbreak. Has the American embassy contacted you?"

"Because of COVID, they do not make personal visits," the police clerk answered. "They typically telephone on a weekday for our American guests." The clerk smirked as Faye adjusted her surgical mask, the only person wearing one in the bustling office.

"We will not wait two more days for their help," Uncle Kumi said, raising a hand to warn Faye off. "Let us see Dr. Lewis now."

The clerk bowed and laughed. "Of course. We always give Americans special treatment."

"What do you think he meant?" Faye whispered to Uncle Kumi as they followed the clerk to the next building. "His tone gave me the creeps."

Uncle Kumi leaned his head down close to Faye's. "The government encourages Black Americans to resettle in Ghana. As long as you have money, members of the diaspora are welcomed home."

After only a week in the country, she'd learned that Ghanaians often joked about everything, so the clerk likely intended nothing ominous.

People needed a sense of humor if jailed, she thought when led to the cell that housed four men in addition to Taylor. Fortunately, Taylor had been allowed to stay dressed in the kente robe which hid the small breasts formed by decades of hormones. Taylor must not have objected to incarceration with men. Admitting to being trans would be scarier.

All five of the cell's residents squatted on a concrete floor—no beds or chairs in sight. One man held a gray blanket over his head. Taylor slammed a cockroach with a bare heel before rising to greet Faye and Uncle Kumi.

"My God, Taylor, how did you sleep?" Faye hadn't intended to start with a negative remark but couldn't help it, seeing the bug guts spread on the floor and likely on the bottom of Taylor's foot.

"Not well," Taylor answered. "It's hot and clammy during the day, cold and clammy at night." Taylor gestured to the ceiling. "The worst is the spiders that drop from their webs onto your head as you doze off. I talked the guard into providing me a blanket for protection, and we take turns using it."

Uncle Kumi banged his fist on the cell bars. "This is unacceptable! And bathroom facilities, what are you doing for that?"

Taylor gestured to a dark hole in the wall. "A pit toilet's back there, but we don't like to use it—it's crawling with worms."

A two-foot brown snake slithered out of the cell and down the hall. Growing up on a Colorado ranch, Faye had never been snake-phobic, but didn't like the thought of lying on the bare ground with one crawling over her body. "Ugh, so you slept with that, too?"

Taylor smiled. "A Cape House Snake. I hope he's eating the roaches, but he prefers bigger prey like rodents. Not venomous, so little risk to us."

"Have they told you the charges?" Uncle Kumi asked, uninterested in the local fauna.

Taylor glanced around. "I'd rather not discuss them here, and you might have more success in getting the details."

"Well, we're glad you're okay." Faye yearned to touch Taylor's hand through the bars but their limited public displays of affection in the castle and on the beach might have led to this horrid incarceration.

"I will talk to the head man," Uncle Kumi announced, "and get you released before nightfall."

Being a Chief held no sway. "Dr. Lewis will see the judge at the arraignment on Monday," the prison director said. "Come again that morning and your embassy can make its arguments then."

Once in the limo with Faye in the back seat next to Uncle Kumi, he ordered, "Give us some privacy." The chauffeur stepped outside, leaving the engine running for the air conditioning.

"Is there anything you omitted when you told me what happened?" Uncle Kumi asked.

Faye was glad she wasn't facing him—it was easier to dissemble. Uncle Kumi might not realize Taylor was trans female, and it wasn't her right to reveal it now. There were only a few brief moments when she and Taylor touched on the slave castle tour, until he spun her in a hug on the beach.

"This is a conservative and religious country—we should have been more careful to avoid PDAs." She glanced at him, then clarified. "I mean public displays of affection." With their lengthy part-time and now full-time relationship, touching each other was second nature, but they hadn't been kissing or making out.

"When I met you, I assumed you were a matronly mentor to my nephew." Uncle Kumi wiped his hand across his brow. "I don't know why Taylor has never married."

Matronly mentor, what an insult, even though Faye occasionally wondered what Taylor saw in her. Uncle Kumi's question was confirmation that he hadn't suspected Taylor as anything other than a single male physician. Probably he thought USAID was paying for her separate room at the hotel and they weren't sharing the one he was covering for his nephew.

Taylor's arrest could have been related to the kid's comment on the bus or Taylor's effeminate mien. Being open about it might be necessary to mount a good defense or could seal the government's case, and Taylor's fate.

FORTY-EIGHT

Biko held Nneka's elbow as they strolled the banks of the canal, sheltered from the afternoon sun by the massive foliage of a rubber tree. A canopy of red flowers brought a touch of beauty to the scene, counteracted by the smell of the dump. Lagos, Nigeria, Africa's largest city with more than sixteen million people, had too many polluted waterways.

But it was nature, however poor its condition. A week after waking up in Guinea from his Ebola coma, Biko relished his first stroll outside in somewhat fresh air. During his medical residency, he had lived in a tiny one-bedroom flat near the University Teaching Hospital. Nneka now used it as her home base between nature treks to the Cross River National Park.

Panting heavily, he put one foot in front of the other as they climbed the muddy embankment to the street, crowded with autos, trucks, pushcarts, bicycles, and pedestrians. "Maybe this was too much too soon," he muttered.

"I told you so," Nneka mocked.

They navigated hawkers chasing after stalled vehicles to sell bottled water, snack bags, even small paintings. One blocked their way, holding up a scruffy yellow puppy.

"Please give it a good home." The young man in his white-striped red shirt and black jeans looked similar in age to Nneka. He pressed the animal into her arms.

Nneka, a pre-eminent animal lover, cuddled it close and kissed its dirty nose. "What do you think, brother? We have no pets since Father died."

The young man tried to take the dog back. "She is a valuable

Golden Retriever, worth 200000NGN. I am a poor boy supporting my family of nine. My mum is sick and home alone. Please be kind and help me."

For a purebred, although Biko doubted its pedigree, the price was reasonable. No more than the cost of a night in a 4-star hotel. But he had no desire to care for an animal. He had all he could do to care for himself, with Nneka's assistance.

"I am very sorry, but we cannot provide a home for this animal at this time." He pulled out his handkerchief and patted his brow. "Sister, I need to sit down."

Nneka pouted but didn't contradict him, and handed the dog back. Once they were home inside the living room with Biko settled on the sagging couch, Nneka prepared two glasses of a Chapman cocktail, a nonalcoholic mix of local soft drinks and black currant, garnished with slices of orange and cucumber.

"Thank you for making this." Biko took slow sips. "Very refreshing on such a hot day." He turned toward the table but couldn't quite reach it. "Nne, can you hand me my phone? I want to check in with Dr. Duda."

Stefan answered the call immediately. "I got your text—so happy to hear you're back home."

"And you, Dr. Duda, how was the reunion with your family?"

After a pregnant pause, Stefan responded, voice strained. "I'll see them tomorrow when I pick up Paula. I'm taking her to the Museum of Science & Technology. She loves their music machines." A moment later, he added, "And please drop the Dr. Duda crap. After all we've been through together, you can call me Stefan."

Biko had difficulty in ignoring the Igbo tradition of respect for elders, but he was only a few years younger. "You are right, Stefan, we are now brothers. We both survived Ebola infection." *Unlike poor Dr. Kreischer.*

Biko had advised Stefan about the risk of semen shedding, which might account for Stefan's hint that he hadn't moved home yet. Stefan's personal challenges only reinforced Biko's decision to stay celibate. College and medical school allowed no time for courting, and his conservative Christian upbringing didn't permit unmarried sex. Perhaps Stefan was being punished by God for his civil partnership. Biko squelched the uncharitable thought.

"How much time off is Dr. Shah giving you?" Stefan asked.

"It depends on my recovery. Nneka is with me so I have good nursing care, although she has no formal training."

"We're lucky that Ebola settled back to its endemic state with almost no new cases." Stefan's voice then changed from reassuring to cautious. "Stay alert for long-term sequelae, which can impact half of all patients up to two years later."

Clouds still floated in Biko's brain—he didn't recall that problem. "But you are feeling fine now, Stefan?"

"Ah, I had some chest pain my last evening in Conakry. Doctors confirmed it as angina. I didn't mention it when I saw you later that night—I was barely putting one foot in front of the other."

Heart damage from Ebola infection? "Angina is from fatty deposits in your coronary arteries. Perhaps it is your diet."

"I'm relearning how to eat healthy. Kondrat . . ." Stefan choked, then continued. "Kondrat is an incredible cook, but my food habits deteriorated when traveling."

Biko remembered sampling local foods with Stefan, even when they didn't know the origin. And Stefan often finished the night with a strong drink.

The comforting odor of coconut milk and nutmeg drifted over from the small kitchen range along the side wall of the living room. Nneka was cooking jollof rice, a West African one-pot dish with tomatoes, chilis, and onions. She usually added chicken and cabbage. Nigeria and Ghana had lively Jollof Wars over the best recipe.

"Speaking of dinner, Stefan, ours is ready." Nneka said. "There is an Igbo proverb worth considering. It translates to 'A lean goat cannot be fattened on market day.'"

Stefan laughed. "Are we still talking food?"

Biko carried his phone to the table. "Perhaps, but it also means that we need to be patient. Both of us for our health, and you for your family's forgiveness. In the end, we will get what we want."

Stefan sighed. "From your mouth to God's ear. Take care, my friend."

Biko smiled at Nneka as he hung up and settled in for his meal. Together, he and his sister could handle anything.

FORTY-NINE

Maya relaxed with a contented sigh on the green metal bench in Santa Fe's Plaza. Under the shade of an aspen tree, the breeze ruffled her hair, like Mark's gentle strokes to wake her up that morning. After sharing breakfast, Maya headed home to face the challenge of packing. She'd soon leave New Mexico behind, so she made a goodbye bike ride to the heart of town.

A child chased a ball down the brick-paved walkway, recalling for Maya a similar excursion with Manolo, four years earlier. He'd flown over from Phoenix for Halloween, his first time visiting her at home. An abortive trip—Maya blew up after discovering he was still married, finalizing a divorce. An encapsulation of their relationship—super hot alternating with icy cold.

She couldn't recall ever getting cross with Mark, despite his being older and more confident than Manolo. He seemed bent on accommodating her wishes. Perhaps he was too good to be true, but she didn't need to figure that out now. She was off to Europe with no home commitments. A strange feeling—very unlike her disposition for planning, reinforced by her mother's instilled discipline.

Her parents planned to drive over from Flagstaff on June 29 to help transfer her belongings into storage and clean her apartment before the lease expired. Just a week and a half for Maya to organize everything into boxes. Mark had recommended a mover to handle the heavy stuff. In thanks, she promised to bring her parents over to dinner at his ranch the next time they were all in the area.

Her mom always enjoyed Mark's company, flirting like a teenager while her dad rolled his eyes. As a serious retired scientist,

Barbara Robinson never acted that way with anyone else. But she'd despaired at the deaths of her son-in-law and unborn grandchild. Mark's devotion to Maya cheered her up.

The only thing despoiling Maya's pleasure on a summer Saturday was the wooden barrier hiding the damaged Soldiers' Monument, its top pulled down by protestors two years earlier on Indigenous Peoples Day. Its plaque had referred to Native Americans as savages. Since then, the controversy lingered in a city commission and the courts. Perhaps the monument could be housed in a museum, replaced by a gazebo like those in Albuquerque and Taos.

Fences hid the divisive monument's scars, but the damage from conflicting historical viewpoints hadn't healed. Just like Maya's heart, torn between a sexual reawakening with Mark and Manolo's spirit hovering over her shoulder. The conflict reinforced her decision to join Stefan in Oslo. The Southwest was haunted with phantoms of her courtship and marriage.

Would her parents guess at Mark's new status when they visited? Despite Barbara's fondness for him, she was a strict Catholic. She'd been less than pleased when she guessed that Maya had consummated her relationship with Manolo before their wedding.

Maya had surprised herself by giving into her desire for another man's arms. With Manolo, they'd been in love, and that wasn't true for Mark. Safe sex didn't require a commitment in this day and age. The night had been fun, not fraught with emotion. A wonderful release and new perspective. Despite love for her parents and whispers of her own lapsed-Catholic guilt about unmarried sex, Maya made her own choices.

A string quartet rolled out lively tunes from the bandstand as she walked her bike along Palace Avenue. The three violins and the cello played a tango that Maya recognized but couldn't name.

Native American jewelry on blankets under the portal of the Palace of the Governors drew her closer. Fingering the bear claw earrings that Manolo bought for her there, she decided against another purchase. Her phone rang with Faye's name popping up on the screen, and she headed back to another bench in the Plaza.

"I'm out of my mind and don't know who to talk to." Faye's voice was high and frantic.

Unused to consoling her favorite counselor, Maya asked, "What happened, where are you calling from?" She couldn't help but match the urgency of Faye's tone.

"I'm still in Accra. Taylor and I finished our week of Ebola response here. After a tour of a Ghanaian slave castle, Taylor got locked up."

Maya's experience in Africa was limited to a *Borrelia* investigation with Stefan in Morocco. Bandits had been a risk—is that what Faye meant?

"Wait, locked up? What do you mean? Why?"

Faye breathed a ragged sigh. "Local authorities. We're still unclear on the charges. PDA with the opposite sex is a cultural no-no, and Taylor hugged me on the beach. That's when the police showed up."

"Yeah, but Ghana advertises for American expats. They shouldn't be that strict."

"You're right, it's probably more than that. A kid on the tour bus asked if Taylor was a guy or a girl. Taylor was passing as a man, but never totally masks their flamboyance. I wonder if the authorities figured out Taylor is trans. That's definitely illegal."

Maya's skin goosebumped despite the warm afternoon in the Santa Fe sun. "Faye, is it safe for you to be talking about this now?"

"I'm back in our hotel room. Uh, I don't think it's bugged."

Maya got an idea. "Mark Zielinski is the attorney who helped me out of several legal entanglements. Maybe he has overseas connections."

Faye's response was barely audible. "The American embassy is still observing COVID protocols and won't come out to the jail. But they promised to phone in for Taylor's arraignment on Monday."

Maya twisted in her seat, searching for answers. "Taylor has Ghanaian relatives, right? Can they bail Taylor out?"

"Uncle Kumi is a powerful local chief and he's trying. He's paying for our hotel room, and it's a blessing to have someplace comfortable to stay. That reminds me, I need to cancel our flights to New York scheduled for this evening."

Mark had legal cases in Phoenix and was likely on his way to Albuquerque's Sunport. "Faye, hang in there. Call whenever you want to talk things over. I'm texting Mark right now."

Maya didn't know Taylor well but had been impressed with the physician's devotion when Faye was ill with dengue infection in Hawai'i. She said goodbye and typed into her phone, **<My friend's in trouble in Ghana. Know any good lawyers there?>**

FIFTY

After three nights in the hellhole that Accra called a jail cell, Taylor was led handcuffed to a separate room, still wearing the same tunic and pants.

Faye, also dressed in the same conservative black pantsuit she wore on Friday, shifted restlessly in the second row of benches. Next to her sat Uncle Kumi, resplendent in a white robe covered with multi-colored striped squares and his black cap with gold stars. Who wouldn't be impressed?

The district court judge nodded to Uncle Kumi and thanked him for attending. Taylor caught Faye's eyes and she smiled in support. When the heavy-set woman with dark hair introduced herself from a large video screen as the US Ambassador, Taylor took a deep breath of gratitude. The Ambassador herself, not some inexperienced underling.

"Magistrate, I think there's some misunderstanding," the Ambassador began. "Dr. Lewis is in Accra on a humanitarian mission. He's a respected head-of-hospital in New York City."

Taylor wasn't a pronoun purist and didn't flinch with being referred to as 'he.' Safer that way.

"That's not the issue," the judge answered. "You are new in your position here. We have been working for several years on a law imposing a prison sentence of up to three years for anyone convicted of being . . . Queer." The judge flinched as he finished.

Taylor gulped. What was the slipup? Surely it wasn't a family member who filed a report.

The Ambassador flushed. "That's a bill in process. How could it apply?"

The judge tapped his dais with his pen, clearly impatient. "It will be official any day now, and it reflects our cultural values."

"Still, there must be a stronger case for a conviction." The Ambassador's tone became confrontational.

Standing up to dominate the room, the judge's voice also raised in pitch. "You are unfamiliar with our problems. Numerous public protests. A community center for these types was opened, then closed by an angry mob. Churches issued a statement that this lifestyle is alien to our family value system, and our citizens cannot accept it."

Taylor might have insufficiently appreciated the degree of animosity within Ghana but still didn't know how it applied. What would constitute as evidence?

Uncle Kumi asked the question. "My Worship, can you tell us the circumstances of my nephew's case?"

The judge signaled to a policeman who stepped forward, studying his notes. "Several patrons of an Osu Castle tour were startled that the defendant's gender could not be determined. Then the defendant was observed in close physical contact with an older female."

That's crazy. Was Taylor in trouble for being viewed as gay or for showing affection in public to a woman?

The policeman gestured at Faye. "She is here in the room."

Not wanting to pull Faye into this problem, Taylor looked away despite yearning to see her reaction.

A small man wearing a shoulder-length white wig bustled into the room and apologized for being late. Taylor could only catch some of Uncle Kumi's angry words about the amount of money paid for someone who didn't show up on time.

The attorney invited Uncle Kumi to sit back down, then asked, "Can we have the specific charges, My Worship?"

The judge nodded to the policeman who continued. "Section 104(1)(b) of the Ghanaian Criminal Code of 1960 criminalizes unnatural carnal knowledge, with consent and between adults, as a misdemeanor."

Taylor strove to control a visible reaction of disgust. *I swung her in a hug—how does that count?*

The attorney huffed, then glanced at Taylor, Faye, and Uncle Kumi. "Section 104(2) defines unnatural carnal knowledge as sexual intercourse with a person in an unnatural manner or with an animal. What is the evidence?"

The judge snorted in exasperation. "This is not a trial. We only need sufficient cause to hold Taylor Lewis over for one."

Once again the policeman piped up. "Someone overheard the defendant's name and looked him up on the internet. There are photos of splashy homosexual events in New York, including with the woman in this courtroom. We understand the two of them are sharing a hotel room, despite the age and racial differences and the defendant's uncertain sexual status."

Taylor's muscles and mind, strengthened by a lifetime of exercise and adversity, puddled like a melting candle. Who would pursue that line of inquiry with such a vengeance? Surely not the boy on the bus. Maybe the kid's father?

Faye looked close to tears as she grasped at Uncle Kumi's arm.

"I fail to see the relevance of Dr. Lewis' lifestyle in America," the lawyer replied. "What evidence is there for Ghana? You must have more to keep him detained."

"We are still investigating all his activities while here," the judge said. "Officer, could you share the results of your inspection?"

A guard stepped forward, shuffling his feet. "Your Worship, when the defendant was strip searched for weapons, his genitalia were confusing." He paused and composed himself. "The male parts were smaller than usual, and there are small female breasts."

At the loud gasp from those in the courtroom, Taylor recalled the search with a shiver, unnerved by the public pronouncement and its role in the imprisonment.

"The hotel maid found these," the policeman went on, holding up a bag of prescribed pills. "We will consult a physician today to confirm what they are."

Taylor could have told them—spironolactone as an anti-androgen and estradiol for estrogen to enhance hormonal levels and outer projection as a trans female. Taylor scratched at a mosquito bite—malaria infection from *Plasmodium falciparum* was also a risk without daily atovaquone-proguanil tablets.

The attorney attempted to regain control of the proceedings in spite of the obvious distaste reflected on his face. "I still fail to see how this 'evidence' meets the definition of unnatural carnal knowledge. Are there cameras in Dr. Lewis' hotel room? Did anyone witness him having sex with an animal when he was out saving lives from Ebola this week?"

Taylor couldn't help but smile at the level of sarcasm coming from the man's lips. The guy showed up late but Uncle Kumi's wealth had purchased someone brash and clever.

"Besides," the attorney continued, "even if convicted, this is only a misdemeanour. Dr. Lewis can be allowed out pending trial."

"A misdemeanour with a penalty of three years imprisonment under Article 296(4)," the judge interjected in a commanding voice. He banged his gavel. "The court needs more time to investigate these charges. The defendant will remain incarcerated until I set the trial date."

The Ambassador, silent throughout the proceedings after her initial inquiry, finally spoke up. "That's unreasonable for someone in Ghana as the guest of your chief. We will pursue further options."

Uncle Kumi stamped his foot and nodded vigorously. Taylor mouthed "Don't worry" to Faye and tried to display a confident posture despite the handcuffs. A confidence that didn't match internal feelings. If the guards revealed any of the hearing room revelations to the others in the cell, Taylor's safety might not be guaranteed.

FIFTY-ONE

A wrinkled woman with gray hair protruding from a duku, a turban-like head wrap, cooked at a stove in the ornate earthen home. A second younger woman placed a plate of ivory dough balls on the wooden table in front of Faye. Uncle Kumi indicated his thanks.

"Dr. Simpson, this is Esi, my stool wife. She joined my family when I became installed as Chief after my father's death."

Faye felt her eyebrows rise before she could control her expression, and Uncle Kumi smiled. "Esi sits in front of me on a stool during ceremonies as a place of honor. Your meal is prepared by Mánsã, my first wife and queen mother for our clan."

Esi poured Faye a cup of a familiar, creamy drink. "Brukina." Then she dropped a dough ball into a vegetable broth.

"You need to eat—you are too pale," Uncle Kumi said. "Today's hearing must have disturbed you."

With no appetite, Faye had intended to bury herself under the hotel room blankets for a good cry. The last time she felt this bad was a year earlier when she was fired by the NYC health department. But Uncle Kumi insisted on hosting her for dinner, and acquiescing to the meal would keep her in his good graces.

She took a careful sip of the brukina and relaxed back into the chair. It reminded her of kombucha—a NYC neighbor swore that fermented drinks improved mental health.

"I am sorry that I did not have you and my nephew to my home before now. You worked so many hours, I postponed the invitation. Now it is too late, at least for Taylor."

Surprised by his statement, Faye's pulse quickened in panic. "Too late? What do you mean?"

Uncle Kumi waved his hand in dismissal. "Taylor visited us on past trips, and we will have him again before you fly back to America. But he may be in jail for a few days—our legal system is slow and careful."

"Hardly careful, considering the lack of evidence that Taylor has done anything illegal." Faye felt uncomfortable challenging Uncle Kumi, but needed to understand the process.

"The photographs from New York—they are surprising. I did not know that part of my nephew's life."

Taylor had been active at the clubs when younger, unconcerned about any risk to the hospital position. Now with Faye, nights cuddled at home watching PBS were the norm.

"Those aren't relevant to what Taylor did here," Faye insisted. "I assume the attorney will reinforce that argument."

Uncle Kumi nodded. "I am unfamiliar with him but he comes highly recommended."

Faye wondered if Maya's lawyer had assisted with the connection. She'd check in when back at the hotel.

After taking a sip from his own mug, Uncle Kumi said, "Ghana is changing rapidly, but as Chief, I still have considerable power. In Botswana and South Africa, chiefs are protected in legislation. But here, our traditional leadership system is even stronger, sealed within our constitution."

"Will your influence extend to a judge?"

Uncle Kumi shrugged. "Our role is to manage the land on behalf of our communities. That comes with a level of respect."

He didn't ask any clarifying questions about Taylor's gender or relationship with Faye. She wouldn't reveal details but was frantic about Taylor's safety. As a trans female, Taylor might be at less risk of attack in a cell with other women. But when passing as male, making such a request would increase legal jeopardy.

Making a fist under the table, Faye wondered if the arrest was her fault. Taylor's previous trips to Ghana without her resulted in no problems. Being with Faye, someone so distinctively different— that change might have led to more attention and greater scrutiny.

FIFTY-TWO

Maya was knee-deep in books when Faye called. Fiction by Tony Hillerman, Edward Abbey, and Robert Heinlein; nonfiction by Robert Graves, Robert Caro, and John McPhee. All books gifted over the years by her father.

In a separate box, she'd organized more recent novels by Tess Gerritsen, Barbara Kingsolver, and Chris Bohjalian that she purchased herself, along with some tattered Harlequin romances picked up cheap at a library sale.

She rarely devoured any of them in one sitting. But late at night in bed, especially after Manolo's death, reading distracted her hamster-wheel brain and allowed her to drift off. At the ring of her phone, she grabbed it.

"Hi, Faye, did you get Taylor released? Are you back in New York?"

"Should have been." Faye sounded like she'd been crying. But Maya knew Faye as a badass woman, ever since she lectured nine years earlier to Maya's vet school class about Middle East Respiratory Syndrome transmitted by camel semen in Saudi Arabia.

No longer the introvert with long hair covering her face, Maya wanted to share with Faye the monumental step she'd taken with Mark. But something much more important was going on with her friend.

"I asked Mark to get you a lawyer, so what's the holdup? When we talked earlier, they didn't have any real evidence of wrong-doing."

"Well, your request worked. Uncle Kumi says we have the best attorney in Ghana. But the authorities found old pictures on the internet of Taylor at some New York queer dance parties. Everything's on hold while they do more 'investigation.' They take sexual and gender differences seriously here."

Maya's fingers tightened around the phone in anger. "Those photos weren't taken in Ghana—they can't possibly use them."

"You're right." Faye sighed. "But the immediate risks freak me out. Taylor's in close quarters without masks, mosquito protection, or medication—in danger of COVID and malaria. Or Taylor could get hurt by one of the male prisoners. It's dangerous."

Maya got up from the boxes on the floor and settled into her couch. Pulling an afghan over her body, she shivered. "Play up Taylor's role as an Ebola savior. Lean on Uncle Kumi and the embassy to get the meds and a private cell."

"You're right, we'll keep trying. Uh, excuse me a second."

Maya heard a loud knock and muffled conversation, then Faye came back on the call. "Uncle Kumi had me to dinner after the jail visit. Can you imagine, he has two wives? I haven't been married once. Sorry, too scattered. I just got key lime pie from room service."

Faye was overweight but Maya wouldn't begrudge her the neurochemical comfort of food. She yearned to share with Faye some of her big changes, but it felt too selfish while Taylor was in jeopardy. On the other hand, it might be a distraction.

"Stefan invited me to Norway so I'm taking a work break." She decided to omit turning down the New Mexico job, and the deepened personal connection with Mark.

"I remember him from Columbia. Tall, brownish hair, well-built. During your internship with me, he did one with … I forget the name." Faye's voice began to slur—she might have dipped into the minibar already.

Faye seemed to forget Stefan's role in Maya's abortive trip to China. She and Faye were both pissed off after that one, but Maya didn't retain any animosity.

"My parents are helping put my stuff into storage," Maya continued, "and my flight's on July 2. I'm getting international phone service so you should be able to reach me in Oslo."

"I'm glad you're taking a work break," Faye said. "Get yourself in a whole new head space."

"That's the plan," Maya answered. "Please keep in touch. I'm worried about you."

FIFTY-THREE

As Taylor's imprisonment stretched beyond a week, the days for Faye became mirror images of the previous ones. Each dawn, she greeted the sunrise with a prayer that Taylor would be released by nightfall. With her Pentecostal upbringing, praying came naturally, even if she wasn't convinced it would be effective.

Every night, she marked the card to order a croissant and yogurt for breakfast. Every morning after it was delivered, she placed a call at nine a.m. to her USAID contact. She'd decided to stay useful by continuing Ebola surveillance and control.

Before setting out on her daily USAID journeys, she always checked with Taylor's attorney and the American embassy. Neither were able to arrange for her to visit the jail, although they reported Taylor was in good shape. Informed that the trial date had been set for late September—a three-month wait—she'd yanked on a fistful of hair in frustration. The declining number of new Ebola cases worked against her staying that long. USAID could likely support her position for only another week or two. The Ghanaian justice system proceeded slowly, Uncle Kumi apologized, but he vowed to continue paying her hotel bill and personal expenses for the duration.

She was impressed by the American Ambassador who appeared to be a real professional, not someone who bought their job with a campaign donation. And USAID weighed in as well, dismayed that a respected physician they had invited to Ghana for Ebola would be arrested on such flimsy charges. Despite Uncle Kumi's reassurances about the legal negotiations, she saw no tangible evidence of the lawyer's accomplishments, other than securing the trial date.

After the routine of morning calls, she spent most days jostled about in a Jeep Wrangler to reach remote villages. Its hood was covered by a large colorful poster titled **Kick Back Ebola!** followed by cartoon-type pictures showing signs and symptoms, how to prevent infection, and treatment options.

When emerging from the vehicle in her claustrophobic moon-suit, the village children invariably screamed and hid in their homes. They weren't her first audience for interviews, blood draws, and the ring vaccination program, targeted to anyone providing care for the suspected or confirmed Ebola cases. Fortunately, she always had a local USAID staff member to smooth over fears generated by her strange appearance.

On some evenings, Uncle Kumi and his two wives hosted Faye for dinner. She enjoyed meeting Taylor's extended family members and played tag with rambunctious grandchildren.

On the last day of June, the morning's journey dangled a glimpse of benign nature rather than mysterious microbes. Near the Densu Delta Protected Area, Faye's USAID driver waved at nesting egrets as they passed a marsh area. "If we had time, I would show you three marine turtles—Olive Ridley, green, and leatherback. But I must get you to the dead girl."

Trying to slow her rapid breaths at his dire reminder, Faye glanced over to a roseate tern perched regally on a rotting wooden boat. Zayaan, the male caseworker in the backseat with Faye, said, "I am worried about how the family is handling the situation." Within minutes, they parked next to a complex of white-washed homes topped by metal roofs, rusting from the sea air.

A mass of people crowded the path in front of one dwelling. Several women were prostrate in the dirt, keening. In contrast, the men were stoic, giving orders about a planned funeral and collecting cash donations from the neighbors.

"Any female who does not lament loudly enough is labeled a witch who caused the death," Zayaan whispered. "But males are not allowed to display emotion, no matter how we feel."

Grateful that neither she nor Taylor were obliged to follow such strict gender roles in New York, Faye tried to honor divergent cultural norms, even when she didn't agree with them. If only they'd been more careful. She still didn't understand how the "evidence" mentioned at the arraignment supported a violation of the penal code.

Zayaan approached the local chief. Not being a physician like Taylor, Zayaan had less success in garnering cooperation, and rejoined Faye with a resigned shrug. "They request being left alone to honor the dead child. He wants us gone."

Despite never having children, Faye tried to put herself in their shoes. When accompanying Taylor, she'd adopted a subservient role. Here, she needed to display more leadership, which was unwelcome. She pulled out her cell and dialed Uncle Kumi.

"I will take care of it," he told her after she explained the situation. "Ask Zayaan to hand your phone to the chief. We are well-acquainted."

After several moments of the local chief raising his voice and gesticulating, he handed the phone back. "You may talk to the women. We have other priorities."

As Faye and Zaayan entered the home in full PPE, the women didn't look up. Two knelt on either side of a cot, bathing the body of a young girl with soft cloths and their bare hands. They collected the dripping liquid in some bowls under the cot.

"Sometimes they sell the mixture of oil, water, and herbs to others for its spiritual potency," Zayaan said quietly to Faye. "New chiefs believe it gives them strength during their installation ceremony."

Faye shuddered at the risky process but hated interrupting such a solemn ritual. "I understand wanting to handle this in the family, but we're on the outskirts of Accra. Surely there is a mortuary they can call."

Zayaan nodded. "Let's find out how much they know about Ebola."

He bowed to the older of the two women kneeling on the floor. "Mama, I am Zayaan from Teshie." Faye recognized it as an Accran suburb along the coast. "And this is our esteemed Dr. Simpson. We work for the United States Agency for International Development. Can we ask you some questions?"

The woman didn't extend her hand but answered yes.

"Madame," Faye said, "are you this child's mother?"

She shook her head side-to-side. "No. Ama—grandmother."

"What is your granddaughter's name?"

"Dzifa." The woman teared up.

Faye continued. "Zayaan and I are both so sorry for your loss. Was Dzifa sick for long?" She didn't see any obvious injuries, but the girl's body was partially hidden under a robe that the women lifted as they bathed her.

Again the grandmother shook her head. "She complained of pain in her chest when running. Then her eyes became red. She had a convulsion a couple of hours ago and stopped breathing."

Faye remembered that people who died from Ebola infection often developed more severe signs and symptoms early in the illness. Without a laboratory test, they couldn't be sure of Dzifa's diagnosis.

"We are wearing these protective suits because of Ebola virus," she said. "Do you know that USAID is helping your government stop it from spreading?" The women shook their heads no.

"Perhaps it's something else." Faye tried to sound reassuring. "Can I get a small amount of Dzifa's blood for testing?" She'd never taken it from a human cadaver—blood thickening could pose a challenge. But the death was so recent, she was confident of success.

As the woman nodded and gestured the second woman away, Zayaan opened his kit and handed Faye a syringe. She inserted the needle in the median cubital vein inside the child's elbow, the most prominent superficial vein in the human body and one she typically used for blood draws on live people.

Grieving relatives watched every move. Despite her intense focus, she had an empty syringe no matter how she angled it.

Calm down, take your time. It's not like the patient is going to faint, walk away, or report you to your supervisor. No one knows you're a vet.

"I'm so sorry," she said to the women. "Let me try the other arm." She couldn't see or feel the vein, then massaged the area and tried once more. Zayaan didn't offer to take over, so maybe he also had little to no experience. Almost ready to give up, she finally filled the syringe. Her nerves didn't lead to the shakes or any needle slip with exposure to blood likely contaminated with deadly virus.

"We won't know for a few days if Dzifa had Ebola," she informed the women. "Was she around anyone who has been sick, or did she have a meal of bushmeat?"

"Last week, my son brought home monkey meat for my birthday and we shared it," the grandmother answered.

Oh God. Faye's heart sank at the number of potential cases. "I need to talk with all of you before we leave. First, can we take Dzifa to a mortuary? That may not be what you prefer, but I don't want someone else getting sick."

Zayaan cleared his throat. "We won't find an ambulance crew to take that risk."

"Even in the city?" Faye's heart pounded with the complications. "Can we ask our driver? I have a backup set of PPE he can use for protection." The man wasn't one of Uncle Kumi's chauffeurs, so she didn't have the clout to compel him, but he worked for USAID so likely respected the mission.

She remained with Dzifa and her relatives while Zayaan headed outside to the jeep. Head bowed, she shared in silence the atmosphere of grief, in honor of Dzifa's spirit. But if others were incubating the virus, a review of possible symptoms with them was urgent.

Pulling up the survey form on her phone, she decided to plunge ahead with her interviews of the women as a group. More than three-quarters of Ghana's population spoke English so she was optimistic they understood her, but having a respected local woman's help couldn't hurt. The chief's college-aged daughter offered to assist.

Faye hated having someone new inside the hut without protection, but Zayaan was offering the backup PPE to the driver.

The girl said she wasn't worried, she'd been inside before, so Faye interviewed her first.

Unable to persuade anyone to step outside the small room, Faye recorded the names and contact information for the eight women, then read through each prodromic sign and symptom. Few said yes to any of them but if they did, she noted the date of onset.

Zayaan returned to the home with the driver fully geared up. The chief's daughter convinced the women to let Dzifa go. They wrapped her in a heavy robe and carried her body to the jeep, followed by a procession of children that Faye had difficulty keeping at a distance. When the vehicle drove away, Faye stayed behind.

As she proceeded through the list of serious complications with the women, her translator hesitated over more challenging terms like sepsis and disseminated intravascular coagulation. For those reporting compatible clinical signs, Faye took blood specimens, which went more smoothly than with Dzifa.

Armed with information on others to check on who'd attended the birthday feast, her breathing rate settled down. Neither she nor Taylor had caught Ebola despite investigating numerous cases, and this group might not add new ones beyond Dzifa. Whatever the little girl died of, Faye struggled to feel good about the day's work in the face of so much sorrow.

FIFTY-FOUR

Taylor blinked rapidly, blinded by the sun in the open courtyard of the Accra jail. Facing months of anxiety pending trial, the unexpected release after only a couple of weeks was exhilarating. Taylor grinned so broadly, it hurt.

Flanked by Faye and Uncle Kumi, the attorney strutted like a rooster. "A mishmash of allegations spun into a spider web, ripped apart by my legendary powers of persuasion. Thank the Lord you are still healthy, Dr. Lewis."

Taylor's muscles with limited exercise said otherwise, although pushups and situps with the other inmates had headed off additional deterioration. First on the New York agenda—a long run through Central Park.

The attorney turned away when Taylor offered a handshake in thanks. Taylor had been careful to offer only the right hand because the left was considered unclean. Without a bath or shower the entire time, Taylor nonetheless had prioritized using the limited drinking water to wash hands, but forgave the uncivil gesture.

Taylor recovered by shaking Uncle Kumi's hand from right to left as a sign of respect. Faye's tear-stained freckled cheeks cried out for a kiss, but Taylor had no stomach for another arrest. Wait until safely home.

Was the lawyer squeamish about his client's sexuality? Maybe the pretrial jail time was due to the man's half-hearted effort, but some in the cell had lingered longer. They'd rejoiced in Taylor's release so far ahead of the September trial date.

Taylor had been generous with sharing the limited food, and the others had treated the American as an honored guest. "Ask your legal practitioner if he will help us, too," they'd chanted as if in a choir.

Back at the hotel, Uncle Kumi led them into the lobby, and his eyes teared as he bowed. "Thank you again, nephew, for risking your life to help Ghana conquer Ebola. Dr. Simpson handled the death of a young girl yesterday. No more, inshallah. Without you and USAID, things would be much worse."

"Risking my life is a stretch," Taylor answered, tone sardonic. "But I'm grateful that jail didn't gift me COVID, malaria, or a long list of foodborne and waterborne diseases."

"I meant your being homosexual," Uncle Kumi snapped back, voice low as he glanced around the lobby, momentarily quiet after the busy morning checkouts.

So he still didn't realize that Taylor was trans female, or he didn't have the vocabulary. If that had been confirmed, sexual relations with Faye might be labeled as lesbianism, strengthening the prosecutor's case. With a plane flight home in six hours, this was not the time and place for clarifications.

"Africa is too dangerous for people like you," Uncle Kumi added in a whisper. "You can be killed in multiple countries, even stoned to death in parts of Nigeria with sharia law. Our penalties will be worse when the president signs our new laws. It is not safe for you to come here again."

Taylor hated saying goodbye on a sour note, but couldn't disagree. "For our next visit, you should come to New York. Thank you again, Uncle Kumi, for everything you've done for both of us."

When entering the air-conditioned hotel room with Faye, Taylor broke out in a shiver. "I stink like a pig. Join me in a hot shower?"

She wrinkled her nose. "Wasn't going to complain, but you're right." Then she frowned as she glanced around. "The maid grabbing your medications on court order has me paranoid. Could they bug the room?"

Taylor gestured to the table and the plastic bag the attorney had handed over. "I have my meds now—I'd like to think all this is behind us."

"The whole episode doesn't leave me with a good feeling about Ghana," Faye muttered as she slipped off her shoes. "Not seeing you, and the death of that child, set me back. Uncle Kumi's hospitality and the hope of your release kept me going. This morning's call from the Ambassador about your dropped charges—the best words I've heard in forever."

Taylor suddenly felt faint and sank to the sofa. "Hand me a glass of water, sweetie."

After swallowing the pills, Taylor said, "I'm relieved my uncle treated you so well. Without a lot to occupy my mind, I worried that he was complicit in my arrest. It didn't make sense, but occasionally my thoughts went to a dark place."

"Two weeks—that seems way too long for bogus accusations." Faye took Taylor's hand. "I freaked out when they mentioned your strip search. Nothing bad happened with the guards and the other inmates?"

"No. Some of the guys in the cell were facing crazy charges too. One man, returning from months away working in the gold mines, came across his mother in a public square. He broke out into a little dance before hugging her. It was Sunday, and dancing is illegal on that day. And a younger guy was arrested because his sagging pants exposed his underwear."

Taylor leapt up to get warm, undressing quickly and dragging Faye into the shower. Her skin reddened and Taylor turned the temperature down. "Can we just stay forever in each other's arms?" Taylor placed a kiss on Faye's limp graying curls. "Safe from all the intrusions and dangers of the world."

Weakened from the limited prison diet and exercise, Taylor exited the shower to Faye, waiting with a plush hotel robe. When curled up on the couch, Taylor studied the room service menu. "Can I try everything?"

"Not unless you want to be vomiting all night in the toilet," Faye groused. "I'm happy they don't serve bushmeat here. I'm betting that's what killed Dzifa, the little girl. A birthday celebration of monkey meat, but none left over for testing."

Taylor picked out an entrée of chicken Kiev and Faye the salmon salad. "A welcome transition back into American food," Taylor said after phoning in the order. "I feel awful that the invite to my family's home country turned out the way it did. I don't want you to think badly of Ghana."

Faye cuddled closer, nestling her damp head against Taylor's warm chest. "It's not like New York is some kind of paradise. People are breaking out of their pandemic lockdowns and major crimes have spiked."

Taylor recalled patients with gunshot wounds in the Staten Island hospital. "Yeah, other than law enforcement, we never saw any weapons here."

"We were lucky the Ebola outbreak was confined to the area around Accra. Your uncle mentioned armed bandits along the border with Burkina Faso."

With a deep sigh, holding Faye close, Taylor whispered in her ear. "I'm getting too old for these travel adventures. When we're home on Sunday, let's order food delivery and read the Times in bed with your cat. A pampered cat, not all the strays in Ghana."

Faye tilted her head up, blue eyes shining. "With your allergies, we've always barred Bosco from the bedroom when you stay over."

Taylor stretched every muscle. "I'll take a Benadryl. If it makes me sleepy, all the better. One day of indolence, then back to the weekly grind of morning runs and afternoon hospital rounds. Never did I ever … relish a routine."

Faye thumbed through the calendar on her phone. "We're about five weeks since our last New York Ebola case. At 42 days, Moshe will officially declare that outbreak over, and we can put Ebola into our long-term memory bank."

"From your lips to God's ear," Taylor answered with a laugh. "I'll happily stick to good-old American diseases."

FIFTY-FIVE

Two women in white leather boots, black dresses, and colorful capes balanced exquisite Zuni pots on their heads as they danced and shook gourd rattles in time to a man chanting and drumming. Maya and her parents sat in the shade on a wooden bench next to the central courtyard of Albuquerque's Indian Pueblo Cultural Center.

When the two o'clock performance ended, Barbara said to her daughter, "I can't believe you've lived in New Mexico for four years and we've never done this."

"Guess I was running around to exotic locales on disease outbreaks," Maya joked.

"Don't worry about it, honey," Tom said. "We know you stopped home to Flagstaff whenever you could."

Maya led the way to the Indian Pueblo Kitchen for a late lunch. Once seated, Tom ordered the Native Superfoods Waffles. "Can't pass this up with blue corn, quinoa, triple berries, currants, and piñon nuts, plus sunflower and pumpkin seeds. Holy cow!"

"This might be my last chance for a New Mexican favorite, so I'm having the Blue Corn Enchiladas with squash and chicken," Maya told the waitress. "Can you add extra sour cream?"

Barbara frowned. "I'm not as hungry as you two. Make mine a Pueblo Turkey Melt with green chile on the side."

"And to drink?" the waitress asked.

"How about Zia sodas?" Maya suggested. "I'd like a Red Chile Ginger Ale."

"Too spicy," Barbara answered. "Sandia Watermelon for me."

"I'll try Prickly Pear Cactus Pad," Tom said. "Did you remove the spines?"

The waitress gave a half-hearted laugh, clearly having heard the quip before.

Maya stretched one leg starting to cramp. "Packing and cleaning wore me out, but I'm glad we made time to spend the day together."

She grabbed one hand of each parent in her own. "I can't tell you how much I appreciate everything you're doing, including this mini vacay for a couple nights in Albuquerque before my flight tomorrow."

"We really haven't done anything like this since you started college in Colorado," Tom said.

A wash of guilt flushed Maya's skin from her toes to her face. Thirteen years, almost half her life. "Tell you what, I promise I'll be back for my big birthday."

Maya knew she'd said the wrong thing by her mother's alarmed expression.

"That's eight months away!" Barbara twisted in her seat, grabbing Maya's arm. "I thought this visit to Norway was a short one."

Maya hastened to correct herself before her mother devolved into one of her famous tirades. "I don't plan to be gone that long, but no matter what I'm doing, we'll celebrate my birthday together."

It might not be the right day, anyway. February 14, 1993 was on the Chinese records, but authorities had been known to falsify them, making an infant appear younger than it really was.

"Are you sticking to your story of hearing an invisible baby cry on the day I was born?" she asked her mom, signaling a lack of confrontation with her teasing tone. "Of course, accounting for the time change."

Barbara's eyebrows formed a caterpillar, then Tom tweaked his wife's ear and both smiled. "

Without a doubt," Barbara answered, her words tender. "I know it was you." The mystery had tremendous emotional resonance within their family. The Red Thread, connecting across oceans and continents.

Maya refocused on her trip. With a one-way ticket, the Norway visit was open-ended, and Stefan hadn't placed parameters on the timing of his hospitality. He sounded desperate for company, scared of the heart problems possibly related to Ebola and the potential failure of his life partnership with Kondrat.

They wouldn't really break up—they'd been together too long and shared a child, who'd been only five when they met, an engaging kindergartner.

"Will your visit to Oslo be a much-deserved rest or will Stefan put you to work?" Tom interrupted Maya's musings.

"I hope to God, no." Barbara's face reddened to match her dyed hair, restrained in a tight bun. "Who can ever forget China, and what he dragged you into?"

Tom squeezed his wife's hand. "We're proud of you as a premiere medical detective, but we worry about the risks."

Maya appreciated the sentiment as an expression of love, but also resented their hovering. "You know how careful I am. Despite numerous zoonotic disease investigations, including Ebola in New York, I only got infected once."

"It only cost you your husband and your baby." Barbara jerked back with a horrified look. "I'm sorry—I didn't mean to say that."

A dagger to Maya's heart. She gulped, then chose to be generous with the parents who rescued her from a Chinese orphanage. "That's always the ten-ton weight whenever we think of COVID."

Those consequences motivated her escape from New Mexico. She had no idea when she'd return. All her limited possessions were in Santa Fe storage, other than Manolo's Southwestern black-and-white photos which her parents would keep in their Flagstaff apartment.

The discussion paused as their meals were delivered. "What did Dr. Grinwold say?" Tom asked. "Will he hold the state public health vet job open for you?"

Maya thought back to the barbecue Dr. Grinwold and Nancy hosted last weekend for all of Maya's colleagues and friends. That was the toughest part. She'd miss daily consultations with Erika on new disease cases and her adorable little cowboy son. With Stephanie—strolling in the Santa Fe National Forest, feeding her loquacious macaw Quetzy, and commiserating over Dr. Grinwold's grumpiness.

"Nancy Bingham, Dr. Grinwold's partner, has lobbied him on my behalf," Maya said. "She told him that veterinary epidemiologists with field and stats experience in multiple states and overseas are as rare as hen's teeth. At least, those willing to work in a small state rather than the big stage of CDC or WHO."

"That's what we like to hear," Tom said. "What about Dr. Becker, your buddy from your CDC training program? As the new Arizona State Epidemiologist, she might want you on board. You'd be closer to us if you were in Phoenix."

Maya wiped her mouth with her napkin. Living in Phoenix had never occurred to her. Sure, she'd worked with their health department on multiple outbreaks, and it was home base for Manolo when they met. Mark had recently relocated his second office from Phoenix to Scottsdale, although he preferred the one in Santa Fe where he could retreat at night to his ranch.

Mark, that was another person she was stringing along. Unless he was a better actor than she suspected, he seemed fine that she postponed a new job commitment.

Perhaps he was just confident she'd be back after their first night together. She had to admit, it was pretty special, one she wouldn't mind repeating. The sex reinforced her interest in maintaining some kind of relationship. She'd always liked and respected him.

"I'll keep in touch with Lila," she answered her dad. "Phoenix isn't my favorite place, but she'd be great to work with."

"We had hoped to run into your friend Dr. Schwartz while we're in Albuquerque," Barbara said. "Is he all done with the monkeys that had Ebola?"

"Ask him tomorrow morning. He offered to buy us breakfast."

No specific job plans for the foreseeable future—that was what Maya welcomed now.

She argued with her dad over the lunch check but let him pay, then followed her parents to the Old Town hotel. Her mom would drive Maya's Prius back to Flagstaff, claiming that a second car would be convenient. Just like them to take care of Maya's loose ends.

By Sunday, she'd be in Oslo to support a friend, albeit a problematic colleague. Hopefully she could put aside their doomed China trip. She didn't want the memories close at hand, not on her first long break without any public health demands since her COVID recovery.

She reached into her purse and fondled a beautiful Korean bookmark gifted by her psychiatrist on a recent visit. Dr. Kim had walked her through some new cognitive therapy exercises and encouraged Maya to go with the flow, an unnatural practice for her. Then Dr. Kim recommended a mantra Maya hoped to follow: "Embrace the unknown and let life surprise you."

With a sigh, she put the bookmark back in her bag. If only life were more comfortably predictable.

FIFTY-SIX

Biko took a ragged breath as the bus passed over the half-mile long Third Mainland Bridge. The open water of the Lagos Lagoon was not far below the roadway, so the height should not make him dizzy. Probably a bit of residual vertigo from Ebola.

Next to him, Nneka asked, "Are you okay?"

"Yes. Thank you for letting me come along on your guided tour."

"Somebody in this family needs to earn a living," she joked.

"Two weeks of convalescence is enough. I am ready to give my university lecture on our outbreak."

"What will you tell them about how it started?"

He shrugged. "I'll say we don't know." Stefan was convinced it was Jan Kreischer's fault, but West Africa had periodic Ebola flareups, so Biko was unsure.

When the roadway joined Lagos Island, he relaxed. It transformed into a narrow boulevard of coconut trees as they approached the parking area for the Lekki Conservation Centre. In front of a triangular-roofed building, Nneka checked off the names of her tour group.

A little boy screamed as a mona monkey dashed by, grabbing the boy's Puff Puff of fried dough. "Please leave all your food on board," Nneka reminded.

The animal ran with the snack in its hands, long black tail arched forward over its brown body. It leapt to the top of the bus, arching one arm to the gloomy sky.

The monkey's hooded orange eyes bore into Biko's, as if to taunt him with his weakness. *You can't do this*, came the clear message.

The monkey's blue-gray face got lost with a flash of white belly as it jumped down and raced for the forest.

"I will lead you now to the canopy walkway," Nneka told the group. "Our 401-metre tour will take about one hour and twenty minutes, and we'll reach 22.5 metres above sea level at the highest point."

Biko wasn't a nature addict like Nneka but his own guide work had funded college classes. Surely he was strong enough by now. The threatening storm lent an oppressive feeling to the initial walk along a wooden platform through the swamp. Exclamations erupted in the crowd as a broad snout pushed through the water close to the boardwalk.

"This is a dwarf crocodile," Nneka said. "Its maximum length is two metres and it weighs only 32 kilograms, less than any of you adults."

Some kids darted behind their parents. "Crabs are their favorite food," Nneka added, "not you."

"Are they a vulnerable species?" Biko knew the answer but allowed Nneka to share her authority.

"Yes. Have you heard of CITES?" At the sea of blank faces, she continued. "The Convention on International Trade in Endangered Species lists those threatened with extinction. We are committed to their protection."

She focused her attention on Biko. "Ready for the next stage?"

He eyed the suspension bridge. The metal walkway and mesh netting on each side allowed a clear view of the forest. The kids ahead got it swinging with their shakes and leaps to increase the thrill. He hung back, hoping that his nausea would decrease if crossing with the older folks.

At an intermediate platform, he hesitated to use a chair. But no one else took advantage so he plopped down. Shading his eyes, he studied the sky.

"I would have cancelled for really bad weather," Nneka assured him.

The wind increased as they moved up to the highest level above the treetops. His fists gripped the braided wire on each side, wind whistling and rocking the entire walkway even more than the jubilant children.

Gasping for breath at the top, his bare arms prickled with the cool air and his stomach threatened to erupt. He leaned over the side, taking slow breaths to calm his system.

"Please do not jump," Nneka joked. "The walk will be easier on the way back." She offered him a drink from her water bottle.

"I will be all right." But he regretted the excursion with every step.

Where the swinging walkway rejoined the wooden boardwalk at the bottom, she thanked the tourists for joining her, then insisted Biko take a break on a shady bench.

"Outdone by my baby sister."

"Unlike you, I am not recovering from Ebola. You almost died."

But Biko wasn't the only one suffering. Nneka hadn't restarted her university classes, a year after her kidnapping by the bandits. Whenever he tried to raise the subject, she put him off.

"Does the fall semester start in September?" he asked—a casual chat, as if she were definitely planning to return.

Her tone became defensive. "I earn enough. The degree may not be worth it."

"Employers like to see that you can complete something." The lack of a credential might hold her back from advancement at the conservation centre, and she was too smart to be content as a guide for her entire life.

"Just because you are older doesn't mean I need to follow in your footsteps." Her eyes flashed, her Bantu knots vibrated, and she stood up to her full five feet, glaring down at him.

He hadn't intended to provoke her—he owed her too much for his care. After their mother's death during Nneka's childbirth and their father's death just two years ago, she was his only remaining relative. They needed to stick together.

"You are right, Nne, you can stay a teenager for a few more weeks. You have plenty of time for college or other options."

Nneka nodded to the next tour as they passed, then handed Biko her bottle. She whispered, "It is hard to forget what happened. That guide—he used to be Boko Haram."

"The young man wearing the Agbada?" Biko glanced down the walkway. The leader in a green wide-sleeved robe, trousers, and pillbox cap contrasted with the tourists in tee-shirts and shorts.

Biko's blood chilled. "Was he one of your captors? Why would this place allow that?"

Her voice was tentative as the group faded down the walkway through the trees. "I never met him before, but he was part of Operation Safe Corridor. It integrates repentant bandits into society."

Unbelievable. Biko did not oppose the program but the man should not work alongside his sister. They must realize Nneka's year-round availability was due to dropping out of college, but perhaps they were not aware of her captivity.

"I have had so much help in my recovery," he said. "Stefan prepared the slides for my presentation, and you do everything for me—cook, clean, shop. Yet you will not let me return the support. I know nothing of what happened to you."

Tears streaked her cheeks. "I no longer felt like me there—they changed our names. If someone protested, they slit her throat."

Biko sucked in his breath. He feared the details, but they still made her cry a year later. It would help her to talk with somebody.

"I was so grateful you had no permanent injuries." He gulped— what about the less obvious ones?

"Most of my classmates survived, but one girl was persuaded to become a suicide bomber. Kids were burned alive in her attack on a nearby village."

"I do not understand how she could do that, after how they treated you."

Nneka twisted her hands. "They groomed us with mangoes and apples. After near starvation from a diet of rice and leaves, fruit tasted like liquid gold. They tried to persuade us to learn Arabic so we could read the Qur'an, then convert and marry a fighter."

Biko had more questions. But perhaps as her brother, he should be careful about anything private. Shifting on the bench, he imagined donning his white doctor coat, interviewing a patient. "Were you sexually assaulted?"

She also squirmed but shook her head no. "They laughed at me, said I looked like a boy. I was a small and skinny pebble in the dirt, not worth it."

Biko made the sign of the cross. "How were you released?"

"I deliberately befriended an older vendor delivering water. He said I reminded him of his granddaughter and he told me how to escape. One night when allowed to go to the toilet, I ran for my life out the back of the compound."

He had assumed Nneka was rescued in a police raid. "You are very brave. I cannot imagine what they would have done if you had been caught." He shuddered—she had risked so much.

"They constantly warned us, 'If you run away, we will break your ribs and legs and leave you in the jungle.' Once I started, failure was not an option. I stumbled into a grave of dead fighters and hostages. The smell—I vomited but crawled back out."

"How long until you reached safety?"

"Days walking through open scrubland, stumbling over rocks and snakes. I finally found a patrol, which arranged for me to be hospitalized. They used my information to free the camp."

A pair of rambunctious monkeys screeched as they hopped tree-to-tree, distracting Biko. He had believed they were rescued using the ransom collected among the relatives, to which he had donated. What really happened to that money?

Overwhelmed by his sister's story, he was irritated that she had withheld it. But he cradled her hands with a gentle squeeze. "You are a hero—you saved others. I will never question your choices again."

FIFTY-SEVEN

Just like her first visit three years earlier, Maya spotted Stefan and his daughter at the Tigerstaden, the bronze tiger statue in Oslo's Sentrum. But Paula could no longer fit under its gaping jaw. At eleven, she could stroke its metallic whiskers.

Stefan ruffled Paula's blonde hair, then embraced Maya in a one-arm hug as Paula threw her arms around Maya's waist. "We should have met you at the airport."

"Nonsense. The Flytoget train is marvelous. Besides, this has become our tradition." Maya's gaze dropped from Stefan's too-thin face to his daughter. "It's a long time since we've seen each other, Paula. I'm glad you remember me."

Stefan laughed. "Well, who could forget our time in Lisbon? Paula and Kondrat sunbathed on the beach while you and I wrestled pigs." He tweaked Paula's cheek.

Maya smirked. "If I recall, you updated your records in the car while I tackled the animals."

"Tatuś texted me pictures to remind me of the trip." Paula showed Maya a photo. The four of them stood in front of the famous Torre de Belém. The tower had been built in the 1500s for defense on the north bank of the Tagus River. Stefan had persuaded someone to take the photo.

"A beautiful day," Maya said. "All the flowers blooming. Except for wildfire smoke in the air, it was paradise."

"Can we go on vacation again?" Paula asked, tugging at Maya's hand. "Please, Tatuś?"

Stefan's pale skin flushed. Maya couldn't recall ever seeing him without a tan.

"I'm sure we'll arrange it sometime. Let's get Maya settled."

He gripped the handle of Maya's roller suitcase but she took it back. They hopped the bus instead of strolling down to the Bygdøy Peninsula ferry. Based on Stefan's slow steps, Maya assumed he wasn't up for a longer walk. It would have been a beautiful day out on the water, but she didn't mind. When passing the verdant Slottsparken where she and Stefan ate lunch after interviewing *Borrelia* patients, she strained for a glimpse of the Royal Palace.

Paula begged to stop at the blue banners announcing the Norsk Folkemuseum.

"Not today, kochanie." Stefan turned to Maya across the aisle. "Kondrat offered to host us for dinner at five. That should give you a couple of hours for a nap."

She was tempted to support Paula. The museum's stave church from Gol was one of her favorite Oslo landmarks, so ornate with its carved animal figures. But seeing Stefan's droopy appearance, she kept her mouth shut. Plenty of time to play tourist later. At the Viking Ship Museum, they hopped off for the walk to Stefan's place. "Can we visit the old ship, Tatuś?" Paula begged.

Maya clasped Paula's hand and urged her along the path, flowers spilling over wooden gates. "You're out of school now? Perhaps we can go tomorrow if it's open."

Paula was sullen and silent. Maya remembered that the girl had executive function problems and learning disabilities, whether from birth or years in the lousy conditions of a Moldovan orphanage, no one knew.

"I can't wait to see your daddy's apartment. Do you think it's nice?"

Paula shrugged. "Guess so. Sometimes I sleep over. You can have my bedroom."

Maya glanced wide-eyed at Stefan. She hadn't realized she'd displace his daughter.

"Not to worry," he answered. "Paula's not sleeping here tonight, but I have a comfortable couch where she can nap." He pivoted to an alleyway, then unlocked a gate. "This is a new accessory dwelling unit. Oslo encourages building apartments in backyards to address housing shortages."

A cobblestone walkway separated patches of lush lawn. After a few steps, he opened a sliding glass door centered in a pale-blue wall protected by an A-framed roof and porch. Inside, the living room and kitchen were designed in the clean lines of Scandinavian style. He guided Maya down the hall to a room with a single bed.

"Small, but comfortable. We have a shared bathroom between the two bedrooms." He gestured to the towel on the end of the duvet. "You're welcome to take a shower—I know how wonderful that feels after a long trip."

When she opened her bag on the floor, Maya heard Stefan and Paula chatting in the kitchen as he fixed her lunch. With plentiful food on the flights, she wasn't tempted to join them. Instead, she lingered under the gentle spray from the rainwater showerhead and rubbed the bath gel over every skin surface. Sensations of Mark's stroking fingers bubbled into her brain, then supplanted by Manolo's.

How could a one-night fling replace her love for her husband? She stepped onto the bathmat and grabbed the towel. Not replaced exactly, just augmented. Hopefully driving out any mysterious hauntings during sleep or daydreams.

No longer hearing voices from the kitchen, she tiptoed into Paula's bedroom. She'd have to find her own lodging before nightfall. Meanwhile, she'd settle like the rest of the household into a welcome nap.

FIFTY-EIGHT

Faye perched at a sidewalk table on Broadway, sipping her black coffee. She needed a full charge to stay awake. She'd left Taylor snoring in her bed, the cat in the living room to spare Taylor's allergies.

Last night when they reached her lower Manhattan apartment after the eleven-hour flight from Accra to JFK, she ordered Taylor on the bathroom scale. A fifteen-pound weight loss, exceeding the recommended 1-2 pounds per week if dieting. Not a huge amount for someone who usually hovered around 180 pounds, all muscle on a six-foot frame. But enough to make a noticeable difference.

This morning, Taylor had a slight fever and headache. Faye provided acetaminophen and sent Taylor back to bed. They'd planned a stroll to Rockefeller Park for views of the Statue of Liberty—a chance to relish Taylor's freedom. But the long walk was too soon. Taylor's intention to start jogging again would have to wait.

Not that she was an expert on all human diseases, but Faye couldn't help running through the possibilities as a pleasant July breeze feathered her bare skin. A foodborne or waterborne microbe would be at the top of the list, but Taylor hadn't reported any nausea or diarrhea.

The two-week break in malaria prophylaxis concerned her the most. The microscopic parasite might be developing in Taylor's red blood cells, then rupturing the cells to release the next stage.

The incubation period between mosquito bite and symptoms ranged from seven to thirty days, so it was possible. Complications of infection could be extreme, including cerebral malaria that progressed to delirium, coma, and death.

But she was getting ahead of herself. Taylor had just a slight fever and headache—nothing to worry about on a Sunday morning. She'd insist on Taylor consulting with a colleague if the symptoms persisted. Lab tests could rule out anything serious.

Her pulse quickened as she remembered tomorrow was the Fourth of July and physicians wouldn't offer normal office hours. Taylor could arrange to consult with someone at the Staten Island hospital, or wait until Tuesday.

She sank her head into her hands—she had no one to call and share her worries about Taylor. Adjusting to the changed social dynamics of being retired was hard. With decades at the city health department, all her friendships had been work-related, and she'd never prioritized after-hours get-togethers.

Maya had helped them locate Taylor's attorney in Ghana, yet Faye hadn't talked to her since Taylor's surprise release on Friday. Maya was an early riser and it was eight a.m. in New Mexico, so she'd be awake. Faye sent a quick text. **<Your attorney did his job. We're back home in NYC. Have time to talk?>**

FaceTime flashed on Faye's phone. With her disheveled hair, Maya looked like she'd had a late Saturday night. "I didn't mean to wake you," Faye apologized.

Maya swiped a hand over her eyes. "I need to get up—it's three in the afternoon here in Oslo, and I just had a nap after my flight. I can't believe your good news!"

"Sorry, I forgot about Norway. Our lives are spookily in sync. I wonder if we were over the Atlantic at the same time, or maybe at JFK."

"How did Taylor get released?"

"The case was always on shaky legal grounds. Between the American Ambassador and the attorney, they finally dropped the charges. Didn't get to trial."

"I'm so relieved. Stefan's not fully recovered from his Ebola infection. How's Taylor doing?"

Faye hesitated to admit her paranoia, but Maya was public health, too—she knew all about having your risk radar on full alert.

"Sluggish, lost weight, and a bit feverish. Didn't fight me about staying in bed."

"Not surprising—I read up on Ghana's jails and prisons. Not the same level of justice as we have in the US. Must have been a strain on you, too."

Before Faye could respond, Stefan's head poked into Maya's phone frame. "Faye, good to see you. I overheard you talking—so happy you're home."

"Sorry, Stefan," Maya said. "Hope I didn't wake up you and Paula."

"Just drew her a bath—she's cleaning up for tonight's dinner. Conditions were a bit rough in Guinea, but I behaved myself and didn't experience their legal system. Ah, I didn't mean to imply Dr. Lewis did anything wrong."

Faye tensed, short-tempered with all the strain. Before she said something undiplomatic, Stefan continued. "Have things quieted down in New York? Maya said you had some dramatic scenarios—a needlestick in Dr. Lewis' hospital, a guy throwing up on TV."

"I wouldn't say we're totally out of the woods," Faye answered. "With such a long incubation period, Ebola could still rear its ugly head. I'll check with my previous colleagues on Tuesday to see if anything's percolating here."

"If only we could have started vaccinations earlier in Conakry," Stefan said. "I was one of the first cases so by the time we got our shipment from WHO, I was already infected and recovered."

Faye breathed a thankful sigh. USAID had authorized their Ebola vaccinations before they headed to Ghana. One less risk to worry about for Taylor's nonspecific prodrome.

"Anyways, I'll hand you back to Maya." Stefan appeared a bit sheepish. "I didn't mean to take over her FaceTime, but it was awfully good to see you so many years after grad school."

Faye remembered Stefan's big puppy energy, all long limbs and bouncing around without a complete thought process. But six years after she first got to know him in NYC, he would have matured. Maya respected his judgment and abilities as a WHO physician epidemiologist, with the exception of the disastrous trip to China. Faye prayed that he'd offer Maya a public health break while in Norway, not drag her into another investigation. With Stefan's slow Ebola recovery, a true vacation was in order. With any luck, she'd persuade Taylor to do the same.

Maya came back on screen. Her shoulder-length locks were now neatly brushed and pulled into a short ponytail. "We're heading over to Kondrat's house for dinner. He's quite a chef."

Faye was startled by Maya's statement. What did she mean about Kondrat's house? Stefan and Kondrat were legal partners, weren't they? But Faye wouldn't pry today.

"Maya, I'm glad to see you escaped the rat race to one of the healthiest and wealthiest countries in the world. You deserve a holiday. Talk to you soon."

She hung up, more focused on her own partner than Stefan's. After placing her empty coffee cup on the café's tray of dirty dishes, she picked up her bag of croissants and hurried back to check on Taylor.

FIFTY-NINE

A pinch of tightness in his chest, Stefan ambled down the street, arm in arm with Maya. Paula raced ahead.

With little auto traffic on the narrow, curvy lane, he didn't worry much about his daughter's safety, but cursed his slow recovery from Ebola-inflicted angina. Maybe he was just being a hypochondriac. The first dinner with Kondrat since Stefan's return to Oslo was bound to be stressful.

The invitation was likely only due to Kondrat's friendly inclinations toward Maya. Kondrat was always a good host. Stefan opened the gate to the backyard, letting Paula and Maya enter first. Away from home only one night, Paula nevertheless screamed in delight and threw her arms around Kondrat.

Kondrat stretched out a hand of welcome to Maya. Stefan got a nod. Under the late afternoon light piercing the leafy cover, gray hairs gleamed in Kondrat's coppery locks. Did Stefan put those there?

Maya laughed as she took a seat on the patio. "I remember that fabulous dinner three years ago during our relapsing fever outbreak. Your salmon was incredible. I promise, this time, that we won't talk about sick people to spoil anyone's appetite."

Paula set crackers and multe berries on Maya's plate. Maya sighed after her first taste. "Heavenly—they taste like angels made them on a cloud."

Paula dissolved in giggles. "Silly, that's why they're called cloudberries."

Stefan dropped to the chair next to his daughter and smiled. "I think Maya knows that, kochanie."

Kondrat returned from the kitchen with a colorful platter. "Sild og poteter," he said. "Herring and potatoes." Small pieces of fish encircled bite-size chunks of yellow potatoes, topped with slices of red onions and beets, then garnished with dill and dabs of sour cream. "One of Norway's most popular summer dishes," he added.

"I don't think I'll get this at Stefan's place." Maya's dig was softened by her wink in Stefan's direction.

He relaxed with her open acknowledgment of the living situation. No reason why they couldn't all be civilized. As promised, Maya kept the conversation directed away from deadly diseases. She showed Paula photos from Friday in the Indian Pueblo Cultural Center.

"For jewelry, Zuni is my favorite." Maya paused at one picture. "See the mosaic inlay turquoise and coral in this squash blossom necklace?" She fingered her bear claw earrings. "These were a gift from my late husband, symbolizing his strength and protection." She side-eyed Stefan while responding to his family. "Just like your fathers give you, Paula."

Stefan squeezed her hand in gratitude for trying to mend fences.

"So is this truly a vacation for you?" Kondrat asked Maya as Paula cleared the table.

"I swear, I didn't lure her under false pretenses to help me with work." Stefan handed Paula his utensils.

"I didn't see much of Norway last time," Maya answered. "But we haven't planned any excursions out of Oslo."

"I understand you also worked on Ebola in New York."

Stefan frowned at Kondrat's bringing up the subject banned from the evening's discussion.

"Yes, I helped a colleague there. The infections are related to Stefan's cases in Conakry, but I think they're snuffed out."

Stefan shifted uncomfortably in his seat. He was sure Maya didn't mean to imply that he had anything to do with starting the outbreak, even if he still suspected their gorilla trip as the origin.

Kondrat stared at Maya. "Does Stefan pose a threat to this family?"

Stefan crumpled his napkin and tossed it on the table, then glanced around for Paula who was still in the kitchen. He couldn't believe Kondrat had stabbed him in the heart like that.

"I'm not in a good position to answer that." Maya leaned over, a look of sympathy on her face. "Kondrat, I understand why you worry. Ebola is frightening, but Stefan is super-conscientious about disease prevention. I trust his judgment."

Stefan nodded an implied 'thank you' in her direction, then stood up from the table. "We should head back to my place."

"Thank you so much for another amazing meal." She reached her arms forward and Kondrat accepted her embrace. Paula emerged from the house and hugged Stefan and Maya goodbye, in turn.

Maya relished the golden sunset while Stefan headed to his refrigerator for bottles of Ringnes Pilsner. She clicked her bottle to his in a toast for Scandinavian summers, then kicked out her legs in a plastic chair on the small patch of grass.

"You see what I'm up against with my love life," he said.

"Fear for one's life or even worse, your child's life, can make someone irrational."

"Let's drop the subject of my fucked-up relationship. You mentioned a certain compelling attorney—the guy in Paris. What's happening on that front?"

Maya blushed. She hadn't really discussed Mark with anyone. If she'd had time before she left, she might have talked to Stephanie and Erika, her closest work girlfriends. Dr. Grinwold's party had not been the time or place. She wasn't ready for that then.

Stefan, on the other hand, was right in front of her, asking a question. He was hurting, and it might help him to focus on someone else.

"Well, when I got back to Santa Fe from New York, Mark and I reconnected. One thing led to another ..." She hesitated to be more explicit.

"Whoa, that is big news. Do you have a picture of this guy?"

On her phone, she flipped to a pensive portrait of Mark on

horseback. A black cowboy hat hung low on his forehead, shielding his eyes from the brilliance of a New Mexico sunrise.

"I thought he'd been in a wheelchair."

She nodded. "We worked really hard together on physical therapy—COVID recovery for me and his spinal problems from a spooked horse."

Stefan looked puzzled. "Why would he get back on a horse if that's what injured him?"

She searched for words to capture such a larger-than-life personality in a few sentences. "He's an advocate of facing down your biggest fears."

"So why did you leave him behind in New Mexico?"

That question had been niggling in the back of Maya's brain. She didn't have sufficient experience to establish a pattern with her sexual or love relationships. It felt funny thinking of love in relation to Mark. Mutual respect and physical attraction, yes, but nothing else. Too soon, despite their years of knowing each other.

Almost two years since Manolo's death. That ought to be enough time to let go.

"My job with CDC finished up, so it's time to explore other options. The relationship with Mark hasn't had a soft or hard launch." She blushed, not intending a sexual innuendo.

Stefan handed back her phone. "So you're not Insta official."

"No." Maya was uncomfortable with the trend of posting everything one was doing on social media. Besides, she didn't have time to curate her public persona. She didn't mind Stefan's curiosity on her personal status, but it was time to turn the tables.

"Tell me why you aren't trying harder to win back Kondrat."

SIXTY

A hacking cough in the teaching hospital's lecture hall interrupted Biko's presentation. He paused and searched the audience. Just in front of the coughing but masked woman, he spotted WHO's Regional Director for Africa shifting in his seat. Dr. Shah hadn't mentioned he'd be in Lagos for Biko's Ebola talk.

Using the laptop on the podium, Biko displayed a worldwide map. "As you can see, 3,146 *Zaire orthoebolavirus* cases were reported worldwide starting in May. Guinea had 53%, followed by Ghana with 31%. Other African nations reported 12%, including Nigeria. The remaining 4%—travelers to other continents."

He clicked on the epi curve. "The bars on this chart represents the number of new cases confirmed each week. This is good news. Cases dropped dramatically once WHO supplied vaccines to Guinea and Ghana. The most recent death was a Ghanaian child, confirmed July 1."

The next slide read **2014-2016 Ebola Outbreak, West Africa.** "In contrast, more than 28,600 cases were reported six years ago before vaccines became available in limited areas on an experimental basis. The case fatality rate in the earlier outbreak was much higher, 56% in one analysis among those unvaccinated. Currently only a quarter of our vaccinees have died, so vaccination reduces serious infections and deaths."

Biko glanced again over to Dr. Shah, who raised his arm and pointed to his watch.

"Uh, I need to wrap up." Biko stumbled over his words. "I appreciate your earlier questions about clinical manifestations but now I have run too long. In summary, we do not know how this outbreak started, but the vaccine has been a huge success. Thank you for your time and attention."

As the audience dispersed, Dr. Shah approached, a white kufi cap covering his short dark hair, reflecting his Sunni Muslim heritage. He'd told Biko that a great-grandfather was an indentured laborer from India imported by the British to work South African sugar-cane fields in the late 1800s.

"That's the danger of allowing discussion during your presentation, rather than reserving time at the end." Dr. Shah tempered the critical words with a kind expression.

Biko flexed his fingers that automatically clenched with any criticism. *Do not let your ego interfere with a learning experience.* He stepped down from the raised stage. "This is my first big talk. Do you have other suggestions?"

Dr. Shah nodded. "Look up from your notes at the audience more often. Glance back to verify you're talking about the slide we're seeing. Try to reduce the ums and ahs—that's a tough one. But the slides themselves—expertly designed."

Biko wanted to take credit but his conscience wouldn't allow it. "These were developed by Dr. Duda. We are recovering from our Ebola infections but he is healthier. He also has more experience with creating presentations."

"No problem. How are you doing?"

His medical leave completed on Monday, Biko projected confidence. "Fantastic, thank you for asking, sir. I am working to regain my strength with exercise."

Dr. Shah guided him to an empty corner. "We have a complication that changes what you presented here today."

Biko's heart fluttered with the news, as if he were back on the conservation centre's upper platform in the wind on Saturday. "A new Ebola case?"

Dr. Shah's lips tightened. "Nigeria arrested a poacher this weekend in Cross River National Park. Your government must do more about that scourge of Africa. Now he's hospitalized with Ebola—confirmed last hour."

Nneka with her full-time guiding work knew more about illegal hunts, so he wished she was in the room to consult. But her tour schedule kept her from attending the talk. "What kind of poaching?"

"Ten days ago, he cut the hands off a gorilla to make ashtrays. One he shot first."

Biko almost fainted. Even though he was aware of the gruesome products, the mental image was still shocking.

Dr. Shah rubbed the back of his neck. "Stefan Duda expressed concerns that our outbreak started from Jan Kreischer's disturbing a gorilla carcass in that park. But human cases predominated in Guinea, not here, so that was the priority. With those under control, we have time to follow this thread."

"Of course. Do you want me involved?"

"Yes, we need to assemble a team. Call Stefan and check on his availability."

SIXTY-ONE

Taylor rolled over in bed. Ten o'clock, according to the alarm clock. Fourth day in a row of sleeping late after Saturday's return from Accra. Midafternoon, Ghana time. Shouldn't still have jetlag.

Faye's voice drifted under the bedroom door from the living room. "How many horses? Oh, I'm sorry to hear about their deaths. It's been several years since you last had eastern equine encephalitis."

Chamomile tea might ease the stomach roiling. Wrapped in one of Faye's pink robes, Taylor padded out to the kitchen and opened the cabinet. Bosco stretched up to place her six-toed foot on Taylor's bare knee, begging for food. Taylor opened a bag of treats and dropped one to the kitty's bowl. A soothing stroke of soft fur would be nice, but runny eyes on top of nausea wouldn't be.

Faye said, "Call you back in a few minutes," then encircled Taylor's waist with her short arms. "What are you doing? I can get you whatever you want."

"I hope to God I can still make myself a cup of tea," Taylor snapped, then regretted the churlishness. Faye had anticipated every one of her partner's needs, and seldom left the apartment. "But one of your herbal blends would be lovely." Taylor settled onto the couch.

"Someone rolled out from the wrong side of the bed." Faye headed for the kitchen and put a pot of water on the stove.

"Sorry, still waking up. What was your call about?" Taylor asked.

"Long Island has four dead horses from triple-E. Record heat led to a skyrocketing number of *Culiseta melanura* mosquitoes that circulate the virus among birds. Unusually early—cases are typically reported in late summer to early fall."

"Why are they calling you?" Taylor wondered if Faye would ever truly retire. The Chief of Staff position brought in enough money to support both of them, but Faye was Colorado rancher-stubborn. With her state pension and retirement savings, she didn't need more income, and usually refused Taylor's offer to pay for anything.

Faye poured the hot water into two cups with tea bags. "Well, if anyone's prepared to deal with mosquito problems, it's Suffolk County. But they haven't identified any positive bridge vector mosquitoes like *Culex salinarius* that spread the virus to horses and people. It's a bit of a puzzle."

She handed a cup to Taylor and also settled on the couch. "Most important, how are you feeling this morning?"

"I threw up once overnight, and I'm glad I didn't wake you." Taylor envied Faye's ability to sleep, unless something big was happening.

Faye's freckled skin reddened and she frowned. "You should have got me up. Vomiting alone ain't fun."

"Ain't fun no matter how it happens." A ringtone interrupted Taylor's joke.

"Let me get that." Faye leapt up, then handed over Taylor's phone.

"Hi, Dr. Lewis," Marie, the hospital lab clerk, said. "Wish I didn't have to tell you this, but we found *Plasmodium falciparum* on your peripheral blood smear and confirmed it with a rapid diagnostic test."

Malaria. One of the damned *Anopheles* mosquitoes in the Accra jail must have been infected. A different species than the ones Faye discussed for EEE, and rarely implicated in spreading the parasite within the US.

Regardless, Taylor could establish a new local focus if bitten by a mosquito that then bit someone else. Or if Taylor became sick enough to be hospitalized, the parasite could spread through contaminated medical equipment. At least Taylor didn't pose a direct threat to Faye.

"My partner can bring me over," Taylor said. "I'll start on ACT."

"ACT?" Marie asked.

Faye, privy only to Taylor's end of the conversation, looked puzzled, likely having the same question.

"Artemisinin-based combination therapy," Taylor answered. A lab clerk shouldn't be expected to keep up on all the treatment modalities. "Give a heads-up to Dr. Cruz—she'll know what I'm talking about."

Taylor said goodbye and set down the phone. "You're right, I'm sick. Fortunately not Ebola—my vaccination worked. But I have malaria, so you should bring me to my hospital."

"Shit. I knew you couldn't escape that jail time unscathed." Faye grabbed her keys from the counter.

SIXTY-TWO

Maya and Stefan stopped by the Fram Museum's Arctic and Antarctic exhibits, then boarded the ferry. She offered him a hand which he refused with a wide smile.

"I'm glad you don't need a wheelchair," she teased as the early evening sun sparkled on the inner Oslofjord. In about ten minutes, they disembarked at the central harbor, then meandered along the waterfront past the Akershus festning, Oslo's medieval castle and World War II museum.

At the tip of the peninsula, industrial warehouses sported huge banners on the doors to their delivery bays. One depicted the evening's scene, a single puffy cloud highlighting a crystal sky above olive-green hills cradling Oslo. On a two-story steel compartment, a mustachioed giraffe wearing a fez played a guitar.

"Do you think Norway is the happiest place on the planet?" Maya took a deep breath of the soothing sea air.

Stefan laughed. "Depending on the survey, Denmark and Finland sometimes beat us out. And then there's Bhutan with its Happiness Index."

They settled at an outdoor table in front of a massive welcome mural. Jellyfish and octopi dotted the blue sea below a bearded and turbaned human head. On the other side of the restaurant door, red and pink hearts crowded a diagram of the area.

"I hope this isn't too casual for your anniversary celebration." Stefan passed Maya menus from multiple restaurants sharing the food court.

Celebration wasn't the right word. If Manolo were still alive, they'd go out to dinner on July 6 and reminisce about their beautiful wedding in the Santa Fe rose garden. Even in 2020 during COVID quarantines, they'd pulled off a romantic ceremony with a few friends appropriately distanced and everyone else on Zoom. But then he died that fall, so they never reached a first anniversary, let alone a second.

She appreciated Stefan recognizing the day's importance, despite the mourning mood layered on the warm remembrance. "Right now, there's nowhere else I'd rather be." She was startled by her admission. Not back in Arizona with her parents, or in New Mexico with Mark? An ocean view in summer with a good friend to cheer her up—something special.

Holding the menu, she pointed to the Biang Biang noodles with Zhejiang meat sauce. "If I order this spicy dish, can I stab you with my chopsticks and complain once again about China?" She modulated her words with a wide grin.

Stefan leaned back, stretching out his long legs under the table. "We helped on a great study of COVID in Thai bats, and you met that Chinese wildlife biologist who's from your hometown. Overall, the trip was a success."

"For you and your family's sake, I hope your optimism rubs off on Kondrat soon."

"The magic of an Oslo summer won't fail," he answered. "Besides, having you visit puts him in a good mood. Did you see him accept my little hug when we brought Paula home after the Viking Museum?"

She wasn't surprised. Kondrat, a good guy, would eventually regret not being more supportive during Stefan's Ebola recovery. "Pick out something before I starve to death."

He flagged down a waiter and ordered the Souvlaki Pork plate and Maya's noodles. "I'm heading back to the office next week—we can do things together on the evenings and weekends. You're welcome to play tourist by yourself."

"Sounds wonderful." Unscheduled time was weird, like playing hooky, but in sync with her new attitude. Earlier, she'd turned off her cell to engage in the moment, but felt guilty being out of touch.

"Mind if I check my phone while we wait for our food?" she asked.

"No problem," he answered. "I'll do the same."

An avalanche of messages from her parents and closest work friends lit up the screen. Mark had texted, **<Important day for you. Watching the clock until you come home and share all your new adventures.>** Her stomach dropped. She'd enjoy their reunion too, at some point, but wasn't sure how to interpret the clock-watching.

A text from Mu Jiang surprised her, when Stefan had just mentioned him. She couldn't remember if she'd told him about her anniversary date. **<I am thinking of you today. My grandparents keep asking when you will visit Tongling so they can meet you.>**

A year since they sampled Chinese bats for COVID, she'd tackled dengue, then Ebola. The outbreak roller coaster never halted, until now. Then her FaceTime screen lit up with a call from Faye.

"Hey, Maya. I saw the photo of your lovely wedding ceremony from two years ago on Facebook. How are you doing?"

Maya slanted the phone to show Stefan. "We're relaxing at the seaside, anticipating a delicious meal."

"Hi, Faye," Stefan said. "Is your partner still recovering from that awful ordeal in Accra?"

"Yes," Faye answered. "I'm at the Staten Island hospital, waiting for Taylor to begin malaria treatment."

Bad news—apparently Faye wasn't successful at getting Taylor back on malaria prophylaxis while in the jail. Did dangerous diseases target her and her colleagues? Maya squashed the morbid thought.

"I hope Taylor's recovery goes smoothly," Maya said. "I was lucky to avoid all those African disease risks by tackling Ebola at home."

Faye turned from her screen. "Well, kiddo, I'm being paged. Hang in there and I'll talk to you later."

Their dinners delivered, Maya and Stefan set their phones aside and discussed local landmarks to prioritize for a visit.

Forty-five minutes later, Stefan put down his fork. "Maybe it's too soon to ask, but do you have room for dessert? This place is treasured for Pannekaker, authentic Norwegian pancakes. They're thin and sweet like French crepes."

"I loved the ones in Paris. Strawberry would be divine."

"Jordbær. You've got it."

She wasn't sure how she finished them, but licked every morsel of whipped cream off her spoon. Stefan's phone rang with a call and Maya joked, "Should have kept them turned off."

He grimaced. "Sorry, it's from Biko, my Ebola colleague—I need to see how he's doing." He stepped away to the waterfront.

Maya studied Stefan's body language. She prayed that Biko's health hadn't taken a turn for the worse, an unfortunate consequence of their Guinea work.

When Stefan returned to the table, she asked, "Everything okay?"

Using his hand, he shaded his eyes from the sun, his expression unclear. "Not exactly. There's a new Ebola death in Nigeria—a gorilla poacher. WHO wants me and Biko back in the national park we visited in April. They figure it's about time we determine if there's an animal origin for this outbreak."

Maya's mouth dropped open. With no new cases, she'd assumed that Ebola was behind them.

Stefan sat down on the chair next to her. "And they asked for my recommendation on a public health veterinarian to help us out."

SIXTY-THREE

A huge white bird with an orange bill and black face floated on the placid surface of the Oslofjord near the outdoor food court. Maya last saw a Mute Swan in Central Park Lake while investigating Ebola in New York. Those birds sure traveled. And once again, Stefan wanted Maya to fly off to a new country, adding another stamp to her passport.

She put her napkin on her plate. Her psychiatrist had emphasized listening to her body when she was anxious, so she reinterpreted each symptom as normal, not imminent death. The slight churning of her stomach might reflect fullness from that final bite of strawberry pancake. Her heart pounded—excitement or worry? Perhaps some of both. Her thoughts raced.

How quickly would they need to go? Would she have time to get vaccinated? Was this another of Stefan's ill-planned boondoggles?

But their time in Thailand was a fabulous learning experience and her blood-drawing prowess had been valuable. She combined an analytic mind with the competent hands of a clinician. And if sudden swerves in her life warred with her desire to plan, she should have chosen another line of work.

"It's less than two months since you became infected," she said, "and neither you or Biko is 100% recovered. Surely WHO has other experts to lead an animal investigation."

Like a nervous twitch, Stefan jangled the keys in his pants pocket. "Our experience is why they want us. Jan Kreischer was the first case that we know of after we visited the national park. We were with Jan when he found the gorilla and Biko is familiar with the park from previous trips."

His answer made sense, plus he and Biko should be immune against new infection. "But why me? WHO must have African veterinarians. Not that it doesn't sound intriguing."

He leaned forward, invading her personal space, his competitive-swimmer's torso even more imposing. "I'm unaware of another veterinary epidemiologist with your skills and experience. I have no proficiency in handling primates, whereas you just finished an investigation of Ebola in macaques."

Her colleague was convincing. The more she thought about it, the more she wanted to leap in. No specific job opportunities or personal agenda to be interrupted, unlike Stefan.

"Maybe you should stay here in Oslo," Maya said. "From what you've told me, your time away caused your rift with Kondrat as much as your small chance of spreading Ebola."

He shrank back in his seat, expression like a disgruntled child. "It's not like he welcomed me back with open arms."

She agreed—no matter her fondness for Kondrat, he was unreasonable. For a few more months, they could wear condoms, or abstain from sex, while maintaining a loving relationship in their home. Kondrat's reaction felt like emotional blackmail.

Maya made her decision. "If you're going, I am too. Our third major disease outbreak together." At least with *Borrelia* and coronavirus, she'd spent some days considering his invitation. Not this time.

The next afternoon, Maya shifted restlessly in the clinic chair. Stefan had arranged for her Ebola vaccine, and staff would review any other travel requirements or recommendations. Families jammed the waiting room in the summer season, and some kids teared up as they awaited their shots.

She decided to text Faye while killing time. A Nordic noir novel she borrowed from Kondrat rested on her lap but she was too revved up to concentrate. **<Headed to Africa—checking out Ebola in animals. You have more experience there—want to go in my place? ☺ >**

Her phone pinged with Faye's immediate response. **<No shit! Call me.>**

Maya let the desk clerk know she'd be in the foyer, then stepped through the first set of glass doors as she clicked on Faye's number. "Hi Faye, how is Taylor doing today?"

"Intermittent vomiting and a bloody nose. No evidence of renal failure or pulmonary edema, but some drowsiness that could be a first sign of cerebral involvement."

"Sounds alarming." Manolo's COVID symptoms came on while she was unconscious with her own infection, so she had no experience with a partner's severe illness. Absolutely terrifying.

"They kept Taylor hospitalized overnight. The blood film shows more than two percent parasitemia, so they want to be aggressive with treatment. Once the vomiting is under control, they'll switch from IV injections to pills."

"God, Faye, you must be worried sick. I'm in a travel clinic right now and they'll include malaria prophylaxis." She carried the phone as she walked back inside. "Just a sec, Faye." After verifying they still weren't ready for her, she headed back to the foyer.

"Sorry about that—checking on my appointment."

Faye's tone changed from morose to enthusiastic. "An Ebola animal investigation—what's the game plan?"

"Not sure yet. Stefan's developing our itinerary with his WHO colleagues. You might be a better veterinarian for the team, with your recent Ebola experience in Ghana and your tackling Arabian camels ten years ago."

Faye laughed. "Yeah, you helped me track people exposed to our MERS case while you were still in vet school."

Unsure whether to encourage Faye's interest in the Ebola field work, Maya felt duty-bound to loop her in. She couldn't recall any major career-related decisions she'd made without Faye's insights.

She envisioned tiny Faye browbeating Olympic athlete-built Stefan. "You and Stefan would butt heads, so I'm not leaning on you to take my place." Not that Maya was a pushover for Stefan's choices, but age and experience dynamics were always in play.

"This is an exciting opportunity," Faye said. "Don't pass it up. Long days interviewing and vaccinating in Ghana don't compare with mountain field work. My body's not up to that anymore. Besides, I can't leave Taylor during this medical crisis, and Suffolk County is trying to rope me into some EEE deaths in horses."

"Of course, you need to be in New York."

"Don't forget yellow fever vaccine. Nigeria had confirmed cases last year, and some probable ones this year."

"I can imagine mosquito-borne diseases are fresh in your mind after Taylor's malaria infection. But I'm already vaccinated against YF. Got it before my previous work with Stefan."

She was up-to-date on all the childhood and adolescent vaccines, including rabies for her job as a veterinarian. For the *Borrelia* trip, she'd arranged vaccines for cholera, Japanese encephalitis, and typhoid. Long-time campers or hikers in Scandinavian forests risked tickborne encephalitis, but if they decided to do anything like that when back in Norway, she'd get the vaccine then.

Flu vaccination in the fall—always on her calendar. With each COVID booster, she thanked the pharmacist, memories of her pre-vaccine COVID coma and the deaths of Manolo and their baby running through her like hot lava.

"Listen, kiddo," Faye said, "I need to check on Taylor's progress. Keep me posted on your adventures. You know with my aching joints and porous brain, I live vicariously through you."

"I don't think you've been put out to pasture, Faye."

"Good, I might have an outbreak or two still in me." Faye suddenly became silent, and Maya wondered if they'd been cut off.

"I realize Stefan has been working in West Africa for a number of weeks," Faye finally said, "but Taylor getting jailed is a warning to take their different laws seriously."

"What do you mean?"

"Stefan being gay—I don't know how that would be received in Nigeria."

Maya hadn't thought about it, although perhaps she should have after hearing about Taylor's and Faye's ordeal in Ghana. "But Stefan's not in a relationship with me, and he's not traveling with Kondrat." Plus neither of them were African—perhaps the authorities would be less suspecting, or the public less affronted, if they didn't present as a biracial couple. Maya got the impression that some Africans thought of Asians as white.

"I'll mention it to Stefan, but he's an experienced WHO physician who has traveled the world. He didn't tell me about any previous problems. I'll text when I have more details about our trip. Give Taylor my regards."

"Will do. Let's be careful out there."

Maya smirked at the *Hill Street Blues* reference. Too young to have seen the cop show during its initial run in the eighties, she'd viewed a handful of streaming episodes. Her predilection for old movies and TV allowed her to catch most of Faye's obscure cultural observations.

"You know how cautious I am," she answered. "WHO is planning a rigorous scientific study. I'm sure we'll have no problems."

SIXTY-FOUR

Eleven days later, seated next to Stefan in the air-conditioned car sent by the Nigerian government, Maya answered Mark's **<Good luck, stay safe>** text with a quick **<Thanks>**, then she turned off her phone. She eagerly took in the wide, orderly avenues of Abuja, the capital city.

"Look at that," she exclaimed when they passed a huge edifice glowing in the morning sun. A gold dome topped a rectangular building with four narrow pillars at its corners, soaring into the sky.

The driver glanced back. "The National Mosque."

"Reminds me of the Conakry Grand Mosque," Stefan said, "but this one is more ethereal. I like it."

"It is open to the non-Muslim public," the driver added, "except for prayer time."

"I don't think we'll be here long enough to play tourist." Stefan turned to Maya. "Sorry about that."

During their visit to Morocco's mausoleum of the kings on the *Borrelia* trip, their local hosts squeezed in other cultural highlights. The married couple had offered welcome advice about juggling work and a personal life. But Maya lost touch with them and she had no family to require that balance. A wash of sadness flooded her veins.

Stefan gave up more by returning to West Africa, but Kondrat had looked resigned rather than angry when getting the news. "Go ahead, get that damned virus out of your system," he said. "When you come home, maybe we can put it all behind us." Paula had studied Africa in school and begged for a stuffed animal, preferably one of the big cats.

The government vehicle pulled up to the multistory Federal Ministry of Health, then the driver hopped out to open their doors. "This building, and the entire Federal Secretariat Complex, was completed in the 1980s," he said, "in preparation for Abuja taking over from Lagos as the capital city in 1991."

As they showed their identification inside the front door, Maya asked, "Why isn't it Lagos?"

"Too big, crowded, and vulnerable to rising sea levels," the driver answered. "For a modern country, we wanted a modern capital city." He dropped them off at a conference room, where Stefan's expression brightened at the glimpse of an African, similar in age and height to Maya. The young man with a smooth, shaved head flashed an easy smile and shook Stefan's hand.

"I'm pleased to see you doing better," Stefan said. "It must be from the tender ministrations of this little lady." He gestured to a girl who looked like a teenager and didn't clear five feet.

"Biko and Nneka," he continued, "this is Maya Maguire, my favorite veterinarian." Turning to Maya, he added, "You remember I talked endlessly about these devoted siblings."

Maya nodded. "I'm happy to work with all of you on this investigation." When her phone rang, she excused herself to the hall.

The call was from Lila Becker, the Arizona State Epidemiologist who'd done her CDC training in California at the same time as Maya in New Mexico.

"Hi, Maya, are you in Nigeria already?"

"I'm in Abuja, the capital city." She guestimated the time in Phoenix as sometime after midnight. "What are you doing awake at this hour?"

"Hantavirus has kept us busy. This call is the final item on my checklist before I turn in. Unfortunately, it's bad news. UC-Davis can't spare staff to help you."

Lila had been intrigued with Maya's new disease hunt. She'd promised to check in with a friend at the vet school who'd done research on bat viruses in the Congo Basin. Maya herself had Zoomed with a veterinarian at Colorado State University who had similar experience. He supported the investigation goals but could offer no resources despite Maya being a fellow CSU vet school graduate. With the pandemic not officially over, many groups still focused on coronavirus work.

"Don't worry, Lila, I appreciate your checking. We're meeting with multiple groups today and might generate additional interest."

Maya realized that seeking the outbreak origin would be like looking for a needle in a haystack, but she didn't care. Since the call from Biko, the team had reviewed the scientific literature nonstop, consulted with experts worldwide, and planned their attack. She was torn between her commitment to determine Ebola's origin and her reservations about pulling it off unless they got more support. However, no matter the size of their expedition, the hunt would be thrilling.

SIXTY-FIVE

Biko studied the public health leaders seated around the conference table. His presentation to the university about the Ebola outbreak had been daunting, but informational only. This talk was more consequential. He nodded to an older, stately woman representing the Africa CDC. Next to her sat a young American man from the Carter Center, considering support for Ebola control in addition to their programs on parasites like Guinea worm and river blindness.

"Let's get started, Dr. Okeke." Vazir Shah, Biko's WHO supervisor, dimmed the room lights with the wall switch.

Biko's review of the outbreak rolled off his tongue. He'd repeatedly practiced with Nneka and took into account Dr. Shah's suggestions from last time. The final slides were about the most recent case, a poacher from Calabar, capital of Cross River State. He and Nneka had grown up in Odukpani, a small town near there.

Jamal Uka. Biko didn't release the patient's name, although he identified with him. Like Biko, Jamal was an Igbo man in his mid-to-late twenties. During the height of the Atlantic slave trade in the 17th to 19th centuries, the Igbo were subject to raids by more powerful tribes in the region. The sense of being underdogs carried down through the generations. From what Biko learned, they each had a grandfather who died battling the Nigerian navy in the 1967 Biafran independence movement.

Biko's father had been the manager for a western-chain hotel and encouraged his children's college education. Without similar family ties, Jamal had done maintenance at a local resort, which closed and fell into disrepair during COVID. Then he became a groundskeeper at a nature reserve for highly endangered drill monkeys, related to baboons and mandrills. A couple of the drills and orphaned chimpanzees had been killed and desecrated, some body parts missing, but no one was charged with the crime.

For the presentation, Biko focused first on Jamal's clinical outcome and presumed exposure. "Based on an interview with a coworker, the patient was ill for a few days before he was found in a Calabar alley. At the hospital, he was diagnosed with hypovolemic shock due to loss of fluid from oral bleeding and severe diarrhea."

Thinking of his own infection and Stefan's, he added, "Perhaps he could have survived with support if he had come to the attention of the medical system sooner."

His slides switched from patient information to a silverback male gorilla. "These beautiful animals are richly significant in our culture. Gorillas are native only to Africa, although maintained in zoos worldwide."

The next photo showed a ceramic ashtray formed like a gorilla's hand, a half-smoked cigarette leaning on the edge. "These are common tourist souvenirs." Then he followed up with a wooden ashtray in the shape of a gorilla head.

His final slide displayed a single gorilla hand, sawed off its body. It was dried out with the leathered palm facing upward, large fingers curled toward the middle. "Unfortunately, this is the gorilla ashtray found in the patient's apartment. It was too desiccated to yield Ebola virus in testing. Park rangers have not yet located any more of the carcass. The patient's coworkers said he had more money recently, so we suspect the second hand was already sold."

Deep sighs, ducked eyes, and crossed arms from the attendees. The image was likely familiar to the mostly African audience, but few could see such an aberrance again without being affected.

He tried to relieve the tension with a joke. "One more reason to stop smoking." Only Stefan's face indicated a tiny smile. Biko adjusted his glasses and his legs weakened as he feared the reaction of higher-level staff. Time to wind things up.

"In conclusion, the patient's interaction with gorillas is a possible source of his Ebola exposure. However, we have no proof.

After lunch, Dr. Maguire will present in detail the animal aspects, a key component of this investigation. Then Dr. Duda, who was a major contributor to my slide set, will share information about Ebola trends."

In case there were questions related to specific slides, he left the projector on. The discussion continued for an hour, serious and urgent in the dim room haunted by the appalling image of the gorilla hand ashtray.

SIXTY-SIX

Stefan leaned back in his chair and eyed the dull green hue of Abuja's Jabi Lake. Hard to breathe with the suffocating humidity. He missed Oslo's breezes from the fjord. A thick layer of clouds blocked the relentless African sun and dampened the temperature.

Maya had argued for a quicker lunch but Stefan supported Dr. Shah's choice of the lakeside restaurant as an opportunity for decompression and diplomacy. Nneka, unfamiliar with the glad-handing necessities of international planning, was quiet.

He turned to Dr. Shah. "Will we have enough laboratory resources?"

Dr. Shah paused to swallow a mouthful of pineapple rice, then answered. "Let me worry about that."

Stefan picked at his chicken shawarma. He didn't want to rock the boat but needed clarification. "I hope we don't collect specimens that are thrown away due to lack of capacity."

His supervisor gave a taut smile. "If you check in with me daily, I'll make sure everything is coordinated."

Biko leaned over from across the table. "Dr. Shah, will you stay here in Nigeria or return to your office in Brazzaville?"

"Neither—Ghana has Marburg virus disease, the first cases ever reported there. Two farm workers—both dead."

Maya fixed Dr. Shah with a look of surprise. "High death rate, similar to Ebola. Infection is from exposure to Egyptian rousette bats and nonhuman primates."

Stefan recalled that Marburg spread through semen like Ebola, and shuddered at the unpleasant reminder of his possible risk to Kondrat.

The two women paused between bites of a shared pizza, concern on their faces. "I never heard of Marburg in Nigeria," Nneka said.

Maya chimed in. "Has a vaccine been approved, like for Ebola?"

Stefan shook his head. "No vaccine, and cases have been reported from multiple African nations."

Dr. Shah added, "People from other countries have been infected through travel or lab accidents."

"Excuse me, I have to make a call." Maya grabbed her phone and stepped away to the grass. Stefan wondered why she was being so rude.

Dr. Shah redirected the conversation to personal matters, inquiring about Stefan's and Biko's health. Although Stefan, like Maya, tended toward impatience when investigation decisions loomed, he had cultivated a greater appreciation of social conventions.

He encouraged Dr. Shah to share photos and stories of his children. One daughter worked for USAID on HIV prevention in Ethiopia.

"My physician friend from New York just returned from Ghana and was diagnosed with malaria," Maya reported as she rejoined the group. "I needed to confirm that Taylor was also evaluated for Marburg."

Stefan was relieved that Maya could once again concentrate on their expedition. He shared her dedication to their professional and personal lives, sometimes in that order, but she tended to obsess too much.

Suddenly, the skies opened up with a dreary drizzle. Dr. Shah paid the lunch bill, then called his limo driver for the ride to the Ministry of Health.

Back in the conference room, Maya swallowed as all eyes swung to her. Intimidated by the knowledge that their investigation rested on her review of Ebola animal issues, she nonetheless plunged ahead.

"Forgive me if I repeat anything you already know. Some of these animal aspects may be new because your agencies emphasize human health." She was glad they decided to discuss the topic around the table—standing up behind a podium always made her nervous.

"We have strong circumstantial evidence, but no definitive proof, that bats are the reservoir species. Here are photos for three of the implicated species."

She removed the lens cover from the projector at her side. "Hammer-headed bat, Franquet's epauletted fruit bat, and the little collared fruit bat. Eating meat from infected bats can cause infection, although cooking kills the virus. When people are infected by bats, it's more often during the butchering process."

She showed another bat species. "This is a greater long-fingered bat, a species that eats insects. One-fifth of the genome for Ebola Zaire, which caused our outbreak, was isolated from an oral swab of this species in Liberia. Other types of Ebola have been found in different insectivorous bat species."

The USAID representative straightened his tie and spoke up with a bragging tone. "As part of our EPT program—that's Emerging Pandemic Threats—we funded the University of California's PREDICT project to collect evidence related to zoonotic diseases and wildlife."

Dr. Shah nodded. "Impressive results—hundreds of novel viruses detected, personnel trained, lab enhancements."

Maya knew that USAID stopped support for that program in 2020. To avoid the man's embarrassment, she didn't bring it up.

"We'd like to build on that initial wonderful work funded by USAID," Maya said. "We'll focus on both fructivorous and insectivorous bat species for sampling. However, we need to consider other species with potential infection, including bush pigs, rodents, porcupines, and forest-dwelling antelope. Infected NHPs—nonhuman primates—can include gorillas and chimpanzees. Based on previous studies, it's worth assessing domestic animals like pigs, guinea pigs, goats, horses, and dogs. Birds also have several viruses similar to Ebola."

"How about feline species?" Nneka asked. "In Nigeria, we

have lions, leopards, servals, caracals, and the African wildcat. They might feed on infected bats in the caves."

"Good thinking," Maya said. "Could our budget include camera traps to capture that?"

"Don't get ahead of yourself," Dr. Shah interrupted, and the other agency reps nodded. "Our pimary targets are gorillas. This may have started because of someone's ill-planned jaunt to see them in the national park."

Maya blanched at his terse remark and the sheepish looks on Stefan's and Biko's faces. Uncertain what to say, she paused in the silent but electric room, waiting to see how they'd respond.

SIXTY-SEVEN

At Dr. Shah's heavy hint that Stefan and Biko started the Ebola outbreak, the individuals around the table ossified like mounds in a termite castle. His previous kind inquiries about Biko's and Stefan's health were long forgotten. Not for the first time, Biko blamed himself for agreeing to the gorilla tour two months earlier. Even worse, Nneka narrowed her eyes, clenched her hands, and jumped in.

"My brother knows I'm a more experienced guide than he is. He should have asked me to lead his gorilla trip. I never would have allowed Dr. Kreischer to get so close to a dead animal, unprotected."

Biko's jaw dropped. The May excursion was a prickly topic and they rarely spoke about it. Clearly his baby sister had an artesian well of resentment that, at this moment, gushed to the surface.

Even worse, she continued, adopting a power beam of a smile directed at his supervisor. "Thankfully, Dr. Shah invited me to coordinate the logistics of this research trip. I promise to bring everyone home safely."

Biko had been the one to suggest his sister as their guide, and Dr. Shah had approved it. Now she implied the arrangements were made without him. It was hard to stay upset at such an appealing little sprite who nursed him back to health, his only living relative, but she was pushing it. Or perhaps she had learned quickly about the benefits of buttering up the big boss.

Before he could respond to his sister's dig, Maya said, "Of course we'll prioritize the gorillas. However, bats are believed to be the reservoir species, not NHPs, and I have experience collecting serum specimens from them."

Stefan followed Maya's lead on emphasizing the research. "Our work plan will be as ambitious as the support WHO gets from other agencies."

Dr. Shah eyed those in the room. "Why don't we—"

"Let me clarify the stakes," Stefan interjected. "Climate factors like temperature and rainfall may change Ebola risk. Although rising temperatures will decrease viral stability outside of the body, changes in bat migration may lead to increased interaction with humans."

Maya looked down at her notes. "Nigeria is a key area for future epidemics, with the potential for many small outbreaks. By 2070, it's possible there will be a 3.2-fold increase in animal-to-human spillovers of Ebola, with a 1.63-fold higher likelihood of epidemics."

Stefan continued. "Another study indicated a potential 29% increased risk for Ebola in Nigeria."

Biko studied Dr. Shah, who appeared unperturbed by the interruption. He decided to join the chorus. "Climate change is already causing migration of human populations, which can increase the introduction of Ebola virus to other parts of the world."

The Carter Center representative tapped his pen on the table. "I'm not a climate denier so I won't dispute your data. However, our mission emphasizes practical steps to improve public health. For example, we fund the SAFE program for trachoma prevention."

The woman from Africa CDC adjusted her turban and frowned. "Investigation of the animal origin for Ebola is basic science, with insufficient direct relevance to public health protection."

Biko tended to agree with her, but needed to get the discussion refocused on what was feasible at this point. "Dr. Duda and I admit that our trek to the national park was ill-planned and foolish."

He glanced over to see if Stefan would object. "As the Nigerian native among the three WHO staff on the trip, I bear the greatest responsibility. Dr. Kreischer is our index case—the first confirmed illness in the Conakry-centered outbreak. Currently, we have nothing definitive linking his death to the gorillas."

"That's right," Stefan added. "And that's the purpose of our proposed expedition. If popular animals like gorillas are infected, management of gorilla tours should be reconsidered."

Maya leaned forward. "I'd still argue for bat testing because they are likely to be the ultimate source. If we find sufficient evidence, we could consider vaccination of valuable animals like the gorillas."

Dr. Shah shook his head. "I'm aware of no studies justifying such an effort."

"No practical applications yet," Maya said, "but injecting chimps or squirting the vaccine into their mouths caused them to develop antibodies."

"The immune system is more complex than simply the antibody response," Dr. Shah said. "We should table that discussion for now. First, we need to learn how many NHPs are infected."

Biko tried to get them back on task. "If I'm hearing everyone correctly, the other agencies aren't interested in this particular Ebola investigation at this point. So our team is the four of us." He looked around at Stefan, Maya, and Nneka.

Nneka was the only one who didn't appear to agree. In fact, she stood up and waved her hand. "We can't pull this off without protection. At least 50 Nigerian park rangers have been killed in the line of duty since 1991. Wild animals and poachers—don't forget Jamal Uka. When arrested before he died from Ebola, he had an assault rifle. WHO must keep us safe."

Biko was humiliated by her outburst, especially naming the patient. Her paranoia was understandable after her kidnapping last year, but Boko Haram was entrenched further north. Although he had encouraged her earning money as their paid guide for the WHO research, she was reaching beyond her level of expertise and authority.

Looking around at faces shocked by the nagging voice and finger of a nineteen-year-old, he tugged his sister down to her chair. Less than a year with WHO, he felt vulnerable. The men's expressions appeared to question Nneka's role on the project—at least, that's how Biko interpreted them. But they all remained silent, condemning with their eyes.

Maya broke the tension. "I agree with Nneka. As our local coordinator in the national park, she must look out for us. Ebola has caused too much suffering already. Dr. Shah, can we prioritize a driver and guard to make sure everything goes as intended?"

Dr. Shah hesitated, then nodded his approval.

SIXTY-EIGHT

A week later, local arrangements almost completed, Maya got up to answer the pre-arranged knock … knock … knock/knock signal. Opening the door of a hostel room she shared with Nneka at the University of Calabar, she was happy to see Stefan and Biko. "The Malabresses welcome you to our humble abode. That's what they call the female students here."

Nneka laughed and waved from an uncomfortable wooden chair, pulling on her tennis shoes. She looked every inch like a college student on a summer break. Multicolored ribbon in her Bantu knots, bamboo hoop earrings, a sleeveless flowered shirt, and lime green shorts. Maya hoped that Biko would keep any comments about his sister's modern outfit to himself.

When getting dressed this morning, Nneka had told Maya that she was rebelling. With the country's turn toward more religiosity among many groups, universities were increasingly banning 'unacceptable' clothing and hair. But the students were gone and there were few employees to enforce any standards.

Stefan stared out the small window streaked with grimy dust. The walkway for the floor above prevented the daily rains from washing it clean. "Every time I see this dorm room, I feel guilty."

Nneka stepped closer to the door. She nodded to Stefan and hugged her brother. "Don't remind me of the splendid accommodations for you male medical Malabites."

"When I was an undergraduate," Biko said, "I never lived on campus. I wish our childhood home in Odukpani had not burned down. We could have all stayed there."

"I am tired of you blaming me for that." Nneka's voice was

choked and her eyes misted, but not a single tear leaked to her cheeks.

Biko's tone and expression settled. "Not blaming, just missing what we used to have."

Maya wondered how much of their brother-sister banter reflected genuine resentment. In an intense week of trip preparation, she and Nneka had bonded. Neither of them had sisters, so they welcomed the close female companionship.

Nneka had revealed she was angry with Biko about his behavior during the planning meeting, but Maya had been dismayed by both of them. Of course, Nneka was only nineteen, and inexperienced.

Maya chalked up Biko's attitude to the male-dominated culture. Even if he was basically a good person, he'd grown up with men assuming leadership, whereas women were considered weak and vulnerable.

Nneka's guilt over the loss of their home remained unabated. She'd rented it out during her first year at college to a man later identified as a gang leader for the Skolombo Boys. Because of their thievery, the group got their name from the Jamaican slang "Skolo" which meant "to obtain." A fearful public called them psychopaths. The gangs recruited kids with disabilities, branded as witches or wizards, who'd been kicked out of their homes.

Maya remembered Brandon, Dave Schwartz's little brother, expelled from the polygamist community for smoking. Boys on their own at a young age invariably fell into trouble, which in Nneka's situation left their home a burned-out ruin.

Stefan knocked his knuckles on the wood-framed bunk bed. "It's good luck that Dr. Shah arranged our stay in empty school dorms. All the money we saved on housing went to supplies for the expedition."

Maya shrugged. "No complaints here, even if we are jealous of your better digs." She grinned to soften the jibe. "At least with the students gone for the summer, we don't have two more roommates."

"We're headed off to our lunch with Biko's biology professor," Stefan said.

Biko smiled. "Without his guidance and recommendation, I would never have been accepted to medical school. I cannot wait to see him again."

"Sure it's okay for us to do that without you?" Stefan's forehead wrinkled.

"I would hate to sit through another lunch of medical jargon." Nneka shook her head emphatically.

Maya wondered if Nneka was covering for being made to feel inferior again. She put her arm through Nneka's. "We gals have our own date."

Biko headed for the door. "All right, just be careful. Calabar South is not as safe as it used to be. Is Sinachi available to escort you?"

"He went to the airport for another load of specimen collection kits." Maya would have preferred a younger driver/guard, although Sinachi Wabaranta was solid and strong as a jaguar. Graying at forty-five, he never seemed to tire.

Nneka pushed the two men out to the walkway. "No need to worry. We will walk to a local restaurant near the campus."

Once they were gone, Nneka said, "I have a special place to show you. Later, on our last night in the city, we can see a Nollywood movie."

"Nollywood?"

"Nigeria's film industry, second only to India's Bollywood in size. A modern American woman might be surprised by their sexism. Me and my friends make jokes about them."

Always curious for new cultural experiences, Maya replied, "If we have time, I'm game." It might be nice to take her mind off an incessant worry that they had forgotten something important for their expedition.

They headed west down Mary Slessor Avenue, named after the Scottish missionary who in the late 1800s stopped the superstitious practice of leaving twins out in the bush to die of starvation or to be killed by animals. Maya purchased a bag of chicken wings which she put in her daypack along with two bottles of water. Nneka led her to a bench under a huge old tree in the botanical gardens.

"My father, raising Biko and me alone, sometimes had no place for us when school was closed," Nneka said. "So he dropped us here before going to his hotel job. We both enjoyed spending Saturdays on the nature trails, turning over rocks to find tiny creatures. The one cool place in the city."

She pulled a pair of binoculars from her daypack. "Look, that's one of the rare hornbills."

Maya slipped off her own pack and rested it on the bench between them. She took the binoculars from Nneka and studied the bird in the tree whose bill was shaped like a cow's horn.

"Which one is that?"

"Nigeria has 13 different hornbill species. That's *Ceratogymna elata*, the yellow-casqued hornbill. It's threatened by all the clearcutting and loss of habitat."

Maya's heart was warmed by the dramatic-looking bird, blue leathery skin surrounding its black eye, extending down his throat. The body was a deep, rich brown with a long tail, gray on the underside. Most impressive—the fluffy reddish feathers on its head, like a lion's mane.

"Look up high in the branches for others," Nneka said. "It usually travels in pairs or small groups. Mostly it eats fruit, but sometimes insects."

Maya slowly swept the binoculars from left to right through the canopy while Nneka searched with her naked eyes. A sudden dark shape swooshed between them, then darted away. Maya swung the binoculars down and noticed her daypack missing.

Nneka leapt up for a chase, then froze when a child no older than ten turned, brandishing a knife. A tattered orange dress draped over one shoulder, exposing the other with a large, irregular lesion, so pink it glowed against her black skin. Her hair was pulled into loose Bantu knots like Nneka's, and her feet were bare. Sunken eyes widened as she shouted, "Onye out nsi!"

"Onye ohi yoruba!" Nneka shouted back.

Maya stood to pull her friend back. "Not worth getting hurt."

When the kid limped into the congested street, Maya led Nneka back to their seats. "What did you say to each other?"

"In Igbo, she labeled me a worthless person, literally a poisoner. I called her a Yoruba thief."

Maya was confused by the different Nigerian ethnicities. "How did you know she was Yoruba, especially since she spoke your language?"

"Yoruba are dark, Igbo fair."

The words were spoken with derision. The child hadn't appeared that much darker. She wondered if Nigerians, like some other ethnicities including the Chinese, favored lighter skin. "She wasn't in good shape. Do you think she's on her own?"

Nneka shook her head no. "Remember the Skolombo Boys who torched my family home? Well, this was a Lacasera Girl. They're lured into sex work and robbery during our December carnival, often from rural communities like Odukpani. Once in a gang, they can't get out."

"LaCasera, isn't that one of your popular soft drinks?"

Nneka nodded. "That's the payment a man gives these girls for their services."

Maya gasped at the backstory for the abandoned kids, and trembled at the memory of the flashing blade, wielded by an exploited child who looked ill and drugged. "I lost nothing valuable, just my water bottle and our lunch."

"A good excuse to find a safer place to eat." Nneka pulled Maya to her feet. "I'm sorry that happened. We're lucky she didn't insist on our money."

Maya had never been threatened on previous outbreaks, except for the time her colleague tried to force intimacy in the Grand Canyon, which was long behind her. The theft by a knife-wielding child triggered panicked heart palpitations despite the calm face she showed Nneka. She hadn't worried about herself on this trip—only Stefan after Faye's warning about him being gay.

SIXTY-NINE

At the lunch with Biko's Calabar University professor, the man complimented him on his accomplishments profusely, as if handing out merit badges for scouting achievements. Biko had graduated medical school with honors, served as chief resident during his community health training, then shut down a major Ebola outbreak.

Biko hadn't vanquished the virus without help, but Stefan abstained from claiming any credit. Who didn't want to play the hero when visiting old school haunts?

As they reached the women's hostel in a downpour, Stefan's African-print shirt clung to his chest, although the warm glow of one-too-many Heinekens countered his cool, drenched skin. Biko looked pleasantly buzzed.

Stefan did the coded knock on the door of the hostel room. No reason to let down on security, even after they'd been Maya's and Nneka's only visitors for a week. During summer recess, the dorms were spookily quiet. Despite the absence of earnest or rambunctious undergrad women, their driver still avoided the building that normally forbade men. After Sinachi picked up Dr. Shah's latest supply shipment, they'd be ready to head out into the field tomorrow.

"Did you boys have a good reunion?" Maya asked when opening the door. "Unfortunately, I need you to head out again and help me find a new pack."

Stefan sat on a rickety chair and slicked his hair back out of his eyes. Biko initially perched on Nneka's lower bunk but she yanked him over to another chair, then dabbed at the wet spot on her blanket.

"Ewu." Nneka handed Biko the towel dampened from her effort. He quickly wiped it over his bald head, then combed his fingers through his close-cropped goatee.

Stefan checked for the meaning of her Igbo explective on his phone as Maya returned from the bathroom with a second towel. *Goat.* Oh, it also meant stupid. Stefan hoped the afternoon wouldn't devolve into another of their fraternal spats.

"I'm happy to go shopping," he told Maya when draping her towel over his shoulders. "What happened to your old pack?"

"I got absorbed in bird-watching and it was snatched from my bench in the park."

"That witch was barely school-aged," Nneka blurted, "and she dared to pull a knife on us."

"What?" Biko jumped up, voice at the level of thunder. "How could you be so careless? Maya is your guest—it is your job to keep her safe from those hallucinating gangster kids."

Play peacemaker, second nature in Stefan's work, although less successful at home. "Important thing—everyone's safe." He was dismayed by the incident, but pickpocketing and purse-snatching happened worldwide. Flashing a weapon, especially by a child, was less expected.

He'd never seen Biko drunk before, so maybe that accounted for his overreaction. Protective of his younger sister—predictable. Yelling at her as if the incident was all her fault—not appropriate. Reminded once again of Nigeria's patriarchal culture, he was surprised Biko allowed Nneka on the expedition at all.

"Did you lose anything valuable, Maya?" he asked.

She shook her head no. "I'm always careful to keep important stuff close to my body, covered by my clothes."

"Then no big impact on our research timeline. Should this be reported to the police?"

Biko sighed deeply, appearing to release his emotions. "No, this is considered minor, and they won't bother to follow up."

Stefan agreed. Wiser to get out of town on their scientific work as soon as possible, away from the criminal elements. "Nneka has been fantastic at handling all our arrangements, and she should continue. I prefer that our next rainforest trip works out better than the last one."

All three of his colleagues nodded and the tension wafted away with a light breeze through the open window. Stefan relished brandishing his skills to get his way.

SEVENTY

Maya, wearing only a lap belt, hung onto Stefan's forearm as the Ford F-250 pickup slipped and slid through gashes in the dirt road of Cross River National Park. The windshield wipers created a swift, clacking noise. From the front seat, Nneka directed Sinachi, their driver. Maya, as the smallest of the other three, had squeezed into the uncomfortable middle rear seat, although she didn't weigh that much less than Biko.

Water cascaded down the steep right bank, eroding the roadway and threatening to wash their vehicle down the hillside. She shuddered, remembering the stricken faces in yesterday's newspaper of parents who lost four children to a storm-related landslide in the Calabar outskirts.

On the news this morning as they left the university, the governor of Cross River State warned about a plot among the Hausa/Fulani communities to establish a separate emirate. Research into Ebola origins felt sufficiently daunting without torrential rains triggered by climate change and religious/ethnic differences leading to political instability.

Maya maintained her grip on Stefan. In her mind she composed a text to Mark, even though she couldn't send it until they had cell service again. **<Remember when I was down in the dirt helping your ewe deliver a lamb? Today I'll get even more mucky.>**

She couldn't guess his reply. Maybe he'd write her a new poem—it had been a long time since he'd done that. Or perhaps out of sight, out of mind.

The gears ground like a blender on high as Sinachi tried to force the truck up the rough path, running with a foot of water. He muttered something to Nneka, who turned and translated. "We are stuck."

When investigating anthrax, Maya had been stranded in a vehicle near the Arizona/Mexico border. A scary nighttime rescue by border patrol agents with guns drawn ended the harrowing experience. In Nigeria, they'd be as likely to run into bad guys as law enforcement, so they'd better solve the problem themselves.

Sinachi kept the engine going and ordered Stefan out to grab the winch. He tripped while pulling the cable, then hooked it to a tree strap. Barely visible in the mist and covered with mud, he appeared like a character from *The Walking Dead* as he windmilled his arm, urging Sinachi on.

The tires struggled to gain purchase. The gears screeched, rivaling the winch in discord. Maya, never fond of loud noises, stuck her fingers in her ears. They made unbearably slow progress, but the truck crept up the road. Without warning, the hillside let go. A river of dirt and debris swept under them. The vehicle slipped backward and the cable snapped away at the tree, its loose end flailing at high-speed toward the windshield.

Everyone ducked and the cable smacked the hood with a bang. "Holy cow, that was close. You guys okay?" Maya asked Nneka, whose head angled beneath the dash with her body still constrained by the seatbelt.

Nneka's voice was shaky. "Yes, thank God."

Sinachi lowered his window and Stefan slid down to the truck. "I'm so sorry. The shock load separated the cable from its hook."

Biko and Sinachi conferred in Igbo. Maya was frustrated that she wasn't in the loop. Then Biko reached behind their seat for rain gear.

"Should have thought of that before I hopped out," Stefan said.

Biko translated Sinachi's instructions. "We need wood in front of and behind the tires to drive out of the gully."

For a half-hour, they exhausted themselves laying out a platform of broken branches, until Sinachi indicated he would give it a try. Stefan and Biko each put a shoulder to the back of the truck. Maya and Nneka, drenched on the sidelines, offered to push on the frame through the front windows, but Biko ordered them to stay back.

Expletives in Igbo, Norwegian, and English forced the vehicle forward until the worst of the deep potholes were behind them. They looked like hippos immersed in a mud bog, and Sinachi waved them inside.

One leg of Stefan's pants was different, reddish. "Let me see that," Maya ordered.

He tugged up the bottom to expose a six-inch area of scraped skin below his knee, bleeding profusely.

"Why in hell didn't you say something about that earlier?" She pivoted for the first aid kit.

"Guess I had more on my mind. Let's keep going. I want to get to our campsite before dark."

Biko traded seats with Maya, moving into the middle so he could clean Stefan's wound and bandage it as they bumped along. With tires struggling to gain purchase in the waterlogged road, the truck still shimmied but didn't get stuck again. Close to the Cross River, they parked and unloaded their gear.

"I'm glad we're starting with the small mammal trapping," Maya said. "That will give us time to hear back from tour groups if they've spotted any gorillas."

Sinachi called Nneka and Biko into a huddle. Then they joined Stefan and Maya, who'd been setting up separate tents for the men and women.

"It is not safe to continue without a winch," Nneka said. "Sinachi will return to Calabar and get it fixed."

Stefan, ruddy and sweating, ran his fingers through sloppy hair. "He'll be in big trouble if he's alone and gets stuck again. Maybe I should go too."

Maya's body felt heavy, perhaps from exhaustion but more likely nerves. On the other side of the river was Cameroon, with violent border conflicts over oil reserves in the Bakassi Peninsula.

"If you think that's best …" Concerned about the risk to both groups if they split up, Maya's tone was discouraging.

Nneka wrapped her arm around Maya's waist. "Biko and I have camped in this park. You will be safe with us."

Maya glanced at Sinachi's rifle mounted on the rear window. As far as she knew, he was the only one who had experience with firearms.

"All right, Stefan," Maya said. "Once the gear's unloaded, you should get going to reach Calabar before dark. And we need to set our traps."

They didn't stop for lunch but kept emptying the eight-foot truck bed. Nneka passed out snack bars as they waved goodbye to Sinachi and Stefan.

Crouching close to the ground, Nneka picked out trails in the undergrowth that looked favorable for their prey. Biko carried the larger collapsed live traps to each location before setting them up, while the women wrangled the smaller ones. They spaced out the cages so a captured animal's cries wouldn't scare off others.

For bait, Nneka mashed berries onto a piece of paper. She placed it in the opposite end from the open door which automatically closed when an animal stepped inside, capturing it unharmed. For the smaller cages, they used commercial rodent food.

Sunlight filtered low through the thick canopy of leaves as they completed the setup for twenty cages. Nneka led Maya to a small cove at the side of the river, leaving Biko at the camp to heat an ofe okra soup over the firepit. In deference to the Okeke family's conservative Christian faith, Maya followed Nneka's lead and left on her underwear.

"This is the best bath I've ever had." Maya felt embarrassed by the keloid scar on her upper right leg from the childhood car/bike accident, but Nneka also had one on her back. Dark, thick scars weren't unusual for persons of color.

They scrubbed dirt out of their clothes against rocks rimming the pool and put them on again. Biko took his turn cleaning up while Nneka finished cooking. After a quick dinner, they settled into their sleeping bags, Maya comforted by Nneka's presence in their shared tent.

She dozed off, then startled awake at an abrupt rustling of leaves outside. Tempted to awaken Nneka and Biko in case someone needed to do something, she decided against making anyone else lose sleep and tamped down her rapid breathing. A leopard would be noisier, and uninterested in them. Fingers crossed that it was only a small, benign animal, Maya willed herself to sleep again.

SEVENTY-ONE

A symphony of bird song woke them at dawn. Steamy heat hugged the riverbed and threatened a scorching day. Biko passed out hard-boiled eggs from the ice chest to Nneka and Maya for their brief breakfast.

Still irritated by his sister's irresponsible visit to the botanical gardens, resulting in her and Maya being accosted, he nevertheless recognized he should support Nneka's independence. Calabar used to be their home turf, and she was comfortable on her own after their father died and Biko was in Lagos for his residency training.

Screeching from a Spanish cedar drew their eyes up to a family of Preuss' red colobus monkeys. "Wow, they're beautiful," Maya said. "Maybe that's what I heard outside the tent last night."

Biko admired their long red tails, limbs, and cheeks, contrasting with black heads and backs sprinkled with orange.

"Remember mona monkeys at my conservation centre?" Nneka snapped photos with her old Canon camera, inherited from their father. "No wildlife like this in America."

Maya laughed. "You're right, this is heaven for a veterinarian."

With Nigeria's richness of flora, fauna, and culture, Biko didn't envision living anywhere else. WHO work could take him on short visits to other nations, but at some point he'd like to buy a modern home on the outskirts of Calabar near the national park.

He'd spent too many years away from home during medical school, internship, and residency, amassing considerable debt. After her kidnapping and his almost fatal case of Ebola, he never wanted to leave Nneka alone again.

"Let's get going," Maya said. "We can't keep the animals caged up in this heat." She donned a pack filled with sedation drugs and syringes, Nneka carried the specimen collection kits, and Biko transported the gear to measure each animal's size.

Their pants legs were soon wet from foliage soaked by yesterday's storm. Biko tread carefully to avoid slipping. He felt fine, other than occasional bouts of dizziness. It would not be advisable to get injured so far from help when Stefan and Sinachi were gone with the vehicle.

He stopped to catch his breath and checked his phone. No signal. Nneka should have chosen a less remote area for their first collection.

"We got one!" Maya sounded like she'd won the lottery. "What is it?"

"*Dasymys rufulus*, the West African shaggy rat," Nneka answered.

Biko had never seen one before. Its dense brownish fur was tinged with red. The animal's small ears were alert and its tiny nose wriggled as it sniffed for signals about the huge people.

Nneka snapped photos for study documentation and her own digital library. Then Maya asked, "Biko, can you make some movements close to the other side of the trap? That will back it up toward me." Wearing a mask, gloves, and disposable gown, she filled a syringe with sedative and injected it in the rat's back leg through the cage wires.

"Well, that was easier than expected," she said as the animal collapsed in sleep. "I based the dose on rodents we monitor for our plague and hantavirus work in New Mexico."

Nneka's experience as a wildlife guide didn't extend to capturing them, so Biko donned his own PPE to serve as the wildlife handler. Unlike Nneka, he was used to wearing it in the heat after all the Ebola work in Guinea, although never for animal sampling. He pulled the rat out and laid it on the cage top.

Maya cleaned the tail with disinfectant. "Biko, observe its respirations and let me know if it tries to wake up. I need to hold the tail for a moment to get it warm and dilate the lateral vein."

On her first try, she got a drop of blood to leak onto a piece of filter paper. She handed it to Nneka. "Put this in a test tube labeled with the species, date, location and the same number as on this paper. We can keep it at room temperature for up to a month without any decrease in antibody titer."

Maya held the tail to stop the bleeding, then draped the rat in a cloth sling while Biko dangled the scale. He read the weight to Nneka who added it to her notebook with the other data, along with the animal's length that he and Maya measured.

"I got the GPS reading," Nneka bragged, teasing her brother about his constant checking for a phone signal that stubbornly remained at zero.

Biko was confused. Didn't both systems use satellites? There must be something different, but he wasn't that kind of scientist.

"Too bad we can't take a larger amount of blood to clot and centrifuge," he said.

Maya removed a glove to brush hair out of her eyes, her forehead already beaded with sweat. "Yeah, without reliable refrigeration and rapid transport to the lab, we can't pull that off." Once again, she wondered about Sinachi and Stefan taking off for winch repair. But at least they could pick up more ice for the food chest, even though it melted rapidly in the heat.

Biko placed the rat belly-down on the ground, counting on it to wake up soon and scamper to safety. Maya had warned them that the procedures weren't without risk to the animals. They could die of stress in the cage, or she could misestimate the sedation dose. At least with the filter paper technique, the animals wouldn't lose too much blood, jeopardizing their health.

This guy, more appealing than the lab rats he'd seen, didn't want to recover. Maya also appeared worried. "If we were in a lab, the animals can be trained to accept a tail vein stick through the wires without sedation."

At that moment, the rat shook itself and darted away into the bushes.

"Thank goodness." Biko smiled at Maya and glanced over to a beaming Nneka.

"I hope they all go that well," Maya said. "We'd better move onto the next one. If every one of our twenty traps is full, we have many hours of work, and it's getting hotter by the minute."

Biko silently prayed for some empty cages, even if it would impact their study results. Otherwise, the sun might do in some animals, and him too.

SEVENTY-TWO

The crested porcupine was the cutest, and Maya allowed Nneka a couple of minutes for numerous photos. Its quills, striped black-and-white like a zebra, extended from its head all the way to the tail.

Maya handed a piece of cloth to Biko—the material might be thick enough to protect them from flying quills. He stepped away when the animal vibrated its tail with a snake-like rattle.

"I need these hands for surgery," he said.

"You are a coward." Nneka laughed and grabbed the fabric. At Maya's instructions, she made loud noises and advanced toward one side of the cage, catching the animal's attention. Maya snuck up behind. She held her own cloth higher and slipped in her injection under it, trying to avoid the barbs.

"Fuck!" She rarely swore but three quills penetrated her latex glove. Shouldn't be a source of exposure if the animal were infected, but it still hurt like hell.

Biko used hemostats from the first aid kit to grab each quill and pull it out. He applied antibiotic ointment and handed her a fresh glove.

"Your sedative worked." Nneka wrapped the unconscious animal with her cloth.

"Not sure why I thought keeping this animal in the study was a good idea." Puncture wounds aching, Maya plucked out enough quills from the tail to locate the vein for a tiny blood sample.

Nneka helped with the weight and length, then gently placed the porcupine on the ground under a tree.

Maya waited impatiently for the animal to wake up. She had reversal agents but was saving them for times when really needed.

Hopefully, the pain wouldn't distract her during the next blood draws. The safety procedures she'd used on the porcupine were similar to those she'd deployed in New Mexico for skunks.

It was clearly easier to protect against skunk spray than quills. They should have just released it without sampling.

Suddenly, the porcupine sprang to life and darted away. They all applauded. Maya began to overheat as the jungle foliage closed in around her, as if it were trying to eat her alive. After all, there were carnivorous plants. She appreciated the forest's inherent beauty but yearned for the wide-open vistas of the Southwest. *Stop that*, she chided herself. *Stay in the moment.*

The next cage contained an animal she didn't recognize. "*Potamogale velox*, the giant otter shrew," Nneka said. The teenager was an encyclopedia of local nature knowledge.

"Pretty big shrew," Maya said.

"It is not a true shrew or otter. It only looks like them."

"Does it feed on land or in water?"

"Usually water—crabs, frogs, fish."

Biko squatted on the ground, leaning against a tree covered in vines. "You two look like you're on top of this one. I'm taking a break."

His lack of energy prompted Maya to question the expedition's timing. With Biko and Stefan still recovering from Ebola, they should have waited a few more months. But the rainy season made July cooler, and any further delays would reduce the chance of tying the Ebola outbreak in Conakry to Nigerian wildlife.

"Nneka and I can handle this alone." Maybe the creature was less aggressive than true otters. Using the same technique as for the porcupine, Maya successfully sedated it. Nneka tugged out the animal and positioned its body on top of the cage.

When Maya pierced the skin of its tail, it awoke in an instant. A scream from Nneka, then the animal fled toward the river.

"What happened?" Maya asked. "Are you hurt?" It was one thing to goof up and get a minor injury herself. Much worse if something happened to her assistant.

Nneka held out her hand as Biko pulled himself to his feet. Blood oozed through her glove. "It bit me." Nneka sounded fragile.

"Both of you are idiots. These risks are unacceptable." Biko grabbed his medical kit again and hurried over. After examining Nneka's hand, his tone turned less hostile. "Only two puncture wounds, and not deep. No stitches required, fortunately."

Maya felt a wave of guilt. She should have insisted that Nneka wear thicker gloves, but taking notes would have been difficult.

"What's the risk of rabies in this area?" Maya asked.

"Dogs and people—I do not recall any specific spillover to wildlife here," Biko said.

"Biko and I were immunized before the trip," Nneka said.

Biko brightened. "Yes, that is right, so Nneka may be fine."

"In the US, even for someone vaccinated, we recommend two doses of postexposure treatment," Maya said.

"If you hadn't let it escape, we could get it tested." Biko kicked at the empty cage.

Nneka waved her injured hand at him. "It did not look rabid, and it is my health we are discussing."

Maya was surprised how quickly the discussion became contentious. Biko didn't have as much experience working outside as Nneka, and he appeared weak.

Maya tried to ease the friction. "A dog bite would be a bigger concern. Let's talk it over with Stefan when he gets back. There should be a clinic where you could get two booster shots."

She continued. "Look, it's my fault for underestimating the amount of sedation. I'm really sorry." With new species, the dose was always a guestimate without the body weight before they could check it.

"Let's finish all the traps as soon as possible." Maya guessed this type of work wasn't Biko's cup of tea, based on his demeanor. If they'd had time and resources to organize a bigger expedition, wildlife biologists would have been helpful.

Nneka checked her notes. "Just two more to go, down that path toward the river. Do we need to reset the traps?"

Maya nodded. "Yes. I expected Stefan back by now so we could discuss how long to stay in this area."

Biko pulled out his phone. "I don't have a signal, how about you?"

Both women were in the same boat.

"Barring unforeseen circumstances, they will return soon." A vision filled Maya's mind—their truck crumpled on its side down an embankment, the two men injured, no way to seek help.

SEVENTY-THREE

Stefan, dragging from a rough night attempting to sleep in the medical hostel room, paced the tile floor of the repair shop. He'd hung around there all morning, expecting any minute to hear that the winch had been fixed and they'd be on their way back to Cross River. Then the owner admitted it would be another day until they received the parts. What parts? They only needed to attach the hook to the cable so it wouldn't break off again.

After a cab ride back to the university, Stefan called to inform Sinachi, who answered from the Tinapa Waterpark.

"Delay is no problem," Sinachi said. "I am happy to spend the time with my grandchildren."

Of course Sinachi would say that. He'd spent every minute of the previous week driving the team around. Getting stuck yesterday had been harrowing, more for Sinachi since he was responsible for the rental and all of them. It was probably a loss of face.

"Should we rent another vehicle?" Stefan asked.

Sinachi made a funny noise. "You do not know the difficulties. We cannot exchange it because we do not have it. Does the World Health Organization want to pay for two trucks?"

"No." For Stefan, patience was a learned quality, not one he was born with. "Do you think they'll be okay a second night without us?"

"Of course. Bandits operate north of the park."

Stefan didn't understand why the park boundary would make a difference, other than having rangers. However, he wasn't in a position to contradict Sinachi.

The call to Maya wouldn't go through. He didn't even get a

chance to leave a message. The same thing happened when he tried Biko. His shoulders slumped—he felt totally helpless. Maya almost broke off their friendship after he coerced her into entering China for bat work without him. He never intended to leave her alone again on one of their joint investigations.

He looked out the hostel window at the brilliant sky. Not a cloud to block the sweltering sun as an African blue flycatcher flew by. Biko had pointed it out to him in Conakry. He'd never seen such a beautiful color on a bird in Europe, from its crest to the long tail. Maybe the Eurasian blue tit came close, but this bird had it beat.

Something had to be done to distract his mind but he couldn't focus on local tourist attractions, like Sinachi was doing with his family. A video chat with Kondrat and Paula would be just the ticket, and move him up a notch on an invisible checklist Kondrat seemed to keep about who did more to maintain their relationship.

"Kochanie!" He greeted Kondrat with the ultimate endearment in Polish.

It must have been warm in Oslo too—Kondrat's face was almost as red as his hair.

"Where are you?" Stefan asked.

Kondrat rotated his phone to show off *The Angry Boy*, one of the larger-than-life bronze sculptures on the bridge in Vigeland Sculpture Park. "Paula looks like this at the moment. I refused to buy her a second ice cream."

"Oh, I don't envy you. Where is she now?"

"Off to the *Man Attacked by Babies*. Perhaps she wants to see the tables turned on me."

Stefan laughed with the memory of the naked statue, two babies attacking his right hand, a third on his left one, and a fourth tackling his leg.

Somehow Paula's terrible two's, lasting all the way to the current terrible eleven's, were more humorous and bearable with his partner. Her challenges with learning disabilities and emotional control required two parents to manage. Kondrat definitely took the largest load.

"I wish I was there to chase her around and wear down that excess energy." Stefan genuinely wanted to be home. What was he as a physician doing on a research study of Ebola in animals?

He scuffed a foot in anger, wincing from the pain. A small amount of blood oozed from the dressing on his leg. Better not tell Kondrat what happened yesterday, even though keeping secrets always got him into trouble.

If his wound hadn't healed by the time he returned, Kondrat would fear he could transmit Ebola that way. Not true—only semen and the central nervous system seemed to harbor the virus that long. Still, Kondrat wouldn't be able to relax around him.

"What are you up to?" Kondrat asked as he carried the phone over the bridge, dodging other tourists.

"I'm headed to one of Nigeria's national parks tomorrow. We're collecting specimens from rodents, bats, and gorillas for the database about Ebola in animals."

Kondrat frowned. "I thought you were trying to determine the origin of your outbreak to prevent it from happening again."

"That's true, but numerous studies beyond our scope must be done to get the ultimate answer. We'd need a biosafety level four lab and an inoculation study that would never be approved for great apes."

"Then I don't know why your time away from home is worth it." Kondrat's voice was soft, not challenging, just sad.

Stefan didn't try to explain his sense of responsibility for Biko's infection and Jan's death, plus an innate curiosity for new information. WHO thought it a worthwhile effort, within the limits of their funding, and he was a WHO epidemiologist with African Ebola experience.

"I'm the first on Dr. Shah's list whenever an outbreak requires travel. I will promptly disabuse him of that assumption."

But for now, no matter how badly he felt about the separation from his family, he wouldn't abandon his team, especially Maya. As a veterinary epidemiologist, she was the most enthusiastic for the expedition.

After chatting with Paula when Kondrat caught up to her in the sculpture park, Stefan brought a smile to his daughter's face. Before saying goodbye, he promised to bring home a stuffed animal, the species of her choice.

Back in his room, he consumed his takeout meal of plantain and grilled fish with little attention. This time he avoided alcohol, in no mood to repeat his drunken excursion to the Conakry casino when he freaked out about a rat and Lassa fever. Instead, he quaffed kunu aya, a cool drink with tiger nuts, coconut, dates, and ginger. Very health conscious.

Despite his leg wound, to which he applied another dose of antibiotic cream, he was determined to be fully awake and ready for tomorrow's drive back to Cross River National Park. If he had to be away from his family, he would do the best job possible. His team shouldn't be on their own without him any longer.

As he lay down in bed, a familiar ache in his chest accompanied his worry about them. He took another pill for his angina, and turned off the light.

SEVENTY-FOUR

Hello, Judy! Hello, Judy! The haunting, high-pitched cry woke Biko up at dawn. He levered himself up on one elbow from his thin foam pad in the tent. The nonsense noise came from the direction of an image floating in front of him. It looked like Ogbanje, an evil spirit associated with misfortune.

He couldn't make out any details beyond electric eyes and a contorted, caped body. Was he hallucinating or dreaming? Why was the threat so clear since all he could hear was screeching nonsense? Sweat dripped from Biko's forehead. Twisting, he looked around for Stefan and Sinachi.

Was the sorcerer warning him about Nneka? As Biko struggled to his knees and put on his glasses, Ogbanje vanished.

Biko unzipped the tent flap and startled a yellow bird with a fluorescent green head and wings. It flapped away from the tent pole, continuing its haunting *Hello, Judy* cry. An African emerald cuckoo—he should have recognized its rhythmic call, if his mind hadn't been preoccupied by the evil spirit.

Nneka's and Maya's tent was far enough away to give them privacy if they had to get up in the middle of the night. Dizzy, Biko wasn't certain whether to walk or crawl there.

He pulled himself up to lean against a tree and call out, "Nneka, are you okay?"

A frustrated wail emanated through the nylon fabric of her tent. "Brother, why can't you wait another half hour? I am dead tired."

Nneka did not answer his question directly, but if there were a problem, she or Maya would have mentioned it. Biko crawled back inside his tent to the medical kit and took his temperature. Maybe his fever triggered seeing things. He swallowed two paracetamol tablets and finished the cup of water.

Perhaps low blood glucose, too. He slowly headed to the back of the truck and grabbed a LaCasera soft drink from the ice chest. The hard-boiled eggs were warm to the touch but his stomach growled. Risk food poisoning or hold off eating anything substantial? Stefan and Sinachi would bring more supplies, whenever they returned.

His shout had triggered stirring in the women's tent. Maya emerged first, shoulder-length hair in a ponytail. She wore khaki shorts and a white tee-shirt in deference to the heat.

"Thanks for waking us up, Biko. We need to check on the traps."

He envied her energy level. "I do not know whether to wish for fewer animals to reduce our workload," he said, "or more to provide us better data." His previous wildlife trips were a single day, like the one in May with Stefan and Jan Kreischer. Once he had assisted on a higher-end excursion where staff provided fancy meals and cots for sleeping. The WHO budget didn't allow for anything like that.

Nneka soon joined them. "I need to examine your bite wound," Biko said. The sorcerer might have been warning that the shrew otter infected her with something.

"It is fine," Nneka answered.

Maya agreed. "No redness, swelling, or pain."

Biko admired Maya's unending eagerness for the trip but in the too-early hour, it became irritating. Plus he resented a veterinarian commenting on a human injury, let alone his sister's. Certainly, Maya was a type of medical doctor, and an epidemiologist too, but still should stay in her lane.

"Did you check Nneka's temperature?" he asked Maya. A trick question, because he had the only thermometer. Why he was trying to provoke her into a lie, he didn't know.

"No need, I feel fine," Nneka said. "However, you don't look well."

"I am off my game today—a slight fever, that is all."

"Stay here and rest," Maya said. "Nneka and I have the routine down by now. Since we still don't know when Stefan and Sinachi will show up, we'll reset the traps for a third day." She smiled and winked. "We won't need your muscles to haul them out."

"I still don't know why we are catching these smaller animals," Biko said. "They are not the host species."

"No," Maya answered. "But we don't know how much time they spend in bat caves. They could pick up the virus there, then spread it to people."

A horde of mosquitoes descended and Biko retreated to his tent. He could hear the women talking outside as they set up their packs.

"A friend became infected with malaria in Ghana so it makes me wonder about Biko," Maya said. "Do Nigeria's residents take prophylaxis like us visitors?"

"Yes." Nneka laughed. "If you have a brother for a doctor."

"Maybe Biko's still recovering from his Ebola infection."

"I hope it is nothing more," Nneka answered. "I am used to him being the strong one."

Biko resented their chatting about him, although they had not been negative. Women were natural gossips, anyways.

Maya called out. "Biko, come find us if the guys show up. That is, if they ever get their butts in gear."

Nneka's laugh had the hint of guilelessness that only someone short of twenty and raised in a strict Christian home could pull off. "Maya, I cannot believe you said that."

Let them have their morning of female bonding. With a few hours of rest, he could assume his responsibilities as a member of the team. A short reprieve from specimen collection would be wonderful. Despite his love of nature, he'd spent his years of medical training in antiseptic environments. This type of field work held little appeal.

SEVENTY-FIVE

In camp after the day-long specimen collection, Maya gently stretched. For Nneka, she demonstrated Single Whip and White Crane Spreads Wings. Tai chi was one of her favorite forms of exercise and honored her Chinese heritage. Despite her lithe strength, Nneka was unfamiliar with the postures. She stumbled and giggled when moving into Step Back and Repulse Monkey.

"Trying this when we're exhausted probably doesn't make sense," Maya joked.

As the lights of the F-250 sliced through the forest, Nneka exclaimed, "They are back." She and Maya finished with Grasp Bird's Tail and the closing.

Biko emerged from his tent in a fresh pair of shorts and tee-shirt. To save space, they'd each brought two sets of clothes, far fewer than Biko needed to feel pulled together. Dirty ones hung from the branches after they'd washed them in the river.

Maya waved to Sinachi and hugged Stefan as he stepped out the passenger side. "About time you showed up." She eyed the dressing on his leg. "Any problems?"

"We tried a different route, hoping to avoid getting stuck again. But the other road was even more flooded. Fortunately, they'd strung a wire and built a wooden raft to ferry us across." Stefan held her lightly bandaged right hand. "And what happened here?"

Nneka joined them, a twin to Maya with her injured hand.

"Looks like an epidemic." Stefan glanced at Biko who meandered over. "Do you also have any souvenirs of your field work?"

"Not me," Biko answered. "The ladies monopolized my doctor skills. Maya got porcupine quills and Nneka was bitten by a shrew otter. Minor wounds for each of them."

"I'm sorry to hear that, but glad it wasn't worse." Stefan led the way to the truck. "Our time in Calabar was productive. We refreshed all our medical, lab, and food supplies."

"Anything yummy to eat?" Using her good hand, Maya clutched one handle on a new ice chest with Nneka grabbing the other. "The fufu's getting old—tastes like wallpaper paste. Or maybe we were supposed to use it for a paper mâché project?"

Nneka laughed. "Fresh vegetables would be wonderful."

"You are in luck, Miss Nneka." Sinachi opened one of the bags. "Okazi and water leaves—we will make afang soup."

"I can help," Nneka answered.

Maya and Stefan positioned their portable chairs at a distance from the heat of the cooking fire. She tried to relax, swatting away mosquitoes. "I didn't want to sound too grouchy in front of Sinachi, but you really took your time."

"I'm sorry—we had to wait on the winch repair. I worried about you out here on your own. Then you and Nneka got hurt—I hope it wasn't because you were short on manpower."

Maya shook her head. "The womanpower did just fine, although we could have collected more specimens with you and Biko as a separate team. He was MIA today."

Stefan's face creased with concern. "Why was that?"

"He mentioned a fever and he slept a lot. Put your medical degree to work and find out."

She showed him the logbook with Nneka's meticulous notes. "We have plenty of rodent and small mammal specimens. After pulling the traps, we should move on to the bat caves."

"Do you think our efforts will make any difference?"

With so many things going wrong on their expedition, Maya masked her anxiety and showed him an enthusiastic face. "Any positive samples might cause us to modify our public health warnings."

"Similar to Thailand, we'll do blood collection on the bats?"

"Yes, and I need some organ tissues for virus isolation. That will provide more information than just the antibody titers."

Euthanasia and field necropsy had been included in overall expedition preparations, but she hadn't emphasized it with Nneka or Biko yet. Until Sinachi guaranteed a cold chain for future tissue samples, it wasn't part of the plan. When first mentioned, Biko was dispassionate. On the other hand, Nneka, with her enthusiasm for nature, had been opposed.

"Dinner is on the table." Nneka's shout triggered grumbling in Maya's stomach.

"Hmm, I don't see a table." Maya winked at her friend and grabbed a steaming bowl. The first spoonful was bitter but her tongue and stomach were accustomed to unusual dishes, so she slurped the soup as if it were her last meal.

Despite his earlier nap, Biko fell into a daze after setting his bowl on the ground.

"Let's hold off on finalizing tomorrow's schedule until I figure out what's going on with him," Stefan whispered to Maya.

"No problem. Maybe Sinachi can locate a health clinic."

Nneka followed Maya into their tent. "Is Stefan going to check on my brother?"

Maya hugged her. "Nothing better than traveling with one or more physicians. I'm sure Biko will be fine."

Despite her reassurances, Maya tossed and turned all night. Biko's symptoms didn't appear serious, so he was unlikely to be threatened by Ebola at this point. However, Stefan had been advised about cardiac arrhythmias, and that would apply to Biko as well.

Manolo's and her grandmother's deaths while battling COVID gave Maya first-hand experience with the reality of cardiac arrest after a viral infection. The chance of an aborted research trip weighed as nothing compared to Biko's health.

SEVENTY-SIX

Down the mountain from the bat caves, Maya and Sinachi arranged for transport of her rodent and small mammal specimens to the Lagos University Teaching Hospital. Nneka agreed to an examination of her bite wound at the Agbokim clinic. As she waited for her rabies booster shot, Stefan accompanied Biko on a checkup.

The elderly primary care physician draped his stethoscope around his neck. "I don't find anything wrong, Dr. Okeke. It's likely you have residual symptoms from your Ebola infection. Blood samples may help with diagnosis of other issues. Results will be available in several days."

"Do you think our Ebola work is safe for him?" Stefan asked.

"I am hardly an invalid." Biko's voice displayed his irritation. "Did Maya or Nneka complain about me yesterday?"

Stefan shook his head no, even though Maya had brought it to his attention.

"You are the best judge of whether you can continue." The physician put on his reading glasses and pulled up a document on his phone. "I'll send you this report. Almost half of Ebola patients had fatigue and headache up to four years after acute infection. However, other studies found a decrease in symptoms over time, so there is reason for optimism."

"Any treatment recommendations?" Biko asked.

"There is no link in this study to markers of inflammation or immune activation, so I cannot recommend anti-inflammatories or steroids due to their side effects and risks."

Not one hundred percent back to normal after his own Ebola infection, Stefan was disturbed by the report. "And Biko's fever?"

"That is not a common Ebola sequela and he is fever-free today. Nigeria has a long list of viral haemorrhagic fevers that could arise from mosquito bites in our forests."

"I use repellent and our clothes are treated with permethrin," Biko said.

"Are you aware of a tick bite?" the physician continued. "Ticks can transmit Crimean-Congo haemorrhagic fever, which has a case-fatality rate of fifty percent."

Biko answered, "No tick bites."

Stefan added, "We're doing tick checks on each other, although we couldn't pull that off for a couple of days."

"Inshallah, the lab tests will rule out all those diseases." The physician ushered them out. "Base your decision about working on how you feel."

"I am not worried." Biko glared at Stefan. "I would not have stopped by here except at the urging of my colleague."

"I hope that we're friends in addition to colleagues." Stefan leaned down to place an arm around Biko's shoulders as Nneka rejoined them and the truck pulled into the parking lot.

Biko appeared uncomfortable with Stefan's friendly gesture. Was it anger over the unplanned clinic visit or something else? Stefan had never sensed any homophobia from Biko, but he was a conservative Christian. Come to think of it, Biko had argued about the nightly tick checks in the shared tent, and Sinachi had refused them altogether. Perhaps Stefan should heed Maya's warning from Faye Simpson and avoid any physical contact with another man while in Nigeria.

"Sinachi and I got our samples shipped." Maya, leaping out of the truck, appeared like a firecracker ready to launch. "We also topped off our provisions. How is the Okeke family doing?"

"Load off my mind that we stopped here," Stefan said, adopting her tone. "So we're a go for the rest of the expedition?"

Nneka gave a thumbs up and Biko nodded.

"Sinachi suggested a break at the Agbokim waterfalls," Maya said.

"Yes, only ten-minute drive." Sinachi opened the rear passenger door for her.

Nneka clapped her hands in excitement. "It's been years since Father brought us there."

"Sounds like a plan." Stefan was optimistic that a short time playing tourist would put the stresses of the investigation and its medical challenges behind them.

SEVENTY-SEVEN

Finally afebrile, Biko was soothed by the seven thundering streams cascading off the high cliff into the tropical rainforest. The angle of the sun created a faint rainbow on the other side of the rocky stream at the base.

Nneka tugged on his arm but her voice was swallowed by the noise. "Did you say something?" he asked.

She handed him a sardine sandwich and he wolfed it down.

A flash of color drew his attention. A malimbe—beautiful black bird with a solid red cap extending to the back of its neck. Perhaps appreciating wildlife from a distance was more in line with his interests than the backbreaking early morning work of setting traps for them.

Being new to WHO, he hadn't felt in a position to refuse the job. Surely Dr. Shah could have found people with more experience. Only Maya truly had the training and skills for it.

He glanced over at Sinachi who had a hunk of sandwich in each hand. Biko envied his lean, muscular frame. The driver might lift weights to maintain it, but perhaps his job was sufficient. He had done the lion's share of work in collapsing all the cages and carrying them back to the truck. Fortunately, his competence as a guard remained untested.

The last time they talked on the phone, Dr. Shah was annoyed with the winch delay and staff injuries. Distracted by management of multiple outbreaks, including the latest Marburg cases, he ordered Biko to wrap up the field work. Tracking down the origin of the Conakry Ebola outbreak was not his top priority, two months after their initial illnesses.

Similarly, Biko would have avoided the field investigation if not for Stefan's obsession over their possible responsibility for starting the outbreak. Although still short of thirty, Biko's career preference was becoming clearer—clinical research in a hospital for best treatments.

His negative reaction to working with his sister was a surprise. Dealing with her adult-to-adult required an adjustment. Despite being geographically apart for his medical training, he was protective of her since their father passed away.

He wished he had persuaded her to start college in Lagos so they could live together while both were in school. Agreeing to her enrollment in the forestry college up north, closer to Boko Haram, had been a major mistake.

Nneka waved her hand in front of his eyes to get his attention. "I want to swim."

Biko spotted other people enjoying the pool and spray below. "Not my cup of tea."

Maya grabbed Nneka's hand. "I'll go with you if the guys are wussies."

Biko arched an eyebrow at Stefan, who said, "I'm up for it."

Sinachi had remained with the truck to guard the supplies, so he couldn't guide them to the pool. But Biko remembered the way. Nneka might also, although she had been much younger when their father had taken them.

They started down a steep path next to a cliff lined with ferns. Water sprayed over the edge, cooling their journey but fogging Biko's glasses.

Closer to the bottom, they needed their hands to climb over black rocks, partially covered with bright green vines and lichens in the bare spots. Biko worried about one of them slipping, adding to their expedition's bad luck with multiple injuries.

All four wore hiking boots and were extremely careful. Biko offered a hand to Nneka when her short legs had trouble stretching between the rocks, and Stefan did the same for Maya.

Nneka winced once or twice when using her right hand to

steady herself. Even with only two small bite wounds, she still had some pain. Maya appeared to have no disability from the porcupine quills, and Stefan's leg scrape was scabbed over.

Several young men, wearing only shorts or swim trunks, scrambled over the rocks behind the base of the falls. None of Biko's group were prepared or courageous enough for that, so they removed their boots and rested on the embankment, feet in the water and misty spray washing over them.

"I have to get wet," Nneka said after fifteen minutes of relaxation. She waded through the grasses at the pool's edge and gingerly stepped over the rocks on the bottom of the pool.

"Me too." Maya joined her, then Stefan. Unlike the men hooting and hollering under the waterfalls, they remained fully dressed in shorts and tee-shirts.

Nneka shrieked in pleasure and ducked her head. After Maya and Stefan followed her lead, Nneka yelled up to Biko. "What is wrong with you? You should join us."

Despite a desperate desire to wash away the sweat, Biko was content to remain on the shoreline. Walking into the pool fully dressed felt unseemly, and he was at one with nature as his body melted into the moist vegetation. Hoping that he was not infected with any terrible mosquito-borne or tickborne disease, he prayed that their expedition challenges were over. This side jaunt was really a blessing.

SEVENTY-EIGHT

Two nights later, Maya fretted about Biko as they trudged up the Obudu Plateau trail. Of the team members, he appeared least excited by their detective work. Finally, they would spend the evening taking bat samples and potentially answering big-picture questions about the Ebola host species. Maya was over the moon in anticipation, even though clouds obscured the real moon and the stars.

Sinachi stayed behind to guard their vehicle and camp. Locals hunted the bats for food and might not be happy about anyone disturbing their larder.

He put their minds to rest about the other threat to bat caves—wildfires. Along park boundaries, villagers used deliberate burns to rid themselves of weeds ahead of planting. Sinachi said that was unlikely on the last day of July during rainy season.

Given the frequency of sibling conflict, Maya decided to work with Nneka, leaving Biko as Stefan's bat handler.

Nneka, despite being the smallest, insisted on carrying a similar load of supplies as Maya. But Stefan outweighed both women, and they happily agreed to his shouldering the heaviest materials.

The previous evening, Maya had selected the cave openings after counting bats flying out. Each team member held a clicker to record an estimate.

Now they began their bat work in the cave with the largest number, entering about an hour before dark. Their headlamps were inadequate for spotting the specific cave rooms with bats hanging from the ceiling. None of them had much experience spelunking and didn't want to waste time crawling around. So Maya rotated a handheld ultrasonic bat detector to verify bat presence. It converted bat ultrasounds used for echolocation into audible noises for humans.

Before leaving Calabar, Maya had visited with a Nigerian biologist to learn about the different patterns of signals emitted by various local bat species. His work focused on conservation and he was reluctant to aid an expedition that would capture and euthanize some bats for organ tissue samples. Maya assured him that the study mainly collected blood samples to check antibody levels, with minimal tissue collection for any endangered species.

Fifty feet inside the man-sized opening, Maya listened to the pattern on the bat detector. A music fan and pianist when she had time, she had an ear for audio patterns.

"Wow! If I'm hearing the signal correctly, we have the short-tailed roundleaf bat, one of the world's most endangered bat species. They haven't been found in this area for two years, and there's only about fifteen hundred left anywhere."

The Okeke siblings hung nets across the smaller cave openings, anchoring the end poles with rocks. Maya and Stefan set up their blood-drawing, euthanasia, and necropsy equipment on two portable tables that Stefan had hauled. When ready, they checked each other's PPE, taping some holes in Biko's and Nneka's coveralls from scrambling to install the nets. Then all four tugged on heavier leather gloves to protect themselves from bites.

Maya wiped away perspiration beading her forehead after the lengthy preparations in hot humidity. Cave temperatures were fairly stable but perhaps a bit cooler near the entrance with the onset of nightfall.

Nneka squealed in delight to pry the first bat out of the netting. It had intended to fly out to feed on local fruits, or pollen and insects as a backup. "I promise we'll be quick and let you get back to it."

With Nneka's words, Maya decided to only collect sera from this one. She couldn't euthanize it with Nneka cooing over its pale, flattened nose, dark eyes, and large ears, almost the size of its head. Nneka was gentle at stretching out one wing for Maya to suck less than 1 cc of blood from the vein using a heparinized syringe to avoid specimen clotting.

Nneka cradled the bat in her hand while applying pressure to the venipuncture site as Maya took measurements of the bat's size and recorded them on a notepad. The Nigerian government required them to apply a prenumbered band on each animal's forearm. Maya was careful not to close the ends completely, leaving a gap between the band and the wing membrane to reduce any irritation.

"I'm excited we have these," Nneka said as Maya applied a tiny GPS tracker to the back of the bat with medical glue that would stick for a few days. The bat biologist had supplied the equipment. Sinachi had established a battery-powered base station for storing data when the bats flew near, which was uploaded to the biologist through a satellite network.

"We won't be the ones tracking the bats," Maya said.

"I can join the team that does it." Nneka was almost bouncing on her toes in anticipation.

"Not for this one. Bats can only be tracked until the transmitter falls off. You'll be tied up on our project. With the skills you're gaining, I bet they'll snap you up for future studies."

While Nneka held the bat, she asked Maya to take a photo. In the dark, lit only by portable lamps, Maya was uncertain if she'd taken an adequate one. Then Nneka carried the bat to an uncovered cave opening and released it with a "Good hunting" call. Maya stepped over to Stefan and Biko's table.

"I didn't realize you were going through with a necropsy," she told them. "Nneka won't want to see this." Her heart and brain battled in a civil war. This was an essential part of the field investigation, yet every bat's life counted when the species was so vulnerable.

Stefan completed his dissection while Biko held the bat's body in place. Nneka returned as Maya put organ tissues into containers.

"How dare you kill an endangered species?" Nneka slugged her brother.

Maya jumped in to defend Biko and Stefan. "We need fresh

tissue to look for the virus. That's one of the most important ways to learn if this is a host for Ebola. I mentioned earlier we'd need to do that on at least one."

Nneka burst into tears. "With so few left, I expected you would change your minds."

Through Biko's facemask, Maya saw him roll his eyes. Human or veterinary medical school inured people to such strong reactions when working in the name of science. You'd never make it through if every death swamped your emotions. Public health research required tradeoffs, weighing the potential risks against the benefits of finding the truth about ways to fight microbial threats.

Maya stripped off her dirty gloves and pulled Nneka in for a tight hug. "I promise this is the last necropsy for this species. Can you help me get more blood specimens? You're so careful when you hold them, and I can't do this without you."

She directed Nneka to the net and pointed at a bat that struggled with their approach. "Let's process this guy quickly so you can return him to his hunt for dinner. Sound like a plan?"

Nneka sniffled, then gently pried it out. "If these bats have Ebola, do you think we could find a cure for them?"

"Don't worry," Maya assured her. "Even if they're infected, the bats won't get sick." But maybe they would find something to reduce bat infections that would then reduce human risk. Even though there hadn't been a cure for Biko or Stefan, they both made it through by caring for each other. With continued research support by the US government and international organizations, anything was possible.

SEVENTY-NINE

In a cabana of a cattle ranch catering to tourists, only a couple of hours from the bat caves, Stefan stepped out of the shower, revived by hot spray and jasmine-infused body wash. After dressing, he headed out to the covered wooden deck to find Biko. "I appreciate your friend letting us stop by to clean up."

Biko looked down, appalled at his own clothes streaked with two nights of cave dust. He'd washed his face in the sink. Now if only he had a razor to trim his goatee and shave his head. But the brief stop at the resort improved his mood.

"If our work reduces Ebola risk here, the resort may benefit with more customers." He smiled. "And our project is endorsed by the Nigerian health ministry. All businesses want to keep the government happy."

When Biko disappeared inside for his own shower, Stefan reclined on a chair overlooking the green grass of the massive hillside. In the distance, jungle-covered mountains where they'd collected bat specimens were cloaked by a gauzy blanket of fog.

He waved to Maya, who'd showered first and now explored the grounds. Sinachi and Nneka had gone to the Ogbakoko health post for specimen shipment and Nneka's final rabies booster. The two would do their own washing up at a relative of Sinachi's, then return after purchasing new supplies and a picnic lunch. Biko's friend had offered them all a fancy, free meal at the resort but that additional favor made Stefan, as a government employee, uncomfortable.

He thumbed **<home>** on his cell.

"Thanks for calling." Kondrat's greeting was a disappointment— no terms of endearment. But at least he answered the phone.

"It's good to hear you," Stefan said. "Our phones didn't work in the jungle. How are you and Paula doing?"

"We're at a cabin in Løvøya. She loves swimming off their white beach. This afternoon we'll explore the nature reserve, and tomorrow a kayak lesson."

Stefan was surprised. They'd discussed a trip to the island in the Oslofjord, yet Kondrat hadn't waited for Stefan's return. He couldn't begrudge them a wonderful time while he chilled out, although only for an hour, in his own luxury digs.

"We should all plan something for next year," he said.

Kondrat's voice increased in pitch. "It's August 1st and Paula starts school in three weeks. Are you saying we won't have any time as a family this summer?"

Pissed about Kondrat chiding him again, yet thrilled his partner wanted a family vacation, Stefan said, "I hope to finish things here soon. Can I talk to Paula?"

At the sound of children in the background, his heart twinged. Hopefully from joy, not angina, but he swallowed a pill just in case. Paula came on the line.

"Tatuś, we're having so much fun! I wish you were here. How are the animals?"

"Good. We got to see the cutest rodents, even better than guinea pigs. This week, gorillas. What do you think of that?"

Sinachi had received a call from one of his contacts. A gorilla troop was spotted on Afi Mountain, not far from the area of their May visit. They should be able to set up camp there by the evening.

"Aw, Tatuś, you do the most exciting things. Me and Pappa haven't been on one of your work trips since Portugal."

The *Borrelia* investigation with Maya had been an unusual opportunity to combine work and pleasure. He hoped Paula didn't expect that too often. Certainly not while investigating a disease with a case fatality rate up to 90%, depending on the Ebola strain.

He spotted Nneka with Maya on the lawn, then finished up his call. "Kochanie, I need to get going. I'll be home soon."

"Promise?"

Stefan recognized the thick emotion in Paula's final question.

"Yes, sweetheart. Nothing will keep me from getting back to you."

EIGHTY

They set up camp in a remote spot on Afi Mountain where gorillas had been spotted. Biko regretted leaving the comfort of the resort, but no more tourist groups were anticipated on the mountain and their research would be undisturbed.

He was hot, miserable, and ashamed of being the least-capable man on this expedition. None of the rodent or bat work had prepared him for the reduced oxygen at this altitude. He was unable to unload as many supplies as Stefan. Sinachi, almost twenty years older, carried more from the truck to the campsite.

Nneka heard panting hoots of chimpanzees and hissed at their team to be quiet in hopes of seeing some, but they weren't successful. However, the Cross River gorilla subspecies was their priority. Biko didn't think Dr. Shah wanted to include other species, but Stefan assured them they were approved to add more nonhuman primates if they found them.

Only their fire illuminated the looming jungle foliage when they finished camp setup. First to collapse on the foam pad in the men's tent, Biko checked his temperature again. One degree elevated. Perhaps it was the cloying heat locked into the small clearing by thick, thrusting vegetation, trying to reclaim the open grassy area.

Wildfires cleared out these spots in the jungle that were then filled in with the ground-hugging plants gorillas favored for their meals and rest. The charred ground replacing his home near Calabar had fire on his list of things to worry about. But villagers usually waited to build fires to prepare their fields in October, the start of the dry season.

Despite increased fire danger in autumn, Biko wished they had waited until then for their expedition. Nothing was worse than the constant soaking on this trip, skin chafing with every step.

Sinachi held the tent flap for Stefan to enter, then paused to study Biko. "Are you unwell, Dr. Okeke?"

"I dey fine." In his exhaustion, Biko lapsed into Nigerian Pidgin. He yearned to unload his misery on his companions, but they already might think he was not pulling his weight.

"Are you sure?" Stefan asked. "Sometimes I still feel like the Ebola virus has me in its grip."

Biko held his thumb and pointer finger close together. "Tiny bit weak and fever. Perhaps we should have waited until we were healthier."

Stefan used his handkerchief to wipe sweat from his face. "We couldn't delay—we're already two months out from the spillover incident that may have started our outbreak."

Sinachi cleared his throat. "Doctors, I will prepare for my watch."

If he felt stronger, Biko would alternate shifts, although he was unsure why standing guard was important. Then he remembered the gorilla poacher who died from Ebola in Calabar. Security was Sinachi's job, and the others needed sufficient rest to do theirs.

"Have the ladies gone to bed?" Biko asked as Sinachi turned to leave the tent.

Sinachi nodded. "See you in the morning."

"I'm not sure what time we should get up tomorrow." Stefan dropped to the middle bed pad.

Biko shrugged. "Nneka or Sinachi will likely wake us when it's time."

Once again, he regretted the timing of their trip. It would be easier to spot them in the dry season when hiking trails were not a soupy mess. The animals would also be at a lower altitude, so less climbing to find them.

Stefan turned on his side away from Biko, who could barely make out Stefan's outline. It jumped around like a spirit in the dancing firelight that illuminated the tent wall.

Unaware of how much later, he was awakened by a piercing repetitive grunt, half snarl and half sinister laugh. Sinachi would be on guard duty so they were safe, but the sound was horrifying.

Unable to find his glasses, Biko could only see a blurry monkey image. Was a mandrill in the tent? Orange eyes peered out under a heavy, dark brow. Its long nose flamed like a raging fire, bordered by swelling blue-striped patches on either side. Its wide mouth threatened with four canine daggers, although the animal mimicked an old man with its white beard.

Had Sinachi left the flap open, or was this just a horrifying dream? Both spirits and the natural world were out to get him, one way or the other.

He roused enough to crawl to the entrance, and verified with his fingers that the zipper was down. His muscles relaxed—the creature hadn't been real. Still Stefan slept, dead to the world.

EIGHTY-ONE

In the rosy dawn, smoke from the small campfire merged with a mist that cloaked the trees and dampened their bare skin. As the two women emerged from their tent, Sinachi finally joined the men in theirs.

Grateful that Sinachi had replenished their larder, Maya mixed up two bowls of acha porridge flavored with ground peanuts and milk, then handed the second one to Nneka. Despite the drab camouflage they wore for the gorilla trek, Biko's sister looked as cute and perky as a meerkat.

"Will you continue guiding wildlife trips?" Maya asked.

Nneka lifted her cup of spiced tea in a toast. "Definitely. I know nothing else, and I love nature."

"How about when it turns on you?" Maya pointed to Nneka's hand and its healing bite marks.

"I will lead photography safaris. Stressing or killing an animal like you have to do for your studies—it is too much for me, even for the greater good."

Maya understood that Nneka didn't mean to criticize her or their research program. She welcomed time to bond with her African sister.

"I would love for you to visit me in New Mexico." The Southwest still felt like home although she hadn't decided when or if to return. "If you'd prefer New York, one of my best friends lives there."

Nneka's face glowed. "I would like that, either one."

They couldn't focus on arrangements now, but they'd have plenty of time after the expedition.

"And college—will you go back?" Maya realized that was Biko's preference for his sister.

Nneka shrugged. "I am not sure how that will help me." She flashed a coy smile. "I assume you will give me an outstanding work reference, so I might need no more classes."

"Count on it, but there's value to school for other things. I concentrated on pre-vet classes and wish I'd also studied psychology. Dealing with people is the toughest part of my job."

Nneka looked down at her hand. "Other than this injury, I never had any problems with animals. You are right, people are scarier."

She turned quiet, perhaps recalling her kidnapping. How awful it must be to harbor those memories.

"Yes, humans are the apex predators," Maya said. "But we each have family members to protect us and prove that there are lots of good people."

"Such as bossy big brothers." Nneka's tone edged the line between peevish and humorous.

"I'd give anything to have a brother, even a bossy one."

"You and Stefan seem close. Is he like a brother for you?"

Never having formed the thought before, Maya acknowledged it was true. She had several friendships with men like that. Perhaps she was drawn to older, confident guys with whom she could joke and relax. Avoiding social anxiety.

Speaking of older, confident guys—but not the brotherly type—she owed a text or call to Mark. He'd emailed another silly poem when she was in Calabar. During her COVID recovery at his ranch, they read the works of famous poets and tried writing their own. He kept up with his practice; she had not.

"Thank God it stopped raining." Stefan stumbled out of the men's tent, followed by Biko.

"Ready to see some gorillas?" Nneka asked her brother as she handed him a cup of tea.

"We already saw one in May," he grumbled.

"Without a better attitude, I will never bring you along again on my guided trips," Nneka replied.

"Is that a promise?" Biko said.

"Okay guys, this is the final step in our expedition." Stefan rested his hand on Biko's shoulder. "If all goes well, we'll collect gorilla samples for a couple of days, then call it quits."

"As long as we do not hurt them." Nneka's expression turned serious. "Cross River gorillas are the rarest great apes on Earth— only about 300 are left. You must promise not to surprise me by euthanizing one for tissue samples."

Maya scuffed her boot in the dirt. At the initial meeting in Abuja, they had discussed sacrificing a few animals of various species for virus isolation, on top of the serum samples for antibody testing. But maybe Nneka forgot what she didn't want to know.

"We won't do that with the gorillas," Maya said. "The last study located only thirty here on Afi Mountain."

Nneka didn't look convinced, so Maya added, "I'll be very careful with my sedation procedure, adjusting the dose for estimated body weight."

Sinachi emerged from his tent looking like roadkill. Maya hoped his nap would be sufficient for him to function, but he could have caught snatches of sleep while on guard duty.

She grabbed her dart gun, its muzzle sticking out from her pack. "I've never worked with gorillas but this is similar to what I used on another investigation."

Sinachi chimed in. "I assisted other veterinarians on gorilla trips and will advise Dr. Maguire on their handling." He looked at his watch. "I recommend we leave in thirty minutes."

After all their extensive planning, Maya prayed that Nneka hadn't developed cold feet. With just the five of them, their group was already very small. From Nneka's photographic safaris, she was experienced at recognizing when they were getting close to gorillas and how to approach them without frightening them away. They could get by without Nneka, but Maya preferred not to.

"Please be our leader in the forest." Maya held Nneka's uninjured hand. "You are our gorilla whisperer, and I don't want to do this without you."

"Gorilla whisperer?" Nneka's eyebrows drew together in puzzlement.

Maya laughed. "It's an American expression. People who are good at working with horses are called horse whisperers."

"I have never been close enough to a gorilla to whisper to her." Nneka broke out into a smile. "But maybe this time."

EIGHTY-TWO

Nneka carefully pushed the vegetation aside on the steep, muddy trail. Sinachi was close on her heels, his assault rifle slung across his chest for protection against rogue humans or animals. Maya followed, her dart gun at the ready. Stefan and Biko took up the rear.

Biko appeared out of breath. Maya wondered about the wisdom of including two recent Ebola patients on the trip, but they were the ones who had been on this specific mountain with the gorillas before. Nneka and Sinachi had been on other gorilla trips, but not in this area. Maya was brand new to this environment, yet she had the most critical role. She prayed she was up to it.

Nneka halted, Sinachi almost tripping over her. Nneka held her finger in front of her mask, indicating silence. Then she pointed to a small clearing to her right.

A mother relaxed on the ground, tearing up leaves and bringing them to her lips, while an infant nestled on her belly. Nneka mimed a baby rocking in her arms, then emphatically shook her head no. Maya was clear that Nneka didn't want to disturb the pair in the name of science.

The gorilla's golden hair was startling. According to Nneka, Cross River gorillas had shorter hair, sometimes lighter, than other species. A thin area of bare skin was distinct on the animal's wrist. Staring intently, Maya could make out a strand of wire. The female had been caught in a poacher's snare, and was injured.

Maya pointed to Nneka's own injured hand, then to the gorilla's. "She's hurt." She looked to Sinachi, who nodded. He pulled out a small notebook and wrote "~100 kg," then handed it to her.

Two hundred twenty pounds. Maya estimated the sedative dose

and pulled it up in the syringe. The other four members of their team watched her in silence, holding their breaths. To avoid any chance of hitting the baby, she raised the dart gun and aimed for the gorilla's back.

Luck of the Irish Maguires—she hit it on the first shot. The gorilla stretched her good arm, trying to reach the dart, but it had already fallen into the leafy undergrowth. Within three minutes, she relaxed into the ground, the infant still clinging to her body.

"I will take care of the baby," Nneka announced, the first to speak out loud. "Its fur looks silky." She let the infant suck on her gloved finger.

Sinachi used a pair of wire cutters to remove the metal snare.

Stefan held up the gorilla's swollen hand. "It's infected."

Maya used an antiseptic sheet to clean the reddened bare skin, then applied a topical antibiotic and an anti-inflammatory.

"Respirations are 27 per minute." Biko monitored the animal's level of sedation and health.

"Thank you." Maya cleaned inside one of the gorilla's legs and Stefan rested a finger near the groin to allow the femoral vein to fill. Maya's luck continued and she drew the blood sample on her first try.

"You're on a roll with this," Stefan complimented.

"Anything else?" Biko asked.

"Take a photo for our records," Maya said.

Biko lifted the camera from around Nneka's neck and took a shot, capturing his sister and the infant clinging with arms blacker than the mother's tawny fur. Its dark eyes stared directly at him.

"Aw, that will be massively cute." Nneka giggled, still stroking the baby's head. "Show it to me when we get back to camp."

Sinachi, alert as a leopard in a tree, swiveled from side-to-side. "Dr. Maguire, can we hurry this along? That wound is fresh and we have no idea if poachers are still in the area."

"Yes, I'm giving the reversal agent now." She made the injection and moved everyone away. "She'll stir in about five minutes, then recover in twenty."

Nneka reluctantly followed the others back to the trail. "Could the baby get hurt if she thrashes around?"

Maya had no way to guarantee the infant's safety, but if they were quiet, perhaps the mother wouldn't become agitated. This time instead of Nneka, Maya was the one who signaled silence with a finger to her masked lips.

The mother woke up as if from a hangover. She brought her injured wrist to her nose and sniffed it. When she became aware of her human audience, she ambled slowly away into the forest, leaning on her uninjured arm and cradling the infant with the other.

"Look, she's able to carry her baby," Nneka whispered as the pair disappeared into the haze creeping down the mountainside.

"My injections should reduce inflammation and pain," Maya said. "Unlikely to be working this quickly, but she appears to be in good shape."

But their luck didn't hold. On the day-long challenging slog through the jungle, they didn't find another animal. Maybe they never saw the silverback or the rest of the troop because the mother had isolated from them with her injury.

EIGHTY-THREE

Despite only collecting one blood sample, the team celebrated their success at removing the snare from the female gorilla. In a pot over the campfire, Stefan stirred a stew Sinachi had made the day before at his friend's house, then stored in the ice chest. Efo Riro—African spinach mixed with palm oil, locust beans, crayfish, and spices.

Stefan would have liked a glass of palm wine with dinner. The thought brought him back to the beachfront meal in Conakry and the cleansing smell of salt air as he anticipated his flight home. But later that night, he'd collapsed at the casino with his first bout of angina. Even when you thought you had everything sorted, life had a way of biting you in the ass.

Maya raised her cup of mango juice in a salute to the team. "Everyone did such a great job—we pulled off our first sample without a hitch."

"Quite a change from the way this expedition started," Stefan said with a hint of irony.

"Do you imply our initial efforts were a dumpster fire, Sir?" Maya joked.

Stefan pointed to the reddened and scabby area on his lower leg. "Our truck got stuck, the winch broke, I got dinged up. Then you were nabbed by a porcupine and Nneka by an otter shrew."

Biko rubbed a rough area of his scalp, scratched by overhanging branches. "Not to mention that I slept the day away while you collected more rodent samples. I'm sorry about that."

"You still lagged a bit today," Nneka observed. "Are you sure you are feeling well?"

"Somebody had to guard our rear flank," he answered.

"Well, I'm happy to have Biko's clinical skill for monitoring the gorillas," Maya said. "Nneka, you would never forgive us if something went wrong with them."

"I am neither an emergency room doctor nor a veterinarian," Biko said. "I am unsure how we would respond to any problems."

Biko seemed determined to argue, despite his apology about sleeping through a workday. But Stefan, as the titular leader of the expedition, wanted to bandage any sore feelings. "We're all a bit out of our element. Except of course Nneka and Sinachi—they're on top of their respective roles."

He should have mentioned Maya. She had done everything right, but admittedly had only some applicable experience. In the worst-case scenario, she didn't have resources for saving the gorilla's life in a sedative overdose or a more severe injury. Leaning over to her with a wink, he added, "You done good, too, my friend."

They'd only planned for two days of gorilla samples, so the next day would be their last. Stefan had phoned Dr. Shah before dinner, who wasn't pleased with their sampling success despite Maya's saving one gorilla from possible sepsis and death. Stefan suggested that they extend the trip if they struck out again, but Sinachi would have to go back into town for more supplies.

Stefan noticed that Sinachi barely took a bite out of his own excellent stew. Rifle still strung across his chest, he studied the jungle between chews. Clearly he was nervous. He'd warned them not to wander away from camp on their own, even for the privacy of bathroom functions. The poacher who set the snare that hurt the mother gorilla could still be nearby.

But dinner passed uneventfully, with everyone more confident of their role in the expedition and their chances of finding additional animals in the morning. After saying goodnight to the women, Stefan and Biko retired to the men's tent. Despite limited sleep the night before, Sinachi decided to stand guard near the campfire.

Stefan had a difficult time staying asleep, his mind in an endless loop as he anticipated the end of the trip. Suddenly he became alert to a rapid unzipping of the tent. Sinachi poked his head inside.

"Grab the women and get them into the truck." Sinachi tossed his keys to Stefan.

"What's going on?" Stefan asked as he shook Biko awake.

"I heard an engine. I want us together in our vehicle to escape if necessary."

Stefan was groggy and his limbs leaden. Every muscle ached after hours of climbing, with more hiking for at least one more day. The last thing he wanted was to head to the truck without more provocation. "It could be Dr. Shah sending someone to help. Let me try to call him."

"No time. Get out now. That is an order."

Stefan respected Sinachi's experience, so he ran outside to rouse the women. Fortunately they'd all been sleeping with their clothes on to reduce mosquito bites. Sinachi stood guard in the narrow, rutted road, assault rifle aimed toward the increasing roar of an engine. Stefan practically dragged a bare-footed Maya toward the front of the truck while Biko tugged his sister around the back to the other side.

As Stefan grabbed the door handle, gunfire burst from the approaching vehicle, a Jeep draped in camouflage. Sinachi went down before he got off a single shot, then Stefan slammed Maya to the ground just as something pierced his foot.

The pain was worse than anything he'd ever experienced. Bolts of lightning flashed repeatedly from his toes up to his ankle. For a moment, he couldn't see a thing, but he could feel. One of his hands was caught between his torso and Maya's. He could sense her trying to catch a breath, and her quiet cries.

A cackling laugh redirected his attention to the vehicle. An arm emerged, swinging a torch which landed on the women's tent. The nylon burst into flames immediately. They'd erected the tent closest to their truck, and the acrid chemical fumes burned Stefan's eyes and inflamed his lungs.

The jeep spun 180° and sped back down the hill. After the brief moments of thundering chaos, the jungle became eerily quiet except for the crackling flames—no sound from a single forest creature.

Stefan tried to push past the pain in his foot to wake up his brain. Other than Maya's whimpers, the only thing he could hear was Biko howling his sister's name, over and over.

"Get off of me." Maya poked Stefan's ribs, then both hands went to her temple. "Oh, Jesus, I think you gave me a concussion."

Stefan's instinct to flee the fire energized his brain but he couldn't get his body to respond. Did he have another wound that paralyzed him? Maybe it was the fist in his chest, hopefully just angina. He removed his pill bottle from his pocket and took the dose dry. Looking down at his foot, he was startled by the amount of blood. Had he been shot?

The heat of the flaming tent yanked his focus away from his own agony. Water, that's what they needed to douse it, but they didn't have enough. During the rainy season, the flames shouldn't ignite the forest, but the truck? In the light of the flames, he spotted Sinachi motionless on the ground, blood seeping from a wound in his arm, rifle next to him.

Maya shoved Stefan again. "I can't see anything. If we need weapons, I can get my tranquilizer gun from the backseat."

A ridiculous suggestion—how would she have time to load it with sedative? At least she had experience with it. He loved her bravery, despite the naivete of her idea. No other alternatives for self-defense—Sinachi should have trained them in how to use his rifle.

Stefan shifted his weight away from her, increasing the dagger-like pain in his ankle. "I saw them speed away. But your tent is burning, and it's dangerously close to our truck."

"Okay, let me get up. I can move the truck away." Protected by Stefan's body, she had no idea of anyone's injuries.

"Maya, can you hear Biko?" Stefan used his arms to steady her as she pushed up to a standing position. "Find out what's happening with him and Nneka."

She wobbled, one hand again to her head. "I can't see straight." She leaned against the truck frame and disappeared through the smoke to the other side.

Eyeing Sinachi, Stefan crawled toward him through the mud. With shaking hands, he verified slow and shallow breathing. Thank God Sinachi was unconscious, not dead. Stefan slipped his belt from his pants and looped it above the wound as a tourniquet, then ripped off his shirt and applied it as a pressure dressing.

Blocked by the truck, he couldn't make out Maya's conversation with the Okekes. But her wails soon melded with Biko's.

EIGHTY-FOUR

Two days after the attack, Biko sat in the first pew of the Catholic Church in Calabar. Not having any living relatives, he was joined by Stefan, Maya, and Dr. Shah, with Stefan's crutches leaning against the wooden seat.

Other pews were filled with Nneka's coworkers from the conservation centre and fellow students on vacation from the university to the north. They hadn't seen Nneka since she dropped out after her kidnapping, but still they came.

Without his glasses, left back at the crime scene in the chaos, Biko wasn't sure he'd recognize anyone. He didn't hear the music, hymns, and prayers. He was left to the sounds in his head of her childish laughter and their frequent fights. Some mourners had approached him last night at the wake to share their respect and sorrow, and he mumbled his thanks.

Stefan had to prod him when the service ended. Following the hearse draped with colorful garlands, Dr. Shah provided the team a ride to the cemetery.

Sinachi was still hospitalized pending surgery. By the time Maya had driven them down the mountain, he'd lost a lot of blood. She drove as fast as she could, but with a mild concussion, she had a hard time seeing the road in the dark.

Biko had been uninjured, but was incapable of doing anything beyond cradling his sister's body as he moaned and leaned against the passenger door. In the backseat, Stefan had maintained pressure on Sinachi's wound until an ambulance he called met them on the highway.

At the graveyard, Maya held the car door open for Biko. He

trembled. Despite a day to clean up, he still felt contaminated by the splatter of blood and brains from Nneka's head wound. She never had a chance. Biko had tried to protect her. He had failed.

The Inspector-General of Police for Cross River State held up his hand to stop Biko from joining the funeral procession. "I am sorry to interrupt, Doctor, but we still have not spoken at length about the attack. With the weekend approaching, we are losing time to investigate."

Biko's voice became high-pitched. "I have no information. We could not see the type of vehicle, or any of the men inside it. It all happened so quickly, and I was preoccupied by my deceased sister."

"Religious fundamentalism or scaring you away from their illegal poaching—those are our top theories. But cattle rustling has been reported near there. Perhaps they were afraid you would stumble on their activities."

Biko felt the heat rise in his face. He could not believe that he needed to focus on this during Nneka's burial. "That is your responsibility to determine, not mine. We all know that political leaders have diverted to their own campaigns the resources intended for fighting Boko Haram."

Of course he wanted to know who murdered Nneka, but an average of a thousand Nigerians per year died in ethno-religious clashes and armed robberies. The authorities wouldn't care about one more. But in this time of viral social media, Nneka had become a martyr overnight for the national park and its wildlife. The press had requested a picture, and Maya provided the one with Nneka holding the baby gorilla's hand as it clung to its anesthetized mother's chest.

"We do have one clue," the Inspector-General continued. "We found shotgun shells at the scene. We're attempting to determine if they came from a Nigerian manufacturer, like the one in Awka."

Maya and Stefan had hovered nearby to offer Biko support. He turned to them and Maya stepped forward, taking his arm.

"I promise to stop by your office before flying back to Norway," Stefan said. "Please let Dr. Okeke lay his sister to rest now."

Six male students from Nneka's university, all dressed in white suits, removed her casket from the hearse. They raised it high over their heads and began to dance, accompanied by two other men in yellow shirts playing a drum and a horn. Older women wearing bright, patterned head scarves matching their full skirts encouraged the dancers, who lowered to their knees vibrating in time with the music while balancing the casket on their necks. They extended their legs and performed two pushups, then in sync stood up and proceeded to the gravesite.

Biko nodded in thanks to the pallbearers. Maya had downloaded all the photos from Nneka's camera, and he had placed it in her coffin this morning, a common practice to allow the spirit personal effects they might need in their reincarnated life.

He felt like he was in another universe as they completed the burial. With no home in the Calabar area to return to, he acceded to Dr. Shah dropping him at the hotel where all of them were staying.

"I will see you on Saturday for the celebration of Nneka's life," Biko told the team in the lobby. "Thank you for being here for me."

Almost forty-eight hours of peace and quiet until Ikwa Ozu, the final rite of passage to guide her spirit to her place among their ancestors. Often it took many weeks to organize such a ceremony, but Biko wanted it scheduled while his friends were around to share it. Besides, he yearned to get back to their Lagos apartment. Calabar with its tragedies—the deaths of his parents and now his sister—no longer felt like home.

EIGHTY-FIVE

A week after Nneka's funeral, Maya relaxed on the cabin's back porch. She closed her eyes and inhaled the salty air. A seaside vacation in Norway's northwest corner was just what the doctor ordered, even though her trauma was psychological, not physical. Paula played on the beach, Kondrat grilled salmon on the barbecue, and Stefan provided unwelcome direction from his hammock.

"Maya, keep your partner-in-crime away from my cooking," Kondrat gently chided, then reached down to kiss Stefan on the forehead.

As Stefan started to get up, Maya swung her legs to the deck, but Stefan waved away her help and grabbed his crutches. "I can manage myself," he huffed.

Maya took in the view while Stefan hobbled over. The cabin's sod roof of lime-green grasses, sprinkled with yellow from the cooler temperatures, crowned reddish wooden walls. Mid-August above the Arctic Circle, autumn already threatened.

Behind them, jagged peaks loomed, and in front, gentle waves of the deep blue sea lapped, matched in intensity by the cloudless sky.

Stefan had quickly found this place to rent after they flew to Oslo from Nigeria. He was obsessed with taking a long-planned vacation to the Lofoten Islands, one of the most spectacular areas of Norway.

Kondrat's hostility finally thawed after the horrible threat to their lives in Nigeria. He insisted that Stefan immediately move home for more personal care, and Maya stayed in Stefan's rental apartment for the few days before the vacation. Something about the shotgun wound in Stefan's foot seemed more motivating to Kondrat than the occasional angina attacks from Ebola, even if heart problems were potentially a bigger risk.

Other than Stefan making the cabin reservation, Kondrat did all the work to book them on a two-hour flight to Tromsø, then the ferry to Finnsnes. Maya at first demurred, not wanting to crash their first family vacation in a while. But Stefan and Kondrat touted the Lofotens as a major wonder of the world, and insisted that she absolutely had to see them.

Her parents and Mark encouraged her to make the trip. Such a huge change in the environment would help her decompress, Mark promised. But once the week in the far north was over, he insisted she come home to Santa Fe. "Our beautiful aspen trees in the fall— you can't miss the mountains exploding in color."

She said she would think about it. Her mind spun like a gyroscope from all the recent life events. At the moment, her only desire was to hear the cry of sea gulls circling overhead.

Stefan lowered himself to the chair next to her. "A penny for your thoughts, that's the correct American saying, isn't it?"

"Our expedition wasn't worth losing Nneka. And they still haven't arrested anyone."

"With the snare around the gorilla's hand, we can guess who attacked us. Nneka's now the face of poaching problems in national parks. She'd be proud of the public campaigns rallying support for more park rangers and gorilla protection."

In the late afternoon breeze, Maya pulled her sweater tighter. Stefan was right, Nneka would love the attention, and knowing she'd done good for the animals. But Biko hadn't been comforted by the memorial accolades. He'd admitted his guilt over not protecting her. He was devastated by her loss.

Maya opened a phone photo of Nneka cradling a bat. She was wearing gloves and a mask to protect the animals and herself— Maya was proud that the pictures demonstrated respectful and safe practices.

The one of Nneka consoling the gorilla infant while its mother was sedated, Maya had released to the press. Nneka's eyes expressed a pure, uncomplicated love, not diminished by the team's fears of zoonotic disease transmission.

"I'm on a roller coaster of guilt over what we should have done differently," Maya said. "Biko's pain at the random suddenness—he's inconsolable."

"Dr. Shah will redirect him to a new task," Stefan said. "Biko is dedicated enough that another public health challenge will re-engage his ambition."

Maya wasn't totally surprised by his insensitive attitude. Two years later, she still mourned Manolo and her baby. It had taken months before she was able to work again, although that had been as much from the long COVID recovery as the emotional impact. Stefan first enticed her back to life with the coronavirus bat trip to Southeast Asia. Biko might need something like that, an older mentor to lean on.

"Dr. Shah is excited about our initial lab results," Stefan added, "even for only one gorilla specimen."

"I can't believe she had Ebola antibodies. With such a high death rate in gorillas, she's lucky to have survived and given birth. It looks like Ebola is going through the Cross River gorillas and could have been the source of Jan Kreischer's infection."

"Then we have the seropositive rodents and bats, plus virus isolation from the bat I put down. That's huge news, worthy of a paper. Thank goodness Dr. Shah got the specimens analyzed in just a week—we'll just need to wait for confirmation. I wonder if the *New England Journal of Medicine* would be interested in it?"

Maya laughed at his presumption—NEJM was considered by many to be the preeminent publication honor. She still had not first-authored a major peer-reviewed article in a public health or medical journal. Dr. Grinwold, and now Stefan, kept reminding her of its importance in her career.

Kondrat called Paula in from the beach. Maya put public health considerations aside and focused on the happy banter from the vacationers as they devoured another of Kondrat's fabulous meals.

After dinner, Maya agreed to take Paula on a beach walk, toes in the frothy waves. Stefan and Kondrat were reconnecting, cherishing some moments of privacy.

Maya found a large log to perch on with Paula as the blue sky purpled near the horizon. Ten p.m., the Arctic sunset in August. The sun would be up again by 4:30 a.m., hardly enough time for a good night's sleep. But that could wait until Oslo. There were too many fun things to do in the Lofotens, and she was determined to blot out the harrowing memories of Africa

"When we got off the ferry," Maya said, "I saw a brochure for horseback riding with Icelandic ponies. What do you think, you and me tomorrow?" She'd already checked with Stefan and Kondrat for permission to suggest the outing. Paula loved riding horses.

"I wish Tatuś could come, too." Paula hung her head, clearly distressed by Stefan's injury.

He'd have other opportunities in the future to do it when he healed. For the moment, Maya wanted to keep Paula occupied while Stefan and Kondrat fortified their renewed connection.

"Let's make it a girls' excursion, just the two of us. I bet we'll have loads of fun."

Paula, elated, leapt up for a graceful pirouette. They wandered back to the cabin hand-in-hand as the skies darkened and stars began to twinkle. Maya wasn't sure which of them looked forward to the horseback ride more. She wondered what it might have been like to share the experience with her child, if she or he had lived.

They interrupted Stefan and Kondrat cuddled on the couch, sharing mugs of glögg, Nordic mulled wine. With Stefan's leg on a stool and a wool blanket across their laps, the couple epitomized kos, cozy togetherness that savored the moment.

"My phone app says it might be a good night for the aurora borealis," Maya said. "Anyone else want to get up at 2 a.m. to see it?"

Kondrat handed Paula her stuffed cheetah, Stefan's homecoming gift for their daughter. "This one needs beauty sleep. See you soon, kjæreste?" He winked at Stefan as they headed down the hall.

"Hmm, I wonder if Kondrat meant Paula or himself when he said beauty sleep," Stefan joked.

"I don't think you can improve either one of them," Maya said. "You're a lucky man, Stefan."

He embraced Maya in a goodnight hug. "Don't I know it. Kondrat's always happier when you're around, so thank you for your part in his mood elevation. See you tomorrow."

She set the alarm on her phone. No way would she miss the northern lights.

The phone going off at two o'clock startled her awake. Groggy, she silenced it and threw on her robe. Despite the week of recovery in Norway, she still felt fatigued from the tragedy after weeks of planning meetings and difficult field work.

Out on the cabin porch, she scanned the sky for telltale swashes of green and purple. Clouds hung low over the ocean and obscured the horizon. Disheartened, she went back into the cabin for a jacket. Her phone said the temperature was 13°C, so only about 55°F.

On the way back outside, she grabbed the blanket from the couch. Might as well be cozy for the wait. Hard to get excited about anything when Nneka was dead.

Not having any siblings, Maya had relished her relationship with Biko's sister. Usually Maya hung around with older people, constantly being guided by them. This time, she'd served in that role for Nneka. They'd talked about their hopes and dreams. Nneka preferred guiding and photography but was proud of her improved skills helping Maya, despite the one bat they'd sacrificed.

Now Nneka would never fulfill her destiny. But the Igbo people believed in the soul's return to complete its journey. That was likely of great comfort to Biko. He'd be on the lookout for any physical resemblances or personality traits that indicated her presence. Maya could, too.

Suddenly, a sword of green shot from left to right across the sky, reflected in the still water of the ocean below. It split into two streams with a band of purple between them. The stars sparkled through the wash of color. A pinwheel of blue rose up behind the mountain peaks, as if birthed from a volcanic caldera. The light shimmered, never freezing for long.

Not a single sound except for a low "Ooooooh." Maya realized it came from her mouth, an involuntary reaction to such dramatic beauty. Tempted to rush in and wake the others, she realized they'd seen it before. Not that Maya could imagine ever tiring of this spectacle. Tiny hairs on the back of her hands tickled. Caused by dancing particles hurled from the Sun and colliding with the Earth's upper atmosphere, or the magnetic field directing them toward the North Pole?

Some sort of whooshing began in her ears. She didn't think it was tinnitus, and the clouds clustered over the ocean in the distance weren't close enough to generate wind. Her imagination, or the northern lights?

With a jolt, she remembered the phone in her pocket. She lifted it to capture a few memories of rapture. The leap into the unknown when she left New Mexico was worth it. Different paths in the woods, as Robert Frost had written. She'd chosen the one less traveled by, and that made all the difference.

CODA

Parasites sound even more gnarly than bacteria or viruses. *Fasciola* is a multicellular flatworm with complex organ systems and hermaphroditic sexual reproduction.

It's also visible to the naked eye. *Fasciola gigantica*, the giant liver fluke, can be three inches long. Very appetizing if you're a vegetarian hoping to eat healthy and you don't wash away the worm's larvae from your salad.

Some infected people get that 'ick' feeling as the flukes migrate from the intestine through the abdomen and liver. The parasite can debilitate months after infection. Anything you should worry about?

[Look for "*Fasciola*," MayaVerse novel #6, in Summer 2026.]

About the Author

Millicent Eidson is the author of the alphabetical Maya Maguire microbial mysteries. The MayaVerse at https://drmayamaguire.com/ includes references and links to prequel and side stories. Author awards include Best Play in Synkroniciti and Honorable Mention from the Arizona Mystery Writers.

Dr. Eidson's work as a public health veterinarian and epidemiologist began as an EIS Officer (like Maya Maguire and Faye Simpson) with the Centers for Disease Control and Prevention, and continued at the New Mexico and New York state health departments. She has authored over a hundred scientific papers, articles, and book chapters. Currently, she is a public health faculty member at the University at Albany and the University of Vermont, and teaches a UVM course on zoonoses and climate change in its Larner College of Medicine.

With formative years in the Southwest, Millie enjoys reconnecting with Arizona family, heritage trips to Norway, Ireland, and China, and wider travel worldwide. In retirement from full-time public health work, she has settled in Vermont with her husband Tom Henderson and daughter Lian Henderson, inspiration for Maya Maguire.

Other interests are photography, painting, hiking, and bicycling along the beautiful Burlington, Vermont waterfront.

Social media links: www.linkedin.com/in/eidsonmillicent

Maya Maguire Media | Facebook

Millie Eidson (@drmayamaguire) • Instagram photos and videos

Millicent Eidson - Microbial Mystery Author (@meidson-author.bsky.social) — Bluesky

Author Note

Inspiration for the MayaVerse comes from collaborative work at the Centers for Disease Control and Prevention and the New Mexico and New York state health departments. If these stories capture even a small part of their ceaseless devotion to excellence and duty, I'll be happy. I also benefit from veterinary medical training at Colorado State University and training in research design and statistics at Michigan State University and the University of Colorado.

The MayaVerse relies on my family team of Lian Henderson, inspiration for and feedback on the Maya Maguire character, and Tom Henderson, audio and visual media advisor for Maya Maguire Media.

My primary scientific consultant for "Ebola: A Microbial Mystery" is nurse epidemiologist Susan Schoenfeld who shared numerous materials from her Ebola rotation in West Africa. Paige Rudin Kinzie, Purdue University DVM-MPH student (class of 2026) provided a photo of West Africa from her research in 2024, which was modified for the book cover. Dr. Laura Rothfeldt, Arkansas State Public Health Veterinarian, shared photos from her Ebola work in West Africa which provided inspiration for the text.

The novel benefited tremendously from a critique workshop of authors associated with the national Sisters in Crime (SinC) (https://www.sistersincrime.org/). They include Amy M. Reade https://www.amymreade.com/), Susan Cory (https://susancory.com/), and M. R. Dimond (https://dimond.me/). For mystery and suspense fans, I recommend you check out their wonderful novels.

The second workshop includes writers of multiple genres. Feedback on all chapters was received from poet Carol Shillibeer (https://gargoylemagazine.com/carol-shillibeer/) and author Liz Teuber. Other authors in the workshop who provided insightful critiques to some chapters include Case Israel, Karen Edwards, and Barbara Westwood Diehl.

Additional supportive organizations are the Grand Canyon Writers ((https://grandcanyonwriters.com/) and the Tucson Old Pueblo Chapter (https://www.tucsonsistersincrime.org/).

My continued growth is fostered by academic affiliations as an emeritus epidemiology professor at the University at Albany and instructor for a zoonoses and climate change class at the University of Vermont.

Provision of information or feedback by agency employees or other individuals does not imply endorsement.

Scientific nomenclature, including when to italicize organism names, can be confusing. For more information, see https://wwwnc.cdc.gov/eid/page/scientific-nomenclature. When words are spelled differently in the US and UK-associated countries, the spelling appropriate to that country and character is used.

The Ebola virus on the cover is based on image 10816 at https://phil.cdc.gov/. The Maya Maguire Media logo is based on image 2871. The Prologue quotation is from https://www.nobel-prize.org/prizes/peace/2004/maathai/lecture/.

Hundreds of nonfiction resources were consulted. A curated list for general education is provided at https://drmayamaguire.com/.

For updates on the MayaVerse, join the Reader List at https://drmayamaguire.com/. See https://books2read.com/millicenteidson/ for a universal link to all MayaVerse story formats and distributors.

Readers who would like to consult on future MayaVerse stories or provide feedback are encouraged to email: drmayamaguire@gmail.com. Ratings and reviews are critically important to help others discover the MayaVerse. Share impressions of this novel at https://www.bookbub.com/authors/millicent-eidson or your favorite bookseller.

EBOLA *Discussion Questions*

Book groups interested in discussions with the author should email drmayamaguire@gmail.com. "EBOLA" crosses genres, with multiple themes in the framework of a zoonotic disease. These questions may help in thinking about and discussing the novel.

1. The genre elements include medical thriller, crime fiction, mystery, women's fiction, and romantic suspense. How do each of these elements contribute to the overall arc and your enjoyment of the story?

2. The novel, with the complexity of the disease and narrative, provides the point-of-view of six characters. How do the alternating POVs expand your identification with the story?

3. Geographic locations are intended as characters in themselves. How do geography and history influence the story?

4. How do culture and personal background influence the character's goals, challenges, and successes in life?

5. What are the roadblocks to achieving a work-life balance based on gender and economic status?

6. Zoonotic diseases are those in common between humans and nonhuman animals. How are transmission, investigation, prevention, and control more complex for zoonotic diseases than those infecting only humans?

7. What is the role of climate change in the story and for zoonotic diseases?

 8. How can someone with a veterinary medical degree contribute to disease investigations?

 9. How should society balance protection of nonhuman animals against risks they may pose to humans?

10. For authenticity, writers often rely on personal experience, while protecting the privacy of those sharing life events with the author. Writers also use research and close consultation with others to create characters, plot events, and settings not their own. As a reader, do you have a preferred balance of work informed by an author's imagination, research, and representation of their background?